A BYZANTINE NOVEL

DROSILLA AND CHARIKLES

by Niketas Eugenianos

A BILINGUAL EDITION

Translated with an Introduction and Explanatory Notes by

Joan B. Burton

Bolchazy-Carducci Publishers, Inc.
Wauconda, Illinois USA

General Editor
Laurie Haight Keenan

Cover Design & Typography
Adam Phillip Velez

Cover and Title Page Illustration
Thirteenth-century Byzantine plate, c.34.54
American School of Classical Studies, Corinth Excavations,
I. Ioannidou and L. Bartziotou

Greek Text
Il romanzo bizantino del XII secolo, a cura di F. Conca, UTET, Torino 1994.

A Byzantine Novel
***Drosilla and Charikles,* by Niketas Eugenianos**

Translated by Joan B. Burton

Bolchazy-Carducci Publishers, Inc.
1000 Brown Street
Wauconda, IL 60084 USA
www.bolchazy.com

Printed in the United States of America
2004
by United Graphics

ISBN 0-86516-536-X

Library of Congress Cataloging-in-Publication Data

Nikåetas, ho Eugeneianos, 12th cent.
  [Kata Drosillan kai Chariklea. English & Greek]
  Drosilla and Charikles : a Byzantine novel / by Niketas Eugenianos ;
translated with an introduction and explanatory notes by Joan B.
Burton.— A bilingual ed.
    p. cm.
  ISBN 0-86516-536-X
  I. Burton, Joan B., 1951- II. Title.
  PA5319.N5D7613 2004
  883'.02—dc22

                                                    2003025758

CONTENTS

FOREWORD

In recent years the study of the ancient Greek novel, a once neglected and fringe genre, has found reputable entry not only into the work of scholars, but also into the classroom. The five canonical novels, sophistic or not, are now studied as vehicles through which one can gain important insight into that turbulent period of the Graeco-Roman world that spans from the end of the first century BC to the fourth century A.D. This bilingual edition of Niketas Eugenianos' *Drosilla and Charikles* now similarly affords us sound access to the literary fictions of the twelfth-century Byzantine novels and the characters, events, myth, customs, ideas, social norms, and history in which this type of literature developed.

Joan B. Burton has created a text that will help bring to completion the ongoing transformation of modern opinion on the Byzantine novel. Previously, most views of these fictions were similar to the one famously expounded by Ben Edwin Perry, who stated that the authors of these novels were "miserable pedants . . . trying to write romance in what they thought was the ancient manner. Of these no account need be taken" (*The Ancient Romances: A Literary-Historical Account of Their Origins* [Berkeley and Los Angeles 1967, 103]). This text shows that Roderick Beaton was right in writing that the "Byzantine romances of the twelfth century are works of remarkable, and surely deliberate, refinement . . . Rhetoric and the power of artifice (whether verbal or visual) become the central props of the stories" ("The Byzantine Revival of the Ancient Novel" in Gareth Schmeling's *The Novel in the Ancient World* [Leiden, New York and Koln 1996, 716]).

This text, the only English translation of Niketas Eugenianos' *Drosilla and Charikles*, faithfully adheres to the Greek narrative. *Drosilla and Charikles* is a story that includes "flight, wandering, storms at sea, abductions, violence, robbers, prisons, pirates, hunger, dreadful dark houses full of gloom under a bright sun, iron fetters wrought with the hammer, a pitiable, unlucky separation from one another, and in the end bridal chambers and nuptials" (Summary.2–8). The plot is equal to or surpasses most modern stories of love, intrigue and adventure—Burton's translation does an excellent job of conveying the action and pace of the Greek original. If one prefers to read the Greek, the explanatory notes help nudge the translator in the right direction.

EDMUND P. CUEVA
Xavier University

ACKNOWLEDGMENTS

It is a pleasure to be able to thank the people who have helped me with this project. I am especially grateful to Dr. Ladislaus (Lou) J. Bolchazy for welcoming this project warmly and giving it a good home: Dr. Bolchazy has long been an important advocate for Classics in and beyond the classroom. Laurie Haight Keenan, my editor, provided support and thoughtful guidance throughout the publication process; her patience and good humor were much appreciated. I should also like to thank Adam Phillip Velez and the anonymous reader for their enthusiasm, valuable suggestions, and care with the manuscript.

Trinity University generously awarded me an academic leave to complete this project. I am grateful to my students for reading a preliminary draft of this translation and learning about the Byzantine novels with me, and to my colleagues and friends, particularly Victoria Aarons, Maud Gleason, Alida Metcalf, Laurie Taylor-Mitchell, Jenny Ring, Willis Salomon, Carolyn Valone, Amelia Van Vleck, and Colin Wells, for supporting and encouraging my move to study medieval Greek literature. I wish to thank David Stinchcomb and Amelia Van Vleck, who read through early drafts of this translation, and Carolyn Valone, who provided timely help at the end of this project. I am also indebted to all the friends, colleagues, and anonymous readers of journal articles who urged me to publish this translation.

Thanks are due to Edoardo Pia and Unione Tipografico-Editrice Torinese for their kind permission to append the Greek text from their volume *Il romanzo bizantino del XII secolo*, edited by Fabrizio Conca, whose excellent text smoothed the way for this translation. I wish to thank Ioulia Tzonou-Herbst and the American School of Classical Studies Corinth Excavations for allowing reproduction of the charming Byzantine plate c.34.54.

I am grateful beyond words to my family and friends for their kindness, understanding, and support (even through missed vacations). My love of reading and scholarship emerges directly from the rich and warm intellectual life provided by my parents, Nancy and Ben Burton. To my husband, David Stinchcomb, I owe more than I could ever say. This book is dedicated to the memory of my grandmother Clara P. Higgins and her "Duke of Dudley," who could have starred in their own romance novel.

INTRODUCTION

The popularity of the ancient Greek and Roman novels has increased greatly in recent years, and courses on the ancient novel are now becoming standard parts of undergraduate and graduate programs around the world. The rise of interest is in part due to the rich forum these novels offer for discussions of such topics of contemporary interest as gender relations, social customs, narrative technique, and ethnic diversity in the ancient world. Encouraging the growth of scholarly and classroom attention to the ancient novels are the many translations into modern languages, including English, available in affordable volumes for classroom and personal use.[1] Western medieval romances, such as *Sir Gawain and the Green Knight*, have long been part of school curricula. Yet in the upsurge of world interest in the ancient and medieval novels and romances, the twelfth-century Byzantine novels have received little notice.

These four Byzantine novels represent a rebirth of the genre of the novel after a hiatus of eight centuries. Written in Christian Constantinople under the Komnenian dynasty and during the time of the crusades, these remarkable novels both revive the pagan Greek world with its pagan gods and beliefs and also reflect customs and beliefs of their own time. Three of the four Byzantine novels survive in their entirety—Niketas Eugenianos's *Drosilla and Charikles*, Theodore Prodromos's *Rhodanthe and Dosikles*, and Eustathios Makrembolites' *Hysmine and Hysminias*—and one survives in fragmentary form: Constantine Manasses' *Aristandros and Kallithea*.[2] Recent scholarly

---

1. Translations into modern languages (including English) began appearing in the sixteenth century and include an excellent, recent collection of new English translations of ancient Greek novels (Bryan P. Reardon, ed., *Collected Ancient Greek Novels* [Berkeley: University of California Press, 1989]), as well as a fine volume of facing-page translations of the fragments into English (Susan A. Stephens and John J. Winkler, eds., *Ancient Greek Novels: The Fragments* [Princeton: Princeton University Press, 1995]).

2. Modern editions of the Greek texts are Fabrizio Conca, ed., *Nicetas Eugenianus: De Drosillae et Chariclis amoribus*, London Studies in Classical Philology 24 (Amsterdam: J. C. Gieben, 1990); Miroslav Marcovich, ed., *Theodori Prodromi de Rhodanthes et Dosiclis amoribus libri IX* (Stuttgart: Teubner, 1992); idem, ed., *Eustathius Macrembolites: De Hysmines et Hysminiae amoribus libri XI* (Munich: Teubner, 2001). A reconstruction of the fragments of Konstantinos Manasses has also been published (Otto Mazal, *Der Roman des Konstantinos Manasses* [Vienna: Hermann Böhlaus Nachf., 1967]). For a useful collection of all four Greek texts, with Italian translations, see Fabrizio Conca, *Il romanzo bizantino del XII secolo* (Turin: Unione Tipografico-Editrice Torinese, 1994).

publications reflect an increasing interest in these novels;[3] heightened interest is also shown by their recent translations into French, German, Italian, Russian, Serbo-Croatian, and Spanish.[4] But English translations of the Byzantine novels remain long overdue.

This English translation of Eugenianos's *Drosilla and Charikles* is a first attempt to address that need. The translation is intended for use by students and teachers of ancient and medieval literature, the novel, as well as medieval culture and society. A Greek text is provided to make the volume also useful for students and teachers of ancient Greek who seek attractive alternative texts. I hope that this will be the first of a series of translations of the Byzantine novels. My aim is to make these exciting novels available for use in the classroom.

I have taught my own English translations of these novels repeatedly with great success in a course on the ancient novel at Trinity University. I have also taught these novels in an upper-division course in Greek language. Students in both courses have expressed delight to be reading a text outside the usual run of classical literature. They were entranced with the Byzantine novels in their own right and felt that these novels offered a fascinating bridge from the pagan to the Christian world and also to the Western medieval novel. Class discussions were lively and rich.

Ancient novels—extended, mostly prose narratives of fictional love and adventure—seem to have arisen in the late Hellenistic or early imperial periods (first century B.C.–first century A.D.). It is difficult to speculate about causes for the rise of the Greek novel. Chronology would be important to such a discussion; yet most of the novels cannot be definitively dated, some even to the century. Still, different factors have been emphasized in different discussions: for example, an increasingly privatized society, an increase in literacy, the rising visibility of women, a desire for escapist fiction.[5] Persistent

---

3. See, for example, Roderick Beaton, *The Medieval Greek Romance*[2] (London: Routledge, 1996); Suzanne MacAlister, *Dreams and Suicides: The Greek Novel from Antiquity to the Byzantine Empire* (London: Routledge, 1996); Panagiotis A. Agapitos and Diether R. Reinsch, eds., *Der Roman im Byzanz der Komnenenzeit*, Referate des Internationalen Symposiums an der Freien Universität Berlin, 3. bis 6. April 1998, Meletemata 8 (Frankfurt am Main: Beerenverlag, 2000); Ingela Nilsson, *Erotic Pathos, Rhetorical Pleasure: Narrative Technique and Mimesis in Eumathios Makrembolites' Hysmine and Hysminias* (Uppsala: distributor, Uppsala University Library, 2001). For annotated bibliographies of recent scholarship, see C. Jouanno, "The Byzantine Novel," a report that has appeared annually in *The Petronian Society Newsletter* since volume 30 (2000).

4. Theodore Prodromos's *Rhodanthe and Dosikles* is available in Italian (1994), Serbo-Croatian (1994), German (1996), and Spanish (1996); Niketas Eugenianos's *Drosilla and Charikles* in Russian (1969) and Italian (1994); Eustathios Makrembolites' *Hysmine and Hysminias* in Russian (1965), German (1989), French (1991), and Italian (1994).

5. Some ancient Greek novels center on heroes and heroines from outside the Greek and Roman world. For example, in Heliodorus's *An Ethiopian Story*, the heroine is an Ethiopian princess, and in *Ninos* (we have only fragments), the hero and heroine are the future founder of Nineveh, Ninos (at 17), and (probably) his cousin Semiramis. On why "the search for origins which dominated much earlier scholarship has now few practitioners," see E. L. Bowie, "The Greek Novel," in *Oxford Readings in the Greek Novel*, ed. Simon Swain (Oxford: Oxford University Press, 1999), 44–45 (quotation from p. 44).

topics addressed in the novels include conflicts between love and society, social instability, the chance nature of the universe, dangers of travel, the loneliness of persons set loose in the world, the problems of adjusting to an expanded world.

Three of the ancient Greek novels (Achilles Tatius's *Leucippe and Clitophon*, Longus's *Daphnis and Chloe*, and Heliodorus's *An Ethiopian Story*) are commonly associated with the Second Sophistic (early centuries A.D.), a period known for rhetorical display and philhellenism.[6] Although these novels share typical plot elements—young hero and heroine, love, abductions, pirates, sea storms, threats to chastity, separations, reunions, and marriage at the end—there are also striking differences. For example, Achilles Tatius's comic novel, presented from the hero's limited first-person perspective, features a hero who fails at first to win the girl's love (she runs away with him to spite her mother). In Longus's pastoral novel, travel is not important; instead the novel focuses on the psychological process of sexual awakening in young adolescents. In Heliodorus's novel, on the other hand, travel and differences of race, language, and ethnicity are central themes (the heroine is a white girl born of black Ethiopian parents).

When the genre of the novel was revived in twelfth-century Constantinople, after an interval of some eight centuries, the Greek novels associated with the Second Sophistic were the primary models. Along with basic themes and plot elements, the Byzantine novels' literary inheritance from the sophistic novels included the use of Atticizing Greek (based on the Greek of fifth- and fourth-century B.C. Athens), an emphasis on rhetoric, experimentation in narrative form and techniques, as well as extended descriptive passages (*ekphraseis*) and allusions to ancient Greek literature of many kinds. Thus both the sophistic and Byzantine novels seem to have been aimed first at well-educated audiences, able to grasp literary allusions and comprehend Atticizing Greek.

We have more information about the immediate context of the Byzantine novels than that of the ancient Greek novels. At least three of the four authors—Theodore Prodromos, Constantine Manasses, and Niketas Eugenianos—were closely associated with the Komnenian court at Constantinople.[7] Although Makrembolites' novel has been variously placed in the relative chronology,

---

6. The other two "ideal" ancient Greek novels (sometimes referred to as non-sophistic) are Chariton's *Chaereas and Callirhoe* and Xenophon's *An Ephesian Tale*.

7. On this association, see, e.g., Alexander P. Kazhdan, "Bemerkungen zu Niketas Eugenianos," *Jahrbuch der österreichischen byzantinischen Gesellschaft* 16 (1967): 102–8; idem, "Theodore Prodromus: A Reappraisal," in *Studies on Byzantine Literature of the Eleventh and Twelfth Centuries*, in collaboration with Simon Franklin (Cambridge: Cambridge University Press, 1984), 87–114; Elizabeth M. Jeffreys, "The Attitudes of Byzantine Chroniclers towards Ancient History," *Byzantion* 49 (1979): 202–3 (on Manasses); idem, "Western Infiltration of the Byzantine Aristocracy: Some Suggestions," in *The Byzantine Aristocracy IX to XIII Centuries*, British Archaeological Reports International Series 221, ed. Michael Angold (Oxford, 1984), 204–5; Paul Magdalino, *The Empire of Manuel I Komnenos, 1143–1180* (Cambridge 1993), 350–51.

there is general agreement that all four novels were written around the mid-twelfth century.[8] Perhaps the comparative political stability and economic prosperity of the Komnenian period (A.D. 1081–1185)[9] helped encourage the blossoming of literary activity during the mid-twelfth century. This period also saw the rise of professional literati—Theodore Prodromos and John Tzetzes being prominent examples—as well as a rise in Hellenism, as shown by the resurgence of ancient genres such as the satire and novel.[10] The fact that all four novels were written in a strong Atticising Greek reflects a desire at court to uphold high standards of purity of speech, a desire exemplified by Anna Komnene, daughter of Alexios I Komnenos and a distinguished writer herself.[11]

The women of the Komnenian family, prominent figures in the cultural world of the twelfth century, may also have played a part in the revival of the genre of the novel. Eirene Doukaina (wife of Alexios I Komnenos, the founder of the Komnenian dynasty) was a patron of Theodore Prodromos; her daughter, Anna Komnene, encouraged the writing of new commentaries on Aristotle.[12] The *sebastokratorissa* Eirene Komnene was also patron of at least two of the four Byzantine novelists, Theodore Prodromos and Konstantinos Manasses.[13] Thus it is not unlikely that educated, elite women were part of the

---

8. MacAlister argues that Makrembolites' novel was written first (Suzanne MacAlister, "Byzantine Twelfth-Century Romances: A Relative Chronology," *Byzantine and Modern Greek Studies* 15 [1991]: 175–210). Magdalino links Makrembolites to the early years of Manuel I's reign (Paul Magdalino, "Eros the King and the King of *Amours*: Some Observations on *Hysmine and Hysminias*," *Dumbarton Oaks Papers* 46 [1992]: 197–204). Beaton places the four romances between 1140 and 1160, in the order Prodromos, Eugenianos, Makrembolites, with Manasses "somewhere in the 1150s" (Beaton, *Medieval Greek Romance*², 80–81, 211–12). For useful recent discussions: Panagiotis A. Agapitos, "Narrative, Rhetoric, and 'Drama' Rediscovered: Scholars and Poets in Byzantium Interpret Heliodorus," in Richard Hunter, ed., *Studies in Heliodorus* (Cambridge: Cambridge University Press, 1998), 144–48 (dating the novels to 1145–55); "Poets and Painters: Theodoros Prodromos' Dedicatory Verses of His Novel to an Anonymous Caesar," *JÖB* 50 (2000), 181–85 (tentatively dating the novels to ca. 1130–45).

9. See, e.g., Magdalino, *Empire of Manuel I Komnenos*, esp. 140–42: "If the Byzantine lands were relatively prosperous for most of the twelfth century, this was demonstrably because the succession of Comnenian emperors provided a century of internal peace and long periods of relative security from invasion" (quotation from p. 141).

10. On the rise in Hellenism, see Magdalino, *Empire of Manuel I Komnenos*, esp. 395–97, 400–1. On the *Timarion* as "a satirical dialogue in the style of Lucian," see Margaret Alexiou, "Literary Subversion and the Aristocracy in Twelfth-Century Byzantium: A Stylistic Analysis of the *Timarion* (ch. 6–10)," *Byzantine and Modern Greek Studies* 8 (1982–83): 29–45 (quotation from p. 30); for an English translation, see Barry Baldwin, trans., *Timarion* (Detroit: Wayne State University Press, 1984).

11. On Anna Comnena's "insistence on the correct use of language," see Magdalino, *Empire of Manuel I Komnenos*, 385, with references.

12. On Anna's "Aristotelian salon," see Magdalino, *Empire of Manuel I Komnenos*, 332; N. G. Wilson, *Scholars of Byzantium* (Baltimore: The Johns Hopkins University Press, 1983), 182–83.

13. See Elizabeth M. Jeffreys, "The Comnenian Background to the *Romans d'Antiquité*," *Byzantion* 50 (1980): 478–81 (with parallels drawn to Eleanor of Aquitaine); idem, "Western Infiltration," 204–7. See too Michael Angold, *The Byzantine Empire, 1025–1204: A Political History*, 2nd ed. (London: Longman, 1997), 246–49.

Byzantine novel's early readership. Direct flattery may also have played a role in a novel's reception: for example, in a wedding poem Eugenianos uses the same lines to describe the beauty of a bride usually identified as the wife of the *sebastos* Stephen Komnenos that he uses in his novel to describe the beauty of the fictive heroine Drosilla.[14]

The proliferation of commentaries in the twelfth century suggests that members of the aristocracy may have been seeking more accessible routes to culture. For example, Manuel I's first wife and an outlander (formerly Bertha of Sulzbach) commissioned John Tzetzes to write a verse summary of Homer's *Iliad* which would have helped her appear educated among the Byzantine aristocracy.[15] The romance novel would also have offered easier avenues to Attic culture than Aristotle and Demosthenes.

Increased contact with the West also characterized the twelfth century, in particular through the crusades, which could have caused some Byzantines to want to assert their Greek identity against the Latins. Further, the West was also experiencing an intellectual renaissance in the twelfth century, and romance fictions were being written there too by the mid-century.[16] Elizabeth Jeffreys has proposed the interesting thesis that the novels of Prodromos and Manasses were already written at the time Eleanor of Aquitaine came to Constantinople in 1147 with the Second Crusade and that through Eleanor these novels could have influenced the rise of the French romances of antiquity.[17] Literary influence might have moved in the other direction as well. Manuel I Komnenos (emperor 1143–80), during whose reign some if not all of these novels may have been written, was highly influenced by the West: for example, he married two Western princesses, jousted, and hired Western military fighters. The Byzantine novels sometimes seem to reflect Western customs as well, for example, the trial by fire at the start of Prodromos's novel (a Western not Byzantine practice in the twelfth century) (1.372–404).[18] In any case, the court of the notoriously amorous Manuel I Komnenos would have offered a welcoming context for the new novels with their focus on erotic love.[19]

---

14. *Drosilla and Charikles* 1.126–32=*Epithalamium* 2.67–73. For discussion, see Kazhdan, "Bemerkungen zu Niketas Eugenianos," 108; cf. Herbert Hunger, *Die hochsprachliche profane Literatur der Byzantiner* (Munich: C. H. Beck, 1978), 2:136 n. 114.

15. On the aim and style of Tzetzes' *Iliad Allegories* in relation to patronage, see Michael J. Jeffreys, "The Nature and Origins of the Political Verse," *Dumbarton Oaks Papers* 28 (1974): 151–57.

16. For a useful, brief overview, see Roberta L. Krueger, "Introduction," in Roberta L. Krueger, ed., *The Cambridge Companion to Medieval Romance* (Cambridge: Cambridge University Press, 2000), 1–9.

17. Jeffreys, "The Comnenian Background," 455–86.

18. Carolina Cupane, "Un caso di giudizio di Dio nel romanzo di Teodoro Prodromo (I 372–404)," *Rivista di studi bizantini e neoellenici*, n.s. 10–11 (1974): 147–68. See also Michael Angold, "The Interaction of Latins and Byzantines during the Period of the Latin Empire (1204–1261): The Case of the Ordeal," *Actes du XVe Congrès international d'études byzantines, Athènes septembre 1976*, 4 (1980), 1–10; Robert Bartlett, *Trial by Fire and Water: The Medieval Judicial Ordeal* (Oxford: Clarendon Press, 1986), 16, 46, 131.

19. Magdalino, "Eros the King," 197–204.

Perhaps too, among sophisticated writers, the revival of the genre of the novel reflected a sense of literary rivalry with the old Hellenic world. Although ancient novels apparently ceased to be written after Heliodorus's *An Ethiopian Story* (third or fourth century A.D.), they continued to be read and discussed. Byzantine writers from the fifth century on attest to the enduring popularity of Achilles Tatius and Heliodorus, both of whom were transformed into Christian bishops, perhaps to make them more acceptable to a Christian reading public.[20] Even less "ideal" ancient novels, such as Iamblichos's *Babyloniaka*, continued to be read, as shown by the patriarch Photios (ninth century) in his *Bibliotheca*, a summary of his reading (for Iamblichos, see codex 94).[21] There seems to have been an ongoing debate regarding the relative merits of Heliodorus and Achilles Tatius; both Photios in the ninth century and Michael Psellos in the eleventh express a preference for Heliodorus but admire Achilles Tatius's style.[22] Psellos attests to the continued popularity of Heliodorus and Achilles Tatius while stressing the importance also of more serious writings in the education of a writer. Again, in the twelfth century, Gregory Pardos (who becomes metropolitan-bishop at Corinth) features these novels among his suggested readings for beginning writers.[23]

But if the ancient novel *per se* seems to have stopped being written in the fourth century, if not sooner, nonetheless the themes and motifs of the Greek "ideal" novel—ordeals, travel, chastity, trials, separations, reunions, miracle rescues—continued to thrive in writings of saints' lives and the apocryphal Acts of the Apostles (for example, *Paul and Thecla*).[24] By the twelfth century, however, there had been a significant decline in the writing of saints' lives in

---

20. For discussion, with references, see, e.g., Hunger, *Hochsprachliche profane Literatur*, 2:121–22; MacAlister, *Dreams and Suicides*, 109–12. For Heliodorus as bishop, see Socrates, *Historia ecclesiastica* 5.22 (fifth century) and Photios *Bibliotheca*, codex 73 (ninth century). For Achilles Tatius as bishop, see the *Suda* (tenth century).

21. Iamblichos's novel is available to us now only in fragmentary and summary form. For an English translation of Photios's summary (as well as the fragments of Iamblichos), see Stephens and Winkler, *Ancient Greek Novels*, 179–245; for Photios's summary, see also Nigel G. Wilson, *Photius*, The Bibliotheca: *A Selection* (London: Duckworth, 1994), 104–13.

22. Photios *Bibliotheca*, codices 73, 87, 94 (for English translations from these codices, see Wilson, *Photius*, 78, 93–94, 104). For Psellos's essay comparing Heliodorus and Achilles Tatius, see Andrew R. Dyck, ed., *Michael Psellus: The Essays on Euripides and George of Pisidia and on Heliodorus and Achilles Tatius* (Vienna: Der österreichischen Akademie der Wissenschaften, 1986), 75–118 (facing-page translation, 90–99); see also discussion, with substantial translation, in Wilson, *Scholars of Byzantium*, 174–77.

23. For translations, with discussion, see Wilson, *Scholars of Byzantium*, 172–74 (Psellos's short essay of recommended readings) and 186–87 (Gregory Pardos's recommendations).

24. For discussion, see Tomas Hägg, *The Novel in Antiquity* (Berkeley: University of California Press, 1983), 154–65. For an English translation of *The Acts of Paul and Thecla*, see Ross S. Kraemer, ed., *Maenads, Martyrs, Matrons, Monastics: A Sourcebook on Women's Religions in the Greco-Roman World* (Philadelphia: Fortress Press, 1988), 280–88.

Byzantium, and this decline may in part have provided an opening for the novel to reemerge and reclaim those themes.[25]

Archaizing fiction, particularly if it shared themes with saints' lives, might also have seemed to offer a safer forum than philosophy *per se* for approaching issues of love, friendship, war, morality, and religion. Despite the sophistication of the Komnenian court, prominent heresy trials would have provided cautionary examples for Hellenizing intellectuals, particularly regarding philosophical inquiry. In 1082, near the start of the reign of Alexios I Komnenos, founder of the dynasty, the distinguished philosopher John Italos (director of Constantinople's school of philosophy) was condemned for paganism and heresy.[26] Then in 1117, another philosopher, Eustratios of Nicaea, who wrote commentaries on Aristotle under Anna Komnene's encouragement, was also convicted of heresy. Later, the reign of Manuel I Komnenos, the period when most (if not all) of the novels may well have been written, was particularly marked by heresy trials.[27] In Theodore Prodromos's novel, when the hero Dosikles declaims upon the nature of Eros to his friends, they admonish him to stop talking that way, "for philosophy is dangerous just now" (ἀπρόσφορος γὰρ ἄρτι φιλοσοφία, 2.434). Dosikles' friends interrupt the hero's philosophizing to urge him to proceed with the business of abduction (a safer enterprise).[28]

---

25. H.-G. Beck, "Marginalia on the Byzantine Novel," in *Erotica Antiqua,* Acta of the International Conference on the Ancient Novel held under the auspices of the Society for the Promotion of Hellenic Studies at the University College of North Wales, Bangor, Wales, U.K., 12th–17th July 1976, ed. B. P. Reardon (Bangor, 1977), 63. Saints' lives were generally simpler narratives, written in a more accessible language than the scholarly Greek of the twelfth-century novels. In the thirteenth century, when Byzantine novels begin to be written again, they are in the vernacular. About a dozen vernacular Greek romances (five of them originals) survive from the 13th to 15th cent.; for an English translation of three of these, see Gavin Betts, *Three Medieval Greek Romances: Velthandros and Chrysandza, Kallimachos and Chrysorroi, Livistros and Rodamni* (New York: Garland, 1995).

26. See Lowell Clucas, *The Trial of John Italos and the Crisis of Intellectual Values in Byzantium in the Eleventh Century* (Munich: Institut für Byzantinistik, Neugriechische Philologie und Byzantinische Kunstgeschichte der Universität, 1981).

27. See Magdalino, *Empire of Manuel I Komnenos,* esp. 276–81: "The first half of Manuel's reign thus witnessed a dramatic increase in the number of trials for heresy, and in the number of patriarchs who left office under pressure, which it is tempting and plausible to attribute to an authoritarian and interventionist outlook on the part of the new emperor" (quotation from p. 281).

28. The word "dangerous" here can also be translated as "unsuitable." Either way, this passage seems double-edged. The fact that this may recall a passage in Achilles Tatius (1.12.1: "We were philosophizing in this way about the god [Eros]") makes it no less pointed in the highly charged context of twelfth-century Constantinople, when philosophy had indeed become a dangerous enterprise. Prodromos's fondness for Plato emerges elsewhere in the novel as well: for example, in book 7, the barbarian king Bryaxes initiates a Socratic dialogue with his captive Dosikles regarding human sacrifice (400–45). For other evidence of Prodromos's strong and lively interest in Plato, see, e.g., Giuditta Podestà, "Le satire lucianesche di Teodoro Prodromo," parts 1 and 2, *Aevum* 19 (1945): 239–52; 21 (1947): 3–25; for discussion, see Magdalino, *Empire of Manuel I Komnenos,* 332–34.

Similarities between the Byzantine and ancient novels include plot, character, themes, descriptions, gods, geography, and narrative technique. Just as the ancient Greek novels are set in an older (pagan) Greek world, so too the Byzantine novels recall the older, pagan Greek world, and Tyche (Fortune) and Eros (Love) continue to play prominent roles. Differences include the use of verse rather than prose[29] and topical elements in characterization and incident: for example, in Theodore Prodromos's novel, the "frogmen" who attack enemy ships from underwater (6.7–38),[30] the impressive throne scene among the pirates (esp. 4.16–29), the trial by fire mentioned above (1.372–404), and the heroine's heavily guarded bath (2.178–87, 440–48). So too contemporary social and political issues color the exploration of certain themes in the novels. For example, Prodromos's and Eugenianos's striking introduction of the theme of the hero's forcible, non-consensual abduction of the heroine is related to a contemporary controversy between church and state regarding control over the institution of marriage.[31]

An important difference between the ancient and the Byzantine novels, of course, is the primary target audience. Although the Byzantine novelists still wrote of pagan gods and pagan themes, their contemporary audience was, for the most part, deeply Christian, and the writers too were steeped in Christian modes of thinking and reading. Thus in addition to the tremendous number of allusions to ancient literature—Homer, Euripides, Plato, Theocritus, Achilles Tatius, Heliodorus, and so forth—there are also allusions to Christian writings and themes.[32] In addition, the striking emphasis on male gods as patrons and guarantors of weddings in the Byzantine novels may be a reflection of the Christian environment in which the novels were written. In the ancient novels female divinities predominantly serve in these roles. Eugenianos's insistence on describing Dionysus, the patron of his hero and

---

29. Only one of the twelfth-century Greek writers uses prose: Eustathios Makrembolites, who is also unusual in presenting the whole story from the hero's point of view and following Achilles Tatius more than Heliodorus.

30. Herbert Hunger, "Byzantinische 'Froschmänner'?" in *Antidosis: Festschrift für Walther Kraus zum 70. Geburtstag*, ed. Rudolf Hanslik, Albin Lesky, and Hans Schwabl (Vienna: Hermann Böhlaus Nachf., 1972), 183–87.

31. Joan B. Burton, "Abduction and Elopement in the Byzantine Novel," *Greek, Roman and Byzantine Studies* 41 (2000): 377–409; on the motif of abduction, see also Corinne Jouanno, "Les jeunes filles dans le roman byzantin du XIIᵉ siècle," in *Les personnages du roman grec*, Actes du colloque de Tours, 18–20 novembre 1999, edited by Bernard Pouderon, with Christine Hunzinger and Dimitri Kasprzyk (Lyon: Maison de l'Orient Méditerranéen, 2001), esp. 335–36.

32. On Christian themes and motifs (including the resurrection and the Eucharist) in the Byzantine novels, see Joan B. Burton, "Reviving the Pagan Greek Novel in a Christian World," *Greek, Roman and Byzantine Studies* 39 (1998): 179–216. Certainly an author writing in such a context might expect at least some of his audience to read erotic language and episodes as allegorical; for an example of a recent strongly allegorical reading of a Byzantine novel, see Karl Plepelits, trans., introduction to *Eustathios Makrembolites, Hysmine und Hysminias* (Stuttgart: Anton Hiersemann, 1989), esp. 29–66 ("Das Werk: mystische Deutung").

heroine's marriage, simply as "son of Zeus" (as if Zeus had no other sons) also seems to bring the pagan deities closer to the Father/Son of Christian theology. Further, the weddings in both Prodromos's and Eugenianos's novels take place inside temples with priests presiding, which reflects common Christian practice in Byzantium.[33]

Sometimes the novels are described as parody. Like Achilles Tatius, Longus, etc., the Byzantine novelists had fun with the genre. But their novels were also able to broach serious and sensitive topics, such as the resurrection and the Eucharist, with a degree of freedom that might not have been possible if the writers were not reviving an ancient genre, imitating the ancient Greeks in a safely distanced world.[34]

Niketas Eugenianos was either Prodromos's pupil or friend; his writings, particularly his monody on Prodromos's death, show his indebtedness to his predecessor.[35] Like Prodromos, Eugenianos wrote his novel in twelve-syllable verse and nine books. Eugenianos too began his novel *in medias res* with an attack on townspeople celebrating a festival outside the town walls. Other elements, familiar from the ancient novels, include stern parents, pirates who capture and separate the lovers, and a best friend with his own tragic love story. But the sheer density of literary allusions as well as the prevalence of love songs, letters, and pastoral motifs set Eugenianos's novel apart from the rest. In fact, for the first time in the history of the Greek novel, a novel has a character directly refer to other novels. An inn-keeper's son attempts to woo the heroine with a courtship speech that names as models of reciprocated love such couples as Heliodorus's Arsake and Theagenes, and Achaimenes and Charikleia (highly unsuitable choices), Longus's Daphnis and Chloe, Musaeus's Hero and Leander, and Theocritus's Cyclops and Galateia (Eug. 6.382–551). Like Cervantes's Don Quixote, the amorous inn-keeper's son looks toward a store of romantic fiction for models of courtship and decorum.[36]

---

33. On Christian aspects of representations of male deities and wedding practices in the Byzantine novels, see Burton, "Reviving the Pagan Greek Novel," 198–200, 205–8 (which includes discussion of linkages between Jesus and Dionysus in Byzantine texts).

34. For example, in his novel, Prodromos has the hero's friend explicitly and at length deny the possibility of resurrection (6.423–35), a speech that would have had special resonance for Christian readers (for discussion, see Burton, "Reviving the Pagan Greek Novel," 190–95).

35. For discussion of their relationship, see Michael J. Kyriakis, "Of Professors and Disciples in Twelfth Century Byzantium," *Byzantion* 43 (1973): 108–19; Louis Petit, "Monodie de Nicétas Eugénianos sur Théodore Prodrome," *Vizantiiskii vremennik* 9 (1902): 446–63.

36. For discussion of this intertextuality, see Joan B. Burton, "A Reemergence of Theocritean Poetry in the Byzantine Novel,"*Classical Philology* 98 (203): 251–73; see also Corinne Jouanno, "Nicétas Eugénianos: Un héritier du roman grec," *Revue des études grecques* 102 (1989), 346-60. On how the novels "show that they conceive of themselves as not merely imitative of the ancient novels, but rather creative and original," see Joan B. Burton, "Byzantine Readers of the Novel," in *The Cambridge Companion to the Greek and Roman Novel*, ed. Tim Whitmarsh (Cambridge: Cambridge University Press, forthcoming).

Christian themes and imagery also come into play in Eugenianos's novel. For example, a kindly old woman's description of the lovers' embrace ("Who could separate those whom a god has joined?" 7.264) echoes Jesus's response to the Pharisees regarding the issue of divorce: "Therefore what God has joined, let no one separate" (Matthew 19.6, Mark 10.9).[37] So too passages of dense, extended imagery of erotic consumption seem to recall the Song of Solomon. For an abbreviated example, compare the blandishment of an amorous woman in Eugenianos (4.285–288):

> I am the tree; come cling to me,
> for you have my arms in place of branches.
> I am the tree; climb me
> and pluck my fruit, which is sweeter than honey.

with a lover's description of his beloved in the Song of Solomon (7.7–8):

> You are stately as a palm tree,
> and your breasts are like its clusters.
> I say I will climb the palm tree
> and lay hold of its branches.[38]

Dense webs of allusion throughout Eugenianos's novel provide forums for meaningful dialogues with earlier Greek literature and culture as well as the biblical tradition.

Eugenianos places his hero, Charikles, in the midst of a vibrant song culture: he and his comrades cavalierly tease promenading women with impromptu songs at a festival; when courting, lovers send letters and sing serenades; enslaved, Charikles beguiles his master with the story of a nymphomaniac gardener. The heroine, a lissome dancer when the hero first sees her, later falls from a cliff into the sea and makes her way alone through a wilderness. Other notable characters include an amorous Parthian queen and her willful son, a gracious Arab king, a kindly old woman who dances raucously at the lovers' reunion, a rival suitor who takes the Cyclops as a model for wooing, a traveling salesman who offers salvation, a "best friend" who turns out to be the most "romantic" character of all. But an introduction should not preempt the joy of discovery for its readers. Enter the adventure world of the Byzantine romance novel. Discover its special pleasures for yourself.

---

37. Cf. Eugenianos 3.12. For discussion, see Kazhdan, "Bemerkungen zu Niketas Eugenianos," 116; Burton, "Reviving the Pagan Greek Novel," 203–4.

38. For discussion, see Burton, "Reviving the Pagan Greek Novel," 201–3; cf. Fabrizio Conca, "Il romanzo di Niceta Eugeniano: Modelli narrativi e stilistici," *Siculorum gymnasium* 39 (1986): 124–25. This scripture quotation is from the New Revised Standard Version Bible, copyright 1989 by the Division of Christian Education of the National Council of the Churches of Christ in the U.S.A., and is used by permission.

NOTE ON THE TRANSLATION

The modern edition of the Greek by Fabrizio Conca (1990) served as the basis for my translation. I also consulted the Greek texts of Boissonade (1819, 1856) and (rarely) Hercher (1859), as well as Boissonade's commentary and translation (1819, Latin) and Conca's translation (1994, Italian).[1] My aim was to translate the Greek into a natural, readable English that also preserves the spirit, style, and thought of the original Greek. I also aimed at an accuracy of translation that might help readers of the Greek.[2] As for the spelling of names, I use Greek forms unless a name is already in common usage in its Latin form.

---

1. Jean François Boissonade, ed., *Nicetae Eugeniani Narrationem amatoriam et Constantini Manassis fragmenta*, 2 vols. (Lugduni Batavorum: Apud S. et J. Luchtmans, 1819); Jean François Boissonade, ed., "Nicetas Eugenianus," rev. ed., in *Erotici scriptores*, ed. Wilhelm Adrian Hirschig (Paris: Ambrosio Firmin Didot, 1856); Rudolf Hercher, ed., *Erotici scriptores Graeci*, vol. 2 (Leipzig: B. G. Teubner, 1859); Fabrizio Conca, ed., *Nicetas Eugenianus, De Drosillae et Chariclis amoribus* (Amsterdam: J. C. Gieben, 1990); Conca, ed. and trans., *Il romanzo bizantino del XII secolo* (Turin: Unione Tipografico-Editrice Torinese, 1994).

2. Useful dictionaries include *A Patristic Greek Lexicon* (Oxford: Clarendon Press, 1961); *A Greek-English Lexicon of the New Testament and Other Early Christian Literature*, 2nd ed. (Chicago: The University of Chicago Press, 1979). Other useful aids include Evangelinus A. Sophocles, *A Glossary of Later and Byzantine Greek*, Memoirs of the American Academy of Arts and Sciences, n.s. vol. 7 (Cambridge, Mass.: Welch, Bigelow, printers to the university, 1860); Sophocles, *Greek Lexicon of the Roman and Byzantine Periods (from B.C. 146 to A.D. 1100)*, Memorial ed. (New York: Charles Scribner's Sons, 1900). The reader might also find helpful (in addition to grammars of classical Greek) F. Blass and A. Debrunner, *A Greek Grammar of the New Testament and Other Early Christian Literature*, a translation and revision of the ninth–tenth German edition incorporating supplementary notes of A. Debrunner by Robert W. Funk (Chicago: The University of Chicago Press, 1961).

CHARACTERS IN ALPHABETICAL ORDER

In parentheses, line in which name first mentioned

Barbition, one of Charikles' friends at the festival of Dionysus held outside Phthia (3.257)

Chagos, lord of the Arabs (5.279)

Charikles, the young hero, Drosilla's beloved, from Phthia (1.74)

Chramos, Maryllis's dead son (7.311)

Chrysilla, Kratylos's wife and a rival of Drosilla for Charikles (1.222)

Drosilla, the young heroine, Charikles' beloved, from Phthia (1.74)

Gnathon, merchant from Barzon (8.188)

Hedypnoe, Drosilla's mother (7.135)

Lysimachos, Kratylos's satrap (1.170)

Kallidemos, Xenokrates' son and a rival of Charikles for Drosilla (6.263)

Kalligone, Kleandros's beloved, from Lesbos (2.50)

Kallistias, Kleandros's father (2.59)

Kleandros, the hero and heroine's friend, met in a Parthian prison; from Lesbos (1.274; character first appears, unnamed, at 1.260)

Kleinias, Kratylos's son and a rival of Charikles for Drosilla (4.73)

Kratylos, Parthian king (1.168)

Krystale, Charikles' mother (3.51)

Kydippe, Kleandros's mother (2.59)

Maryllis, old woman who helps Drosilla when she reaches an unnamed village (6.667; character first appears, unnamed, at 6.236; on her name, see "Explanatory Notes" 6.667)

Mongos, Chagos's satrap (5.282)

Myrtion, Drosilla's father (7.135)

Phrator, Charikles' father (3.51)

Xenokrates, inn-keeper in the unnamed village (6.254)

CHARACTERS BY RELATIONSHIP

In parentheses, line in which name first mentioned

Charikles, the young hero, Drosilla's beloved, from Phthia (1.74)

Krystale, Charikles' mother (3.51)

Phrator, Charikles' father (3.51)

Barbition, one of Charikles' friends at the festival of Dionysus held outside Phthia (3.257)

Drosilla, the young heroine, Charikles' beloved, from Phthia (1.74)

Hedypnoe, Drosilla's mother (7.135)

Myrtion, Drosilla's father (7.135)

Kratylos, Parthian king (1.168)

Lysimachos, Kratylos's satrap (1.170)

Chrysilla, Kratylos's wife and a rival of Drosilla for Charikles (1.222)

Kleinias, Kratylos's son and a rival of Charikles for Drosilla (4.73)

Kleandros, the hero and heroine's friend, met in a Parthian prison; from Lesbos (1.274; character first appears, unnamed, at 1.260)

Kydippe, Kleandros's mother (2.59)

Kallistias, Kleandros's father (2.59)

Kalligone, Kleandros's beloved, also from Lesbos (2.50)

Chagos, lord of the Arabs (5.279)

Mongos, Chagos's satrap (5.282)

Maryllis, old woman who helps Drosilla when she reaches an unnamed village (6.667; character first appears, unnamed, at 6.236)

Chramos, Maryllis's dead son (7.311)

Xenokrates, inn-keeper in the unnamed village (6.254)

Kallidemos, Xenokrates' son and a rival of Charikles for Drosilla (6.263)

Gnathon, merchant from Barzon (8.188)

GODS AND LEGENDARY FIGURES
MENTIONED MORE THAN ONCE

Aphrodite, goddess of love, was married to Hephaestus, the crippled god of blacksmiths. The name "Aphrodite" appears in the Greek text only once, 4.314. Instead, Eugenianos commonly uses the names "Cypris" (13 times) and "Paphia" (2 times) to refer to this goddess (see below).

Ares, god of war, was also Aphrodite's lover.

Artemis, chaste goddess of the hunt, also served as a model of maidenly beauty.

Charon was the ferryman who transported the dead across a lake or river into Hades.

Cypris, "the Cyprian," is another name for Aphrodite; the large Mediterranean island Cyprus was a center for worship of Aphrodite.

Dionysus, god of wine, was the son of Zeus and Semele (a mortal). In Eugenianos's novel, Dionysus is often referred to by his parentage alone: seven times as "son of Zeus," once as "son of Zeus and Semele," and once as "son of Semele."

Eros, god of love, is often represented as a beautiful winged youth, with bow and arrows. He is sometimes regarded as Aphrodite's son (as in our novel at 2.232–34, 4.157–83, 4.313–24 [cf. Moschus poem 1]; see also Apollonius Rhodius esp. 3.85–157, Simonides 575 *PMG*). For Eros as a primordial being, along with Chaos, Earth, and Tartarus, see Hesiod *Theogony* 116–22 (see also Longus 2.5.2–3); this is the tradition recalled at Eugenianos 3.115. For the theme of a plurality of Erotes (Loves), see Eugenianos 5.135–45 (cf. Anacreontea 25; see also Theocritus 15.120–22; Apollonius Rhodius 3.452, 687, 765, 937; Herodas 7.94).

Fortune (Tyche), goddess of luck, fate, or chance, is frequently invoked by characters in the ancient and Byzantine novels. To the heroes and heroines of the novels, she often seems unhappily fickle.

Furies, primordial female creatures, often represented with snakes in their hair, pursued and punished wrongdoers. They were invoked in curses and linked with death.

Graces, usually three in number (after Hesiod *Theogony* 902-11), were minor goddesses often found in association with Eros and Aphrodite. They represent such qualities as charm and beauty.

Helios was god of the sun.

Herakles, the son of Zeus and Alkmene (a mortal woman), was perhaps the greatest of the Greek heroes. He was famous for his labors as well as his sexual potency and gluttony. His second labor was to kill the Lernaian hydra, a many-headed water serpent (Eugenianos 5.315–19; for the story of this labor, see Apollodorus *Bibliotheca* 2.5.2).

Niobe, a mortal woman proud of her many children (twelve or fourteen), boasted that she was better than Leto (who had only two). In response, Leto's children, the gods Apollo and Artemis, killed Niobe's children. Niobe turned into a stone in grief, but even as a stone she kept weeping. (For Niobe's story see Homer *Iliad* 24.602–17, Ovid *Metamorphoses* 6.148–312, Apollodorus *Bibliotheca* 3.5.6.)

Pallas Athena, goddess of war, wisdom, and crafts, was born from Zeus's head. "Pallas" alone also refers to Athena (Eugenianos 6.629, 8.107). As a chaste goddess, she contrasts with Aphrodite, the goddess of love (6.629). She also competed against Aphrodite and Hera in the famous beauty contest judged by Paris (6.622–25, 8.107–9).

Pandion, a legendary Athenian king, had two daughters, Procne and Philomela. He married Procne to King Tereus in exchange for his help in war, and Procne bore Tereus a son, Itys. Tereus, however, raped Procne's sister, Philomela, and removed her tongue to keep her from telling anyone. Philomela informed Procne through a weaving, and in revenge the sisters killed Itys and served him to Tereus for dinner. Tereus, Philomela, and Procne were all turned into birds afterwards, Tereus a hoopoe, and Philomela and Procne a swallow and a nightingale. For this version of their story, see Apollodorus *Bibliotheca* 3.14.8, Ovid *Metamorphoses* 6.424–674.

Paphia, "the Paphian," is another name for Aphrodite; the city Paphos, in southwest Cyprus, was the site of a famous sanctuary of Aphrodite (see Homer *Odyssey* 8.362–63).

Selene was goddess of the moon.

Semele, one of King Cadmus's daughters, conceived Dionysus by Zeus.

Zeus, ruler of the Olympian gods, is also called father of the gods. He begot many other important gods, including Apollo, Ares, Artemis, Athena, Hermes, and Dionysus.

SELECT PLACES AND PEOPLES

Arabs (5.279). The Arabs, having conquered the Persian Sasanids in the mid-seventh century A.D., became major military rivals of the Byzantines until the eleventh century when the Seljuq Turks took over that antagonistic role. Rather than disparage the Arabs as savage barbarians, Eugenianos characterizes his fictive Arab leader, Chagos, as generous, brave, and kindly.

Barzon (1.6). The novel opens with a fierce Parthian attack on the unknown city of Barzon.

Lesbos (2.57). This large Aegean island, close to northwest Asia Minor, was home to the Greek poets Sappho and Alcaeus, and the setting of Longus's novel, *Daphnis and Chloe*. In Eugenianos's novel, Lesbos is Kleandros and Kalligone's home.

Parthians (1.6). Parthia, an ancient realm in southwest Asia, boasted fine horsemen and archers. The Parthian empire, traditionally dated from 247 B.C. to the early third century A.D. (when replaced by the Persian Sasanids), at its height extended from the Euphrates to the Indus and was a major rival to the Roman empire in the East. Eugenianos characterizes his fictive Parthians as savage and intemperate. For the suggestion that Eugenianos could be using an archaizing name to refer to the Seljuq Turks, major rivals of the Byzantines from the eleventh century A.D., see Corinne Jouanno, "Les barbares dans le roman byzantin du XIIe siècle: Fonction d'un topos," *Byzantion* 62 (1992): 266.

Phthia (3.52). A city of this name in southeast Thessaly was home to Achilles, hero of Homer's *Iliad*. In Eugenianos's novel, Phthia is Drosilla and Charikles' home.

A BYZANTINE NOVEL
DROSILLA AND CHARIKLES

ΥΠΟΘΕΣΙΣ ΤΟΥ ΟΛΟΥ ΒΙΒΛΙΟΥ

Αὐτοῦ Δροσίλλης ἀλλὰ καὶ Χαρικλέους
φυγή, πλάνη, κλύδωνες, ἁρπαγαί, βίαι,
λῃσταί, φυλακαί, πειραταί, λιμαγχόναι,
μέλαθρα δεινὰ καὶ κατεζοφωμένα,
5   ἐν ἡλίῳ λάμποντι μεστὰ τοῦ σκότους,
κλοιὸς σιδηροῦς ἐσφυρηλατημένος,
χωρισμὸς οἰκτρὸς δυστυχὴς ἑκατέρων,
πλὴν ἀλλὰ καὶ νυμφῶνες ὀψὲ καὶ γάμοι.

ΒΙΒΛΙΟΝ ΠΡΩΤΟΝ

Νῦν τοῦ φεραυγοῦς ἀστεράρχου φωσφόρου
ἐκ τοῦ κάτω φάναντος ἡμισφαιρίου,
ἐξ ὠκεανοῦ τῶν ῥοῶν λελουμένου
καὶ γῆς τοσαύτης ἐκταθείσης εἰς πλάτος
5   ἀναδραμόντος τοὺς κορυφαίους τόπους,
Πάρθοι παρεμπίπτουσι Βάρζῳ τῇ πόλει,
οὐχ ὡς κατ' αὐτῆς συγκροτήσοντες μάχην,
οὐδ' ὡς βαλοῦντες ῥιψεπάλξιδας λίθους
ἐκ πετροπομπῶν εἰς τὸ τεῖχος ὀργάνων,
10   οὐδ' ὡς κατασπάσοντες ἐκ τῶν ὑψόθεν
πέτραις χελώναις καὶ κριοῖς χαλκοστόμοις
– οὐκ ἦν γὰρ εὐάλωτος αὐτοῖς ἡ πόλις,
κρημνοῦ περισφίγγοντος αὐτὴν κυκλόθεν –
ἀλλ' ὡς ἀφαρπάσοντες ἄνδρας Βαρζίτας
15   οὓς ἐκτὸς ἂν λήψοιντο τῶν ὁρισμάτων,
καὶ πᾶσαν αὐτῶν τὴν τυχοῦσαν οὐσίαν.
Καὶ γοῦν ὑφαπλωθεῖσα καὶ τεταμένη

SUMMARY OF CONTENTS

Here are the contents of Drosilla and Charikles' story:
flight, wandering, storms at sea, abductions, violence,
robbers, prisons, pirates, hunger,
dreadful dark houses
full of gloom under a bright sun,   5
iron fetters wrought with the hammer,
a pitiable, unlucky separation from one another,
and in the end bridal chambers and nuptials.

BOOK ONE

The morning star, bringer of light, leader of the stars,
had just risen from the hemisphere below,
after bathing in Ocean's streams,
and climbed over the peaks of the land,
which extended over a vast distance,   5
when Parthians invaded the city of Barzon.
They did not come to fight a battle against the city,
to hurl against its wall stones that could
knock down battlements, from rock-throwing machines,
or to tear down the wall from above   10
with rocks, tortoise shields, and bronze-tipped battering rams
(for the city was bound tightly on all sides by a cliff
and thus not easily taken),
but to carry off Barzian men
captured outside the confines of the city,   15
with all available property.
A band in the Parthian commander's service,

τῶν τῆς πολίχνης τειχέων ἀποστάδην
ὑπουργικὴ χεὶρ Παρθικῆς φυλαρχίας
20   αἰφνηδὸν ἐσκύλευε τοὺς πέριξ τόπους·
οἱ βάρβαροι δὲ συνδραμόντες αὐτίκα
λείαν Μυσῶν ἔθεντο τὰ πρὸς ταῖς πύλαις.
Τοὺς μὲν γὰρ ἐσπάθιζον ἄνδρας ἀθλίους,
οὓς ἀντιπίπτειν ἔβλεπον πειρωμένους,
25   τοὺς δὲ προῆγον δεσμίους κρατουμένους.
Πᾶν συγκατέκλων δένδρον ἐξ ἀπληστίας,
καίτοι βρῖθον βλέποντες ἐξ εὐκαρπίας.
Τὴν αἶγα, τὴν βοῦν συγκαθήρπαζον τότε,
ἢ μὴ τὸ τεῖχος εἰσδραμεῖν ἐπεφθάκει.
30   Γυναῖκας εἷλκον αἳ συνεῖλκον τὰ βρέφη·
ὤμωζον αὐτῶν αἱ τάλαιναι μητέρες,
καὶ συνεμινύριζον αὐταῖς τὰ βρέφη·
οὐκ ἀπομαστεύειν γὰρ εἶχον εὐκόλως·
τῶν οὐθάτων γὰρ ἡ βρεφοτρόφος ῥύσις
35   εἰς αἱματοστάλακτον ὄμβρον ἐτράπη.
Ἐκεῖ στάχυς ἐτμᾶτο καὶ πρὸ τοῦ θέρους,
τὴν ἵππον ὡς θρέψαιτο τὴν τῶν βαρβάρων·
καὶ βότρυς ἁδρὸς ἐθλίβη πρὸ τῆς τρύγης,
ὄνυξιν ἵππων συμπατηθεὶς ἀθλίως,
40   λεηλατούντων τὴν περίχωρον κύκλῳ
Πάρθων ἀπηνῶν, δυσμενῶν, ἀλλοθρόων.
Τί γοῦν ἐπ' αὐτοῖς; Οἱ μὲν ἐκτὸς τειχέων
ὅσοι φυγεῖν ἔφθασαν ἐκ ξίφους τέως,
φεῦ, τοὺς ἑαυτῶν ἐντιθέντες αὐχένας
45   ζεύγλῃ βαρείᾳ δυσχεροῦς ὑπουργίας,
τὴν σφῶν κακίστην ἐξεδάκρυον τύχην·
οἱ δ' ἐντὸς αὐτῶν εἰσρυέντες τειχέων,
τὴν Παρθικὴν μάχαιραν ἐκπεφευγότες,
πρὸς τὴν ἐφ' ὕψους ἀσφαλῆ τείχους βάσιν
50   ἀναδραμόντες, τοῖς ἀπεξενωμένοις
συμπατριώταις ἀντεπέστενον μέγα
'τίς βάσκανος' λέγοντες 'ἀγρία τύχη
αὖθις διεσπάσατο τοὺς ὁμογνίους;
Φεῦ, τίς Ἐρινύς, τίς ἀλάστωρ, τίς τύχη
55   δουλοῖ κακούργοις βαρβάροις ἐλευθέρους;
Ποίοις ἀπ' αὐτῶν ἐνστενάξει τις μέγα;

which had spread out and scattered
far from the walls of the city,
suddenly despoiled the surrounding area,   20
and the barbarians quickly ran together
and made what they found at the gates "Mysian plunder."*
They pierced with their swords some wretched men
whom they saw trying to resist
and seized others and led them forth in chains.   25
They greedily tore down every tree
although they saw it laden with good fruit.
    They seized the goats and cows
that had not already run inside the wall.
They dragged away women with their babies,   30
the unhappy mothers wailing,
and their babies along with them,
for the mothers could not nurse easily
since the nourishing flow from their breasts
had become a shower of blood.   35
Ears of corn were cut before summer
to feed the barbarians' cavalry,
and dense bunches of grapes were pressed before vintage,
foully trampled by horses' hooves,
as the cruel, hostile Parthians, with their strange speech, 40
despoiled the surrounding countryside.
What else besides? The men outside the walls
who had escaped the sword in the meantime
were placing their necks, alas,
in a heavy yoke of hateful servitude   45
and weeping aloud for their terrible fortune.
And the men who had run inside the walls,
escaping the Parthian sword,
had hurried up to a secure position
on top of the wall and were lamenting loudly   50
over their fellow-countrymen, driven from their homes.
"What malicious, savage Fortune," they said,
"has again torn apart kinsfolk?
What Fury, what avenging Deity, what Fortune, alas,
enslaves free men to villainous barbarians?   55
For whom of these shall we lament loudly?

---

*   Explanatory notes for asterisked items begin on p. 195.

Τοῖς συσφαγεῖσι; Τοῖς ἁλοῦσι δεσμίοις;
Χήραις γυναιξί; Ταῖς ἀνάνδροις παρθένοις;
Ἀπειροκάκῳ τῶν βρεφῶν ὁμηγύρει;
60   Ἡμῖν ἑαυτοῖς; Ὦ κακῶν συγκυρμάτων'.
   Οὗτοι καὶ οὕτω τοῖς πόνοις ἐκαρτέρουν,
καὶ θρῆνος ἦρτο συμμιγὴς βαρὺς μέγας
ἀνδρῶν, γυναικῶν, παρθένων, μειρακίων,
τὸ βάρβαρον δὲ συλλογῆς οὐκ ἠμέλει·
65   πρὸς ἁρπαγῆς γὰρ ἠσχολεῖτο φροντίδας·
ἀνὴρ γὰρ ἐχθρὸς βαρβαρόφρων ὠμόνους
ἀντὶ τρυφῆς εἴωθεν ἡγεῖσθαι πάσης
ἄνδρας σκυλεύειν μηδὲν ἠδικηκότας.
   Τοὺς οὖν ἁλόντας συμπεδήσαντες μόλις
70   ἀπεῖδον ὀψὲ πρὸς τρυφὴν καὶ πρὸς πόσιν.
   Τούτοις συνῆν θήρευμα καὶ τοῦτο ξένον,
οἷς καὶ συνεξέσφικτο δεσμοῖς ἀλύτοις
καὶ συγκατεστέναζε τοῖς πεδουμένοις,
καλὸς Χαρικλῆς καὶ Δροσίλλα καλλίων.
75   Καὶ δὴ συνιζήσαντες ἐν πεδιάδι
προκειμένης ἥπτοντο τῆς ἐδητύος.
   Λειμὼν γὰρ ἦν ἥδιστος αὐτῆς ἐν μέσῳ,
οὗ κυκλόθεν μὲν ἦσαν ὡραῖαι δάφναι
καὶ κυπάριττοι καὶ πλάτανοι καὶ δρύες,
80   μέσον δὲ δένδρα τερπνὰ καὶ καρποφόρα.
Πόα τε κρίνων καὶ πόα τερπνὴ ῥόδων
πολλὴ παρῆν ἐκεῖσε, λειμῶνος μέσον·
αἱ κάλυκες δὲ τῶν ῥόδων κεκλεισμέναι
ἢ μᾶλλον εἰπεῖν μικρὸν ἀνεῳγμέναι
85   ταύτην ἐθαλάμευον ὥσπερ παρθένον.
Τούτου δὲ πάντως αἰτίαν λογιστέον
θερμαντικὴν ἀκτῖνα τὴν τοῦ φωσφόρου·
ὅταν γὰρ αὕτη – καὶ καλῶς οὕτως ἔχει –
μέσον καλύκων φλεκτικῶς ἐπεισβάλοι,
90   γυμνοῦσιν αὗται τὴν ῥοδόπνοον χάριν.
Καὶ νᾶμα πηγιμαῖον ἦν ἐκεῖ ῥέον,
ψυχρὸν διειδὲς καὶ γλυκάζον ὡς μέλι.
Κίων δέ τις ἀνεῖχε τῆς πηγῆς μέσον,
ἔσωθεν οὕτω τεχνικῶς γεγλυμμένος·
95   σωλῆνι μακρῷ δῆθεν ἐξεικασμένος,

For those slain? For those captured and chained?
For widowed women? For unmarried maidens?
For the throng of babies ignorant of evil?
For ourselves? Oh, what terrible misfortunes!"   60
    These men endured their sufferings thus,
and a loud, mournful lament was raised by all together—
men, women, maidens, and lads.
But the barbarians did not forget their booty,
for they were preoccupied with plundering   65
(a savage and cruel enemy
typically considers robbing innocent men
superior to any pleasure).
Then, after chaining together their captives,
they turned at last to revelry and drink.   70
    The captives also included this unusual prize,
shackled with the others by unbreakable bonds
and moaning along with the rest:
beautiful Charikles and Drosilla even more beautiful.
And so the barbarians sat together in a level field   75
and ate the food set before them.
    In the middle of this field was a very pleasant meadow,
with lovely laurels all around
and cypresses, plane-trees, oaks,
and, in the middle, delightful fruit trees,   80
along with an abundance
of lilies and lovely roses.
The roses' calyxes, being closed
or rather a little opened,
shut the flower within like a maiden in her chamber.   85
One must certainly regard the sun's warming ray
as the cause of this,
for whenever the sun's ray—at a fitting time—
penetrates with its heat among calyxes,
the calyxes open to reveal the rose's fragrant beauty.   90
Water from a spring was flowing there,
cold, clear, and sweet as honey.
In the middle of the spring stood a pillar,
skillfully hollowed within,
like a long pipe,   95

δι' οὗ τὸ ῥυτὸν ὑπανήκετο τρέχον·
πλὴν ἀετός τις τοῦτο προσδεδεγμένος
– χαλκοῦς γὰρ ἦν ἄνωθεν ἑστὼς εὐτέχνως –,
ἐξῆγε τοῦ στόματος αὖ καταρρέον.
100 Λευκῶν δὲ πετρῶν τῆς καλῆς πηγῆς μέσον
ἀγαλμάτων ἕστηκεν εὐξέστων κύκλος·
οἱ δ' ἀνδριάντες ἦσαν ἔργα Φειδίου
καὶ Ζεύξιδος πόνημα καὶ Πραξιτέλους,
ἀνδρῶν ἀρίστων εἰς ἀγαλματουργίαν.
105 Τῷ δεξιῷ δὲ τοῦ παραδείσου μέρει
ἔξωθεν αὐτῶν τῶν ξυλίνων θριγγίων
βωμὸς κατεσκεύαστο τῷ Διονύσῳ,
οὗ τὴν ἑορτὴν εἶχον ἄνδρες Βαρζίται,
καθ' ἣν τὸ πλῆθος τῶν ἀθέσμων βαρβάρων
110 ἄφνω παρεισέπνευσε τοῖς ἐγχωρίοις,
φυλακτικῶν ἔξωθεν οὖσι τειχέων
ὁμοῦ μετ' αὐτῶν τῶν γυναικῶν καὶ τέκνων
καὶ τὴν ἑορτὴν τοῦ θεοῦ Διονύσου
ἐκεῖ τελοῦσι καὶ συνεστιωμένοις
115 σκηνορραφικῶν ἔνδοθεν στεγασμάτων.
Δι' ἣν ἑορτὴν καὶ Δροσίλλα παρθένος
σὺν ταῖς κατ' αὐτὴν καὶ κόραις καὶ παρθένοις
τὸ τεῖχος ἤδη τῆς πολίχνης ἐξέδυ,
χοροῦ καλὴν τόρνωσιν ἐνστησαμένη.
120 Ὡς οὐρανὸς γὰρ ἦν ἔναστρος ἡ κόρη,
χρυσοῦν, φαεινόν, λευκοπόρφυρον φάρος
πρὸς τὴν ἑορτὴν δῆθεν ἠμφιεσμένη.
Εὔρυθμος ἥβην, λευκοχειροσαρδόνυξ,
χείλη, παρειὰς ἐξέρυθρος ὡς ῥόδον·
125 ὀφθαλμὸς αὐτῆς εὐπερίγραφος μέλας,
πυρσὴ παρειά, ῥὶς γρυπή, στιλπνὴ κόμη,
ναὶ καὶ χλιδῶσα καὶ διευθετισμένη,
κάλυξ τὰ χείλη, σίμβλον ἀνεῳγμένον,
θυμῆρες ἐκρέοντα τοῦ λόγου μέλι,
130 γῆς ἄστρον ἐξαστράπτον, οὐρανοῦ ῥόδον·
εὔρυθμος ὁ τράχηλος ἐκτεταμένος,
τὰ πάντα τερπνά· κυκλοειδεῖς ὀφρύες,
καὶ πυρσὸν ἀστράπτοντα λευκερυθρόχρουν
αἱ τῶν παρειῶν ἐξέπεμπον λαμπάδες,

through which the flowing water rose.
But an eagle received this water
(for a bronze eagle had been artfully placed on top)
and released the liquid from its mouth to flow back down again.
In the middle of the lovely spring's white rocks   100
stood a circle of well-carved statues,
the works of Pheidias,*
Zeuxis, and Praxiteles,
the finest creators of sculpture.
On the right side of the garden,   105
outside the wooden fences,
an altar for Dionysus had been built,
where the Barzian people were holding his festival
when the crowd of lawless barbarians
suddenly made their breaths felt upon the inhabitants,   110
who were outside the protective walls,
with their wives and children,
celebrating the festival of the god Dionysus
and feasting together
under the shelter of tents.   115
Because of this festival, the maiden Drosilla too,
with girls and maidens of her own age,
had just come out from the city's wall
and begun a lovely, circular dance.
    The girl was like a starry sky,   120
for she was dressed for the festival
in a splendid purple-white cloak, adorned with gold.
Graceful and young, she had hands as white as a sardonyx,
and lips and cheeks as red as a rose.
Her dark eyes were well-outlined,   125
her cheeks rosy, her nose aquiline, and her hair shining,
soft, and well arranged.
Her lips were like a rose-bud or an opened beehive,
as they poured forth the sweet honey of her speech.
She was a sparkling star of the earth, a rose of the sky.   130
Her neck was long and graceful—
her whole body a delight. Her brows were arched,
the torches of her cheeks sent out
a gleaming, rose-white fire,

135   χιὼν δὲ τἄλλα τοῦ προσώπου τῆς κόρης·
       ὁ βόστρυχος χρύσειος, αἱ πλοκαμίδες
       ξανθαί, μελιχραί, χρυσοειδεῖς, κοσμίαι,
       τεταμέναι τε καὶ πνέουσαι τοῦ μύρου·
       ἡ γνάθος, ὁ τράχηλος ἐστιλβωμένα,
140   τὸ χεῖλος αὐτῆς νέκταρ ἦν ἀπορρέον,
       τὸ στέρνον ἄλλην εἶχεν ὀρθρίαν δρόσον,
       ἥβης τὸ μέτρον ὡς κυπάριττος νέα,
       εὔτορνος ἡ ῥίς, τῶν ὀδόντων ἡ θέσις
       ὡς σύνθεσίς τις μαργάρων λευκοχρόων,
145   τὰ κυκλοειδῆ τόξα τὰ τῶν ὀφρύων
       ὡς τόξον ἦν Ἔρωτος ἐγκεχαρμένου,
       ἔοικεν ὡς ἔμιξε γάλα καὶ ῥόδα,
       καὶ συνδιεχρώσατο καθὰ ζωγράφος
       ταύτης τὸ σῶμα λευκέρυθρον ἡ φύσις·
150   θάμβος γὰρ αὕτη συγχορευούσαις κόραις
       λειμῶνος ἐντὸς τοῦ νεὼ Διονύσου.
       Οἱ δάκτυλοι δὲ καὶ τὰ τῶν ὤτων ἄκρα
       ἄνθρακας εἶχον, ὡς τὸ πῦρ ἀνημμένους,
       χρυσῷ καθαρῷ συμπεπηγότας λίθους·
155   ἤστραπτον αὐτῆς χεῖρες ἐκ τοῦ χρυσίου,
       ναὶ μὴν σὺν αὐταῖς ἀργυροσκελεῖς πόδες.
       Οὕτω τοσαύτην ἡ Δροσίλλα παρθένος
       καινὴν ἐπευτύχησε καλλονῆς χάριν.
       Ἐπεὶ δὲ μακροῖς τοῖς πότοις ἐνετρύφων
160   καὶ μέχρι δυσμῶν καὶ βαθείας ἑσπέρας,
       οἱ δυσμενεῖς χαίροντες ἐξηρπαγμένων
       – τὸ βάρβαρον φύσει γὰρ ἐγχαίρει μέθαις,
       φιλεῖ δὲ τρυφαῖς ἐκδίδοσθαι καὶ πότοις,
       καὶ μᾶλλον εἴπερ εὐχερῶς ἀφαρπάσοι,
165   ἀλλοτρίαν ὕπαρξιν εὑρὸν ἀθρόαν –
       ἐκ τῆς τραπέζης ἐξανέστησαν μόλις
       ἐφ' ᾧ τραπῆναι καὶ πρὸς ὕπνον αὐτίκα.
       Ὁ γοῦν Κρατύλος – τοῦτο γὰρ ὁ Παρθάναξ –
       τῆς συνθολούσης μικρὸν ἐκνήψας μέθης
170   τῷ Λυσιμάχῳ ταῦτά φησι σατράπῃ·
       ἡμεῖς μὲν ἤδη καὶ πότου καὶ σιτίων
       ἐλάβομεν νῦν ἀλλὰ καὶ μέθης κόρον,
       ἢ καὶ τὸν ὕπνον ἐντίθησι ταῖς κόραις·

and the rest of her face was like snow.   135
Her hair was golden-yellow, and her plaits
blond, honey-sweet, golden, well-ordered,
long, and fragrant with perfume.
Her cheeks and neck were gleaming,
nectar flowed from her lips,   140
and her breasts glistened with morning dew.
Her youthful body was like a young cypress.
Her nose was well turned, her teeth
like a set of white pearls,
and her brows curved   145
like the bow of joyful Eros.
It seemed as if Nature, like a painter,
had mixed milk with rose
and thus colored the girl's body white-red,
and the girls who were dancing with her in the meadow   150
of Dionysus's temple wondered at her.
Her fingers and ears
were adorned with rubies that gleamed like fire,
gems set in pure gold.
Her hands glittered with gold,   155
and her silver feet glittered too.
Thus the maiden Drosilla was extraordinarily well blessed
with beauty's grace.
    The enemies reveled in long drinking-bouts,
which lasted until sunset and late into the evening.   160
Then, rejoicing over their booty
(for the barbarian by nature delights in drunkenness
and enjoys abandoning himself to revelry and drinking-bouts,
especially if he's easily carried off
an abundance of property belonging to others)   165
they stood up with effort from the table
so that they might turn directly to sleep.
    Then Kratylos, the Parthian king,
having recovered a little from the confusion of drunkenness,
said the following to his satrap Lysimachos: 170
"We've now had enough of wine and food
and also drunkenness,
which puts sleep into the eyes.

καιρὸς τὸ λοιπὸν συγκλιθῆναι, σατράπα,
175   πρὸς ὕπνον ἡμᾶς τῇ τρυφῇ δεδωκότας.
Σὺ γοῦν, ἀληθῶς φιλάγρυπνε καρδία,
μὴ συγκαθευδήσειας ἐξ ἡμῶν μόνος·
λαβὼν δὲ σύν σοι καὶ στρατοῦ τοὺς ἐκκρίτους,
ἵππευε κύκλῳ τῶν ἁλόντων δεσμίων,
180   τηρῶν, φυλάσσων, προσκοπῶν, περιτρέχων,
μή πως ἀποδράσαιεν ἐν λεληθότι
καὶ μακρὸν ἡμῖν ἐμπαράσχοιεν γέλων
ἢ καὶ νεανικόν τι δράσαιεν τάχα
ἐς τοὺς ὑφ' ἡμᾶς ἡδέως κοιμωμένους.'
185   Τοιοῦτον ἐξ ἄνακτος ἀλγεινὸν λόγον
ὁ Λυσίμαχος σατράπης δεδεγμένος,
ἤδη τὸν ὕπνον ἐκτινάξας μακρόθεν
εἰς φυλακὴν ἔσπευδε τῶν κρατουμένων.
Ἐπεὶ δ' ὁ λαμπρὸς ἥλιος διφρηλάτης
190   ἁπανταχοῦ γῆς τὴν ἑαυτοῦ λαμπάδα
ἐξῆπτε, φαιδρὰν δεικνύων τὴν ἡμέραν,
ἀνίσταται μὲν εὐθέως ὁ Παρθάναξ
καὶ Λυσίμαχον τῆς φυλακῆς θαυμάσας
λαμπροῖς τὸν ἄνδρα δεξιοῦται τοῖς λόγοις,
195   πολλὰς πρὸς αὐτὸν ἐκτελῶν ὑποσχέσεις·
ναὶ μὴν σὺν αὐτῷ καὶ τῆς λείας πλέον
αὐτὸς παρασχεῖν τοῖς ὑπ' αὐτὸν ἐξέφη·
'τοὺς γὰρ πονοῦντας ὑπὲρ ἄλλους τι πλέον
καὶ δωρεῶν χρὴ δεξιοῦσθαι μειζόνων'.
200   Τοσαῦτα λέξας ἐξανέστη τῆς κλίνης·
ἀνίσταται δὲ καὶ τὸ βάρβαρον φῦλον
οὐ βραδέως ἕτοιμον ἀνθυποστρέφειν,
καὶ δὴ συνάξαν τὰ προεξηρπαγμένα,
τὴν αἶγα, τὴν βοῦν, τοὺς ἁλόντας δεσμίους,
205   αὐτῇ κελεύσει τοῦ κρατοῦντος Κρατύλου
ἰθυτενῶς ἤλαυνε πρὸς τὴν πατρίδα.
Φθάσαντες οὖν ἐκεῖσε πεμπταίῳ φάει,
εἰς φυλακὴν ἔδοντο τοὺς κρατουμένους,
μίξαντες αὐτοὺς τοῖς προεγκεκλεισμένοις
210   ἐκ πρωτολείας αἰχμαλώτοις ἀθλίοις·
οἳ καὶ φυλακῆς ἔνδον ἐμβεβλημένοι,
χαμαὶ πεσόντες καὶ κλιθέντες εἰς γόνυ,

It's time, then, Satrap, for us to turn
to sleep, after our enthusiastic revelry.   175
But you, most wakeful heart,
don't sleep with the rest (you alone among us)
but take with you the army's best men
and ride among the captives—
observing, guarding, watching, moving quickly about—   180
so that they may not somehow secretly escape
and make us great laughingstocks
or perhaps even commit some violent act
against our men in their sweet sleep."
    When the satrap Lysimachos heard   185
this unwelcome speech from his king,
he at once shook off sleep
and hurried to guard the captives.
Then, when the shining Sun in his chariot
shone his torch over all the earth,   190
thus illuminating the day,
the Parthian king at once rose from sleep,
marveled at Lysimachos for his careful watch,
greeted him with splendid words,
and fulfilled the many promises he'd made to him.   195
Indeed, the king proclaimed that he would give
the greater share of the booty to Lysimachos and his men,
"for those who work more than others
ought to be honored with greater gifts."
    After he said this, the king rose from his couch,   200
and the barbarian host rose too,
eager to return speedily home.
They gathered together all that they had seized—
the goats, the oxen, and the captives—
and by command of Kratylos, their ruler,   205
they headed straight for their fatherland.
    When they arrived home on the fifth day,
they put their captives into prison,
where they joined unhappy prisoners
confined from a previous raid.   210
These captives, thrown into prison,
cast themselves to the ground, fell to their knees,

τὴν σφῶν ἀπωδύροντο δυσμενῆ τύχην,
μόνους ἐμακάριζον, αἴνων ἠξίουν
215   οὓς ἔργον εἰργάσατο τὸ ξίφος φόνου,
τούτων καλοῦντες τὴν σφαγὴν εὐεργέτιν·
ψυχὴ γὰρ ἀνέραστός ἐστι τοῦ βίου
λύπαις ἀμέτροις ἐμπεσοῦσα πολλάκις.
Τὴν δὲ Δροσίλλαν δυστυχῶς δυσδαιμόνως
220   διαζυγεῖσαν ἐκ παλαμναίας τύχης
τοῦ μέχρι φωνῆς νυμφίου Χαρικλέος
ἡ τῆς Χρυσίλλας εἶχε γυναικωνίτις·
γυνὴ γὰρ ἡ Χρυσίλλα Πάρθου Κρατύλου.
    Ὁ γοῦν Χαρικλῆς ἔνδον ἐγκεκλεισμένος
225   τῆς φυλακῆς, ὡς εἶπον, ἤρξατο στένειν,
καί 'τίς Ἐρινύς, Ζεῦ, Ὀλύμπιον κράτος,
Δροσίλλαν ἐξήγαγεν ἐκ τῆς ἀγκάλης
τῆς τοῦ τοσαῦτα δυστυχοῦς Χαρικλέος;'
εἰπὼν Χαρικλῆς μεῖζον ἀντεκεκράγει·
230   'ὤμοι, Δροσίλλα, ποῦ πορεύῃ; Ποῦ μένεις;
Ποίαις ἐτάχθης δουλικαῖς ὑπουργίαις;
Ἀνῃρέθης πρὸς τίνος ἐχθρῶν ἀγρίων;
Ἢ ζῇς ἀμυδρῶς, ὡς σκιὰ κινουμένη;
Κλαίεις; Γελᾷς; Ὄλωλας; Ἐρρύσθης φόνου;
235   Χαίρεις; Θλίβῃ; Δέδοικας; Οὐ φοβῇ ξίφος;
Ἀλγεῖς; Κροτῇ; Πέπονθας; Οὐ πάσχεις φθόρον;
Τίνος μετέρχῃ λέκτρον ἀρχισατράπου;
Ποῖός τις ἐχθρὸς νῦν φανείς σοι δεσπότης
ἐκ δακτύλων σῶν τὸν κρατῆρα λαμβάνει;
240   Ἢ πού σε πολλῆς ἐμφορούμενος μέθης
τυχὸν πατάξει βαρβαρώδει κονδύλῳ
πταίουσαν οὐχ ἑκοῦσαν; Ὤμοι τῆς τύχης·
ἢ καὶ Κρατύλος οὗτος ὀφθαλμὸν λίχνον
ἐπεμβαλεῖ σοι καὶ φθονήσει τοῦ γάμου;
245   Πρὸ τοῦ τυχεῖν δὲ τῆς Χρυσίλλας ὁ φθόνος
διαφθερεῖ σκύφῳ σε δηλητηρίου.
Ὦ τοῦ Διὸς παῖ, Διόνυσε, πῶς πάλαι
τὸν τῆς Δροσίλλας ἀνθυπέσχου μοι γάμον,
ἐπεί σε πολλαῖς ὑπὲρ αὐτῆς θυσίαις
250   ἐδεξιούμην τὸν κακάγγελον τότε;
Ἆρ᾽ οὖν ἔχεις ἔννοιαν ἐν τῇ καρδίᾳ

and bitterly lamented their cruel fortune,
proclaiming only those slain by the sword
happy and worthy of praise,   215
and calling their slaughter a kindness
(for a spirit that's often fallen into limitless grief
is not a lover of life).
But Drosilla, who'd been unluckily and unhappily
separated by malicious Fortune   220
from her promised bridegroom, Charikles,
was being kept in the women's quarters of Chrysilla,
the wife of Kratylos, the Parthian king.
        Charikles, then, who had been confined
in the prison, as I said, began to groan,   225
saying, "What Fury, O Zeus, Ruler of Olympus,
has taken Drosilla from the arms
of Charikles, so very luckless?"
Then Charikles cried again, even more loudly,
"Oh, Drosilla, where are you going? Where are you staying?   230
To what slave duties have you been assigned?
By what fierce enemy have you been killed?
Or do you live obscurely, moving like a shadow?
Do you weep or laugh? Are you dead or rescued from death?
Are you rejoicing or oppressed? Are you afraid? Do you not
        fear the sword?   235
Do you grieve? Are you being beaten? Have you suffered? Are you not
        suffering ruin?
What chief satrap's bed are you sharing?
What enemy, now your master,
takes the wine bowl from your fingers?
Will he, full of much strong drink,   240
perhaps strike you with a barbarous fist
for making a mistake, though unintentionally? What bad luck!
Will this Kratylos also cast a lustful eye
upon you and grudge us our wedding?
But before he gains his purpose, Chrysilla's jealousy   245
will kill you with a cup of poison.
O Dionysus, Child of Zeus, why long ago
did you promise me marriage with Drosilla,
when I honored you with many sacrifices
for her sake—you, a messenger of evil?   250
And you, Drosilla, do you have a thought in your heart

καὶ σύ, Δροσίλλα, τοῦ φίλου Χαρικλέος
θρηνοῦντος, οἰμώζοντος ἐγκεκλεισμένου;
Ἦ μὴν λέλησαι τοῦ θεοῦ Διονύσου
255   καὶ τῆς δι᾽ αὐτοῦ πρὸς Χαρικλῆν ἐγγύης,
ὡς τῶν ἀναγκῶν ἐμποδών σοι κειμένων,
τῆς αἰχμαλώτου συμφορᾶς καὶ τοῦ πάθους;᾽
    Οὕτω Χαρικλεῖ πρὸς Δροσίλλαν ἀσχέτως
πολύστονον πλέκοντι τὴν τραγῳδίαν
260   ἐφίσταταί τις ἀγαθὸς νεανίας,
τὸν φθόγγον ἡδύς, εὐγενὴς τὴν ἰδέαν,
συναιχμάλωτος, συμφυλακίτης ξένος,
καὶ συγκαθεσθεὶς πλησίον Χαρικλέος
παρηγορεῖν ἔσπευδε συμπεπονθότα
265   λέγων· ᾽Χαρίκλεις, λῆξον ὀψὲ τῶν γόων·
ἐμοὶ λόγον δός, ἀνταπόκρισιν λάβε,
ὡς ἂν τὸ πλεῖστον τῆς ἀθυμίας βάρος
ἐκ προσλαλιᾶς κουφίσῃς αὐθαιρέτου·
λύπης γάρ ἐστι φάρμακον πάσης λόγος,
270   ψυχὴ δὲ πάντως οὐκ ἂν ἄλλως ἰσχύσοι
πῦρ ἐξαναφθὲν θλίψεως κατασβέσαι,
εἰ μὴ πρὸς ἄλλον ἐξαγάγῃ τὸ θλίβον,
παρηγορεῖν ἔχοντα τοὺς λυπουμένους.᾽
    ᾽Καλῶς λέγεις, Κλέανδρε,᾽ Χαρικλῆς ἔφη
275   ᾽πλὴν ἀλλὰ νῦν πρόσρησις ἡ σὴ καὶ μόνη
ἀρκεῖ τὰ πολλὰ τῶν παθῶν μου κοιμίσαι.
Ἐπεὶ δὲ καὶ νὺξ ἀντεπῆλθεν, ὡς βλέπεις,
καὶ νυκτὶ πεισθῆναί με, φιλότης, πρέπει,
ἔα με λοιπὸν ἠρεμοῦντα συγκλῖναι,
280   εἴ πως βραχὺν τὸν ὕπνον ὀφθαλμοῖς λάβω,
λήθην μικρὰν σχὼν τῶν ἐμῶν παθημάτων·
ἐς αὔριον δέ, νυκτὸς ἐκχωρησάσης,
ἐπακροάσῃ συμφορῶν Χαρικλέος.᾽
    Οὕτω τραπέντος πρὸς ὕπνον Χαρικλέος,
285   Δροσίλλα πικρῶς ἐστέναζεν ἐκ βάθους
ἐν παρθενῶνι τῆς Χρυσίλλας κειμένη
– οὐ γὰρ κατασχεῖν ἠδυνήθη τὴν κόρην
νήδυμος ὕπνος ἐκχυθεὶς κατ᾽ ὀμμάτων –
᾽ψυχὴ φίλη᾽ λέγουσα ᾽Χαρίκλεις ἄνερ,
290   ἄνερ Χαρίκλεις μέχρις οὖν φωνῆς μόνης,

for your beloved Charikles,
as he wails and laments, a prisoner?
Have you forgotten the god Dionysus
and the pledge you made through him to Charikles,   255
because you are oppressed by necessities—
the misfortune of captivity, and suffering?"
    While Charikles thus spoke his tragic lament
to Drosilla, without pause and with many groans,
a well-born young man appeared—   260
sweet in voice, noble in form,
a fellow-captive and prisoner, a stranger—
and sitting down by Charikles,
tried to console him, a fellow sufferer,
by saying, "Charikles, stop your groaning at last.   265
Let me speak and give me a response in turn
that you may lighten the great weight of your despondency
through free conversation.
Talk is a cure for every pain;
a soul could not otherwise   270
quench a fire that burned with grief
unless it revealed its distress to another
able to console those in pain."
    "You are right, Kleandros," Charikles said,
"but now your speech alone   275
is enough to soothe most of my sufferings.
And since night has come, as you see,
and it is fitting, my friend, that I obey night,
let me lie down and rest, then,
in the hope that a brief sleep may settle upon my eyes   280
and I may forget my sufferings for a while.
In the morning, when night has passed,
you shall hear about Charikles' misfortunes."
    Thus Charikles turned to sleep.
Drosilla, meanwhile, groaned bitterly from deep in her soul,   285
as she lay in Chrysilla's chambers
(for sweet sleep had poured
over her eyes in vain),
and said, "Charikles, beloved soul, husband
(though in name only),   290

σὺ μὲν καθυπνοῖς τῆς φυλακῆς εἰς μέρος
Δροσίλλαν εἰς νοῦν οὐδὲ μικρὸν εἰσφέρων,
ἀλλ᾽ ἀμελήσας ἐκ κακῶν προκειμένων
καὶ τῆς καθ᾽ ἡμᾶς ἐγγύης αὐθαιρέτου
295   καὶ τοῦ θεοῦ με τοῦ συνάψαντος πάλαι
σοὶ τῷ Χαρικλεῖ, πλὴν ὑποσχέσει μόνῃ·
ἀλλ᾽ ἡ Δροσίλλα πολλὰ τοῦ Χαρικλέος
καταστενάζει δακρύων πληρουμένη
καὶ μέμφεταί σε καὶ πρὸ τοῦ τὰ τῆς Τύχης
300   ἀμνημονοῦντα τῆς προηγγυημένης.
Κἂν γὰρ τοσοῦτον ἡ παλαμναία Τύχη
ἀντιστρατεύῃ δυστυχῶς σοι, Χαρίκλεις,
ἢ καὶ πρὸ σοῦ μοι τῇ Δροσίλλᾳ παρθένῳ,
ὡς τὴν ἀδιάρρηκτον ἀλληλουχίαν
305   ἡμῶν διασπᾶν καὶ μερίζειν εἰς δύο
– τί γάρ, Τύχη βάσκανε, μὴ κόρον δέχῃ
τῇ προφθασάσῃ ποικίλῃ περιστάσει
καὶ τῇ κατασχούσῃ με νῦν τιμωρίᾳ,
ἀλλ᾽ ἐκτὸς ἐγκλείεις με τοῦ Χαρικλέος;
310   Ὑπὲρ τὸ φῶς μοι τῆς φυλακῆς τὸ σκότος,
εἰ συγκαθῆσθαι Χαρικλεῖ κατεκρίθην
καὶ χθὲς σὺν αὐτῷ τὴν φυλακὴν εἰσέδυν –
ἐχρῆν, Χαρίκλεις, κἂν τοσοῦτον ἡ Τύχη
ἀντιστρατεύῃ πρὸς διάστασιν φίλων
315   καὶ μηχανᾶται συμμερισμὸν τῶν δύο,
ἀγωνιᾷ δέ, φεῦ, διασπᾶν εἰς τέλος
τοὺς εἰς ἓν ἐμπνέοντας ἀλληλεγγύως,
μὴ καταπίπτειν, μηδὲ λήθῃ διδόναι,
ἀλλὰ πρὸς αὐτὴν τὴν παλαμναίαν Τύχην
320   ἀλκὴν μεγίστην ἐνδιδύσκεσθαι πλέον.
Σὺ δ᾽ ἀλλ᾽ ἐφυπνοῖς καὶ Δροσίλλαν οὐ στένεις,
ἡ δὲ στενάζει καὶ θεοὺς μαρτύρεται
διαρραγῆναι μηδαμῇ Χαρικλέος.
Κισσὸς γὰρ εἰς δρῦν δυσαποσπάστως ἔχει·
325   ἐθίζεται γὰρ συμπλοκαῖς ταῖς ἐκ νέου
καὶ σωματοῦται καὶ δοκεῖ πεφυκέναι
ἓν σῶμα, διπλῆν τὴν ἐνέργειαν φέρον·
οὕτω Δροσίλλα πρὸς Χαρικλῆν νυμφίον
ἓν σῶμα καὶ φρόνημα καὶ ψυχὴ μία,

you sleep in a corner of the prison
and are not even a little mindful of Drosilla.
Your present evils have made you heedless
of both our pledge to one another, freely undertaken,
and the god who long ago united me   295
with you, my Charikles—though by promise only.
Drosilla, however, filled with tears,
groans much over Charikles,
and blames you—and even sooner Fortune's cruelty—
for your forgetting the woman betrothed to you.   300
Fierce Fortune wages so great a war,
unluckily, against you, Charikles—
or even sooner against me, the maiden Drosilla—
that she tears apart
our unbreakable union, splits it in two.   305
Why, envious Fortune, are you not satisfied
with the many difficulties that came before
and the punishment that now oppresses me,
but keep me confined far from Charikles?
The darkness of prison would be dearer than the light to me   310
if I had been condemned to stay with Charikles
and yesterday had entered prison with him.
Even if Fortune fights hard
to separate lovers, Charikles,
plots to divide us,   315
strives (alas) to part completely
those who breathe as one through mutual pledges,
it would be best not to give way or yield to forgetfulness,
but to put on the greatest courage
and confront fierce Fortune herself.   320
        "But instead you sleep, Charikles, and don't grieve for Drosilla.
She, on the other hand, groans and calls the gods to witness
that she should never be torn from Charikles.
Ivy clings tenaciously to an oak,
for it is accustomed to intertwinings from the start   325
and takes on form and seems to be by nature
a single body with a double force.
Thus Drosilla and her bridegroom Charikles
were one body, one mind, and one soul,

330   κἂν χθὲς τραπέζης κειμένης ὁ Κρατύλος
       ἔκδηλος ἦν ἔρωτα δεινὸν ἐκτρέφων
       καὶ βάσκανόν μοι βλέμμα δεικνύειν θέλων.
       Ὤμοι, Χαρίκλεις, κλῆσις ἡ φιλητέα,
       πῶς αἱ καθ᾽ ἡμᾶς συμφοραὶ σχοῖεν τέλος;
335   Ὡς νῦν ἐγώ, σοῦ κἂν διῄρημαι, κρίνω
       μικρὸν παρηγόρημα τὸ βλέπειν μόνον
       καὶ τὴν φυλακὴν ἧς κατεκλείσθης ἔσω
       – ναὶ τοῦτο μικρόν – καὶ τὸ πάντως εἰδέναι
       ποῦ νῦν διάγεις, ποῦ καθεύδεις, ποῦ κάθῃ.
340   Ἄφες τὸν ὕπνον, εἴπερ ὑπνώττειν ἔχεις·
       γνῶθι Δροσίλλαν· σὲ στενάζει, σὲ κλάει·
       σύγκλαιε, συστέναζε, συγκατηφία.
       Ἦ που, Χαρίκλεις, οὐκ ἀπὸ δρυῶν ἔφυς·
       καὶ σὲ στενάζειν ἐννοῶ καὶ δακρύειν
345   καὶ μὴ διυπνώττειν σε νυκτὸς ἐν μέσῳ
       πολλὰ Δροσίλλας παρθένου μεμνημένον.
       Ὦ δεῦρο, μικρόν, Ὕπνε, συγκάτασχέ με,
       εἴ που φανεὶς ὄνειρος ἐγκαθηδύνει,
       ἐμοὶ παριστῶν τὸν φίλον Χαρικλέα·
350   οἱ γὰρ ποθοῦντες ἢ φιλοῦντες πολλάκις
       θέλουσιν, οὐ βλέποντες ἀλλήλους ὕπαρ,
       ἐν τοῖς ὀνείροις συλλαλεῖν καὶ συμπνέειν.᾽
           Οὕτω λεγούσης τῆς Δροσίλλας παρθένου,
       καταστεναζούσης δὲ καὶ γοωμένης,
355   τοῖς αἰχμαλώτοις ἀντεπῆλθεν ἡμέρα
       τοῖς ἐν φυλακῇ δυστυχῶς κοιμωμένοις,
       κἂν καὶ τὸ ταύτης ὡς βαθύτατον σκότος
       κατακρατοῦν ἦν καὶ ζοφοῦν τὴν ἡμέραν.

       ΒΙΒΛΙΟΝ ΔΕΥΤΕΡΟΝ

           Τῆς ἡμέρας δὲ θᾶττον ἀντιλαμψάσης
       καὶ τοῦ γίγαντος καὶ φεραυγοῦς ἡλίου
       ἐκ τῶν στενωπῶν τῆς φυλακῆς νυγμάτων
       ἀκτῖνα μικρὰν ἐμβαλόντος τοῖς ἔσω,
5   εὐθὺς Χαρικλῆς ἐξανίσταται μόνος·
       ἰδὼν δὲ πάντας βαθέως κοιμωμένους,

even if yesterday, when the table was set, 330
Kratylos clearly nurtured a terrible love for me
and repeatedly cast entrancing glances my way.
    "Oh, Charikles, name that I adore,
what will be the end to our misfortunes?
Now, even though I'm separated from you, 335
I consider it a small consolation just to see
the prison in which you're confined—
yes, a small consolation—and to know
where you now live, sleep, and sit.
Shake off sleep (if indeed you are able to sleep). 340
Think of Drosilla; she is moaning and weeping for you.
Weep with her; moan with her; sorrow with her.
Truly, Charikles, you were not born from oak trees;
you are moaning, I think, and weeping—
not sleeping in the middle of the night— 345
filled with memories of the maiden Drosilla.
Come, Sleep, take hold of me a while,
on the chance that a dream may appear and sweeten my sleep
by placing my beloved Charikles beside me.
Those who feel desire or love are often accustomed, 350
when they don't see one another while awake,
to converse and breathe together in dreams."
    While the maiden Drosilla was speaking thus,
with laments and groans,
day came upon the captives 355
who were unfortunately sleeping in prison,
even if the prison's profound darkness
defeated and obscured the day.

BOOK TWO

    As soon as the day became bright,
and the giant, light-bringing sun
through the narrow cracks of the prison
cast a great beam of light upon those inside,
Charikles alone rose up, 5
and when he saw all the men sleeping deeply,

ταχὺ στενάξας ἐκ βάθους τῆς καρδίας,
ἔφησεν· 'ἄνδρες συμπεφυλακισμένοι,
ἐοικὸς ὑμῖν ἐστιν ὑπνοῦν εἰσέτι·
10   ὧν καὶ γὰρ οὐ κατέσχε καρδίας πλάτος
τὸ δριμὺ φίλτρον οὐδ' ὁ τοῦ πόθου πόνος,
ὧν οὐ κατεκράτησε τῆς ψυχῆς ἔρως,
τί καινὸν εἰ τὸν ὕπνον ἀσπάζοισθέ μοι
ἐκ νυκτὸς ἀρχῆς ἄχρι φωτὸς ἡλίου;
15   Ὁ γὰρ Ἔρως εἴωθε νύκτωρ τὸ πλέον
ἀναπτεροῦσθαι τοῖς ἐρῶσιν εἰσρέων,
ψυχῆς ἐρῶντος ἐνσχολαζούσης τότε
ὅλης ἐκείνῳ δῆθεν ἀνακειμένης.
Ὡς ὤφελες γοῦν εὐσθενῶς ἔχων, Ἔρως,
20   ποιεῖν ἐρᾶν μὴ τοὺς χαμαὶ κινουμένους·
ποιῶν δὲ πάντως καὶ τυχεῖν πῶς οὐ δίδως,
πολλῶν δὲ πολλοὺς ἀξιοῖς παθημάτων,
ἕως τυχεῖν γένοιτο τοῦ ποθουμένου;'
      Οὕτω Χαρικλῆς καθ' ἑαυτὸν ἠρέμα
25   θρηνῶν ὑπεστάλαζε ῥεῖθρα δακρύων·
πολύδακρυς γὰρ γίνεται πάντως Ἔρως
ψυχαῖς ἐπαχθὴς ἐμπεσὼν τεθλιμμέναις.
Ἀλλ' οὐκ ἔλαθε τὸν Κλέανδρον δακρύων·
ἐφίσταται γοῦν ἐξαναστὰς εὐθέως
30   ὅπου Χαρικλῆς εἶχε τὴν γῆν ὡς κλίνην,
καὶ 'χαῖρε' φησί 'συμφυλακίτα ξένε.
Λέγοις ἂν ἡμῖν τὰ προϋπεσχημένα,
τὰς σάς, Χαρίκλεις, συμφορὰς καὶ τοὺς πόνους·
ἐνταῦθα δ' αὐτὸς συγκαθεσθεὶς πλησίον
35   τὰς ἀκοὰς διδοῖμι τῇ τραγῳδίᾳ.
Καὶ γὰρ σὺ σαυτὸν κουφιεῖς στεναγμάτων
ἐμοὶ παριστῶν δῆλα τὰ θλίβοντά σε
καὶ τὸν Κλέανδρον τὸν συνεγκεκλεισμένον
ἐλαφρυνεῖς με τῶν ἐμῶν παθημάτων·
40   οὐ γὰρ μόνος σὺ τὴν φυλακὴν εἰσέδυς.
Ἢ καὶ πρὸ ταύτης αἰχμάλωτος ἐσχέθης
ψυχὴν ἔχων ἔρωτι πυρπολουμένην;
Οὐδ' ὁ Κλέανδρος ἀνέραστος ἐσχέθη,
οὐ τὴν φυλακὴν δυστυχῶς προεισέδυ
45   ἐρωτικῶν ἄμοιρος ἐννοημάτων

he groaned at once from the depths of his heart
and said, "Fellow prisoners,
it is fine for you to be still sleeping,
for neither bitter love nor the pain of desire   10
has filled the breadth of your hearts;
love has not prevailed over your souls.
What is strange if you welcome sleep
from start of night to light of sun?
Eros is accustomed more at night   15
to spread his wings and enter into lovers,
since a lover's soul is then at leisure
and wholly receptive to love.
If only you, Eros, who are so strong,
did not make those who walk the earth fall in love!   20
But since you certainly do, why don't you also grant them to succeed,
instead of requiring many to endure many sufferings
until at last they can attain the objects of their desire?"
        Thus Charikles lamented softly to himself
and wept rivers of tears,   25
for Eros certainly causes many tears
when he grievously attacks souls in distress.
But Charikles' tears did not escape Kleandros's notice.
At once he rose, went to where
Charikles had his ground as bed,   30
and said, "Morning, stranger, fellow-captive;
tell me the things you promised—
your misfortunes, Charikles, and your sufferings—
and I myself will sit here by your side
and listen to your tragic tale.   35
You'll ease yourself of your grief
by telling me clearly the things afflicting you
and ease me, Kleandros,
your fellow prisoner, of my sufferings,
for not alone have you entered this prison.   40
And if even before this prison you were held captive,
inflamed in your spirit with love's fire,
Kleandros too was not taken captive ignorant of love;
he did not unluckily enter this prison
without experiencing amorous thoughts   45

καὶ συμφορῶν ἄγευστος, αἷς παίει Τύχη
ἐρωτικοῖς με συμπλακέντα δικτύοις.
Ἀλγεῖς; Συναλγῶ· δακρύεις; Συνδακρύω·
ποθεῖς; Ποθῶ, καὶ ταῦτα καλὴν παρθένον,
50   Καλλιγόνην μοι τὴν προεξηρπαγμένην'.
        Κλέανδρε, σῶτερ τληπαθοῦς μοι καρδίας'
ἔφη Χαρικλῆς 'τίς σε τῶν Ὀλυμπίων
θεῶν ἀφῆκεν εἰς ἐμὴν εὐθυμίαν;
Λέγοις τὰ σαυτοῦ, ταυτοπάθειαν λέγοις.
55   Λέγειν χρεών σε τὸν προεγκεκλεισμένον,
ἔπειτα κἀμὲ συμπεφυλακισμένον.'
        ' Ἐγώ, Χαρίκλεις, Λέσβον ἔσχον πατρίδα·
σεμνῶν προῆλθον κοσμίων φυτοσπόρων,
μητρὸς Κυδίππης καὶ πατρὸς Καλλιστίου.
60   Ἐγειτνία μοι παρθένος Καλλιγόνη,
τὴν ἀρρένων μὲν ὄψιν εὐλαβουμένη,
μυχαιτάτῳ δὲ θαλάμῳ φρουρουμένη.
Ταύτης τὸ κάλλος – οὐ γὰρ ἴσχυον βλέπειν –
ἐκ τῶν ὑπ' αὐτὴν ἐξεμάνθανον κλύων.
65   Οὐκ αἰσχύνη μοι ταῦτα, Χαρίκλεις, λέγειν
πρὸς τὸν νοσοῦντα ταυτοπαθῆ μοι νόσον.
Ἐπεὶ δὲ δώροις δεξιῶν δι' ἀγγέλων
Καλλιγόνην κατεῖδον ὀψὲ καὶ μόλις
ἐκ θυρίδων ἄπλαστον ἐκκρεμωμένην,
70   ταύτης ἑάλων ἁπαλῆς οὔσης ἔτι,
οὕτως ἐχούσης τοῦ προσώπου τῆς θέας,
ὡς μακρὸς ἐξήγγειλε τῆς φήμης λόγος.
Βαβαί, μὰ τὴν Ἔρωτος ὁπλοποιίαν,
φεῦ φεῦ, μὰ τὰς Χάριτας, εἶπες ἂν βλέπων
75   καὶ σύ, Χαρίκλεις, τὴν Δροσίλλαν οὐ βλέπων,
μητρὸς Σελήνης, πατρὸς Ἡλίου τέκνον.
Τὰς τῶν ὁρώντων ἐξελίθου καρδίας,
ὁδοιποροῦντας ἐξετόξευε πλέον,
οὐκ ἔβλεπε βλέποντας ἐξ ἀπληστίας
80   ἀλλ' ἔφλεγε ξύμπαντας ἐξ εὐμορφίας.
Παῖς ἦν ἐκείνη, παῖς ἁπαλή, παρθένος·
πλὴν δυσκινήτους ἐκ χρόνων ἀμετρίας
γέροντας εἷλκε πρὸς ἔρωτα τῇ θέᾳ,
οὐ πῦρ μόνον πνέοντας εὐζώνους νέους.

or tasting the misfortunes with which Fortune strikes me,
entangled in nets of love.
Do you suffer? I suffer with you. Do you weep? I weep too.
Do you feel desire? I feel desire, and that for a beautiful maiden,
Kalligone, who was snatched from me."   50
        "Kleandros, savior of my suffering heart,"
said Charikles, "which one of the Olympian gods
sent you to cheer me up?
Tell of your own experiences, your similar suffering.
It is right that you speak first since you were imprisoned first;   55
then I will, your fellow prisoner."
        "Lesbos is my fatherland, Charikles.
I was born from noble, honorable parents:
Kydippe, my mother, and Kallistias, my father.
The maiden Kalligone was my neighbor,   60
kept secluded from men's sight
in the inner recess of the women's quarters.
Her beauty—for I wasn't able to see it—
I learned by hearsay from her servants.
I'm not ashamed to say these things, Charikles,   65
to one who's suffering from a sickness like mine.
But when, after sending gifts through clever messengers,
I beheld Kalligone at last and with effort,
as she leaned unaffectedly out a window,
I was conquered, for she was still a delicate beauty;   70
the appearance of her face was
just as persistent rumor claimed.
Ah, by the weaponry of Eros
and by the Graces, too, you'd have said on seeing her—
you too, Charikles, if you weren't looking upon Drosilla—   75
that she was the child of Selene and Helios.
She turned to stone the hearts of those who saw her
and shot with arrows even more those who walked by.
She did not look at those gazing at her insatiably,
but inflamed all with her beauty of form.   80
She was a girl, a delicate maiden,
but her appearance drew even old men
(hard to excite due to excessive age) to love—
not just ardent, active young men.

85   Ἔρωτος ἦν ἄγαλμα, τέκνον Ἡλίου,
        φέρουσα πατρὸς ἐμφέρειαν Ἡλίου
        ἢ καὶ πρὸς αὐτὸν ἀντερίζουσα πλέον.
        Ἔμελλες, ὦ γέννημα θηρίων Ἔρως,
        ἐμὴν πατάξαι καὶ σπαράξαι καρδίαν·
90   γάλα λεαίνης ἐξεμύζησας ἄρα
        καὶ μαστὸν ἄρκτων ἐξεθήλασας τάχα.
        Ὡς εἶδον οὖν, ἔπαθον εἰς ψυχὴν μέσην·
        ἔτρυχεν, ἐστρόβει με δυστυχὴς πόθος,
        ἐβαλλόμην, ἔπιπτον, ἐσπαρασσόμην,
95   οὐ γὰρ συνεῖχεν ἄγριος πόθος μόνον
        – ἢ μᾶλλον αὐτὸς ἦν κατατρύχων Ἔρως –,
        στοργὴ δὲ πολλὴ παιδικῆς ἀπλαστίας
        καὶ τῶν ἐκείνης οἶκτος αἰωρημάτων.
        Ἦν εὐσθενὴς ἂν ἐκ φιλήματος μόνου
100   ἀντιστρατεύειν ταῖς Ἔρωτος σφενδόναις·
        οὐκ ἤθελον σχεῖν ἐξ ἐκείνης τῆς κόρης
        οὐδὲν πλέον τι τοῦ φιλήματος τότε,
        καὶ τοῦτο φίλτρον πάντως ἐξ οἴκτου μόνου.
        Τοίνυν προσεῖπον – οὐδὲ γὰρ ἠνεσχόμην –
105   "ἔργου πάρεργον μεῖζον, ὦ κόρη, βλέπω·
        στόμα φιλεῖν σου κρεῖττον ἢ λείχειν μέλι."
        Ἀλλ᾽ ἐθροήθη καὶ μικροῖς ἡ παῖς λόγοις·
        ἐρωτικῶν γὰρ ἀδαὴς ἦν εἰσέτι.
        Εὐθὺς μὲν οὖν κέκρυπτο – φεῦ μοι τῆς φρίκης –
110   καὶ τὰς παρειὰς τῶν ἑαυτῆς δουλίδων
        ἔτυπτεν ἐγγελῶσα· καὶ γὰρ αἰσχύνη
        κατέσχεν αὐτήν· οὐ γὰρ εἶχεν ὃ δράσοι
        ἡ νηπιόφρων, ἁπαλόχροος κόρη.
        Εἰώθασι γὰρ ὠχρίαν προσλαμβάνειν
115   αἱ μὴ βλέπεσθαι προσδοκῶσαι παρθένοι,
        ὅταν τις αὐταῖς ἀπροόπτως ἐγγίσῃ
        καὶ προσλαλήσῃ μᾶλλον ἀξυμφωράτως.
            Ἐντεῦθεν ἐλθὼν εἰς τὸν οἰκεῖον δόμον
        ἐμαυτὸν ἐκδίδωμι τῷ κλινιδίῳ,
120   ἁδρὰν λαβὼν ἔρωτος ἀνθρακουργίαν
        – δι᾽ ὀμμάτων γὰρ δὺς Ἔρως τὴν καρδίαν
        οὐ μέχρι ταύτης ἵσταται φλέγειν θέλων,
        μέλη δὲ πάντα πυρπολεῖ περιτρέχων –,

She was an image of Eros, a child of Helios;   85
she resembled her father, the sun,
or rather she rivaled him.
You, Eros, child of beasts,
were about to beat and tear my heart—
you who'd drunk milk from a lioness   90
and perhaps sucked the breasts of bears.
When I saw her then, I suffered deep in my soul.
An unfortunate desire afflicted me, distracted me.
I was being struck, I was falling, I was being torn apart,
for not only was fierce desire afflicting me—   95
or rather, Eros himself was tormenting me—
but also much love for her childlike unaffectedness,
and sympathy for her willingness to lean out the window.
I should have been able from a kiss alone
to wage war against the missiles of Eros.   100
I did not wish to have from her
anything more than a kiss then—
even though this kiss should come from pity alone.
Accordingly I addressed her (for I did not hold myself back),
'I consider the secondary act greater than the act itself, maiden: 105
to kiss your mouth better than to lick honey.'
But the girl was troubled even by little words,
for she was ignorant still of love.
At once, then, she hid herself (to my horror),
and laughing, she struck the cheeks   110
of her slave women, for shame oppressed her
and she didn't know what to do,
the childish, soft-skinned girl.
Maidens who don't expect to be seen
generally turn pale   115
when someone suddenly approaches them
and more, secretly talks to them.
    "Then, having gone to my own house,
I put myself to bed
since I was burning with a great fire of love   120
(for Eros, having entered my heart through my eyes,
did not stop at this in his desire to inflame me,
but running about, he set all my limbs ablaze),

καὶ καθ᾽ ἑαυτὸν ἐτραγῴδουν ἠρέμα·
125   "μηδεὶς πτοείσθω κἂν πεφαρμακευμένα
τὰ τοῦ πόθου βέλεμνα τὰ ξιφηφόρα·
τὴν γὰρ φαρέτραν τῶν βελῶν πληρουμένην
ὅλην καθ᾽ ἡμῶν ἐκκενοῖ μανεὶς Ἔρως.
Μὴ δειλιάτω τῶν πτερύγων τὸν κρότον·
130   Ἔρως γάρ, ὥσπερ ἐμπεσὼν ἐν ἰξίῳ,
τῇ καρδίᾳ μου συγκρατεῖται καὶ μένει.
Ἔρως, Ἔρως δείλαιε, πῦρ πνέων Ἔρως,
ἂν εἶδες ἰξευθέντα τὸν στέρνου τόπον,
οὐκ ἂν καταπτὰς ἀμφεκολλήθης τάλας.
135   Πανδαμάτορ, πάντολμε, παντάναξ Ἔρως,
ποινηλατεῖς πικρῶς με μὴ πταίσαντά σοι·
οὐ χεῖρα κόπτεις οὐδὲ συντέμνεις πόδας
οὐδ᾽ ἐξορύττεις τὰς κόρας τῶν ὀμμάτων,
αὐτὴν διστεύεις δὲ καρδίαν μέσην
140   καὶ θανατοῖς με· δυσμενές, βριαρόχειρ,
σφάττεις, φονεύεις, πυρπολεῖς, καταφλέγεις,
πλήττεις, ἀναιρεῖς, φαρμακεύεις, ἐκτρέπεις.
Τῆς ἰσχύος σου, πτηνοτοξοπυρφόρε."
Οὕτως ἐγὼ δείλαιος ἐξεκοπτόμην·
145   πλὴν φάρμακόν τι συννοῶ μου τῆς νόσου
μήνυμα γραπτὸν ἀντιπέμψαι τῇ κόρῃ·
ὑπέτρεχον γὰρ συλλογισμοί με ξένοι
ὡς τυχὸν ἀντέπαθε καὶ Καλλιγόνη
ἰδοῦσα τὸν Κλέανδρον ὡραιωμένον.
150   Μὴ γάρ, Χαρίκλεις, τὸν λαλοῦντα κερτόμει
βλέπων ἀμαυρωθέντα τῇ περιστάσει,
βλέπων σκοτεινὸν καὶ κατησβολωμένον,
ἐν πηλοφύρτῳ φυλακῇ κεκλεισμένον·
ψυχῆς γὰρ ἐντὸς θλίψεσι στροβουμένης
155   καὶ τῶν ἱμερτῶν ἔκπαλαι στερουμένης
πάντως ἀνάγκη σῶμα συμπάσχειν ὅλον.'
' Ὡς εὖ λέγεις, Κλέανδρε" Χαρικλῆς ἔφη
'θάλλει νέου πρόσωπον, ὡραῖον μένει,
ψυχῆς ἀφορμὰς χαρμονῆς κεκτημένης.'
160   ' Γράψας τὸ λοιπὸν ἀντέπεμψα συντόμως'
Κλέανδρος ἀντέφησε 'πρὸς Καλλιγόνην,
πειρώμενος σχεῖν πίστιν ἐκ τῶν πραγμάτων,

and by myself, quietly, I told my tragic tale:
    "'Let no one fear the sword-sharp darts of desire,   125
even if they are poisoned,
for in his madness, Eros shot
his entire quiver full of arrows against us.
Let no one be afraid of the noise of wings,
for Eros, as if he'd fallen into birdlime,   130
is held fast by my heart.
Eros, wretched, fire-breathing Eros,
if you'd seen my heart covered with birdlime
you'd not have flown down and been caught fast, poor chap.
All-taming, all-daring, all-ruling Eros,   135
like a fury you pursue me cruelly, a man who's done you no wrong.
You don't chop off my hand, cut off my feet,
dig out the pupils of my eyes;
instead you shoot arrows at the very middle of my heart
and you make me die! Strong-handed enemy,   140
you slaughter, kill, burn, inflame,
strike, destroy, poison, and eliminate.
What great power you have, Eros—with wings, fire, and bow!'
    "Thus, in my wretchedness, I was beating myself up,
when it occurred to me to cure my sickness   145
by sending a written message to the girl,
for the strange thought came over me
that perhaps Kalligone too suffered in turn
when she saw Kleandros in his beauty.
Don't scoff, Charikles, at the one saying this,   150
because you see him weakened by circumstance,
dark, covered with soot,
shut up in a muddy prison!
When the spirit is distressed by afflictions
and deprived of lovely things for a long time,   155
the whole body surely must suffer too."
    "How right you are, Kleandros," Charikles said.
"The look of a young man blossoms and stays beautiful
when his spirit has occasions of delight."
    "Then I wrote the note and sent it to Kalligone   160
at once," Kleandros said in turn,
"in an attempt to learn from her actions

εἴ πού τι συμπέπονθε καὶ Καλλιγόνη.'
         ''Αλλ' ὡς ὄναιο τοῦ πόθου Καλλιγόνης'
165   ὁ Χαρικλῆς ἔλεξε τῷ ξένῳ πάλιν,
'Κλέανδρε, τούτων μηδὲν ἄρρητον λίποις
ὧν γεγραφὼς ἔπεμψας πρὸς τὴν παρθένον.'
         ' Ἄκουε λοιπόν' ὁ Κλέανδρος ἀντέφη'
         ' τῆς σῆς ἐγώ, παῖ παγκάλη, μεμνημένος
170   θέας ἱμερτῆς ἣν ἰδὼν κατεπλάγην,
χθὲς ἐντυχὼν Χάρωνι μικρὸν ἠρόμην
καὶ σὲ πρὸ ἡμῶν, ὥσπερ εἶπεν, εἰδότι'
"ἆρ', ὦ χαρᾶς ἄμοιρε, δυσμενὲς Χάρων,
καὶ τὴν φερίστην ἐν κόραις Καλλιγόνην
175   σὺν τοῖς καθ' ἡμᾶς δυστυχῶς ἀφαρπάσεις
καὶ κάλλος αὐτὸ τὸ προτεθρυλλημένον
διαφθερεῖς καὶ κύκλα τοξεύοντά με
τῶν ὀμμάτων τοιαῦτα, φεῦ, διασπάσεις
ἢ πρὸς τὸ κάλλος συσταλῇς ἀποβλέπων;"
180   Οὕτω μὲν αὐτὸς εἶπον' ἀλλ' ὁ γεννάδας
ὁ τρισθενής "ναί" φησὶ δύσμορος Χάρων.
Καὶ δυσφορήσας εὐθὺς ἀνταπεκρίθην'
"Αἰαῖ, κακῶν κάκιστε, τί δράσεις, Χάρων;"
Τί λοιπόν; Ἀμφίνευσον, ὦ Καλλιγόνη'
185   ἔχεις με τὸν Κλέανδρον ἐξαιτοῦντά σε.'
         'Μικρὸν τὸ γράμμα, μηχανῆς δ' ὅμως γέμον'
ὁ Χαρικλῆς ἔφησεν ἠκουτισμένος,
'ὅπως θανάτου καὶ Χάρωνος ἡ κόρη
μνησθεῖσα νῦν κλίναντος τὰς ἐπηρμένας
190   ἐπικλινὴς γένοιτο τῷ γράψαντί σοι.
Τί λοιπὸν εἰς Κλέανδρον ἡ Καλλιγόνη
ἀντεῖπεν, ἀντέγραψεν, εἰδὼς εὖ, λέγοις.'
         ' Οὐδέν, Χαρίκλεις, ὡς ἔοικεν, ἡ κόρη,
ἢ μὴ τὸ γράμμα τοῦτο προσδεδεγμένη
195   ἢ παισὶ συμπαίστορσιν ἠσχολημένη.
Καὶ δευτέρας οὖν συλλαβῆς ἄκουέ μου.'
         ''Αλλ', ὦ φίλε Κλέανδρε, μηδὲ τῆς τρίτης
ἐμοὶ φθονήσῃς συλλαβῆς πρὸς τὴν κόρην'
ἔφη Χαρικλῆς' ὁ Κλέανδρος ἀντέφη'
200   'ἄκουε' ταύτης οὐ φθονῶ σοι, Χαρίκλεις'
κουφίζομαι γὰρ προσλαλῶν σοι τῆς νόσου.

whether Kalligone perhaps shared my suffering."
    "May you enjoy, Kleandros, your love
of Kalligone," Charikles responded to the stranger,   165
"and leave unsaid none of the things
you wrote to the maiden!"
    "Listen then," Kleandros replied.
    "'Remembering, most beautiful girl,
your lovely appearance (which amazed me the instant I saw it),   170
when I met with Charon yesterday—who said he knew you
before I did—I asked him a brief question:
"Cruel Charon, with no share in joy,
will you take away Kalligone,
best among the maidens, along with people like us,   175
ruin her renowned beauty
and tear out such lovely eyes, alas,
which wound me with arrows;
or will you withdraw when you gaze upon her beauty?"
Thus I spoke, but the noble,   180
thrice-strong, death-dealing Charon replied, "Yes!"
At once, in anger, I answered back,
"Ah, Charon, most wicked of all, what will you do?"
What remains? Nod your consent, Kalligone!
You have me, Kleandros, asking for you.'"   185
    "The letter is short but full of art,"
Charikles said when he heard it,
"so that the girl, reminded now of death and of Charon,
who humbles proud girls,
might yield to you, the writer.   190
What, then, did Kalligone say in response to Kleandros?
What did she write? Tell me, you who know well!"
    "The girl said nothing, Charikles, as it seems,
either because she did not accept my letter
or because she was busy with her playmates.   195
Then hear my second letter also."
    "But, dear Kleandros, don't deny me
even your third letter to the girl,"
said Charikles. Kleandros replied,
"Listen; I don't deny you this, Charikles,   200
for I gain relief from my sickness by talking with you.

Μῦθον τὸ Σειρήνειον ἐννοῶ μέλος,
ἀφ' οὗ τὸ σὸν πρόσωπον εἶδον, παρθένε.
Αὐχεῖς, ἰδού, τὸ κάλλος ὑπὲρ τὸν λόγον·
205   διδοῖς ἐμοὶ τὸ φίλτρον ὑπὲρ τὴν φύσιν·
λιθοῦσα πλήττεις, οὐδὲ γὰρ φεύγειν δίδως.
Ξανθὸν τὸ πλέγμα· δῦθι, χρυσέ, γῆν πάλιν.
Λαμπρὸν τὸ βλέμμα· χαῖρε, λαμπρότης λίθων.
Τὸ χρῶμα λευκόν· ἔρρε, μαργάρων χάρις·
210   τῆς σῆς γὰρ αὐτὸς φωσφορούσης, παρθένε,
θέας ἐκείνης πανταχοῦ μεμνημένος
τοῦ δυσμενοῦς Ἔρωτος οὐ κατισχύω
τοὺς ἄνθρακάς μοι τοὺς ἀναφθέντας σβέσαι.
Καὶ νοῦς μὲν αὐτὸς ἐξελίσσει τὴν θέαν,
215   ἀντιστορῶν ἣν εἶχεν, ὡς εἶδον πάλαι·
ἀλλ' ἔνδον αὐτῆς τῆς ταλαίνης καρδίας
Ἔρως ὁ πικρός, ὁ δρακοντώδης γόνος,
ἑλίσσεταί μοι λοξοειδῶς, ὡς ὄφις,
καὶ στέρνα μοι καὶ σπλάγχνα, φεῦ, κατεσθίει.
220   Σὸν ἔργον ἐστὶ καταπαῦσαι τὴν νόσον.
Τοὺς ἄνθρακας σβέννυε καὶ δρόσιζέ με
καὶ τὸν δράκοντα τὸν περιπλακέντά μοι
ταῖς σαῖς ἐπῳδαῖς ἐξαπόσπα, παρθένε.'
        'Ναὶ ναί, φίλε Κλέανδρε' Χαρικλῆς ἔφη,
225   'ἁλόντος αὐτὰ καὶ παθούσης καρδίας·
ἔπαθες, ὡς φῄς· ἐξ ἐμαυτοῦ μανθάνω.
Τὸν τῶν βροτῶν τύραννον αὐτοδεσπότην
Ἔρωτα τὸν τοσαῦτα συντήξαντά με
δεσμῆσαν αὐτὸ τῶν Χαρίτων τὸ στίφος,
230   ταῖς εὐπροσώποις καλλοναῖς τῶν παρθένων
τὸν δεσπότην δίδωσιν ὡς ὑπηρέτην.
Ἡ Παφίη δὲ πανταχοῦ πλανωμένη
καὶ λύτρα δῶρα προσφέρουσα μυρία
ζητεῖ τὸ τέκνον πολλὰ ποτειρομένη,
235   καὶ κἄν τις αὐτὸν εὑρεθῇ λῦσαι θέλων,
οὐ δραπετεύει· καὶ γὰρ ὡς ὑπηρέτης
τὸ προσμένειν ἔμαθεν ἐκ τῶν Χαρίτων.'
        '"Ακουσον' ὁ Κλέανδρος εἶπε 'καὶ τρίτης
ἡμῶν, Χαρίκλεις, συλλαβῆς πρὸς τὴν κόρην.
240   'Ἐκ σοῦ, σελήνη, καὶ τὸ φῶς δοκῶ βλέπειν.

'Ever since I saw your face, maiden,
I have considered the Sirens' song a fable.*
You boast of beauty beyond words;
you give me a love-charm beyond nature;   205
you strike, turning men to stone, for you don't allow them to flee.
Your braids are blond—plunge back into the earth, gold!
Your eye is bright—farewell, splendor of precious stones!
Your complexion is fair—begone, loveliness of pearls!
Remembering always, maiden,   210
that luminous appearance of yours,
I cannot extinguish cruel Eros's coals,
which burn within me.
And my mind revolves around your appearance,
asking what you looked like when I saw you then,   215
but within my wretched heart,
cruel Eros, the snake-child,
rolls around obliquely, like a serpent,
and devours my heart and inward parts, alas.
It's your job to stop this sickness.   220
Quench the coals, sprinkle me with dew,
and draw off the serpent that's wrapped himself round me,
maiden, with your charms.'"
        "Yes, dear Kleandros," Charikles said,
"these things belong to a person caught and a heart that's suffered.   225
You've suffered, as you say; I understand from my own experience.
The chorus of the Graces fettered
the tyrant of mortals, the absolute master,
Eros, who made me waste away so greatly,
and gave him, a master, as a servant   230
to fair-faced, beautiful maidens.
Paphian Aphrodite seeks her child
by wandering everywhere, offering countless gifts as ransom,
and asking many questions besides;
and even if someone is found willing to release him,   235
he does not run away, for he has learnt
from the Graces to remain as a servant."
        "Listen, Charikles, also to my third letter
to the girl," Kleandros said.
'From you, moon, I think I see my light too.   240

Σοὶ συγκινοῦμαι, σοὶ πνέω, σοὶ συμμένω,
Σὺ χαρμονή μοι καὶ σὺ θλίψεως βέλος.
Σὺ καὶ νόσος μοι καὶ σὺ φάρμακον νόσου.
Σὺ φροντὶς εἶ καὶ θᾶττον ἄφροντις βίος.
245   Σὺ καὶ νεκρὸν ζωοῖς με, τὸ πρᾶγμα ξένον,
καὶ ζῶντα νεκροῖς· θαῦμα. Καὶ γὰρ ἡ φύσις
κεστοὺς ὅλους λαβοῦσα πρὸς τὴν σὴν πλάσιν
ἀγαλματοῖ σε λευκερυθροφωσφόρον.
Ὦ ποῖον ἄστρον λαμπρὸν οὕτω καὶ μέγα,
250   μήτηρ Σελήνη φωσφόρος, φυτοσπόρος,
ἐν τοῖς καθ᾽ ἡμᾶς ἐξεγέννησε χρόνοις.
Νοσεῖς; Νοσῶ· χαίρεις δέ; Συγχαίρω μέγα·
ἀλγεῖς; Συναλγῶ· δακρύεις; Συνδακρύω.
Ἓν τοῦτο πικρόν, ἓν τὸ δάκνον, τὸ τρῦχον·
225   ἀφ᾽ οὗ γὰρ εἶδον, ἐξετοξεύθην τάλας,
ἀεὶ δέ μοι σὺ πετροκάρδιος μένεις·
οὐ φάρμακον γὰρ ἐμπαρέσχες αὐτίκα
τῇ καρδίᾳ μου τῇ τετραυματισμένῃ,
καὶ νῦν σαπέντος τοῦ πεπληγότος τόπου
260   ἐκφύντες οἱ σκώληκες ἐσθίουσί με·
οὕτως ἀεὶ τὸ τόξον ἐντείνων Ἔρως
σφάττει, φονεύει, τραυματοῖ, ξαίνει, θλίβει,
κεντεῖ, τιτρώσκει, θανατοῖ, τέμνει, τρύχει.
Ἔγγισον, ἴδε καρδίαν πεπληγμένην
265   καὶ στέρνον αὐτὸ καιρίως βεβλημένον.
Ἔνσταξον εἰς τὸ στέρνον ἐκ στέρνου δρόσον
ὡς οἶνον, ὡς ἔλαιον εἰς τὸ τραῦμά μου·
τοὺς κρυσταλλώδεις ὧδε δακτύλους φέρε,
ὅλης ἐφάπτου τῆς παθούσης καρδίας·
270   τὸ λεπτοϋφὲς ἐξυφάπλου μοι φάρος,
τοὺς ἑλκεσιτραφεῖς δὲ δακνοκαρδίους
σκώληκας ἁδροὺς θᾶττον ἐκκάθαιρέ μοι.
Οὕτως ὄναιο τῆς ἐμῆς σωτηρίας,
οὕτως ὀναίμην σῆς τόσης εὐποιίας.
275   Ποίησον οὕτως· ἀλλ᾽ ὑπὸ χλαῖναν μίαν
γενοίμεθα ζέοντι καρδίας πόθῳ,
ἐπαινετὴν πλέξαντες ἀλληλουχίαν.
    Ἀλλ᾽, ὦ Χαρίκλεις, εἰ δοκεῖ, σιγητέον·
εἰ δ᾽ οὔ, τετάρτῃ συλλαβῇ δὸς ὠτίον.᾽

I move with you, breathe through you, remain with you.
You are my joy and a dart of affliction.
You are my sickness and a cure for sickness.
You are my anxiety, and instantly, a life without care.
You give me life when I am dead (an extraordinary thing)   245
and make me dead when I am alive (a wonder). Nature too,
having brought all charms to your form,
makes you into a white and red, light-giving image.
What a star, so shining and big,
did mother Selene, light-giving and fertile,   250
bring forth in our time!
Are you sick? I am sick. Do you rejoice? I rejoice greatly with you.
Do you suffer? I suffer with you. Do you weep? I weep too.
This one thing is cruel; this one thing stings and afflicts me.
As soon as I saw you, I was shot with arrows, wretchedly,   255
but you always remain a girl with a heart of stone,
for you did not at once provide a cure
for my heart when it was wounded,
and now, when the wound has festered,
the worms that arose are devouring me.   260
Thus Eros always stretches his bow tight and
slaughters, slays, wounds, mangles, afflicts,
goads, damages, kills, maims, and torments.
Approach and look at a heart that has been struck
and a breast hit with a mortal blow!   265
Drop into my breast from your breast
dew like wine, like olive-oil into my wound.
Bring fingers like crystal,
lay hold of my heart, which has suffered greatly,
spread a finely woven cloth under me,   270
and clear away from me at once
the wound-eating, heart-stinging, thick worms!
Thus may you benefit from my salvation,
and thus may I enjoy your great benefaction!
Make it so. May we lie beneath one cloak,   275
with burning desire in our heart,
and enjoy a splendid coupling!'
    "But, Charikles, if you think it best, I will be silent;
if not, give ear to the fourth letter."

280   'Λέγοις ἄν, ὦ Κλέανδρε' Χαρικλῆς ἔφη.
      ' Ἄκουε λοιπὸν ῥημάτων κατωδύνων,
      ὅσα προσεξέπεμψα τῇ Καλλιγόνῃ.'
      Κλέανδρος εἰπὼν ἦρχε τῆς τραγῳδίας·
         'Χυσοῦν δέχου τὸ μῆλον οὗ γεγραμμένον,
285   ὦ σῶμα συμπὰν εὐφυὲς Καλλιγόνη·
      κἂν ἐγράφῃ δέ, πρὸς σὲ ποία τις ἔρις;
      Δέχου, καλή, τὸ μῆλον, ὡς καλὴ μόνη·
      τῶν παρθένων γὰρ ἐν χοροῖς σὺ καλλίων.
      Συμμαρτυρεῖ καὶ Μῶμος αὐτός, ἀτρέμας
290   ἰδὼν σὺν ἡμῖν εἰς πανήγυριν πάλαι
      ἄνω πατοῦσαν καὶ προκύπτουσαν κάτω·
      καὶ γὰρ τὸ χεῖλος ἐνδακὼν κατεπλάγη.
      Μὴ σφόδρα μοι σύναγε τὰς ὀφρῦς ἄνω·
      ἐκ τῶν Ἔρωτος ἐξετάκην φαρμάκων,
295   ἐκ τῶν ἐκείνου κατεκαύθην ἀνθράκων.
      Ἐξ ἡλίου φλέγοντος ὡς ὁδοιπόρος,
      ὡς σκιερόν τι δένδρον ἐξεύρηκά σε·
      ὡς κισσὸς εἰς δρῦν συμπλακείην παννύχως.
      Εἰπεῖν δέον με τὴν ἀλήθειαν· ὅσον
300   χειμῶνός ἐστι κρεῖττον ἐκκρίτως ἔαρ,
      στρουθῶν ἀηδών, μῆλον ἡδὺ βραβύλων,
      ὅσον γυναικῶν τριγάμων ἡ παρθένος,
      τοσοῦτο τὸ πρόσωπον· ἡ σκιὰ μόνη
      ἔθελξε τὸν χθὲς ἀτενῶς βλέψαντά σε.
305   Ἡ Κύπρις, ὡς ἔοικεν, αὐτή, παρθένε,
      τὰς χεῖρας εἰς τὸν κόλπον ἐντέθεικέ σου,
      καὶ πᾶσα Χάρις ἐξεκαλλώπισέ σε.
      Ἐμοὶ λογισμὸς ἦλθε μὴ σὺ Πανδώρα,
      ἣν εἰσάγει τις μυθικὴ πλαστουργία.
310   Κἂν γοῦν ἐκείνην μῦθος αὐτὸς εἰσάγῃ,
      ὅμως ἐναργὴς τῆς ἀληθείας λόγος
      ἡμῖν παριστῶν ὡς ἄγαλμα δεικνύει
      ἡλιοειδὲς καὶ κατηστερισμένον,
      τὴν παρθένον σε, τὴν καλὴν Καλλιγόνην.
315   Οὕτω, Χαρίκλεις, μηδαμοῦ στέγειν ἔχων
      γραφὰς παρεξέπεμπον ἀλληλοδρόμους.
      Τί γοῦν; Ὁ τάλας ἀντεμηνύθην μόλις
      ἐλθεῖν πρὸς αὐτοὺς παρθενῶνας ἐννύχως,

"Speak, Kleandros," Charikles said.   280
"Hear then the very painful words
that I sent to Kalligone next,"
Kleandros said and began his tragic recitation:
    "'Accept the golden apple, uninscribed,
Kalligone with your altogether shapely body!   285
But even if it were inscribed, what quarrel would you have?
Accept the apple, beautiful girl, since you alone are beautiful,
for you are more beautiful than all the maidens in the choirs.
Blame himself bears witness to this, having looked
quietly with us at the maidens' assembly once,   290
as the girls were walking, heads held high or with downcast eye,
for he even bit his lip in amazement.
Don't knit your brows severely at me!
I wasted away from Eros's poisons;
I was burnt by his glowing embers.   295
Like a traveler out of the burning sun
who finally finds a shady tree, I found you.
May I cling to you, like ivy to a tree, all night long!
I must tell the truth: just as
spring is better by far than winter,   300
nightingale than sparrows, sweet apple than blackthorn plums,
a maiden than thrice-married women,
so great is your beauty—your shadow alone
charmed the man who gazed at you intently yesterday.
Cypris herself as it seems, maiden,   305
put her hands upon your bosom,
and every Grace beautified you.
The thought came to me that you might be Pandora,*
whom mythological stories introduce.
But even if myth itself introduces that character,   310
still truth's clear authority
presents you to us and shows you, the maiden,
the beautiful Kalligone, as a statue
like the sun and adorned with stars.'
    "Thus, Charikles, since I couldn't restrain myself at all,   315
I sent her letters, one after the other.
What then? Finally I was told—lovesick lad—
to come during the night to the maidens' apartments,

ἐν οἷς διημέρευεν ἡ γλυκυτάτη.
320   Καταλαβούσης τοιγαροῦν τῆς ἑσπέρας,
ἀναλαβὼν κίθαριν ἠργυρωμένην,
ἐπέκρουον κρούματα καλλίστῳ κρότῳ
καὶ συγκροτῶν ᾦδευον εἰς Καλλιγόνην
καί – τῶν Ὀλυμπίων γὰρ ὑπερεφρόνουν –
325   τοιῶνδε τερπνῶν ᾀσμάτων ἀπηργμένος.
      "Λαμπὰς σελήνης, φωταγώγει τὸν ξένον.
Ἡ Νιόβη κλαίουσα λίθος εὑρέθη,
μὴ καρτεροῦσα τὴν στέρησιν τῶν τέκνων·
Πανδίονος δὲ θυγάτηρ παιδοκτόνος
330   ἐξωρνέωτο πτῆσιν αἰτησαμένη.
      Λαμπὰς σελήνης, φωταγώγει τὸν ξένον.
Ἐγὼ δ' ἔσοπτρον εὑρεθείην, Ζεῦ ἄναξ,
ὅπως ἀεὶ βλέπῃς με σύ, Καλλιγόνη·
χιτὼν γενοίμην χρυσόπαστος ποικίλος,
335   ὅπως ἔχω σου θιγγάνειν τοῦ σαρκίου.
      Λαμπὰς σελήνης, φωταγώγει τὸν ξένον.
Ὕδωρ φανείην, ὡς προσώπου πᾶν μέρος
σχοίην ἀλείφειν εὐτυχῶς καθ' ἡμέραν·
μύρον γενοίμην, ὡς ἐπιχρίειν ἔχω
340   χείλη, παρειάς, χεῖρας, ὄμματα, στόμα.
      Λαμπὰς σελήνης, φωταγώγει τὸν ξένον.
Τί μοι μεγίστων καὶ τυχεῖν μὴ ῥᾳδίων;
Ἤρκει γενέσθαι χρύσεόν με βλαυτίον
καὶ καρτερεῖν με συμπατούμενον μόνον
345   τῇ λευκοτάρσῳ τῶν ποδῶν σου συνθέσει.
      Λαμπὰς σελήνης, φωταγώγει τὸν ξένον.
Ζεὺς ἀντὶ πυρὸς ἐμπαρέσχε τῷ βίῳ
πῦρ ἄλλο δεινόν, τῆς γυναικὸς τὴν πλάσιν.
Ὡς εἴθε μὴ πῦρ, μὴ γυναικεῖον φύλον
350   κατῆλθεν εἰς γῆν καὶ προῆλθεν εἰς βίον.
      Λαμπὰς σελήνης, φωταγώγει τὸν ξένον.
Τὸ πῦρ γὰρ αὐτό, κἂν ἀναφθείη, πάλιν
καὶ συντόμως σχοίη τις ἐγκατασβέσαι·
γυνὴ δὲ πῦρ ἄσβεστον ἐν τῇ καρδίᾳ
355   ἂν κάλλος εὐπρόσωπον ὡραῖον φέρῃ.
      Λαμπὰς σελήνης, φωταγώγει τὸν ξένον.
Τυχὸν γὰρ οὓς ἔσωσεν ἀνδρεία μάχης,

where the sweetest girl resided.
Therefore, when evening came,   320
I took up a silver cithara,
struck the strings most beautifully,
and made my way to Kalligone, playing music all the while,
starting up (for I thought little of the Olympians)
such delightful songs as this: 325
    "Torch of the moon, guide the stranger with your light.
Weeping, Niobe became a stone*
since she couldn't bear the loss of her children,
and Pandion's daughter, who killed her child,*
became a bird when she asked for flight.   330
    "Torch of the moon, guide the stranger with your light.
May I become a mirror, Lord Zeus,
that you, Kalligone, might always look at me.
May I become a tunic embroidered with gold, variegated,
that I might be able to touch your body.   335
    "Torch of the moon, guide the stranger with your light.
May I become water that I might have the good fortune
to wash every part of your face every day.
May I become unguent that I might be able to anoint
your lips, cheeks, hands, eyes, and mouth.   340
    "Torch of the moon, guide the stranger with your light.
Why do I wish for these great things, not easily gained?
It would suffice for me to become a golden slipper
and simply allow myself to be trampled
by the white soles of your feet.   345
    "Torch of the moon, guide the stranger with your light.
Zeus gave to life, in exchange for fire,
another terrible fire: the female form.
If only that fire, the female race, had not
descended to earth and come to life!   350
    "Torch of the moon, guide the stranger with your light.
Fire itself, if it should be kindled,
could quickly find someone to quench it again.
But a woman is an unquenchable fire in the heart
if she bears a fresh-faced, youthful beauty.   355
    "Torch of the moon, guide the stranger with your light.
Wherefore those whom manliness saved from battle,

ὧν μὴ κεφαλὰς ἐξέκοψεν ἡ σπάθη,
οὓς μὴ κλινήρεις ἀπέδειξεν ἡ νόσος,
360   οὓς δραστικὴ φρὴν ἐρρύσατο κινδύνων,
    Λαμπὰς σελήνης, φωταγώγει τὸν ξένον,
οὓς οὐ κατειργάσαντο κύκλοι πραγμάτων,
οὓς δεσμὸς οὐ κατέσχεν, οὐ κλοιῶν βάρος,
ἀεὶ δὲ χωρὶς τῆς τυχούσης φροντίδος
365   ζῶσι Κρονικὸν καὶ τὸν εὔθυμον βίον,
    Λαμπὰς σελήνης, φωταγώγει τὸν ξένον,
τούτους γυνὴ λαλοῦσα χαρμονῆς χάριν
ταῖς ἐξ ἐκείνης ἀστραπαῖς σελασφόροις,
ὡς ἐν κεραυνῷ πρηστικῷ καταφλέγει,
370   ἄνθος κατατρύχουσα σαρκίου νέου.
    Λαμπὰς σελήνης, φωταγώγει τὸν ξένον.
Σῶν χειλέων κάμινος ἐξῆπται μέσον,
Καλλιγόνη, θάμβημα τοῖς ἰδοῦσί σε,
ὁμοῦ κατ' αὐτὸ πῦρ φέρουσα καὶ δρόσον,
375   τῇ μὲν καλοῦσα, τῷ δ' ἀποτρέπουσά με.
    Λαμπὰς σελήνης, φωταγώγει τὸν ξένον.
Αὕτη τὸν ἐμβλέψαντα μακρόθεν φλέγει,
τὸν δὲ προσεγγίσαντα τῷ στόματί σου,
ἢ καὶ τυχόντα τοῦ φιλήματος μόνου
380   ψυχρᾷ ψεκάδι δεξιοῦται καὶ δρόσῳ.
    Λαμπὰς σελήνης, φωταγώγει τὸν ξένον.
Ὦ πῦρ δροσίζον, ὦ φλογίζουσα δρόσος·
Ἀλλὰ φλεγέντα καὶ πεπυρπολημένον
ἐξ ἄνθρακος σῶν χειλέων παρηγόρει
385   διδοῦσα τὴν σὴν εἰς ἀνάψυξιν δρόσον."'.

ΒΙΒΛΙΟΝ ΤΡΙΤΟΝ

    ' Οὕτω μελίζων, ὡς ἀηδὼν εἰς ἔαρ,
προσῆλθον, εὗρον, εἶδον αὐτὴν τὴν κόρην,
καὶ "χαῖρε" φησίν "ὦ καθ' ὕπνους νυμφίε"
ἐμοῦ προαρπάσασα τὴν ὁμιλίαν·
5   " Ἔρως ἐπιστὰς τῇ πρὸ τῆς χθὲς ἑσπέρα
ἐμοὶ συνῆψε σέ, Κλέανδρε, πρὸς γάμον,
ὡς εἶπε, προσχὼν οἷς ἐπένθεις δακρύοις.

whose heads the sword spared,
whom sickness did not put to bed,
whom a daring mind has saved from dangers—   360
    "'Torch of the moon, guide the stranger with your light—
whom changes of circumstance did not subdue,
whom bonds did not restrain nor weight of prisoners' collars,
but who always, outside the concerns of the day,
live the old-fashioned, cheerful life—   365
    "'Torch of the moon, guide the stranger with your light—
these men are inflamed by a woman of charming speech,
by the luminous flashes that burst from her
like blazing lightning bolts,
as she consumes the bloom of a young man's body.   370
    "'Torch of the moon, guide the stranger with your light.
In the middle of your lips a furnace has been lit—
a wonder to those who see you, Kalligone—
producing fire and dew together,
the one attracting and the other repelling me.   375
    "'Torch of the moon, guide the stranger with your light.
This furnace burns the one who looks from afar,
but welcomes with a cold drop of dew
the one who approaches your mouth
or even obtains only a kiss.   380
    "'Torch of the moon, guide the stranger with your light.
O fire that besprinkles, O dew that burns!
Comfort the one who is inflamed,
wasted with fire from the embers of your lips,
by giving him your dew for relief.'   385

BOOK THREE

    "Singing this song, like a nightingale in springtime,
I approached, and I found her and saw the girl herself.
'Greetings, bridegroom of my dreams,' she said,
taking the initiative by speaking first.
'Eros appeared to me the evening before last   5
and united you with me in marriage, Kleandros,
since he was moved, he said, by your tears.

Καὶ σκεπτέον σοι, ναί, Κλέανδρε, σκεπτέον
πῶς τῶν καθ᾽ ἡμᾶς ἀσφαλῶς φροντιστέον.

10   Ἐγὼ γὰρ οὐ πῦρ, οὐ θάλασσαν, οὐ ξίφος
πρὸς τὴν Κλεάνδρου δειλιάσαιμι, σχέσιν·
οὓς γὰρ θεὸς συνῆψε, τίς διασπάσοι; "
        Τούτων ἀκούσας, ὦ Χαρίκλεις, τῶν λόγων
"Καλλιγόνη, σύγχαιρε" λοιπὸν ἀντέφην,

15   "καὶ δεῦρο δεῦρο πρὸς τὸν ἀγχοῦ λιμένα,
ὅπως ἀποπλεύσωμεν ἄμφω Λεσβόθεν,
Ἔρωτι δόξαν τῷ τυράννῳ, παρθένε. "
Οὐκοῦν ἑαυτοὺς ἐμβαλόντες ὁλκάδι
– οὐ γὰρ βραδύνειν ἐμμανεὶς Ἔρως θέλει –

20   καὶ πέντε συμπλεύσαντες ἡμερῶν πλόον
τοῦ φωσφόρου κλίναντος ἄρτι πρὸς δύσιν
καὶ πνευσάσης λαίλαπος ὠλεσισκάφου
ἄκοντες ἐξήχθημεν εἰς Βάρζον πόλιν,
ἧς καὶ προσωρμίσθημεν ἐν τῷ λιμένι,

25   μόλις φυγόντες τὴν ἀνάγκην τῆς ζάλης.
Οὕτω τυχὸν δὲ δυσμενεῖς Πάρθοι τότε
σφοδρῶς ἐληΐζοντο κύκλῳ τὴν πόλιν
– τοὺς Βαρζίτας γὰρ ζημιοῦσι πολλάκις
ἄφνω παρεμπίπτοντες ἠμελημένοις –,

30   οἳ συλλαβόντες πάντας ἡμᾶς ἀθρόως
τοὺς τῆς θαλάσσης ἐκφυγόντας τὸ στόμα,
Καλλιγόνην Κλέανδρον, ἄλλους ἐμβάτας,
τὴν φορταγωγὸν ἐξέκαυσαν ὁλκάδα.
Καλλιγόνη γοῦν ἐγκρυβεῖσα μυρρίναις

35   – συνηρεφεῖς γὰρ ἦσαν ἀγχοῦ λιμένος –
τὴν Παρθικὴν ἔφυγεν ἀγερωχίαν,
ἐγὼ δὲ μέχρι τῆς παρούσης ἡμέρας,
ἀφ᾽ οὗπερ αὐτῆς, ὦ θεοί, διεζύγην,
εἱρκτὴν κατοικῶ τὴν κατεζοφωμένην,

40   διττὴν πεπονθὼς συμφορὰν βαρυτάτην·
Καλλιγόνης γὰρ ἐστέρημαι παρθένου
καὶ νῦν παρ᾽ ἐχθροῖς εἰμι δυσμενεστάτοις.
Σὺ γοῦν, Χαρίκλεις, ὡς ὑπέσχου μοι, λέγοις
τὸν σὸν πονηρὸν καὶ πολύδακρυν βίον. "

45   " Ποιεῖς μὲν ὄντως οὐκ ἀδακρύτως λέγειν,
Κλέανδρε, τὰ τρύχοντα καὶ θλίβοντά με"

You must consider—yes, Kleandros—
how to provide for the safety of our affairs.
I would not fear fire, sea, or sword   10
to have Kleandros as my husband!
Who could separate those whom a god has joined?'
    "When I heard these words, Charikles,
I replied, 'Kalligone, greetings to you too.
Come to the harbor nearby   15
that we may both sail away from Lesbos,
as Eros, the tyrant, decreed, maiden.'
Then we boarded a ship—
for Eros when maddened does not wish to delay—
and sailed together for five days,   20
and when the sun had just begun to set on the fifth day
and a ship-destroying tempest had started,
unwillingly we retreated to the city of Barzon,
where we came to anchor in the harbor
after barely escaping the violence of the storm.   25
By chance hostile Parthians were then
violently plundering about the city
(for they often inflict injury on the people of Barzon
by suddenly attacking them when they're unprepared)
and they seized all of us together   30
who had escaped the mouth of the sea—
Kalligone, Kleandros, and the others on board—
and burned the merchant ship.
Kalligone hid in myrtle branches—
for they grew thickly near the harbor—   35
and thus escaped the Parthian violence,
but I, up until today
from when (oh gods!) I was parted from her,
have been dwelling in this dark prison,
having suffered a grievous, double misfortune,   40
for I was deprived of the maiden Kalligone
and am now in the hands of hateful enemies.
Now then, Charikles, as you promised,
tell me of your grievous and tearful life."
    "You are making me speak, truly not without tears,   45
Kleandros, of the things that afflict and distress me,"

ἔφη Χαρικλῆς τοῦ λαλεῖν ἀπηργμένος·
"ὅμως ἐπειδὴ καρδίαν ἐλαφρύνει
τὸ τοὺς κατ' αὐτὴν ἐξερεύγεσθαι λόγους,
50   Κλέανδρε, πρόσχες· οὐ κατοκνῶ γὰρ λέγειν.
Μήτηρ μὲν ἦν μοι Κρυστάλη, πατὴρ Φράτωρ,
οὐκ ἐκ γεναρχῶν ἀκλεῶν, πατρὶς Φθία.
Ἤδη δὲ τὸν μείρακα τῆς ἥβης νόμον
ἡλικιούμην εὐγενῶς τεθραμμένος·
55   μείραξι συνέχαιρον οἷς προσωμίλουν,
ἵππευον, ἀμφέπαιζον, ὡς νέοις νόμος,
λαγὼς ἐθήρων, εὐφυῶς ἱππηλάτουν
– συμπαίστορας γὰρ εἶχον εὐπρεπεστάτους –
ἐρωτικῶς γοῦν οὐκ ἔπαθον εἰσέτι,
60   οὔπω γένυν ἴουλος ὑπεζωγράφει.
Διονύσου δὲ τῆς ἑορτῆς ἐνστάσης,
συνεξεληλύθαμεν ἡδονῆς χάριν
βωμὸν παρ' αὐτόν, ὃς παρ' αὐτῇ τῇ Φθίᾳ
ἔξωθεν ὠρόφωτο πλαξὶν εὐχρόοις.
65   Ἦν οὖν κατ' αὐτὸ τοῦ θεοῦ τὸ χωρίον
ἀεὶ τὸ δένδρον οἷον ἀνθοῦν εἰς ἔαρ
βρῖθόν τε καρπῷ καὶ τεθηλὸς φυλλάσι.
Καὶ γὰρ ποταμὸς ἐκρέει Μελιρρόας,
ἰδεῖν μὲν ἡδὺς καὶ πεπόσθαι βελτίων·
70   οἱ πλείονες δὲ τὸν γλυκὺν Μελιρρόαν
καλοῦσι Θρεψάγρωστιν ἄνδρες βουκόλοι,
ὅσοι βόας νέμουσιν ἐν τῷ χωρίῳ,
ὡς ἡσυχῇ ῥέοντα τῆς ὄχθης ἔσω·
οὐ γὰρ χιὼν λυθεῖσα γεννῶσα τρέφει,
75   οὐδ' ἐξ ὄρους πρόεισι πολλὴ πλημμύρα
καὶ τὰς ἀρούρας τῇ ῥοῇ παρασύρει·
μόνος γὰρ οὗτος ἐν ποταμοῖς τῆς Φθίας
ἴσως ἀεὶ ῥεῖ καὶ περιρρέει κύκλῳ·
εὐδαιμονεῖ δὲ πᾶς νομεύς, πᾶς ἀγρότης,
80   ὧν ἔσχεν ἐντὸς τῶν ἑαυτοῦ ῥευμάτων·
ἐκ δ' οὐρανοῦ κάτεισιν ἡδίστη δρόσος,
ἀφ' ἧς συνεστώς ἐστιν ἐξ ἴσου ῥέων.
Τούτου παρ' ὄχθαις χρῆμα χρυσῆς πλατάνου
ἐν θαλλεραῖς ἔθαλλε χρυσαῖς φυλλάσιν.
85   Οὐδὲν πρὸς αὐτήν ἐστιν ἐν παραθέσει

said Charikles as he began to speak.
"Still, since it lightens the heart
to empty out the stories in it,
pay attention, Kleandros, for I do not shrink from speaking.   50
My mother is Krystale, my father Phrator—
both with noble ancestors—and my fatherland, Phthia.
Now, having been reared nobly,
I was coming of age following the custom of youth:
I took pleasure in my friends,   55
rode horses, played about, as young lads do,
hunted hares, and skillfully handled horses—
for I had very noble playmates—
but I had not yet experienced love,
nor was down yet adorning my cheeks.   60
When the festival of Dionysus came,
we went out together for pleasure's sake
to the altar, which was just outside Phthia
and covered with colorful marble slabs.
    "In this place of the god, then,   65
a tree was always flowering as if in spring—
heavy with fruit and luxuriant with leaves—
for the river Melirroas also flows there,
sweet to see and better to drink.
Most of the herdsmen   70
who graze cattle in this place
call sweet Melirroas Threpsagrostis (Grass-Nourisher)
since it flows gently within its bank,
for melted snow does not produce and feed it,
nor does a great flood-tide descend from a mountain   75
and sweep away the fields with its flow.
This one alone among the rivers of Phthia
always flows at the same rate and in a ring;
every herdsman and countryman is happy
whom it holds within its streams;   80
and from the sky descends a very sweet dew,
from which this river, with its equal flow, is formed.
By the banks of this river a great, golden plane tree
flourished, with luxuriant, golden leaves—
in comparison, the celebrated plane tree   85

ἡ Ξερξικὴ πλάτανος ἡ θρυλλουμένη·
τὸ μὲν γὰρ ἀκρόπρεμνον ἐγγὺς αἰθέρος,
τὰ φύλλα δ᾽ ἐσκίαζε τὴν γῆν τὴν πέριξ,
ὅσην συνέσχεν ἡ Μελιρρόου ῥύσις.
90   Ἐκρεῖ δὲ πηγὴ ῥιζόθεν τῆς πλατάνου,
οἵαν ἐοικός ἐστιν ἐντεῦθεν ῥέειν.
Ἡ γῆ δ᾽ ἐπανθεῖ καὶ τὰ θρέμματα τρέφει
τῇ πλησμονῇ τε τῆς βορᾶς καὶ τῷ κόρῳ
καὶ τῷ ῥοθίῳ τοῦ καλοῦ Μελιρρόου·
95   μεθύσκεται γὰρ ἡ μηκὰς αἴξ εἰ πίῃ,
χλωραῖς ἐπεσκίρτησε πολλάκις πόαις.
Νεωκόρος δὲ πρὸς θεοῦ τεταγμένος
μένει φυλάσσων, ἀγρυπνῶν ἀκαμάτως,
τὴν ἱερὰν πλάτανον ἐξ ὁδοιπόρων
100   μὴ ποὺς πρὸς αὐτὴν ἰταμὸς προσεγγίσῃ.
    Συνέδραμον οὖν πάντες ἔξω τῆς Φθίας
πρὸς τὴν ἑορτὴν τοῦ θεοῦ Διονύσου,
ἄνδρες, γυναῖκες, παρθένοι, νεανίαι,
μείρακες ἄλλοι καὶ νεάνιδες κόραι.
105   Ἐγὼ θεωρῶν ἀμύητος ἦν ἔτι
ἐρωτικῶν δήπουθεν ἐκτοξευμάτων.
Ὡς εἴθε τηνικαῦτα μὴ συνεξέδυν
τοῖς γνησίοις μείραξι τῆς Φθίας πύλης.
Προσήλθομεν δὲ συννεανίαι φίλοι
110   τῷ τοῦ τόπου φύλακι καὶ τῆς πλατάνου,
καὶ δῶρα δόντες ἕδραν ἔσχομεν ξένην
καὶ καρδίας τύραννον ἢ ποινηλάτιν
τῆς παρθενικῆς καλλονῆς θεωρίαν.
Εἴωθε καὶ γὰρ ὁ βριαρόχειρ Ἔρως,
115   ὁ πρεσβύτης παῖς, τὸ πρὸ τοῦ Κρόνου βρέφος,
ὡς ἐκ θυρίδων ἐμπεσὼν δι᾽ ὀμμάτων,
τὰ σπλάγχνα πιμπρᾶν καὶ φλέγειν τὴν καρδίαν
καὶ νεκρὸν ὥσπερ τὸν ποθοῦντα δεικνύειν.
Καὶ γοῦν ὑπὸ πλάτανον αὐτὴν αὐτίκα
120   ἡλικιώταις συγκαθήμενος φίλοις
τρυφῆς μετεῖχον ποικιλοψαρτυμάτων,
ἀμφαγνοῶν δύστηνος ὡς γένοιτό μοι
τὴν τηλικαύτην χαρμονὴν καὶ τὸν γέλων
εἰς δακρύων ῥοῦν συμπεριστῆναι τέλος.

of Xerxes is nothing.*
The tree's top reached to the sky,
and the leaves shaded the ground all around,
all that the course of Melirroas enclosed.
From the roots of the plane tree a stream flowed out,   90
of the sort that would naturally flow there.
The land thrives and nourishes its creatures
with a satisfying abundance of food
and with the swell of the beautiful Melirroas,
for the bleating goat becomes inebriated if she drinks,   95
and often leaps on the green grasses.
The temple custodian, appointed by the god,
stays there guarding the sacred plane tree from travelers,
watchfully and without tiring, so that
a reckless foot may not approach it.   100
    "All the people were gathering, then, outside Phthia,
for the festival of the god Dionysus—
men, women, maidens, youths,
lads also, and young girls.
I was watching, being yet uninitiated   105
in love's arrows.
If only I had not gone out of Phthia's gate then,
together with those noble youths!
My young friends and I went to
the guard of the place and the plane tree,   110
and, by giving him gifts, we obtained an exceptional seat
for viewing maidenly beauty—
a tyrant of the heart or vengeful fury.
Strong-handed Eros, too,
the old child, the baby born before Kronos,*   115
typically attacks through eyes as if through windows,
burns up inward parts, inflames the heart,
and makes the lover into a corpse as it were.
Then, sitting suddenly beneath the plane tree,
together with friends of my age,   120
I shared in a feast of foods variously prepared,
and I didn't know, poor me,
that so great a joy and laughter
would turn into a stream of tears in the end.

125   Ὅμως πάλιν ἔχαιρον οἷς συνετρύφων.
       Τοιοῦτόν ἐστιν ἀγνοοῦσα καρδία
       κακὸν τὸ μέλλον ἐν χαρᾷ καθημένη.
       Γελωτοποιῶν ἠκροώμην ῥημάτων
       ἐρωτικῶν, μᾶλλον δὲ τερπνῶν ᾀσμάτων.
130   Ὁ μὲν γὰρ αὐτῶν τῶν συνεστιωμένων
       τοιούσδε τυχὸν ἐξέπεμπε τοὺς λόγους
       πρὸς τὰς ἐκεῖσε συνδραμούσας παρθένους
       ἢ πρὸς γυναικῶν ποικίλας ὁμηγύρεις
       ἐκεῖθεν ἔνθεν τὴν ὁδὸν ποιουμένας·

135   "χθὲς εἶχε πῦρ δίψης με, καὶ λαβὼν ὕδωρ
       – τυχὸν γὰρ οὕτω τὴν ὁδὸν διηρχόμην –
       ὡς ἄμβροτον ῥοῦν ἐξέπινον εἰς κόρον.
       Μέμνησο τῆς χθές· σὺ γὰρ ἡ διδοῦσά μοι.
       Ἀλλ' ὁ πτερωτός, ὁ θρασύσπλαγχνος μόνος
140   Ἔρως δυσαντίβλεπτος ὁπλοτοξότης,
       κώνωψ φανεὶς ὤλισθεν ἔνδον τοῦ σκύφου,
       ὃν καὶ πεπωκὼς γαργαλίζομαι τάλας
       ἐκ τῶν πτερύγων ἔνδοθεν τῆς καρδίας,
       καὶ μέχρι τοῦ νῦν – τῆς ὀδύνης, τοῦ πόνου –
145   κνήθει με καὶ δάκνει με, καὶ κακῶς ἔχω.
       Τέως μαλαχθεὶς οὗτος ὀψὲ καὶ μόλις
       ὁ τῶν βροτῶν τύραννος αὐθάδης Ἔρως
       πέμπει με πρός σε τὴν ἰάσουσαν μόνην
       τὸ τραῦμα καὶ τὸ δῆγμα καὶ τὴν καρδίαν·
150   πέμπει με, καὶ δέχου με ταῖς σαῖς ἀγκάλαις,
       οὐδὲν ξένου ποιοῦσα· ναὶ δέχου, δέχου."

       Ἄλλος μετ' αὐτὸν ἀντέφησεν εὐθέως·
       "ἰού, τί ταῦτα; Τὴν κατάστερον κόρην,
       τὴν πολλὰ βακχεύουσαν ἐν κάλλει πάλαι,
155   ὡς ἡ Λαῒς τὸ πρῶτον ἡ Κορινθία,
       τρύχει νόσος δύστηνος – ὦ κακὴ νόσος –,
       ἡ δ' εὐτραφὴς σάρξ, ὡς ὁρῶ, κατεστάλη.
       Μὴ τοῦτο, μὴ μὴ τοῦτο· ῥῶσιν, σάρξ, λάβε·
       ὄλοιτο πᾶσα τηκτικὴ καχεξία·
160   οὐ γὰρ γυναικὸς σάρξ τις ὄλλυται μία,
       ἀλλ' οὖν σὺν αὐτῇ καὶ φίλων πληθὺς πόση."

Still, I took pleasure with my friends in our shared delights—   125
such is a heart that does not know,
when experiencing joy, the evil to come!
I listened to amusing words of love,
and more, to delightful songs.
One of those feasting with me   130
perhaps uttered such words as the following
to the maidens who had gathered together there
or the various companies of women
making their way on this side and that:

"'Yesterday a fiery thirst held me, and so I took water—   135
for I was thus, by chance, completing my journey—
and drank it up to satiety, as if it were divine.
Remember yesterday, for you gave it to me!
But winged Eros, uncommonly bold,
hard to face, armed with a bow,   140
appeared to me in the guise of a gnat and slipped within my cup.
When I drank it, I felt tickling, poor me,
from the wings within my heart,
and even now—what pain and suffering!—
it scratches and bites me, and I am badly off.   145
Meanwhile willful Eros, ruler of men,
having relented at last and with difficulty,
sends me to you, who alone will cure
my wound, my bite, and my heart.
He sends me; take me in your arms!   150
You'll be doing nothing strange—yes, take me, take me!'

"Another spoke directly after him:
'Ho! What about these things? The heavenly girl
who was on a great rampage with her beauty just now,
like Lais, the Corinthian, before her,*   155
is afflicted by an unhappy sickness—O evil sickness!—
and her well-fed body, I see, has shrunk.
Not this; no, not this! Take strength, Body.
May all the wasting and bad health end,
for a woman's body does not perish alone,   160
but also, with it, what a great number of lovers!'

Ἐντεῦθεν ἄλλην ἄλλος ἰδὼν ἀντέφη·
"νεύεις κάτω, ποθοῦσα καὶ ποθουμένη,
ὁδοιποροῦντος τοῦ φιλοῦντος πολλάκις,
165   καὶ στέρνα καὶ πρόσωπον ἐγκρύπτειν θέλεις,
ζώνην δὲ τὴν σὴν ἀκρολυτεῖς ἀθρόον
καὶ τῶν ποδῶν σου τοῖς ἁπαλοῖς δακτύλοις
τὴν προστυχοῦσαν ἐγχαράττεις γῆς κόνιν.
Αἰδοῦς τὰ σεμνὰ ταῦτα; Πλὴν οὐ συμφέρει·
170   οὐκ οἶδε αἰδῶ Κύπρις οὐδ᾽ Ἔρως ὄκνον.
Εἰ γοῦν θέλεις τοσαῦτα τὴν αἰδῶ σέβειν,
ἐμοὶ χαρίζου κἂν τὸ νεῦμά σου μόνον."

Τορὸν δὲ πάλιν ἄλλος ἀντεκεκράγει·
"ὡς εὐχαριστῶ τῇ πολιᾷ μυρία.
175   Καλῶς δικάζει καὶ καλῶς πάντα κρίνει·
ἀρωγός ἐστι τῆς Κύπριδος, ὡς βλέπω,
ποινηλατοῦσα τὰς σοβαρὰς πρὸς πόθον.
Ἡ γαυριῶσα βοστρύχων εὐκοσμία
ὁρᾷ τὸ μακρὸν πλέγμα νῦν διαρρέον,
180   εἰς λευκὸν ἐτράπη δὲ τὸ ξανθὸν πάλαι·
ἡ τὰς ὀφρῦς ὑψοῦσα καὶ διηρμένη
ἀφῆκε πᾶσαν ἄρτι τοῦ κάλλους χάριν.
Ὁ μαστὸς ἑστὼς ὄρθιος πρὶν τῆς κόρης
ὑπεκλίθη· καθεῖλεν αὐτὸν ὁ χρόνος.
185   Γηραλέον τὸ φθέγμα, φεῦ, σοί, πρεσβύτις·
τὸ πρὶν δροσῶδες χεῖλος, ὡς αὐαλέον·
πέπτωκεν ὀφρύς, ἦλθεν εἰς ἀηδίαν
τὸ πᾶν δέ σοι παρῆλθε τοῦ κάλλους, γύναι.
Τί λείπεταί σοι; Δεῦρο, μαστρόπευέ μοι.
190   Ὕβριζες· ὑβρίσθητι νῦν, τρισαθλία.
Παρέτρεχές με· συμπαρατρέχω δέ σε.
Ἔπληττες, οἶδας· ἀντιπλήττου καιρίως.
Ἀλγεῖς; Προήλγουν. Δυσφορεῖς; Ἐδυσφόρουν.
Παθοῦσα καὶ μαθοῦσα νῦν, τὸ τοῦ λόγου,
195   δίδασκε πάσας τὰς προλοίπους παρθένους
ὑποκλίνεσθαι τοῖς ἐρῶσι ταχέως."᾽

"Ὤμοι, Χαρίκλεις, οἷος ἄρτι μοι γέλως
ἐκ σῶν μελιχρῶν ἦλθε διηγημάτων᾽

"Then another youth saw another girl and spoke in turn:
'You look down (you who love and are loved)
when your lover often walks by,
and you try to hide your breast and face,   165
and you suddenly play with the ends of your girdle,
and with the delicate toes of your feet
you engrave the dust of the earth beneath them.
Are these the seemly signs of shame? But it is no use:
Cypris does not know shame, nor Eros hesitation.   170
If, then, you wish so greatly to honor shame,
grant me the gift of your nod alone.'

"Another cried out clearly in turn:
'How immensely grateful I am to grey hair.
It judges and decides all things well;   175
it is Cypris's helper, I see,
pursuing like a fury women haughty toward love.
The woman who prides herself on the ornament of her curls
sees her great plait now fall away,
and what was yellow before has turned white.   180
The woman lifting her eyebrows up high
has now lost all the grace of her beauty.
The girl's breast, which stood upright before,
has fallen down; time has lowered it.
Your voice is senile, alas, old woman;   185
the lip that was moist before, how dry now!
The brow has fallen, become unpleasant,
and all your beauty has vanished, woman.
What is left for you? Come, be a bawd for me!
You abused me; now be abused, wretched woman.   190
You slighted me, and I slight you.
You struck me, you know; be struck in return, mortally.
Do you suffer? I suffered first. Do you grieve? I grieved.
Having learned now by suffering, as the proverb goes,
instruct all the remaining maidens   195
to yield to their lovers quickly.'"

"Oh, Charikles, what laughter
has come to me just now from your honey-sweet tales!"

Κλέανδρος εἶπεν· 'ὢ κακῶν προκειμένων.
200   Πλὴν ἀλλὰ καί σε μειδιῶντα νῦν βλέπω·
καίτοι προεῖπας ἐν καταρχῇ τοῦ λόγου
τὰ κατὰ σαυτὸν οὐκ ἀδακρύτως λέγειν'.
''Εῶ' Χαρικλῆς εἶπε 'τὸν μακρὸν λόγον,
ὃν εἶπεν ἄλλος συμποτῶν μοι γνησίων.'
205   'Μὴ, πρὸς Δροσίλλας' ὁ Κλέανδρος ἀντέφη.
'Ἄκουε λοιπὸν ῥημάτων μελιρρόων·

"φιλεῖς τὸν ἀνδρόθηλυν, ὡς ἠκηκόειν,
μαινάς[13], σοβάς, τάλαινα, πρέσβα παρθένε.
Θάρρει τὰ γαστρός, οὐ γὰρ ἐγκύμων γένῃ,
210   κἂν καὶ μετ' ἀνδρῶν συγκλιθήσῃ μυρίων,
κἂν Ἡρακλεῖ γὰρ συγκαθευδήσῃς, γύναι,
κἂν καὶ Πριήπῳ τῷ φιλοίφῳ τοῦ μύθου.
Ἄπαις, πολύπαις οὖσα τῶν χρόνων πάλαι,
ἄπαις μενεῖς· καλεῖ γὰρ ὁ Πλούτων κάτω.
215   Παύθητι κουρίζουσα· ναυστόλου, γύναι."
Ἐξεῖπε ταῦτα καὶ πρὸς ἄλλην αὐτίκα·
"βαβαί, παλαιὸς ὡς διεύψευσται λόγος.
Τρεῖς φησι τὰς Χάριτας, ἀλλ' ὁ σός, κόρη,
ὀφθαλμὸς εἷς Χάριτας αὐχεῖ μυρίας.
220   Αἰαῖ, τεφροῖς με τῇ καμίνῳ τοῦ πόθου
καὶ πυρπολεῖς τὰ σπλάγχνα καὶ τὴν καρδίαν.
Ὦ μιαρὰ παῖ, τοῦτο πολλῆς ἀγάπης;
Μὴ τὰς ὀφρῦς ἔπαιρε, τὴν Κύπριν τρέμε·
σύννευε τοῖς φιλοῦσι, μέτρια φρόνει.
225   Κόρης ἀπειλὰς δῆθεν ἐκτινακτρίας
αὐταγγέλους Κύπριδος ἔγνων πολλάκις,
τῶν σχημάτων δὲ τὴν πολύτροπον πλάσιν
καὶ τὴν σιωπήν, ἀνθυπόσχεσιν ξένην.
Καὶ πρός σε ταῦτα τὴν ἀμείλικτον βλέπει
230   σημεῖά μοι κάλλιστα. Χαῖρε, καρδία.
Φεῦ, σῆς ἱμερτῆς προσλαλιᾶς, παρθένε.
Ἀποστροφὴ σὴ δυσπαράκλητος τάχα
καὶ πέτραν αὐτὴν συγκινήσοι πρὸς πόνον.
Τί γοῦν πάθοι τις; Ἀλλ', ὁ τοξεύων Ἔρως,
235   τὴν πλῆξιν αὐτὸς ἐξιῶ μοι καὶ μόνος.
Σοὶ καὶ θαλασσῶν ἐκπεράσω πλημμύραν

Kleandros said. "Oh, what evils lie ahead!
But I see you too smiling now,   200
and yet you stated at the beginning of your narrative
that you would tell of your experiences, not without tears."
    "I am leaving out," Charikles said, "the long speech
given by another of my noble drinking-companions."
    "Don't, by Drosilla!" Kleandros replied.   205
    "Hear, then, words that flow with honey:

'You love the hermaphrodite, as I've heard him called,
you mad, insolent, wretched old maid.
Don't be concerned about your belly, for you won't become pregnant
even if you lie with ten thousand men,   210
even if you sleep with Herakles, woman,
and also with Priapos, the mythical lecher.*
Childless, although you had many children over time,
childless you will remain, for Pluto summons you below.
Stop acting like a girl; cross the water, woman!'   215
    "Suddenly, he spoke these things to another woman:
'Oh, how mistaken the old story is.
It says the Graces are three, but your one eye, girl,
boasts of countless graces.
Ah, you burn me to ashes in the furnace of desire;   220
you destroy my bowels and my heart with fire.
Foul child, is this a sign of great love?
Don't raise your eyebrows! Fear Cypris;
nod assent to your lovers; be modest.
I have learned that a girl's threats are often,   225
in fact, announcers of Cypris the disturber,
and that her shifting gestures and silence
are often a wonderful promise in return.
These signs, which are most beautiful to me,
refer to you, cruel woman. Farewell, my heart!   230
Oh, what lovely talk, maiden!
Your aversion, relentless perhaps,
would move even a rock to suffer.
What, then, will become of me? But Eros, archer,
you yourself alone, cure my wound!   235
For you I will pass over huge swells of seas,

καὶ πῦρ διέλθω τοῦ προσελθεῖν σοι χάριν.
Δὸς χαροπόν μοι νεῦμα, καὶ τὸ πᾶν ἔχω.
Μὴ πλῆττε, μὴ σύντριβε – κέρδος οὐκ ἔχεις –
240   πρὸς τὰς Ἔρωτος λαβυρινθώδεις πάγας."

Οὕτως ἀπαγγείλαντος αὐτοῦ τῷ τέως
ἄλλος πρὸς ἄλλην ἄλλον ἀντέφη λόγον·
"βαρύνεται σὸν ὄμμα τοῦ πόθου γέμον,
πολλὴ δ' ἀμαυροῖ τὰς παρειὰς ὠχρότης.
245   Ἔοικας ὕπνων ἐνδεὴς εἶναι, γύναι.
Εἰ μὲν παλαίστραις ὡμίλησας παννύχοις,
ὡς εὐτυχὴς ἐκεῖνος ὄλβιος μάκαρ
ὁ χερσὶν αὐτοῦ προσπλακεὶς σῷ σαρκίῳ·
εἰ δὲ πρὸς ἧπαρ πῦρ βαλὼν Ἔρως φλέγει
250   εἴης πρὸς ἡμᾶς μᾶλλον ἐκκεκαυμένη.
Σὺ νῦν Ἀχιλλεύς· Τήλεφον βλέπεις, γύναι·
ναί, παῦσον, ὡς ἔτρωσας, ἥπατος πόνους·
εἰ δ' οὐκ ἀρεστόν, ἄλλο βάλλε μοι βέλος,
τὸ δ' ἧπαρ ἄφες ἀλλὰ καὶ τὴν καρδίαν."

255   Τοιαῦτα προσπαίζουσι τοῖς νεανίαις
ἐφίσταταί τις τῶν συνήθων ἡλίκων,
Βαρβιτίων, ἄριστος εἰς εὐφωνίαν,
ὃς καὶ προσεῖπεν ἐγκαθεσθεὶς πλησίον
"ἀεὶ τὸ φιλοῦν αὐτόκλητον, φιλότης·"
260   καλῶς δὲ συνθεὶς τὴν ἀνὰ χεῖρας λύραν
καὶ πρὸς τὸ πλήττειν εὐφυῶς καθαρμόσας
ἔρωτος ᾖσεν ᾆσμα τερπνὸν ἡδύνον·
"Φίλεε Βαρβιτίωνα, εὔχροε πότνια Μυρτώ.
Ἡ Ῥοδόπη ποτ' ἄτιζε τὰ Κύπριδος ἀφρογενείς
265   καί ῥ' ἐς ὅλους λυκαβάντας ἐπήνεε συμβιοτεύειν
Ἀρτέμιδι, ποθέουσα κύνας ἐλάφους τε καὶ ἵππους,
τοξοφόρος δονάκεσσιν ἀν' οὔρεα μακρὰ βιβῶσα.
Φίλεε Βαρβιτίωνα, εὔχροε πότνια Μυρτώ.
Ἡ Κύπρις ἐστύγνασε· τὸν υἱέα τῇδ' ἐποτρύνει
270   τόξ' ὤμοισιν ἔχοντα καὶ ἀντίον ὥπλισεν αὐτῆς.
Ἡ Ῥοδόπη πρὸς ἔλαφον ὀρεινόμον ἔγχος ἐνώμα·
ἐς Ῥοδόπην ὁ Κύπριδος ἀγάστονα τόξα τιταίνει.
Φίλεε Βαρβιτίωνα, εὔχροε πότνια Μυρτώ.

and I will go through fire for the sake of coming to you.
Give me a glad-eyed nod and I have everything.
Don't strike me, don't crush me in Eros's
intricate snares—you gain nothing.'   240

"After he related this story,
another youth made another girl another declaration:
'Your eye is heavy and full of desire,
and a great paleness dims your cheeks.
You seem to be in need of sleep, woman.   245
If you frequented wrestling-schools all night long,
how lucky that fellow is—how happy, how fortunate—
who clung to your body with his hands.
But if Eros burns you by throwing fire at your liver,
may you burn more with love for me!   250
You are now Achilles; you look at Telephus, woman.*
Yes, since you wounded me, relieve the sufferings of my liver.
But if this doesn't please you, throw another missile at me,
but leave my liver and my heart alone.'

"As the young men jested in this way   255
a friend of similar age approached,
Barbition, who had an excellent voice,
and he sat nearby and said,
'Friendship is always unbidden, my friends.'
Then he positioned his lyre well in his hands,   260
adjusted it suitably for playing,
and sang a love-song, pleasant and sweet.
    "'Love Barbition, Myrto, rosy mistress.
Rhodope once snubbed the realm of foam-born Cypris*
and consented to live with Artemis for long years,   265
craving dogs, deer, and horses,
and, armed with bow and arrows, striding up tall mountains.
    "'Love Barbition, Myrto, rosy mistress.
Cypris scowled. She stirred up her son, bow on shoulders,
and armed him against the girl.   270
Rhodope was wielding a lance against a mountain deer;
Cypris's son bent his grievous bow towards her.
    "'Love Barbition, Myrto, rosy mistress.

Ἤϋχεεν, ἀλλ᾽ ἐβέβλητο· ταχύτερον ἔγχος Ἔρωτος.
275   Ἤλγεεν ὦμον ἔλαφος, ἐπέτρεχεν ἐς μέσον ὕλης·
       ἐς καρδίην Ῥοδόπη δὲ καὶ ἐς φρένας ἤλγεεν αὐτάς,
       ἔνθ᾽ ὁλοὸν καὶ ἄτλητον Ἔρως ἐπέπηξε βέλεμνον.
           Φίλεε Βαρβιτίωνα, εὔχροε πότνια Μυρτώ.
       Ἤλγεεν, ἐστονάχιζεν, ἐπὶ πόθον ἤλασεν ἔμπης.
280   Εὐθύνικον φιλέεσκε· βεβλημένος ἦν δὲ καὶ αὐτός.
       Παῖς γὰρ ὅδ᾽ ὠΐστευσε καὶ ἐς πόθον ἤλασεν αὐτῆς·
       ἀλλήλους ἐσέδρακον, Ἔρως δ᾽ ἄρα πῦρ ὑπανῆπτεν.
           Φίλεε Βαρβιτίωνα, εὔχροε πότνια Μυρτώ.
       Ἔργον δ᾽ ἐκτετέλεστο, καὶ ἐς πόθον ἤλυθον ἄμφω·
285   παρθενίην δ᾽ ἀπόειπεν ἄτλητον Ἔρωτος ἀνάγκῃ.
       Φείδεο καὶ σὺ Κύπριδος· ἔγνως ῥά ἑ ὀβριμοεργόν·
       μηδὲ λόγοις ἀνάνευε λυγιζομένη παρ᾽ ἐμεῖο.
           Φίλεε Βαρβιτίωνα, εὔχροε πότνια Μυρτώ."
       "Ἤδυνας ἡμᾶς, προσφιλὲς Βαρβιτίων"
290   ἔφημεν εὐθύς· "ἀλλ᾽ ἐφάπτου κειμένης
       τῆς τῶν συνήθων ποικίλης πανδαισίας."
       Ἔφαγε πεισθείς, μέχρις ἦλθεν εἰς κόρον·
       καὶ δεύτερον γοῦν εὖ διαθεὶς τὴν λύραν,
       τὴν δεξιὰν ἤρεισεν εἰς γῆν ὠλένην
295   – λαιὸς γὰρ αὐτὸς εἰς τὸ πλήττειν ἐξέφυ –
       καὶ τερπνὸν ᾖσε καὶ μελίφθογγον μέλος·

       "Ἤν ποθέω τίς ἔδρακεν; Ἄειδέ μοι, ὦ φίλ᾽ ἑταῖρε.
       Παρθενικὴ χαρίεσσα ἐπήρατος ἦν ποτε Σύριγξ
       κούρη, ψυχοδάμεια, εὔχροος, ἀργυρόπεζα.
300   Πᾶν ἐσιδὼν ἐσέδραμεν ἐνὶ κραδίῃφι πατάσσων.
       Ἐσθλὴ πρόσθε πέφευγε, δίωκεν ὄπισθεν ἀμείνων·
           Ἤν ποθέω τίς ἔδρακεν; Ἄειδέ μοι, ὦ φίλ᾽ ἑταῖρε·
       ἐν λειμῶνι Σύριγξ δὲ προήλυθεν εἰς καλαμῶνα,
       γαῖα δ᾽ ὑπὸ στέρνοισιν ἐδέξατο παρθένον αὐτήν.
305   Αὐτὰρ ὁ Πὰν μεμάνητο· Σύριγγα γὰρ ὤλεσε κούρην.
       Φυλλάδος ἔμπης ἥψατο καὶ καλάμους διέτμηξεν,
           Ἤν ποθέω τίς ἔδρακεν; Ἄειδέ μοι, ὦ φίλ᾽ ἑταῖρε·
       κηροχύτους δ᾽ ἐπέπηξε, συνήρμοσε χείλεσιν ἐσθλοῖς,
       φίλεεν ἠδ᾽ ἄμπνυτο· πνοὴ δὲ κάλαμον ἐσήχθη
310   καὶ μέλος ἡδὺ σύριξε τὸ φάρμακόν ἐστιν ἐρώτων.
       Καὶ σὺ μισεῖς στέργοντα, καὶ οὐ ποθέοντα ποθεῖς με;

She boasted of success but was hit. Eros's lance was swifter.
The deer felt pain in its shoulder and ran to the midst of the woods.   275
Rhodope felt pain in her heart and soul,
where Eros directed his fatal, unbearable dart.
    "'*Love Barbition, Myrto, rosy mistress.*
She felt pain, wailed, and advanced toward love nonetheless.
She loved Euthynikos, and he himself had also been hit,   280
for this child shot arrows at him too and drove him to love her.
They looked at one another, and Eros at once lit a fire beneath.
    "'*Love Barbition, Myrto, rosy mistress.*
The deed was accomplished, and they both came to their desire.
She gave up her insufferable virginity by compulsion of Eros.   285
Pay heed, you too, to Cypris, for you know that she does violence.
Don't reject my pleas and twist away from me!
    "'*Love Barbition, Myrto, rosy mistress.*'
    "'You have delighted us, dear Barbition,'
we said at once, 'Now share in your friends' banquet,   290
lavishly and richly laid.'
He was persuaded and ate until he had his full.
And then a second time he positioned his lyre well,
leaned his right elbow on the ground—
for he used his left hand to pluck the strings—   295
and sang a pleasant, honey-sweet song.

    "'*Who saw the girl I desire? Sing to me, dear friend.*
Syrinx was once a chaste, charming, lovely girl,*
conqueror of souls, with pretty skin and silver foot.
Pan on seeing her ran towards her with his heart pounding.   300
A good runner, she fled in front; faster, he pursued behind—
    "'*Who saw the girl I desire? Sing to me, dear friend—*
and Syrinx came first to a reed-bed in a meadow,
and earth received the maiden within her bosom.
But Pan was driven mad, for he had lost the girl Syrinx.   305
Yet he grasped the leaves and cut the reeds in half—
    "'*Who saw the girl I desire? Sing to me, dear friend—*
and joined the reeds with wax, fit them to his clever lips,
kissed them, and blew forth. And his breath entered a reed
and produced a sweet song, which is a remedy for love.   310
And you, do you hate the lover and not desire me who desire you?

Ἦν ποθέω τίς ἔδρακεν; "Αειδέ μοι, ὦ φίλ' ἑταῖρε.
Σχέτλιος ὅσσ' ἐμόγησα· τί τὸν φιλέοντ' ἀποβάλλῃ;
Ὡς ὄφελές μοι κάλαμος ἠὲ δάφνη τεθαλυῖα
315   καὶ σὺ ἔῃς, κυπάριττε τανύσκιε ὑψικάρηνε,
τήν ποθ' ὁ Φοῖβος ἔνυττε μιγήμεναι οὐκ ἐθέλουσαν·
Ἦν ποθέω τίς ἔδρακεν; "Αειδέ μοι, ὦ φίλ' ἑταῖρε,
καί ποτ' ἐμὸν νόον ἄλγε' ἔχοντα βαρύστονα τέρπων
σαρκοφόροις δονάκεσσι διαμπερὲς ἐκροτάλιζον
320   ἢ στέφανον φορέων σε πυρὸς δρόσον εἶχον ἔρωτος.
Τοίη ἐμὰς κύκλῳ σε περὶ φρένας ἔσχεν ἐρωή.
Ἦν ποθέω τίς ἔδρακεν; "Αειδέ μοι, ὦ φίλ' ἑταῖρε."
Τοσοῦτον ᾄσας ἐξανέστη τοῦ τόπου
καὶ "δεῦτε" φησί "τὰς χορευτρίας κόρας
325   ἴδωμεν αὐτοῖς ἐμπλακείσας δακτύλοις
καὶ κύκλον εὐκίνητον ἐκπονουμένας."
Εἰπὼν ὀπαδοὺς εἶχε τοὺς νεανίας
καὶ πρῶτον ἄλλων τὸν λαλοῦντά σοι ξένον,
τὸν ἐν τοσούτοις τοῖς κακοῖς Χαρικλέα.
330   Τί γὰρ παθεῖν μου τὴν τάλαιναν καρδίαν
δοκεῖς, φίλε Κλέανδρε συμφυλακίτα,
ἐρωτικῶν πληγεῖσαν ἐξ ἀκουσμάτων;
Ὤδευον οὖν, ἔμπροσθεν ἔτρεχον τότε
ὡς ἂν στάσιν σχῶ δεξιὰν πρὸς τὸ βλέπειν
335   τὰς τηνικαῦτα συγχορευούσας κόρας.
Ἐκεῖ σελήνην εἶδον ἐν τῇ γῇ κάτω,
κύκλῳ μετ' αὐτῶν ἀστέρων φορουμένην·
τοῦτο Δροσίλλα συγχορευούσαις κόραις.
Καὶ τοὺς ἐρῶντας ἄχθος ἄλγος λαμβάνειν
340   γνοὺς ἐξ ἐκείνων τῶν προηνωτισμένων
"καλὸν μὲν ἦν, Δροσίλλα" πρὸς νοῦν ἀντέφην,
"εἰ μὴ Χαρικλεῖ νῦν κατέστης εἰς θέαν·
ἐπεὶ δὲ τοῦτο τοῦ θεοῦ Διονύσου
θέλημα – τί; Κλέανδρε, μὴ συνδακρύῃς –,
345   οὐ μέμψις ἐν σοὶ τληπαθῆσαι, παρθένε,
τὸν ἐκ θεοῦ σοι νυμφίον Χαρικλέα
καὶ καρτερῆσαι κἂν φυγὴν κἂν κινδύνους
κἂν ἁρπαγὴν σήν, πρὶν τυχεῖν σου τοῦ γάμου·
καὶ πᾶν τι δεινὸν ἄλλο συγκλώσειέ μοι

"'*Who saw the girl I desire? Sing to me, dear friend.*
Wretched me, how much I've suffered! Why do you reject your lover?
If only you were a reed or a luxuriant laurel
(O cypress, with your long shadow and high top),   315
whom Phoebus once wounded when she refused intercourse*—
   "'*Who saw the girl I desire? Sing to me, dear friend*—
one day, cheering my mind, with its grievous pains,
I too would constantly play on reeds of flesh,
or, by wearing you as a wreath, I would have dew for love's fire.   320
Such a force holds you close to my heart.
   "'*Who saw the girl I desire? Sing to me, dear friend.*'
   "After singing this song, he stood up from his place
and said, 'Come on! Let's see the girls of the dancing choir
as they form a graceful circle,   325
with their fingers entwined.'
   "He spoke, and the young men accompanied him,
and first among them was the stranger who's speaking to you,
Charikles, who's suffering such terrible misfortunes.
How do you think my wretched heart felt,   330
dear Kleandros, fellow prisoner,
when it was struck by tales of love?
I went then, running in front,
in order to have a good place to see
the girls dancing together.   335
There I saw the moon down on the earth,
moving in a circle together with the stars;
such was Drosilla among the dancing girls.
And since I knew from the stories heard earlier
that lovers feel grief and pain,   340
I said to myself, 'It would be good, Drosilla,
if you had not now come into Charikles' view.
But since this is the will of the god Dionysus—'
what? Kleandros, don't weep for me!—
'maiden, you can't be blamed because Charikles,   345
your god-given bridegroom, suffered hardships
and endured flight, dangers,
and your abduction, before marrying you,
and every other terrible thing

350   μίτος πονηρὸς ἐξ ἀλάστορος Τύχης. "
        Τοσαῦτα λέξας καθ' ἑαυτὸν ἠρέμα,
        παλινδρομήσας εἰς τὸ πατρῷον πέδον
        ἀπεῖδον εἰς ἄγαλμα τοῦ Διονύσου,
        ῥίψας δ' ἐμαυτὸν εἰς ἐκείνου τοὺς πόδας
355   πνέοντα νεκρόζωον ἀνεκεκράγειν·
        "ὦ παῖ Διός, νῦν θυσιῶν μεμνημένος
        καὶ λιβανωτοῦ τοῦ πάλαι τεθυμένου,
        ἀρωγὸς ἐλθὲ τῆς Δροσίλλας εἰς γάμον
        ἐμοὶ Χαρικλεῖ τῷ νεαλεῖ πρὸς πόθον·
360   κἂν γοῦν τυχεῖν γένοιτο τοῦ ποθουμένου,
        οὐκ ἀμελήσω πλειόνων σοι θυμάτων.
        Ἐξῆλθον, ὦ παῖ Διόνυσε, σὴν χάριν
        καὶ πικρὸν ἦλθον ἀντικερδάνας βέλος·
        τὸ πῦρ γὰρ ἐντὸς βόσκεται τὴν καρδίαν,
365   ὃ σβεννύει φίλημα πάντως, οὐχ ὕδωρ. "
        Οὕτως ἐπειπὼν τῷ θεῷ Διονύσῳ
        εἰς ἁρπαγὴν ἕτοιμος ἦν τῆς παρθένου,
        ἧς καὶ τυχεῖν ἔσπευδον ἀμφιδεξίως
        καὶ τοὺς ὀπαδοὺς εὐφυῶς λεληθέναι·
370   ἐπεύχεται γὰρ ἡ φιλοῦσα καρδία
        καταλαβεῖν τάχιστα καθ' ἣν ἡμέραν
        κατατρυφᾶν δύναιτο τοῦ φιλουμένου.
        Γνοὺς οὖν τὸ πρᾶγμα καὶ σκοπήσας τὸ θράσος,
        ὡς οὐκ ἂν ἄλλως εὐχερῶς, ἀκωλύτως
375   τὸ πᾶν ἀπαρτίσαιμι τοῦ σκοπουμένου,
        εἰ μὴ συνίστωρ ἡ κόρη γένοιτό μοι,
        δῆλον καθιστῶ τὸν πόθον τῇ παρθένῳ,
        ἀνακαλύπτω τὸν σκοπόν, τὸ πρακτέον,
        καὶ τὴν κατὰ νοῦν ἁρπαγὴν προμηνύω.
380   Αὕτη προλαμβάνουσα τὴν ἐσταλμένην
        – γυνὴ γὰρ ἦν πρὸς ταῦτα δεξιωτάτη –
        ἄλλῳ κατηγγύητο τοῖς γάμου νόμοις·
        εἶπε πρὸς αὐτὴν ἡ κόρη μετὰ πόνου.
        Πρὸς δευτέραν γοῦν μηχανὴν ἀποβλέπω,
385   δι' ἧς συνεργοῖς τοῖς φίλοις κεχρημένος
        ἀκινδύνως λάβοιμι τὴν ἐρωμένην.
        Ἀλλ' ἥδε προφθάνουσα ταῦτα καὶ πάλιν
        ψυχῆς παθούσης ὑπέδειξεν ἐμφάσεις,

that avenging Fortune's evil thread could weave for me.'   350
     "I said this quietly to myself
and then ran back to my father's estate,
looked at the statue of Dionysus,
threw myself at his feet,
gasping as if about to die, and cried out,   355
'Child of Zeus, remember now the sacrifices
and the frankincense I offered to you in time past,
and come help me, Charikles, a boy new to desire,
in my marriage with Drosilla.
And if I obtain what I desire,   360
I will not fail to make more sacrifices to you.
I went forth, young Dionysus, for your sake,
and I gained a cruel dart in return,
for fire feeds within my heart,
and only a kiss can quench it, not water.'   365
     "After I spoke thus to the god Dionysus
I was ready to abduct the maiden,*
eager to seize her with both hands
and cleverly escape her attendants' notice.
The heart in love wishes   370
to seize at once the day on which
it may be able to delight in the object of its love.
Then, after judging the plan, assessing the risk,
and realizing that I could not easily and freely
accomplish the whole of what I contemplated   375
unless the girl were privy to my plans,
I made my desire clear to the maiden,
revealed my aim and what needed to be done,
and disclosed the abduction I had in mind.
When the girl received the messenger I'd sent—   380
a woman most clever in these matters—
she was already betrothed to another by the laws of marriage,
and she told the messenger this with pain.
I looked to a second method then
through which, with the help of my friends,   385
I could take my beloved without danger.
But she, anticipating this development in turn,
showed signs of a soul in love,

δι' ἀγγέλου μοι δῆθεν ἀντεσταλμένης
390   τὰ κρυπτὰ μηνύουσα καρδίας πάθη,
ὡς εἶδεν, ὡς ἔπαθεν, ὡς κατεσχέθη,
ὡς ἀντετρώθη τῇ Χαρικλέος θέᾳ,
καὶ προσλαβεῖν θέλει με τοῖς γάμου νόμοις.
Ὡρισμένον γοῦν ἀντεμήνυσα χρόνον
395   καθ' ὃν συνέλθω πρὸς λόγους τῇ παρθένῳ.
Προσῆλθον, εὗρον, εἶδον αὐτὴν ἀσμένως,
λόγους δεδωκὼς ἀντεδεξάμην λόγους,
ὅρκοις συνεσχέθημεν ἀλληλεγγύοις·
ὁ Διόνυσος ἐμπεδῶν ἦν τοὺς λόγους,
400   ληφθεὶς παρ' ἡμῶν ταῖς ἐνόρκοις ἐγγύαις.
Καὶ μέχρις αὐτοῦ τοῦ Δράκοντος λιμένος
– οὕτω γὰρ ὠνόμαστο τοῖς ἐγχωρίοις –
μετὰ Δροσίλλας ἔδραμον τῆς παρθένου,
καὶ ναῦν ἀποπλεύσουσαν εἰσδεδορκότες,
405   λύουσαν ἤδη τοὺς ἐπὶ πρῴρας κάλως,
ταύτης ἑαυτοὺς ἔνδον ἐντεθεικότες
ἐναυστολοῦμεν οὐριοδρομωτάτως
ὑπὸ προπομπῷ τῷ θεῷ Διονύσῳ·
αὐτὸς γὰρ ἦν μοι νυμφαγωγῶν τὴν κόρην,
410   ἐμοὶ παραστὰς τῇ καθ' ὕπνους ἐμφάσει,
πρὸ τοῦ προβῆναι τοὺς ἐς ἀλλήλους λόγους.'

ΒΙΒΛΙΟΝ ΤΕΤΑΡΤΟΝ

' Ὡδοιποροῦμεν τοιγαροῦν δι' ὁλκάδος
ὑγρὰν θαλάσσης λειοκύμονος τρίβον
ἐς ἥλιον τέταρτον ἄχρις ἑσπέρας,
καὶ θροῦς ἐρετμοῦ ληστρικῆς ναυαρχίας
5   εὐθυπλοοῦσιν ἐμπεσὼν ἐπεκτύπει
καὶ τὸν λογισμόν, οὐ γὰρ ἀκοὰς μόνον,
τῶν ἐντὸς ἡμῶν ἧσπερ εἶπον ὁλκάδος.
Τῆς ἑσπέρας γοῦν πανταχοῦ γνοφουμένης,
τῷ γῆν ὑπελθεῖν τὸν γίγαντα φωσφόρον,
10   οὐκ εἴχομεν σφᾶς ἐντρανέστερον βλέπειν·
ἀλλ' οἴδε συννεύσαντες εἰς μείζω δρόμον
καὶ χεῖρας ἐκτείναντες ἀλλὰ καὶ πόδας,
ὡς τὰς τριήρεις εὐδρομώτερον τρέχειν,

and, through a messenger she sent back to me then,
revealed the secret sufferings of her heart—   390
how she saw, suffered, was conquered,
and was wounded in turn by the sight of Charikles,
and wished to take me as her lawfully wedded husband.
I set a time then, in turn,
at which I could meet the maiden and talk.   395
I drew near, found her, saw her gladly,
and spoke and listened in turn.
We were bound together by mutual oaths;
Dionysus provided guaranty for our words,
whom we called as witness to our sworn pledges.   400
I ran with the maiden Drosilla
to the harbor of Drakon—
for thus the inhabitants call it—
and there we saw a ship starting to sail,
already unfastening the cables at its prow,   405
and we put ourselves on it
and sailed away, with a good wind behind us
and the god Dionysus as our escort,
for he himself gave the girl to me as my bride
when he appeared to me in my sleep,   410
before we'd conversed with one another.

BOOK FOUR

    "We were traveling then by merchant ship
over the watery path of a smooth sea
on the evening of the fourth day,
when the noise of the rowing of a pirate fleet
fell upon us as we held our course, and struck   5
not just the ears but also the minds
of us within the ship which I mentioned.
Since the evening, then, was darkening everywhere
as the mighty sun sank beneath the earth,
we were not able to see them clearly.   10
But these men, bent forward to a faster course,
with arms and legs pulling hard
to make their triremes run more swiftly,

κωπηλατοῦντες ἦσαν ἐξ ὅλου σθένους,
15   τὴν τῆς θαλάσσης συρραπίζοντες ῥάχιν
γυμναῖς πρὸς εὔπλουν εὐσθενούσαις ὠλέναις,
καὶ τῇ καθ᾽ ἡμᾶς ἐγγίσαντες ὁλκάδι
τὰ σφῶν ἑαυτῶν ἐξεγύμνωσαν ξίφη.
Οἱ γοῦν σὺν ἡμῖν, ὡς ἄριστοι ναυτίλοι,
20   καίτοι πρὸς αὐτοὺς τοὺς θρασεῖς ξιφηφόρους
πενιχρὸν ὄντες εὐαρίθμητον στίφος,
ἀναλαβόντες ἀνδρικῶς τὰς ἀσπίδας
τοῖς τὰ ξίφη φέρουσιν ἀντεναυμάχουν·
σφάττοντες ἐσφάττοντο, μὴ πεφρικότες
25   τὴν τῶν τοσούτων πειρατῶν ἀμετρίαν·
τὸ τῆς θαλάσσης ἐξεπορφύρουν ὕδωρ
καὶ μέχρι νυκτὸς ἀντέπιπτον εὐστόχως.
Ἀλλ᾽ ὀψὲ τὴν ναῦν ἑλκύσαντες ἐκ μέσου,
ὡς συμπεσόντων ἐν μάχῃ τῶν πλειόνων,
30   εἰς χέρσον ἐξέδωκαν ἠσθενηκότες.
Ἣν καὶ λιπόντες ἔμπλεων βαρημάτων,
τοῦ κυριαρχήσαντος ἠρημωμένην,
ἔφυγον εἰς φάραγγας, εἰς ὄρη μέσα.
Τούτοις φυγῇ ζητοῦσι τὴν σωτηρίαν
35   κἀγὼ συνεκβὰς ἐκ μάχης τραυματίας
μετὰ Δροσίλλας παρθένου συνειπόμην.
Ἔσπευδον, εἶχον, εἷλκον αὐτὴν τὴν κόρην,
ἐχειραγώγουν εἰς ἐπικρήμνους τόπους,
ἕως συνηρέφειαν εὑρόντες κλάδων
40   ταύτῃ συνιζήσαμεν ἐγκεκρυμμένοι.
Ἐς αὔριον δὲ λαμψάσης τῆς ἡμέρας
ὄρους ὑπερκύψαντες εἴδομεν κάτω
πυρκαϊὰν εἰς ὕψος ἐκτεταμένην·
εἰκάζομεν δὲ πυρπολεῖν τὴν ὁλκάδα
45   λῃστὰς ἐκείνους ἁρπαγαῖς ἐφησμένους,
φόρτου κενὴν ξύμπαντος ἐξειλκυσμένην.
Ὡς γοῦν ἐκεῖθεν ἔνθεν ἠπορημένοι
τὰς φωταγωγοὺς ἐξετείνομεν κόρας,
εὔπυργον ὕψος καθορῶμεν εὐθέως,
50   λεπτῶς, ἀμυδρῶς· ἦν γὰρ ἡμῶν μακρόθεν.
Ἄμφω δὲ συνδραμόντες ὡς πρὸς τὴν πόλιν
ὀψὲ προσεγγίσαμεν αὐτῇ καὶ μόλις

were rowing with all their strength,
beating the back of the sea   15
with arms naked and strong for a fair voyage.
They approached our merchant ship
and drew their swords.
Then our men, the bravest sailors,
though few in number compared to   20
our bold, sword-carrying opponents,
manfully took up their shields
and fought a sea-battle against the men wielding swords.
They slaughtered and were slaughtered, without trembling
at the endless number of pirates.   25
The water of the sea was turning red,
and until night they were resisting successfully.
But at length they drew their ship away
since most of them had fallen in battle,
and they disembarked, weakened, onto dry land.   30
They left their ship, full of cargo
and bereft of its commander,
and fled to ravines in the midst of the mountains.
Together with these men seeking salvation by flight
I too disembarked, wounded from battle,   35
and followed along, with the maiden Drosilla.
I was hurrying, holding and dragging the girl,
leading her by the hand into steep places,
until, finding a thick tangled shade of branches,
we sat there together, hidden.   40
The next morning, when the day shone forth,
we looked over the top of the mountain and saw below
a fire reaching high up,
and we surmised that those pirates,
pleased with their booty, were burning up our ship,   45
emptied of all cargo and dragged to shore.
Then we, being at a loss,
were directing our eyes here and there,
when suddenly we saw a summit, fortified with towers—
although faintly, dimly, for it was far from us.   50
We ran toward the city
from sunrise until evening

ἐκ φωτὸς ἀρχῆς ἄχρις αὐτῆς ἑσπέρας·
ἦν καὶ συνεισέδυμεν ἐκπεφευγότες
55   τὴν ἐν θαλάσσῃ λῃστρικὴν ἀστοργίαν,
κἂν καὶ Χαρικλῆν, ὡς Κλέανδρον, ἡ πόλις
ἔμελλε χερσὶ Παρθικαῖς δεδωκέναι
καὶ τοὺς θαλασσῶν ἐκφυγόντα κινδύνους
πόνων ἀνάγκαις ἐμβαλεῖν με δευτέραις
60   μετὰ Δροσίλλας, ὦ θεοί, τῆς φιλτάτης.
Τῶν γὰρ κατοίκων ἐξιόντων τὴν πόλιν
αὖθις συνεξέδυμεν, ἐκτελουμένης
λαμπρᾶς ἑορτῆς τῶν Διὸς γενεθλίων.
Τὸ Παρθικὸν δὲ δυσμενέστατον φῦλον
65   οὐκ οἶδ' ὅθεν προῆλθε· πλὴν συλλαμβάνει
καὶ τῆς ἑαυτοῦ μέχρι πατρίδος φέρον
εἰς τὴν φυλακὴν τὴν παροῦσαν εἰσάγει.'
      Τοιοῖσδε πολλοῖς ἀσχολούμενοι λόγοις
ἀλληλοπενθεῖς ἦσαν οἱ νεανίαι,
70   Κλέανδρος ἅμα καὶ Χαρικλῆς οἱ ξένοι.
Ὁ βάρβαρος δὲ Κρατύλος μετ' ὀφρύος
αὐτῇ Χρυσίλλᾳ συγκαθεσθεὶς εἰς ἕω
εἶχε πρὸς αὐτῷ καὶ τὸν υἱὸν Κλεινίαν,
καὶ τοὺς ἁλόντας αἰχμαλωσίας νόμοις
75   ἐκ τῆς φυλακῆς ἐγκελεύεται φέρειν.
Ἔστησαν ἐξαχθέντες οἱ φυλακίται·
ἔπαθεν εἰς τὸ στέρνον ἡ τοῦ βαρβάρου
γυνὴ Χρυσίλλα τὸν Χαρικλῆν ἀθρόον
ἰδοῦσα καὶ πληγεῖσα τῷ πόθου βέλει.
80   Ἦν γὰρ ἄχνους τις χρυσόθριξ, ἐρυθρόχρους,
πλατὺς τὰ νῶτα, ξανθοβόστρυχον κόμην
ἔχων φθάνουσαν ἄχρι καὶ τῆς ὀσφύος·
χεῖρας δὲ λεπτὰς εἶχε λευκοδακτύλους,
καὶ τοὺς ἀμέτρως ἐκχυθέντας ἀστέρας
85   κάλλει καλύπτων καὶ προσώπου λαμπάσιν.
Ἑστηκότας γοῦν εἰσορῶν ὁ Παρθάναξ
οὓς μὲν μερίζει τοῖς ὑπ' αὐτὸν σατράπαις
'μέγιστα δῶρα τῆς συνεργούσης τύχης
δέξασθε' φάσκων 'Παρθικὴ φυλαρχία',
90   οὓς δὲ προπέμπει φῶς ἐλεύθερον βλέπειν,
ἄλλους πρὸς εἰρκτὴν δυστυχῶς ἀντιστρέφει,

and reached it at last and with difficulty.
We slipped into the city together, after escaping
pirate cruelty in the sea.   55
But that city was destined to give Charikles too,
like you, Kleandros, into Parthian hands,
and throw me, who'd escaped the sea's dangers,
into a new set of unavoidable troubles,
together with my dearest Drosilla (oh gods!),   60
for when the inhabitants went out from the city
to celebrate the splendid festival of Zeus's birthday,*
we went out too, in turn;
and the cruel tribe of Parthians
came forth, I don't know from where, and seized us,   65
carried us off to their fatherland,
and put us into this prison."
       In the course of these long speeches
the young men grieved for one another,
Kleandros together with Charikles, the two strangers.   70
But in the morning the barbarian Kratylos proudly
sat next to Chrysilla, his wife,
with his son Kleinias also by his side,
and ordered that the captives
be brought from the prison.   75
The prisoners were led out and stood before them.
Chrysilla at once saw Charikles,
was struck by the dart of desire,
and suffered in her heart,
for he was a smooth-cheeked, golden-haired lad,   80
ruddy in face and broad in shoulder,
with curly yellow hair that reached his loins.
He had slender hands with white fingers,
and with his beauty and the light of his face
he eclipsed even the countless stars spread across the sky.   85
The Parthian king looked at the prisoners standing there,
and some he distributed to the satraps under him,
saying, "Receive these greatest gifts
of benevolent Fortune, Parthian leaders,"
others he sent forth to look upon the light of freedom,   90
others he unfortunately returned to the prison

δώροις ὅπως λυθεῖεν ἐκ γεννητόρων·
πολλοὺς δὲ καὶ δίδωσι μοῖραν τῷ ξίφει,
δεκτὸν νομίζων αἷμα θῦμα τῶν ξένων
95   θεοῖς συνεργοῖς εἰς τὸ πᾶν σωτηρίοις·
χαρίζεται δὲ τὸν Χαρικλῆν Κλεινίᾳ,
οὐχ ὡς ἐκείνου τοῦτον αἰτησαμένου
– ὁ νοῦς γὰρ αὐτοῦ τὴν Δροσίλλαν ἐσκόπει
πασῶν γυναικῶν οὖσαν εὐειδεστέραν –
100   ὡς ἐκ πατρὸς δὲ δῶρον εἰς υἱὸν μέγα·
ἦν γὰρ ἁπάντων τῶν προεγκεκλεισμένων
ὡραῖος ἰδεῖν, τῶν καλῶν δὲ καλλίων.
Τοσαῦτα πράξας ἐξανέστη τοῦ θρόνου
καὶ τοῖς θεοῖς ἔθυσε λαμπρὰς θυσίας.
105   Τετρωμένος γοῦν ἐς μέσην τὴν καρδίαν
ὁ Κλεινίας παῖς βαρβάρου τοῦ Κρατύλου
– καὶ γὰρ ἑάλω τῆς ἁλούσης παρθένου –
τοιαῦτα πολλὰ καθ᾽ ἑαυτὸν ἠρέμα
ἐψιθύριζεν, ἐτραγῴδει τῷ πάθει·
110   'δεινὸν πόθος πᾶς· ἂν δὲ καὶ φιλουμένης,
διπλοῦν τὸ δεινόν· ἂν δὲ καὶ κόρης νέας,
τριπλοῦν τὸ κέντρον· εἰ δὲ καὶ κάλλους γέμει,
πλεῖον τὸ κακόν· εἰ δὲ πρὸς γάμον φέρει,
πῦρ ἔνδον αὐτὴν βόσκεται τὴν καρδίαν.
115   Οὐκ ἔστιν ἰσχὺς ἐκφυγεῖν τὸν τοξότην,
τὸν πυρπολοῦντα καὶ τὸν ἐπτερωμένον·
τῷ γὰρ πτερῷ φθάνει με, τῷ πυρὶ φλέγει,
τῇ τοξικῇ βάλλει με κατὰ καρδίαν.
Μῦθος δοκεῖ μοι νέκταρ ἡ θεῶν πόσις
120   πρὸς σὸν γλυκασμόν, κρυσταλόστερνε, ξένον.
Εἰ γάρ σε περκάζουσαν ἄμπελον βλέπω,
τὸ στέρνον ἐκθλίψει τίς ὡς γλυκὺν βότρυν,
ἢ γλεῦκος ἡδὺ νεκταρῶδες ἐκχύσει
ἢ μυελὸν μέλιτος εὐωδεστάτου;
125   Λειμὼν δοκεῖ μοι σὸν πρόσωπον, παρθένε,
δούλη Χρυσίλλας μητρὸς εὐειδεστάτη·
τὸ χρῶμα τερπνὸν οἷον αὐτοῦ ναρκίσου,
ἄνθος παρειῶν ὡς ἐρυθρόχρουν ῥόδον,
ὡς κυαναυγὲς ἴον ὀφθαλμοὶ δύο,
130   οἱ βόστρυχοί σου κισσὸς ἐμπεπλεγμένος.

so that they could be ransomed with gifts from their parents,
and many he handed over for death by the sword
since he thought the strangers' blood would be an acceptable sacrifice
to the gods who helped him return home safely.   95
And he gave Charikles to Kleinias,
not because he'd asked for him—
for Kleinias's mind was contemplating Drosilla,
the most beautiful of all women—
but as a great gift from a father to a son,   100
for of all the prisoners he was
most comely to see, more beautiful than the beautiful.
After doing all this, Kratylos stood up from his throne
and made splendid sacrifices to the gods.
    Then, wounded deep in his heart,   105
Kleinias, son of the barbarian Kratylos—
for the captive maiden had captivated him—
whispering softly many such things to himself,
lamented thus, with passion:
"All desire is terrible. But if you desire a girl already loved,   110
it's doubly terrible; if you desire a young girl,
the sting is threefold; if you're obsessed with beauty,
the evil is greater; and if you aim at marriage,
a fire within feeds on the heart itself.
There doesn't exist a force able to escape the archer god,   115
with his fire and feathers.
He overtakes me with his wings, burns me with his fire,
and hits me in the heart with his arrows.
Nectar, the drink of the gods, seems to me a fable
compared to your extraordinary sweetness, girl with crystal heart. 120
If I see you as a ripening vine,
who will squeeze your breast like a sweet bunch of grapes,
or pour out sweet new wine like nectar
or essence of sweet-smelling honey?
Your face seems to me like a meadow, maiden,   125
most beautiful slave of my mother, Chrysilla,
your delightful color like that of a narcissus,
the blossom of your cheeks like a red rose,
your eyes like a dark-gleaming violet,
and your locks of hair like entwined ivy.   130

Ὦ πῶς ἀφέλκω τὰς κόρας τῶν ὀμμάτων
τῆς καλλονῆς σου, τοῦ προσώπου τῆς θέας;
Ἀλλ' αἵδε προσμένουσιν ἀνθειλκυσμέναι,
οὐκ ἐνδιδοῦσαι πρὸς τὸ μὴ δεδογμένον.
135   Ἔρως φυτῶν γὰρ καὶ σιδήρου καὶ λίθου
κρατεῖν ἔοικεν, οὐ γὰρ ἀνθρώπων μόνον.
Καὶ γὰρ σίδηρος εἰς μαγνῆτιν ἐκτρέχει,
ἐρωτικόν μοι πῦρ δοκῶν ἔνδον φέρειν·
ἔνευσεν, ἦλθεν, ἔδραμε δρόμον ξένον·
140   ἐμοὶ δοκεῖ φίλημα τοῦτο τῶν δύο,
ἐρωμένης ἐρῶντος· ὦ ξένη σχέσις.
Ἐρᾷ δὲ φυτοῦ φυτὸν ἄλλο πολλάκις·
φοῖνιξ δὲ πρὸς γῆν οὐδὲ ῥιζοῦσθαι θέλει,
εἰ μὴ τὸ θῆλυ συμφυτεύσειας πέλας.
145   Καὶ πόντος οἶδεν Ἀρεθούσης τοὺς γάμους,
πρὸς ἣν γλυκὺς πρόεισιν ἀγκυλορρόας
Ἀλφειὸς εὐρύς, οὗ τὸ ῥεῖθρον ἐν σχέσει
ὁ συνδυασμὸς οὐ μετατρέπειν θέλει.
Ἄκουε, πετρόστερνε, χαλκῆ καρδία,
150   καὶ δὸς μετασχεῖν καλλονῆς ἀσυγκρίτου.'
   Οὕτως ἐρωτικόν τι πάσχων Κλεινίας
πρὸς μουσικόν τι θᾶττον ἐτράπη μέλος,
τοιόνδε ποιῶν λεπτολεύκοις δακτύλοις
τὸ φθέγμα καὶ τὸ κροῦσμα τῆς εὐφωνίας,
155   ἐν λιγυρᾷ φόρμιγγος ἡδυφωνίᾳ·
   ' Ὦ πῶς, Δροσίλλα, πυρπολεῖς τὸν Κλεινίαν.
Ἡ Κύπρις εἰς Ἔρωτα τὸν ταύτης γόνον
μέσαις ἀγυιαῖς ἐξεφώνει πρὶν μέγα
"εἴ τις πλανηθὲν συλλάβῃ τὸ παιδίον
160   ἢ που στενωπῶν ἢ μέσον τῶν ἀμφόδων
ὁ μηνυτής μοι λήψεται γέρας μέγα·
τὸ Κύπριδος φίλημα μισθὸν ἁρπάσει.
   Ὦ πῶς, Δροσίλλα, πυρπολεῖς τὸν Κλεινίαν.
Πλὴν ἴσθι μοι τὸν παῖδα τοῦτον τοξότην,
165   τὸν δραπέτην Ἔρωτα, τὸν κακεργάτην,
καὶ πρόσχες αὐτῷ μὴ βαλεῖ σε καιρίως.
Ἄκουε τούτου καὶ διδάσκου τὸν τρόπον.
Ἂν προσχαρές τι μειδιῶντα προσβλέπῃς,
πλήττει τὰ πολλὰ καὶ κατασφάττειν θέλει·

How will I drag my eyes away
from your beauty, from the sight of your face?
But when dragged away, they remain fixed
and don't turn to a sight they didn't choose.
Eros seems to rule over plants,   135
iron, and rock—not only over humans.
Iron runs to a magnet
and seems to me to carry a fire of love within;
it nods, moves, and runs a wondrous course;
this seems to me a kiss of these two—   140
male lover and female beloved (what a strange relationship).
One plant loves another often;
a palm does not even wish to take root in the earth
unless you plant a female nearby.
The sea knows the nuptials of Arethusa,*   145
towards whom, with sinuous flow, wide Alpheios
sweetly advances, whose waterflow in quality
the coupling will not change.
Hear me, girl with breast of stone and heart of bronze,
and allow me to share in your incomparable beauty."   150
        Kleinias, suffering such a love,
quickly turned to music,
producing with slender, white fingers
this song and harmonious melody
on a clear-toned, sweet-voiced lyre: 155
    "Oh, Drosilla, how you burn Kleinias!
Cypris once cried out after Eros, her son,
in a loud voice in the midst of the streets,
'If someone seizes my child when he has strayed
in some narrow passage or in the middle of the street,   160
on informing me, he shall receive a great reward:
he shall have Cyprus's kiss in return.'
    "Oh, Drosilla, how you burn Kleinias!
'But know that my son is this notorious archer,
runaway Eros, the troublemaker,   165
and take care that he does not hit you fatally.
Listen to this and learn his ways.
If you see him smiling pleasantly,
then he strikes the most and intends to kill.'

170   Ὢ πῶς, Δροσίλλα, πυρπολεῖς τὸν Κλεινίαν.
        Ἂν συλλαβὼν θέλοντα προσπαίζειν ἴδῃς,
        βάλλει σε, τοξεύει σε· πρόσχες οὖν κλύων·
        εἰ δὲ προορμᾶν καὶ φιλεῖν σε γνησίως,
        ἔκφευγε· πυρπολεῖ σε καὶ καταφλέγει.
175   Παῖς ἐστι, πῦρ δὲ τόξα καὶ πτερὰ φέρει·
        οὐκ ἐξ ἀδήλων φαίνεται πετασμάτων·
            Ὢ πῶς Δροσίλλα, πυρπολεῖς τὸν Κλεινίαν·
        καίει, τιτρώσκει καὶ διώκει καὶ φθάνει·
        προσμειδιᾷ γὰρ θηριόστερνος μένων
180   καὶ προσγελᾶν ἔοικε παίζων ἀγρίως
        ὁ τοξοχαρής, ὁ θρασύς, ὁ πυρφόρος.
        Ὁ γοῦν ἐφευρών, συλλαβὼν καὶ μηνύσας,
        τὸν μισθὸν οἷον εἶπον εὐκόλως λάβοι."
            Ὢ πῶς, Δροσίλλα, πυρπολεῖς τὸν Κλεινίαν.
185   Μῦθος μὲν αὐτὸς ἐκτοκευθῆναι λέγει
        κόρην Ἀθηνᾶν τοῦ Διὸς τὴν Παλλάδα
        ἀπὸ κρατὸς πάνοπλον ἔννουν παρθένον·
        σὲ ζωγραφεῖ δὲ μᾶλλον ὡραίαν Ἔρως
        σῆς γαστρὶ μητρὸς ἐμβαλὼν τοὺς δακτύλους,
190   βαλὼν τὸ δίχρουν χρῶμα, γάλα καὶ ῥόδα·
            Ὢ πῶς, Δροσίλλα, πυρπολεῖς τὸν Κλεινίαν·
        καὶ ζωγραφεῖ πάντως σε μὴ διδοὺς ὅπλα·
        οὐ γὰρ νέμει σοι τόξον, οὐ τομὸν ξίφος,
        ὡς κρεῖττον ἦν βάλλειν σε πρὸς φονουργίαν·
195   ποιεῖ δὲ τόξα κύκλα τῶν σῶν ὀφρύων,
        βέλος δὲ πικρὸν τὰς βολὰς τῶν ὀμμάτων,
        δι' ὧν ὀιστεύεις με κατὰ καρδίαν.
            Ὢ πῶς Δροσίλλα, πυρπολεῖς τὸν Κλεινίαν.
        Ὡς εὔστοχον τὸ τόξον αὐτό, παρθένε·
200   ὡς εὐφυὲς τὸ πλῆκτρον. Ἐπλήγην· ἔγνων.
        Τὸ τραῦμα πικρὸν οἷον ἀλλὰ καὶ πόσον.
        Τὸ πρᾶγμα καινὸν οἷον ἀλλὰ καὶ ξένον.
        Οὐ θανατοῖ τὸ κέντρον· ὦ ποῖος λόγος·
        βάλλον δὲ ποιεῖ τῆξιν, ἀλλ' αἰωνίαν.
205   Ὢ πῶς, Δροσίλλα, πυρπολεῖς τὸν Κλεινίαν.
        Πλὴν ἀλλ' ἰδοὺ νύξ ἐστι τῷ δοκεῖν, κόρη·
        ἔχω μακρὰς ἐγὼ δὲ τὰς ὁδοὺς ἔτι·
        ἢ προσλαβοῦ σύνδειπνον εὐνατῆρά σοι

"*Oh, Drosilla, how you burn Kleinias!*   170
'If having seized him, you see that he wishes to play,
then he strikes you and hits you with arrows. Hear this and take heed!
If you see that he wishes to run forward and warmly kiss you,
flee! He burns you and consumes you with fire.
He is a child but has fire, bow, and wings;   175
wings are a big part of his appearance.'
    "*Oh, Drosilla, how you burn Kleinias!*
'He inflames, wounds, pursues, and overtakes;
he smiles while remaining fierce in his heart
and seems to be laughing while playing savagely,   180
that bold boy who delights in the bow and brings fire.
He who finds him, then, seizes him, and informs me
will easily receive the reward I mentioned.'
    "*Oh, Drosilla, how you burn Kleinias!*
A fable says that from Zeus's head   185
Pallas Athena was born,
in full armor, wise, and chaste.
But Eros paints you more beautiful
by putting his fingers in your mother's womb
and depositing twofold color: milk and rose.   190
    "*Oh, Drosilla, how you burn Kleinias!*
And he paints you without giving you weapons,
for he doesn't give you a bow or a sharp sword—
how much better it would be for you to strike to kill!
But he makes a bow out of your arched brows   195
and a sharp dart out of your eyes' glances,
and you shoot me in the heart.
    "*Oh, Drosilla, how you burn Kleinias!*
How well-aimed the bow is, maiden,
and how well-made the dart. I've been struck, I know.   200
How bitter and great the wound is!
How new and strange the whole business!
The dart doesn't kill (oh, what a tale!),
but when it strikes, it produces a consumption that won't go away.
    "*Oh, Drosilla, how you burn Kleinias!*   205
But look, it seems to be night, girl;
I still have long roads ahead.
Either take me as a companion for dinner and bed,

ἢ μὴ θέλουσα τοῦτο δευτέρῳ λόγῳ
210   ὕφαψον ἐκ σῶν χειλέων μοι λαμπάδα
– ἐπίσταμαι γὰρ ὡς ἀνάψεις, εἰ θέλεις –,
"Ω πῶς, Δροσίλλα, πυρπολεῖς τὸν Κλεινίαν,
καὶ φαίδρυνόν μοι τὴν παροῦσαν ἑσπέραν
καὶ λάμπρυνόν μοι τὸ κατατρύχον σκότος
215   καὶ δὸς πρὸς οἶκον, ὦ φαεινὴ λυχνία,
δραμεῖν ἄτερ πλάνης με καὶ προσκομμάτων.
Νοσῶ φρενῖτιν καὶ μεμηνυῖαν νόσον·
μή μοι φθονήσῃς παυσολύπων φαρμάκων.
"Ω πῶς, Δροσίλλα, πυρπολεῖς τὸν Κλεινίαν."
220   Ὁ γοῦν Χαρικλῆς γνοὺς ἐρᾶν τὸν δεσπότην
πρόσεισιν αὐτῷ γνησιώτερον λέγων·
'ἐρᾷς, ἐπέγνων, δέσποτά μου Κλεινία,
ἐρᾷς ἀδελφῆς τῆς ἐμῆς τῆς παρθένου,
ἐρᾷς Δροσίλλας τῆς καλῆς, τῆς παγκάλης.
225   Τί τοῦτο καινόν; Σὸς γὰρ αὐτὸς οἰκέτης
δειλὸς Χαρικλῆς, δυστυχής, τλήμων ξένος
δεινῶς ἑάλων ἁπαλῆς πάλαι κόρης,
ᾗ καὶ συνελθεῖν εἰς λόγους οὐκ ἰσχύων,
καίτοι θέλων πως – οὐ γὰρ εἶχον προσβλέπειν,
230   ὁποῖα καὶ σὺ τὴν Δροσίλλαν οὐ βλέπεις –
μόλις θυρίδων εἶδον ἐκκρεμωμένος
εἰς κῆπον ἁδρὸν ἐκ ῥόδων ἐξ ἀνθέων
τὴν πανταχοῦ μοι συμπαροῦσαν εἰς φρένας,
λεπτὴν δρόσον στάζουσαν ἐν τοῖς ὠκίμοις
235   καὶ βάλσαμα βρέχουσαν ἐκροῇ ῥόδων,
λωτοὺς ὑακίνθους τε καὶ φυτῶν στίφη
καὶ κρίνα λευκὰ καὶ κρόκους καὶ ναρκίσους
καὶ πλεῖστον ἑσμὸν ἀνθέων ἡδυπνόων.
Ἐκεῖ κατεῖδον ἡμιγύμνους ὠλένας,
240   αἷς οὐδὲ χιὼν ἀντερίσειν ἰσχύει,
ἐκεῖ κατεῖδον κρυσταλώδεις δακτύλους
καὶ πρὸς τὸ λευκὸν ἀντερίζοντας γάλα.
Ἰδὼν ἑάλων καλλονῆς ἀμετρίᾳ·
μὴ γὰρ δρυὸς προῆλθον ἢ πετρῶν ἔφυν·
245   ἁλοὺς προσεῖπον, μὴ κατασχεῖν ἰσχύων·
"χαίροις, φυτουργὲ τῶν τοσούτων ἀνθέων·
τί καὶ δι' ἡμᾶς οὐκ ἀνοίγεις τὴν θύραν;

or, if you don't wish to do this, as a second option
set my torch on fire with your lips, 210
for I know that you'll light it if you're willing—
    "Oh, Drosilla, how you burn Kleinias! —
and brighten for me the present evening,
illuminate the consuming darkness,
and enable me, O shining lamp, to go quickly home 215
without wandering and stumbling.
I am suffering brain inflammation and delirium—
don't deny me medicines to end my pain!
    "Oh, Drosilla, how you burn Kleinias!"
    Charikles, then, having perceived that his master was in love, 220
approached him and spoke with great sincerity:
"You are in love, I know it, Kleinias, my master,
you love my chaste sister,
Drosilla the beautiful, totally beautiful.
What's strange in this? I too, your household slave, 225
wretched Charikles, the unfortunate, suffering stranger,
fell terribly in love once with a delicate girl,
with whom I couldn't even converse,
although I wanted to—for I could not look at her,
just as you don't see Drosilla. 230
At last, while I was leaning out of a window
into a garden luxuriant with roses and flowers,
I saw her—the one who's always present in my mind—
as she was dropping delicate dew in the basil
and moistening with rose drops the balsam, 235
lotuses, hyacinths, masses of plants,
white lilies, crocuses, narcissuses,
a great throng of sweet-smelling flowers.
There I saw her half-naked arms,
which not even snow can challenge; 240
there I saw her crystal fingers,
which even rival white milk.
I saw and was conquered by her infinite beauty,
for I was not born from a tree or descended from rocks;
and having succumbed, I addressed her (I couldn't contain myself): 245
    "'Greetings, gardener of so many flowers.
Why don't you open your door also for me?

Ἆρ' ἦλθες εἰς νοῦν τοῦ πάθους τοῦ Ναρκίσου,
ἀπορριφέντος ἐξ ἔρωτος εἰς φρέαρ;
250   Μνήμην τε παιδὸς Ὑακίνθου λαμβάνεις
καὶ τῶν ἐκείνου δυστυχῶν δισκευμάτων,
πῶς ἐξεκαρτέρησεν ἐκ φθόνου φθόνον
ἀπὸ Ζεφύρου τῆς ἐρωτοληψίας;
Ἔχεις τε πρὸς νοῦν Κύπριν αὐτὴν τὴν πάλαι
255   τὴν ἐξερυθρώσασαν ἐκ τῶν αἱμάτων
τῶν ἐκρυέντων τοῦ ποδὸς τετρωμένου
ἐκ τῶν ἀκανθῶν τοῦ ῥόδου λευκὴν θέαν,
Ἀδώνιδος μαθοῦσαν ἄγριον φόνον
ἐξ Ἄρεος πεσόντος; Ὦ κακοῦ φθόνου
260   καὶ τοὺς ἐρῶντας θανατοῦντος πολλάκις.
Πλήρης ὁ κῆπος χαρμονῆς καὶ δακρύων·
καλὴν μὲν αὐχεῖ τὴν φυτουργὸν παρθένον,
ἐρωτικῶν γέμει δὲ δυστυχημάτων
σὺ δ' ἀγνοεῖν ἔοικας ἃ ξένα κλύεις."
265   Οὕτω μὲν αὐτὸς εἶπον αὐτῇ τῇ κόρῃ·
ἡ δὲ πρὸς αὐτὰ θᾶττον ἀνταπεκρίθη·
"ὡς ἥδυνάς μου τὴν πονοῦσαν καρδίαν.
Ἐπῳδὸς εἶ πανοῦργος, ὡς ὁρῶ, τάλαν·
ἀθυμίαν τρέπεις γὰρ εἰς εὐθυμίαν.
270   Δείλαιε, πῶς φής; Βαῖνε τῆς θύρας ἔσω·
τὸ κηπίον θαύμαζε· τὴν κλίνην βλέπε
καὶ δεξιοῦ με τοῖς διηγήμασί σου,
πείρᾳ διδαχθεὶς ὡς κακὸν πόθος μέγα.
Ῥοδωνιᾶς τρύγησον ἐξ ἐμῆς ῥόδα·
275   ἀνακλίθητι· συγκατέρχομαι δέ σοι.
Φάγῃς δὲ τί, δείλαιε; Καρπὸς οὐκ ἔνι·
κἂν μῆλον οὐκ ὥριμον ἐν κηπίῳ,
τὸ στέρνον ἡμῶν ἀντὶ μήλου προσδέχου·
εἴ σοι δοκεῖ, δύστηνε, συγκύψας φάγε·
280   κἂν μὴ πέπειρος βότρυς ἀναδενδράδος
στέρνου στρυφνοῦ μοι θλῖψον αὐτοῦ τὰς ῥάγας·
φίλημα τερπνὸν ἀντὶ σίμβλου μοι λάβε·
ἀντὶ περιπλοκῆς δὲ δένδρου καὶ κλάδων,
ἣν οἶδέ τις δρᾶν καρπὸν ἐκτρυγᾶν θέλων,
285   ἐγὼ τὸ δένδρον· δεῦρο προσπλάκηθί μοι·
ἀντὶ κλάδων ἐμὰς γὰρ ὠλένας ἔχεις·

Do you recall the suffering of Narcissus,*
who threw himself into a well for love?
Do you remember the boy Hyacinth*   250
and the unlucky discus throw—
how he endured jealousy after jealousy
because of Zephyros's love?
Does Cypris come to mind, who once,
with the streams of blood that flowed   255
from her foot wounded by thorns,
changed the rose's white color to red
when she learned of the cruel murder of Adonis,*
who fell at Ares' hands? Oh, evil jealousy,
which often kills lovers!   260
The garden is full of joy and tears;
it boasts of having a beautiful maiden as its gardener,
and it is full of love's misfortunes.
But you seem not to know the strange stories you're hearing.'
        "I spoke thus to the girl,   265
and she replied at once,
        "'How you've delighted my suffering heart.
You're a clever enchanter, I see, poor man,
for you turn sadness into gladness.
Wretched man, what do you say? Come in my door,   270
admire my garden, look at my couch,
and entertain me with your tales
since you've learned by experience what a great evil love is.
Gather a rose from my rose-bed;
recline and I will lie down with you.   275
But what shall you eat, wretch? There is no fruit here.
If there is no ripe apple in the garden,*
accept my breast in place of the apple;
if it pleases you, unhappy man, bend forward and eat.
If a bunch of grapes from a vine is not ripe,   280
squeeze the tips of my tart breast;
take a delightful kiss in place of a honeycomb.
Instead of embracing tree and branches,
which one knows to do when wishing to gather fruit,
see, I am the tree: come cling to me,   285
for you have my arms in place of branches.

ἐγὼ τὸ δένδρον· καὶ προσανάβηθί μοι·
δρέπου τε καρπὸν τὸν γλυκὺν ὑπὲρ μέλι. "
      Ἐμοὶ τὰ σαυτοῦ πάντα λοιπὸν ἀνάθου,
290   καὶ πιστὸν ὄψει δοῦλον ἐκ τῶν πραγμάτων.'
      Οὐκ αἰχμάλωτος οὐδὲ δοῦλος, ὡς ἔφης'
τοῦ βαρβάρου παῖς ἀντέφησε Κλεινίας,
ἐλεύθερος δέ, συμπατριώτης, φίλος
καὶ σατραπικῆς συμμετασχὼν ἀξίας
295   πάντως φανήσῃ κύριος κλήρου τόσου,
εἰ τῇ Δροσίλλᾳ συμμιγῆναι καὶ μόνον
τῷ Κλεινίᾳ γένοιτο σῇ συνεργίᾳ.
Ἀλλ', ὦ Χαρίκλεις, ἐντυχὼν τῇ παρθένῳ
ἄγγελλε ταύτῃ τὴν ἐμὴν ἀχθηδόνα.
300   Νόσος με τήκει· σύντομον λόγον μάθε·
Ἅιδης συναρπάζει με καὶ πρὸ τοῦ χρόνου,
ὁ λαμπρὸς αὐτὸς ἀστεράρχης φωσφόρος
ἔδυνέ μοι τοῖς πᾶσιν ἀκτῖνας βρύων.

      Πηγαὶ ποταμῶν συγκινείσθωσαν ἄνω·
305   θνήσκω γὰρ ὡς μόρσιμος, ἀλλὰ πρὸ χρόνου·
ἀνθησάτω καὶ βάτος ἡδύπνουν ῥόδον·
γένοιτο πάντα νῦν ἐναλλὰξ ἐν βίῳ,
τοῦ Κλεινίου θνήσκοντος, εἰ μὴ προφθάσει
ἡ σή, Χαρίκλεις, εἰς τὸ σῶσαι στερρότης.'
310   ' Τὰ πρὸς Δροσίλλαν, Κλεινία, θαρρητέον'
ὁ Χαρικλῆς ἔλεξε, 'μὴ κατηφία'
τούτοις ἐπειπὼν ἄλλον ἀστεῖον λόγον·
'κοιμωμένην μέλισσαν ἐν ῥόδοις πάλαι
τῆς ποντογενοῦς Ἀφροδίτης παῖς Ἔρως
315   οὐκ εἶδεν· ἐτρώθη δὲ δακτύλῳ μέσῳ,
καὶ στυφελιχθεὶς ἐπτερύξατο τρέχων
πρὸς τὴν τεκοῦσαν "μῆτερ, οἴχομαι" λέγων·
"ὄφις με τύπτει μικρὸς ἐπτερωμένος,
μέλιτταν ἣν λέγουσιν ἄνδρες γηπόνοι."
320   Ἀλλ' ἡ καλὴ Κυθήρη τῷ πεπληγμένῳ
ἀστεῖον ἐγγελῶσα λοιπὸν ἀντέφη·
"εἰ τῆς μελίττης συνθλίβει τὸ κεντρίον,
πόσον δοκεῖς πονοῦσιν οἱ βεβλημένοι
ἐκ σῶν, Ἔρως παῖ, δυστυχῶν τοξευμάτων;"'
325   Εἴρηκε ταῦτα Χαρικλῆς τῷ Κλεινίᾳ,

I am the tree: climb me
and pluck my fruit, which is sweeter than honey.'
   "Entrust all your affairs, then, to me,
and you'll see from what happens that your slave is reliable."   290
   "You shall not be a prisoner or slave, as you said,"
the barbarian's son Kleinias replied,
"but a free man, a compatriot,
a friend who shares the satrap's rank,
and an absolute master of a great estate,   295
if only you can arrange that
Kleinias be united with Drosilla.
Go, Charikles, meet with the maiden
and tell her of my distress.
A sickness is consuming me. Here's a brief description of what to say.   300
Hades is seizing me before my time.
The bright sun himself, leader of the stars,
who sends forth rays to all, has set for me.
Let rivers flow back to their sources,
for I am dying as destined, but before time.   305
Let the bramble-bush too bloom with the fragrant rose.
Let all things now be changed in the world
since Kleinias dies, unless you save him first,
Charikles, with your strength."
   "As for Drosilla, Kleinias, be confident,"   310
Charikles said, "not downcast,"
and he added another pretty story:
"Once Eros, sea-born Aphrodite's son,
didn't see a bee that was sleeping
among roses, and he was stung in his finger.   315
He spread his wings, flew to his mother,
and cried, 'Mother, I am dead!
A small, winged serpent has wounded me—
which tillers of the earth call a bee.'
But beautiful Kythera, with an amused smile,   320
then replied to her son who'd been stung,
'If the bee's little sting distresses you,
how much do you think those hit
by your cruel arrows suffer, Eros, my son?'"
   After saying these things to Kleinias,   325

καὶ τὸν Δροσίλλας ἐγγυώμενος γάμον
μικρὸν διέστη πρὸς διάσκεψιν τάχα,
οὐκ ὡς συνάψαι τὴν Δροσίλλαν Κλεινίᾳ,
κακὴν δὲ βουλὴν ἐκφυγεῖν ἠπειγμένος.
330   Ἦν καὶ κατιδεῖν ἰδιάζουσαν θέλων,
ὡς συναποκλαύσαιτο τὴν δυστυχίαν,
λειμῶνος ἐντὸς εὗρε κειμένην μόνην,
κοιμωμένην μὲν ἐκ μεριμνῶν βαρέως,
ἄνθει δὲ λευκῶν ἀντερίζουσαν ῥόδων
335   καὶ μειδιᾶν δοκοῦσαν ἀκροωμένην
φθογγῆς μελιχρᾶς τῶν καλῶν χελιδόνων.
Ὦ θάμβος οἷον ἀλλὰ καὶ φρίκη πόση
ἐκεῖ Χαρικλῆν συγκατέσχεν ἀθρόον,
ὡς εἶδεν ὑπνώττουσαν ἐν τῷ κηπίῳ
340   ταύτην ἀπαστράπτουσαν ἡλίου δίκην
ἐαρινὴν λάμποντος ἀνθρώποις φλόγα.
Ὃς γὰρ Δροσίλλας ἐγκαθισθεὶς πλησίον
– φειδὼ γὰρ εἶχε τήνδε μὴ διυπνίσαι –
ἔφασκε, ταύτην ἀτενέστερον βλέπων·
345   'ἐνταῦθα καὶ Χάριτες, ὦ ποθουμένη,
κοιμωμένῃ σοι συμπάρεισιν ἠρέμα,
ἐπαγρυπνοῦσαι μή τι φαῦλον ἐμπέσῃ
σύγκυρμα πάντως ἐξ ἀποφράδος τύχης.
Ὦ ποῖον αὐτὴ λεπτὸν ἀσθμαίνεις, κόρη·
350   ὦ ποῖον ἡδὺ μειδιᾶν δοκεῖς τάχα·
ἧς ἐξεπορφύρωσεν ἡ φύσις πάλαι
χείλη παρειάς, ὡς δοκεῖν φλόγα τρέφειν,
καὶ βοστρύχους ἔτεινεν ἄχρις ὀσφύος,
οἷς οὐδὲ χρυσὸς ἀντερίσειν ἰσχύει.
355   Σιγῶσι πάντα σοῦ σιγώσης, παρθένε·
οὐ στρουθὸς ᾄδων, οὐχ ὁδοιπόρος τρέχων,
οὐδεὶς ὁμιλῶν, οὐ παρερπύζων ὄφις·
ἔπαυσεν, οἶμαι, καὶ πνοὴ τῶν ἀνέμων
τὸ κάλλος αἰδεσθεῖσα τῆς κοιμωμένης.
360   Ὦ πῶς σιγᾷ νῦν πᾶν μελῳδὸν στρουθίον.
Πηγαὶ μόναι νάουσιν, ὦ ποθουμένη,
ὡς μᾶλλον ἡδὺν ὕπνον ἐμβάλωσί σοι.
Καὶ φθόγγος αὐτῶν ἡ ῥοὴ λέγουσά σοι·
"ὦ καλλονὴν ἅπασαν ἠμφιεσμένη,

Charikles promised to set up marriage with Drosilla,
and then withdrew a little to think,
not about how to unite Drosilla with Kleinias,
but rather about how to escape a disadvantageous plan.
He wanted to see her privately,   330
to weep with her for their misfortune,
and he found her lying alone in a meadow,
sleeping heavily after all her cares.
She rivaled the blossom of white roses
and seemed to smile as she listened to   335
the honey-sweet sound of lovely swallows.
What great amazement and also awe
came over Charikles at once
when he saw this girl sleeping in the garden,
for she gleamed brightly like the sun   340
as he lights the flame of spring for mortals.
He sat down near Drosilla—
for he was reluctant to wake her—
and said, gazing intently upon her,
"Here the Graces too, beloved,   345
stand quietly by your side as you sleep,
and watch that something bad
from cruel Fortune may not befall you.
What a dainty breath you take, girl;
how sweetly you seem to smile.   350
Nature once dyed your lips and cheeks
so that they seem to contain a flame,
and she let fall to your hips curls of hair
with which not even gold can compete.
Everything is still since you are still, maiden: 355
sparrows don't sing, travelers don't run,
people don't speak, snakes don't slither.
The blowing of the winds has also ceased, I think,
from respect for the beauty of the sleeping girl.
How hushed is every tuneful sparrow!   360
The streams alone are flowing, beloved,
to make your sleep sweeter,
and the murmur of their flow is saying to you,
'Girl clothed in absolute beauty,

365   σιγᾷς· σιγᾷ σοι καὶ τὸ τῆς αὔρας ψύχον·
      ὑπνοῖς· ἐφυπνοῖ καὶ τὸ τῆς αὔρας γένος·
      πηγαὶ μόναι νῦν ἐγκελαρύζουσί σοι. "
      Ἐντεῦθεν ἀντᾴδουσαν οὐκ ἔχοντά σε
      σιγῶσι φιλόμουσα τῶν πτηνῶν γένη.
370   Πλὴν ἀλλὰ μή μοι στέργε τὸν λήθης ὕπνον·
      λυπεῖς γάρ, ὡς ἔοικε, τὰς ἀηδόνας,
      αἷς ἀντερίζει σὸν γλυκύτατον στόμα·
      μελισταγὲς γὰρ προσλαλεῖς, ἡ παρθένος.
      Ἀλλ' ὦ συνεργοὶ καὶ συνέμποροι φίλαι,
375   Χάριτες ἐσθλαί, μαργαρόστερνοι κόραι,
      φρουρεῖτε καὶ τηρεῖτε πρὸς σωτηρίαν
      τὰ στέρνα καὶ τὰ νῶτα τῆς κοιμωμένης,
      μακρὰν τιθεῖσαι λίχνα τῶν μυῶν γένη.
      Ἔρωτος οὐδὲν ἄλλο φάρμακον ξένον·
380   ᾠδὴ δέ τις καὶ μοῦσα παῦλα τῶν πόνων.
      Βεβλημένος γὰρ καὶ Πολύφημος πάλαι
      τὸ στέρνον ἐξ Ἔρωτος ἀνδροτοξότου,
      πλατὺ τρέφων τὸ φίλτρον εἰς Νηρηίδα
      ἐφεῦρεν οὐδὲν ἄλλο φάρμακον νόσου,
385   ᾠδὴν δὲ καὶ σύριγγα καὶ θέλγον μέλος,
      καὶ πέτραν ἕδραν, τῇ θαλάττῃ προσβλέπων.
      Πρῶτον γὰρ οἶμαι – καὶ καλῶς οὕτως ἄρα –
      πτηνοδρομῆσαι τοὺς λίθους εἰς αἰθέρα
      καὶ λίθον ἀδάμαντα τμηθῆναι ξίφει
390   ἢ τοξικῆς Ἔρωτα παυθῆναι κάτω,
      κάλλους παρόντος καὶ βλεπόντων ὀμμάτων.
      Λήγει μὲν οὖν καὶ πόντος ὀψὲ τῆς ζάλης,
      λήγουσιν ἤδη καὶ πνοαὶ τῶν ἀνέμων,
      καὶ πῦρ ἀναφθὲν συγκατεσβέσθη πάλιν·
395   ζάλη δὲ καὶ πῦρ λῆξιν ἔσχεν οὐδ' ὅλως
      τοῖς στερνοπλήκτοις ἐξ Ἔρωτος τοξότου·
      τήκειν γὰρ οἶδεν, ὡς τὸ πῦρ τὸ κηρίον,
      οὓς ἔνδον αὐτοῦ τῆς καμίνου συλλάβῃ.
      Ἀνιαρόν τι χρῆμα τοξότης Ἔρως·
400   ἐμφὺς γὰρ ὥσπερ βδέλλα λιμνῆτις πίνει
      τὸν αἵματος ῥοῦν πάντα· τῆς ἄκρας νόσου.
      Ὡς ἐξανάπτεις οὓς λάβῃς Ἔρως, Ἔρως,
      καίεις, φλογίζεις, πυρπολεῖς, καταφλέγεις·

you are still; the cool breeze is also still for you.   365
You sleep; the family of breezes sleeps too.
Streams alone now murmur to you.'
All the song-birds are silent, then,
since they don't have you singing in response.
But don't love the sleep of forgetfulness!   370
You distress the nightingales, it seems,
with whom your sweet mouth contends,
for your words drip with honey, my maiden.
But you, helpers and dear companions,
noble Graces, girls with breasts of pearl,   375
watch and protect the breast and back
of the girl sleeping, by keeping
far away the greedy race of flies.
There is no other strange remedy for love:
song and music alone offer a rest from love's cares.   380
Even Polyphemos once, when he was hit*
in the breast by Eros, murderous archer,
and nursed a strong love for a Nereid,
found no other remedy for his sickness
than a song, a reed pipe, and a charming tune,   385
and a rock for a seat, from which he gazed at the sea.
I think—and I am right—
that sooner would stones fly winged to the sky
and diamond be cut by sword
than Eros cease to shoot arrows to earth,   390
as long as beauty exists and eyes perceive it.
Even storms at sea, then, cease at last,
blasts of the winds soon stop,
and a blazing fire is again quenched.
But storm and fire don't cease at all   395
for those hit in the heart by the archer Eros,
for just as fire melts wax, he can melt
anyone that he seizes within his furnace.
A nasty creature is the archer Eros,
for clinging closely like a marsh leech he drinks up   400
every drop of blood. What a dreadful plague!
How you inflame those you seize, Eros—
ignite, combust, cremate, and incinerate them!

ὡς ἐξ ἐκείνων τῶν προηνθρακωμένων
405   καὶ λύχνον ἁδρὸν ἐξανάψει τις θέλων·
ποιεῖς δοκεῖν γὰρ ὑποκόλπιον φέρειν
ἐρωμένην ἐρῶντα πολλὰ πολλάκις·
οὕτως ἐρῶν πᾶς – ὡς ἄφυκτόν τι πόθος –
ἁλίσκεται γὰρ τοῖς Ἔρωτος δικτύοις,
410   ὡς μῦς πρὸς ὑγρᾶς ἐμπεσὼν πίσσης χύτραν.
Δοκεῖ δέ μοί τις, ἂν παρέλθοι καὶ φύγοι
Ἔρωτα τὸν τύραννον ἐπτερωμένον,
καὶ τοὺς ἐφ᾽ ὕψους ἐκμετρήσοι ἀστέρας.᾽

ΒΙΒΛΙΟΝ ΠΕΜΠΤΟΝ

Τοιαῦτα πολλὰ καὶ τοσαῦτα καὶ τόσα
ἐπετραγῴδει καθ᾽ ἑαυτὸν ἠρέμα·
πλὴν ἐξανέστη καὶ Δροσίλλα τῷ τότε.
Ἔμεινε δ᾽ οὖν ἄφθογγος εἰς πολὺν χρόνον,
5   ὡς εἶδε συμπαρόντα τὸν Χαρικλέα,
ψυχῇ φιλοῦσα καρδίαν ποθουμένην,
καὶ τὸν καταρρέοντα μαργάρων δίκην
ἱδρῶτα λεπτὸν ἀπεμόργνυ δακτύλοις.
Ἦν εἴ τις εἶδεν ὕπνον ἀφεῖσαν τότε
10   εἴρηκεν ἂν ᾽ Ζεῦ, τῶν Ὀλυμπίων πάτερ,
τέρπει μέν, οἶδα, πάντα τερπνὰ τοῦ βίου,
ᾠδαί, τρυφαί, τράπεζα λαμπρὰ καὶ πόσις,
μέγιστος οἶκος, χρυσός, ἄργυρος, λίθος
καὶ πλοῦτος ἄλλος χρημάτων καὶ κτημάτων·
15   ναὶ ταῦτα τέρπει – καὶ τίς ἀντίθρους λόγος; –,
ἀλλ᾽ οὐ τοσοῦτον ὡς ἐρυθρόχρους κόρη,
ὅταν διυπνισθεῖσα πρὸς μεσημβρίαν
θρόμβους περιρρέοντας ἱδρώτων φέρει,
ὡς εἰς ἔαρ ἄγρωστις ὀρθρίαν δρόσον·
20   ἧς εἰ φιλεῖν σχοίη τις αὐτὴν τὴν γνάθον
λεπτὴν ἀποστάζουσαν ἱδρώτων δρόσον,
τὸ πῦρ δροσίζει καὶ μαραίνει τὴν φλόγα
καίουσαν αὐτὴν ἔνδοθεν τὴν καρδίαν
τὴν δυσφοροῦσαν, τὴν πεπυρπολημένην,
25   ὡς δῆθεν ἐξ ἔρωτος ἠνθρακωμένην·

How easily from their ashes
whoever wants could kindle a large torch.   405
You often cause a lover to believe
that he carries his beloved in the folds of his robe.
Thus every lover (how inescapable love is!)
is caught by the nets of Eros,
just like a mouse who's fallen into a pot of pitch.   410
I think that anyone who could pass by
and escape Eros, the winged tyrant,
could even count the stars in the sky!"

BOOK FIVE

    While Charikles was lamenting quietly to himself
many such sorts of things,
Drosilla woke up.
When she saw Charikles beside her,
she remained silent for a long time—   5
a soul loving a beloved heart—
and she wiped off with her fingers the fine sweat
pouring down like pearls.
If someone had seen her then when she'd just dismissed sleep,
he'd have said, "Zeus, father of the Olympians,   10
all pleasures of life, I know, delight you:
songs, luxuries, splendid food and drink,
a great house, gold, silver, precious stones,
and a wealth of other goods and possessions.
Yes, these things delight you—who could deny it?—   15
but not so much as a rosy girl
when she awakes from sleep about midday,
dripping with sweat all over,
like spring grass with morning dew.
If someone should kiss her cheek   20
as it drips with a fine dew of sweat,
he would sprinkle the fire and quench the flame
that burns within his heart—
wretched, wasted with fire,
burnt to ashes by love.   25

ἐξ ἄνθρακος δὲ χειλέων τῶν τῆς κόρης
τὸν ἄνθρακα σβέννυσι τὸν τῆς καρδίας.'
    Μόλις προσεῖπε πρὸς Χαρικλῆν τοιάδε·
'σύ μοι, Χαρίκλεις, σὺ δοκεῖς ἐφεστάναι.
30   Αὐτὸς πάρει νῦν τῆς Δροσίλλας ἐγγύθεν,
ἢ φασμάτων ἔμφασις ἐμπαίζειν θέλει;
Ἔμβαπτε χείλει χεῖλος· ἅπλου δακτύλους·
ἐμῶν ἐφάπτου καὶ τραχήλου καὶ γνάθου.
Δὸς ἀντιφιλεῖν, Χαρίκλεις, φιλοῦντά με·
35   σοῦ μὴ φιλεῖν θέλοντος ἐκ ψυχῆς μέσης,
δοκῶ ποθεινῆς ἥμισυ ζωῆς ἔχειν.
Πῶς τοῦτο χρηστὸν τὴν φιλοῦσαν ἀλγύνειν;
Μίαν καλιὰν πῆξον εἰς ἕνα κλάδον,
οὗ μὴ προβαίνειν εὐχερῶς ἂν ἰσχύοι
40   ἢ πτηνὸς ὄρνις ἢ προσερπύζων ὄφις.
Πρώτην δέ σε στέρξασαν αἰσχύνου κλύων·
ἐν δευτέρῳ με τῆς Χρυσίλλας μὴ τίθει,
μὴ τῆς κόρης πρόκρινε τὴν γηραλέαν.
Ἔρως ὁ πλήττων ὡς ὑπόπτερος μάθε·
45   γυνὴ παρηκμακυῖα πῶς ἂν ἰσχύσοι
πτηνοδρομοῦντα συλλαβέσθαι τοξότην;'
    Ἔφη Χαρικλῆς ἀντιπαίζων μετρίως
καὶ μὴ τὸ μέλλον προσκοπῶν καὶ προβλέπων
– τὸν γὰρ πρὸς αὐτόν, ὃ Δροσίλλα μηνύει,
50   ἔρωτα δεινὸν τῆς Χρυσίλλας ἠγνόει –·
' τοιαῦτα μὲν σὺ κερτομήματα πλέκεις·
οὐκ ἀγνοῶ δέ, δεινὸς ὢν πρὸς τὸν πόθον,
ὡς ζηλότυπον χρῆμα θηλειῶν ἔφυ·
γεννᾶν γὰρ οἶδε ψευδεπιπλάστους λόγους,
55   τὰς ἐν προλήψει τῶν φρενῶν ἀναπλάσεις
ἀεὶ νομίζον ὡς ἐφεστώσας βλέπειν·
δοκεῖ γὰρ αὐτὰς οὐσιῶν ὑποστάσεις.
Πλὴν καὶ φορητὰ κερτομούμενος φέρω·
περιφρονῶν δὲ τὰς προλοίπους ἐμφρόνως
60   μόνην ποθῶ· κέκτησο τὴν ζωὴν ὅλην.'
Ἀλλ' ἡ Δροσίλλα 'ναί, Χαρίκλεις' ἀντέφη,
'εἶχον προφανῶς συντίθεσθαι σοῖς λόγοις,
εἰ μὴ Χρυσίλλα τὸν σύνευνον Κρατύλον
ἐκ φαρμάκων ἔσπευδεν ἀνῃρηκέναι

With the embers of the girl's lips
he quenches the embers of his heart."
　　At last she said the following to Charikles:
"You seem, Charikles, to be beside me.
But are you yourself now near Drosilla,　　　　　　　　　　30
or does a phantom desire to mock me?
Dip your lip in my lip; stretch out your fingers;
touch both my neck and cheek!
Allow me to return your love, Charikles.
If you don't want to love me from the depths of your soul,　　35
I think I have only half the life I desire.
How is this good, to grieve the girl who loves you?
Stick a bird's nest on a branch
that neither a winged bird
nor a slithering snake could easily reach.　　　　　　　　40
Be ashamed at hearing that I loved you first;
don't put me in second place behind Chrysilla;
don't prefer an old woman to a girl!
Know that Eros, who strikes, is winged—
how could a woman past her prime　　　　　　　　　　45
seize an archer who flies swiftly?"
　　Charikles spoke, teasing her a little,
not considering the future and looking ahead,
for he didn't know of Chrysilla's terrible love for him,
which Drosilla revealed,　　　　　　　　　　　　　50
"What snide remarks you are making!
I know, since I am clever at love,
how jealous women are by nature.
They are capable of producing false speech,
for they always think that they see before them　　　　55
things that arise from their minds' preconceptions,
and they believe that these are substances of reality.
But when I am sneered at, the sneers are bearable,
and sensibly despising the rest of women
I desire you alone. Be master of all my life!"　　　　　60
But Drosilla replied, "Yes, Charikles,
I could certainly agree with your words
if Chrysilla were not striving to kill
her husband Kratylos with poisons,

65   ἐρῶσα, φεῦ φεῦ, τοῦ καλοῦ Χαρικλέος.'
     ᾿Ώμοι' Χαρικλῆς τὸν λόγον προαρπάσας
     ᾿Δροσίλλα, τί φής;' ἀντέφησαν εὐθέως·
     λέγεις τι μεστὸν χαρμονῆς καὶ δακρύων·
     τὸ γὰρ θανεῖν μὲν τὸν τύραννον Κρατύλον
70   εὐκταῖον ἡμῖν δυστυχῶς δουλουμένοις·
     ἴσως λυθῶμεν τοῦ ζυγοῦ τοὺς αὐχένας,
     φροντίδα μικρὰν Κλεινίου τεθεικότες·
     τὸ δὲ Χρυσίλλαν τὴν ἐρυτιδωμένην
     ἔρωτα πικρὸν νῦν ἐρᾶν Χαρικλέος
75   ἀπευκτὸν οὐκ ἔοικεν; Οὔ, μὰ τὴν Θέμιν,
     οὔ οὔ, μὰ τὴν Ἔρωτος ἀνθρακουργίαν,
     οὐ προσπλακῇς μοι γραῦς τάλαινα, καρδία
     θάλασσα πικρὰ τελματώδης ἀγρία.
     Ποινὴ τὸ σὸν φίλημα πάντως, ὦ γύναι·
80   σκληρὸν τὸ χεῖλος, ξηρὸν αὐτὸ τὸ στόμα·
     χρόνος δὲ τὰς σὰς ἐξεβύρσωσε γνάθους·
     λημᾷς γὰρ ἤδη, κἂν ὁ κόχλος εἰς βάθος·
     κατωχριᾷς ναί, κἂν τὸ φῦκος εἰς πάχος.
     Καὶ κἂν ἐκείνης Ἀρτέμιδος καλλίων
85   Χρυσίλλα, λυπρὰ νῦν, γενήσεται πάλιν,
     ποῦ ποῦ, Δροσίλλα, τοὺς ἐνωμότους λόγους
     θήσει Χαρικλῆς συζυγεὶς τῇ βαρβάρῳ;
     Φθείρου, τυραννίς· ἔρρε, σατραπαρχία·
     ὁ πλοῦτος, ἐκράγηθι τοῦ Χαρικλέος.
90   Οὐ μὴ προθῶμαι σωφροσύνης τὸ κλέος.
     Συνουσιώθην τῆς Δροσίλλας τῷ πόθῳ·
     ἀποστερηθείην δὲ μὴ σοῦ, παρθένε.
     Ὁρᾷς ὁ καλλίμορφος ἐκ Διὸς γόνος;
     Σύ μοι Δροσίλλας ἠγγυήσω τὸν γάμον·
95   καὶ νῦν γυνὴ γραῦς βαρβαρόφρων ὠμόνους
     ζητεῖ διασπᾶν τῆσδε τὸν Χαρικλέα.
     Βλέπεις ἀνάγκην ἣν φέρει, βλέπεις νόσον.
     Τὸν Κρατύλον φόνευε καὶ τὸν Κλεινίαν,
     ναὶ καὶ σὺ σαυτήν, ὦ Χρυσίλλα κυρία,
100 οὕτω Χαρικλῆν ἡδυνεῖς σὸν οἰκέτην,
     οὕτω Δροσίλλαν εὐφρανεῖς σὴν οἰκέτιν.
     Ταῦτ' οὖν μελήσοι τοῖς θεοῖς, ὦ παρθένε·
     τὸν γοῦν ἔρωτα Κλεινίου τοῦ δεσπότου

for love, alas, of the beautiful Charikles." 65
    "Oh, Drosilla," Charikles replied at once,
cutting off her speech, "what are you saying?
Your speech is full of joy and tears,
for we who are unfortunately slaves
have prayed for the death of the tyrant Kratylos. 70
Perhaps we'll have our necks freed from the yoke,
for we have little regard for Kleinias.
But for the wrinkled Chrysilla
now to love Charikles with a keen love,
doesn't this seem terrible? No, by Themis, 75
no, no, by the furnace of Eros,
you'll not be united with me, wretched old woman,
sea that's hateful to my heart, muddy, and savage.
Your kiss is altogether a penalty, woman,
your lip hard, your mouth dry; 80
time has made your cheeks leathery,
for you're bleary-eyed now, even if your purple dye is deep,
and you're pale, even if your rouge is thick.
Even if Chrysilla, now wretched, becomes
in turn more beautiful than famous Artemis, 85
where, Drosilla, will Charikles, if yoked
to the barbarian woman, put the oaths he swore to you?
Away with you, monarchy! Begone, satrapy!
Wealth, break away from Charikles!
I'll not put fame before decency. 90
Love has joined me with Drosilla;
may I never be deprived of you, maiden!
Do you see, beautiful child of Zeus?
You promised me marriage with Drosilla,
and now an old woman, barbarous and savage, 95
seeks to separate Charikles from this girl.
You see the pain and sickness I suffer.
Kill Kratylos and Kleinias;
yes, and kill yourself too, Mistress Chrysilla!
Thus you'll cheer your slave Charikles; 100
thus you'll delight your slave Drosilla.
The gods, then, will take care of these things, maiden;
but where in our terrible misfortune

ποῦ τῆς καθ' ἡμᾶς θήσομεν δεινῆς τύχης;
105 Λέγοις τι μικρόν· ὡς ἀπέσταλμαι μόνος
ὑμᾶς συνάψων καὶ τὸ πᾶν καταρτίσων.'
　　Πρὸς ταῦτα δακρύσασα μικρὸν ἡ κόρη·
''Ολύμπιε Ζεῦ' φησίν 'οὐρανοκράτορ,
τί ζῆν με κακότητι συγχωρεῖς ἔτι,
110 τὴν λειπόπατριν, τὴν ἄποικον, τὴν ξένην;
Τί μὴ θαλάσσης ὑπεδέξατο στόμα;
Τί βάρβαρόν με μὴ κατέκτεινε ξίφος;
Ἐπεὶ δέ με ζῆν δυστυχῶς θέλεις ἔτι,
τί πρὸς λιθώδη μὴ μετατρέπεις φύσιν;
115 Τί μὴ πτέρυγας ἀντιδίδως καὶ πάλιν,
ὡς Πανδίονος 'Αττικοῦ ταῖς ἐγγόνοις;
Τί μὴ βριαρὸς καὶ θρασύσπλαγχνος λέων
λόχμης προκύψας θᾶττον ἐσπάραξέ με,
ὅτε πρὸς ἄλση καὶ φαραγγώδεις τόπους
120 τὴν λῃστρικὴν ἔφευγον ἀγερωχίαν;
Ὡς κρεῖττον ἦν θανοῦσαν, ὦ θεοί, τότε
ἀπαλλαγήν με τῶν κακῶν εὑρηκέναι
ἢ ζῆν ἀειστένακτον ἐν γῇ βαρβάρων
δούλην ταπεινήν, αἰχμάλωτον ἀθλίαν.
125 'Αλλ', ὦ ποθεινὸν ὄμμα καὶ φίλη θέα,
ἥδιστα ταῦτα πάντα· μὴ δάκρυέ μοι'
– γνοὺς γὰρ δι' αὐτὸν ταῦτα συμπεπονθέναι
αἰδούμενος δάκρυον ἐστάλαζέ τι –
ἔφη Δροσίλλα· καὶ Χαρικλῆς ἀντέφη,
130 ἰδὼν πρὸς αὐτοὺς φωλεοὺς χελιδόνων·
　　'σὺ μὲν μολοῦσα ταῖς ἔαρος ἡμέραις,
καλὴ χελιδών, εἰς ἐπίτροχον μέλος
διττοῖς νεοττοῖς συντιθεῖς χειὰν μίαν·
ὅταν δὲ χειμὼν ἀντεπέλθῃ, φυγγάνεις·
135 ἀλλ' ὁ πτερωτός, ἀλλ' ὁ τοξότης Ἔρως
ἀεὶ καλιὰν εἰς ἐμὴν ψυχὴν πλέκει.
Πόθος δ' ὁ μὲν πτέρωσιν ἁδρὰν ἐκφύει,
ἄλλος δὲ τὴν κύησιν ἤδη μηνύει,
ᾠοῦ δέ τις ἔξωθεν ἄλλος ἐκτρέχει,
140 ἀεὶ δὲ τὴν τάλαιναν ἐντὸς καρδίαν
βοῇ νεοττῶν ἐκθροεῖ κεχηνόντων·
τῶν γὰρ τραφέντων ἐκτοκεύονται νέοι·

shall we put the love of Kleinias, my master?
Speak a little, for I've been sent here alone,   105
to unite you both and arrange the whole thing."
   The girl wept a little in response to this
and said, "Olympian Zeus, ruler of heaven,
why do you still allow me to live in misery,
exiled from my fatherland, homeless, a stranger?   110
Why didn't the mouth of the sea swallow me up?
Why didn't a barbarian sword kill me?
But since you still wish me to live unhappily,
why don't you transform me into stone?
Why don't you give me wings, in turn,   115
as you gave to the daughters of Attic Pandion?
Why didn't a strong, bold-hearted lion
come out of a thicket and quickly tear me apart,
when towards groves and ravines
I was fleeing from pirate cruelty?   120
How much better it would have been, gods,
for me to have died then and found release from my evils,
than to live in perpetual distress in a land of barbarians,
as a lowly slave and a wretched prisoner.
But, dear friend and beloved sight,   125
all these things are sweet; don't cry for me,"
Drosilla said—for Charikles, knowing that she
had suffered these things because of him,
was shedding a tear for shame. Then Charikles
answered, looking towards the swallows' nests,   130
   "You, lovely swallow, when you come
with fluent song in the days of spring,
build one nest for two baby birds,
and when winter comes in turn, you flee;
but winged Eros, the archer,   135
always weaves a nest in my soul.
One Love produces thick plumage,
another is not yet hatched,
while another is running out from the egg,
and always the cry of nestlings with open beak   140
resounds within my wretched heart,
for from those who have grown, new ones are brought forth.

τῇ καρδίᾳ τίς μηχανὴ γένοιτό μοι;
Ἐρωτιδεῖς γὰρ οὐ τοσούτους ἰσχύει
145   ἀεὶ τοκεύειν, ζωπυρεῖν, φέρειν, τρέφειν.
Δεινὸν φιλῆσαι, μὴ φιλῆσαι δὲ πλέον·
δεινῶν δὲ πάντων χαλεπώτερον κρίνω
τὸ τοὺς φιλοῦντας εὐκόλως μὴ τυγχάνειν.
Κέρας μὲν οὖν ἔδωκε ταύροις ἡ φύσις,
150   ἵπποις ὁπλὰς δέ, τὴν ποδώκειαν πάλιν
δειλοῖς λαγωοῖς, τῇ λεόντων ἀγέλῃ
τὸ τῶν ὀνύχων ὀξυκέντητον σθένος,
τὸ νηκτὸν ἔθνει τῶν ἀφώνων ἰχθύων,
τοῖς ὀρνέοις τὴν πτῆσιν, ἀνδράσι φρένας·
155   πρὸς γοῦν Δροσίλλαν, ἄλλο μὴ κεκτημένη,
δίδωσι κάλλος ἀντὶ πάσης ἀσπίδος,
ἀντὶ βελέμνων, ἀντὶ πολλῶν ἐγχέων·
νικᾷ δὲ καὶ σίδηρον εὖ τεθηγμένον
καὶ παμφάγον πῦρ δραστικῶς ἀνημμένον.
160   Ἐγώ, Δροσίλλα, Κλεινίᾳ τῷ δεσπότῃ
τὸν ὄλβιον σὸν ἠγγυησάμην γάμον,
οὐχ ὡς φρονῶν τοιαῦτα μὴ γένοιτό μοι,
πλὴν βαρβάρῳ μὲν καρδίᾳ θυμουμένῃ
ὥραν παρασχὼν ἠρεμῆσαι μετρίαν,
165   ἡμῖν δὲ πάντως τί σκοπῆσαι συμφέρον.
Ἤδη δὲ καιρός, καὶ σκοπεῖν ἀπαρκτέον
πῶς τὸν Χρυσίλλας καὶ τὸν υἱοῦ Κλεινίου
ἔρωτα νῦν σχοίημεν ἐγκατασβέσαι.'
        Τοιοῖσδε λοιπὸν ἦσαν ἠσχολημένοι
170   – ἔρως ὁ σώφρων ἡ φιλάλληλος σχέσις –
αὐτὸς Χαρικλῆς καὶ Δροσίλλα παρθένος·
καί τις παρεισέπνευσεν ἀντίθρους λόγος,
ὡς Κρατύλος πέπτωκεν ἀθρόᾳ νόσῳ.
Οἳ καὶ διασπασθέντες ἀλλήλων τότε
175   ἀντιπροσῆλθον τοῖς ἑαυτῶν δεσπόταις
μαθεῖν τὸ πραχθέν, πενθικῶς ἐσταλμένοι.
Καὶ συρρεόντων τῶν ὑπ' αὐτοὺς αὐτίκα
ἀνδρῶν γυναικῶν σατραπῶν καὶ βαρβάρων·
ὁμοῦ κατ' αὐτό, Κρατύλου προκειμένου
180   ᾤμωξεν ἡ Χρυσίλλα πάντων ἐν μέσῳ,
πρὸς μὲν τὸν ἄνδρα δῆθεν ἠσχολημένη,

What recourse could there be for my heart?
It does not have the strength always to bring forth
so many young Erotes, and to warm, carry, and nourish them.   145
To love is a terrible thing, but not to love is worse,
yet I judge the worst thing of all would be
for lovers not to gain their ends easily.
Nature gave to bulls horns,
to horses hooves, to timid hares   150
swiftness of foot, to the herd of lions
the strength of sharpened claws,
to the class of mute fish the power of swimming,
to birds flight, and to men wits.
To Drosilla, then, Nature, not having anything else,   155
gave beauty in the place of a shield,
darts, and many spears,
but with it she conquers well-sharpened iron
and all-devouring fire's fierce flames.
Drosilla, I promised Kleinias,   160
my master, a happy marriage with you,
not because I intended such things (may they not happen!),
but to provide some time
for a barbarian heart, passionately aroused, to be quiet,
and for us to consider at any rate what we should do.   165
And now it is time, and we must start to consider
how we can quench the love
of Chrysilla and her son Kleinias."
    Charikles and the maiden Drosilla
were engaged, then, in these things—   170
their love was mutual and chaste—
when a rumor breathed its way to them
that Kratylos had died from a sudden illness.
They then separated from one another
and, dressed for mourning, went to meet   175
their own masters to learn what had happened.
The subject people quickly came together—
men, women, satraps, and barbarians—
and in the place where Kratylos was laid out
Chrysilla lamented, in the midst of all,   180
seemingly focused on her husband

τὸ δ' αὖ ἀληθὲς πρὸς Χαρικλέος θέαν·
'σὺ μὲν προοίχῃ καὶ γυναικὸς καὶ τέκνου,
ἄνερ Κρατύλε, δυστυχῶς λελειμμένων,
185 ὃν οὔτε χεὶρ ἔκτεινεν ἀρχισατράπου
τείνουσα τὴν μάχαιραν ἐν καιρῷ μάχης
οὐδ' ἄλλος ἐχθρῶν ἀντιπράττειν ἰσχύσας,
ἀλλ' ἡ θεῶν πρόνοια τῶν Ὀλυμπίων
εἰς κρυεροὺς ἔπεμψε Πλούτωνος δόμους.
190 Ποῖος δὲ τὴν σὴν δέξεται τυραννίδα;
Τίς τῆς Χρυσίλλας κυριαρχήσειέ μου;
Τίς πατρικὴν δείξειε φιλοστοργίαν
τοῖς ἀμφὶ τὴν σὴν καὶ τὸν ἐκ σοῦ Κλεινίαν;'
Τοιαῦτα ῥαψῳδοῦσα πρὸς Χαρικλέα
195 μήνυμα μεστὸν ἀντιπέμπει πικρίας
αὐτῷ Χαρικλεῖ καὶ Δροσίλλᾳ τοῖς νέοις·
'κινεῖς μέν, οἶδα – τὴν ἀλήθειαν λέγω –,
καὶ χαλκοτύπους ἀνδριάντας παρθένων
ἄφυκτον εἰς ἔρωτα, δειλὲ Χαρίκλεις·
200 ἀλλ' οἱ θανόντες ὡς ἀνέλπιστοι σκόπει·
ἐν ζῶσιν ἐλπίς, ἐν θανοῦσιν οὐκέτι.
Σειρὴν μελιχρά, θέλγε τὴν ὁδοιπόρον·
βροτοὺς λιθοῦσα καὶ βροτοῦσα τοὺς λίθους,
ᾄδουσιν ἤχῳ τῶν ποδῶν σου καὶ λίθοι.
205 Ὦ λαμπρὸν ἄστρον, φέγγε κἀμοὶ τῇ ξένῃ.
Ἆισον, χελιδών, εἰπὲ θελκτικὸν μέλος·
Μοῦσαι γὰρ αὐταὶ νέκταρ ἐγχέουσί σοι
καί σου μελιχρὸν συγγλυκαίνουσι στόμα.
Πλὴν ἀλλὰ τί μοι ταῦτα; Τὸν σκοπὸν μάθε.
210 Αὐχμὸς ποταμῷ καὶ χιὼν δένδρῳ βλάβη,
στρουθοῖς τὸ λίνον, ἡ νόσος τῷ σαρκίῳ,
νεανιῶν δὲ ταῖς γυναιξὶν ἀγάπη.
Τί μοι βλεπούσῃ γνησίως τρισασμένως
σύνοφρυς ἑστὼς ἀγρίως ἀντιβλέπεις;
215 Τέττιξ φίλος τέττιξι, ποιμὴν ποιμέσι,
μύρμηξι μύρμηξ· ἀλλ' ἐμοὶ σὺ καὶ μόνος.
Ἔρως δὲ τυφλός, οὐ γὰρ ὁ Πλοῦτος μόνος.
Ζητεῖ τὸν ἄρνα λύκος, αἲξ χλωρὰν πόαν,
λαγὼν δὲ κύνες, ἀμνὸν ἄρκτος ἀγρία,
220 στρουθοῦ νεοσσοὺς ἀγκυλῶνυξ ἱέραξ·

but in reality focused on the sight of Charikles:
"You have gone before your wife and child, Kratylos,
my husband, and they are left unluckily behind.
A chief satrap's hand with outstretched sword   185
in time of battle did not kill you, nor did
another enemy who had power to act against you,
but the providence of the Olympian gods
sent you to Pluto's cold home.
Who will inherit the rule?   190
Who will be master of me, Chrysilla?
Who will show a father's tender love
to your wife and your son, Kleinias?"
      After this impassioned speech, she sent Charikles
a message full of bitterness   195
for young Charikles and Drosilla:
      "You are able (I know; I speak the truth)
to move even bronze statues of maidens
to inescapable love, wretched Charikles.
But the dead, see how hopeless they are;   200
there is hope among the living, but among the dead no longer.
Honey-sweet Siren, charm the traveler,
you who turn mortals into stone and stones into mortals;
stones too sing to the sound of your feet.
Bright star, shine also for me, the stranger.   205
Sing, swallow, utter an enchanting song,
for the Muses themselves pour nectar in you
and sweeten your honey-sweet mouth.
But why do I say these things? Learn my goal.
Drought is harmful to a river, snow to a tree,   210
a net to sparrows, sickness to the body,
and to women love for young men.
Why, when I look at you with affection and joy,
do you look back at me savagely with a scowl?
Cicada is dear to cicadas, shepherd to shepherds,   215
ant to ants; but to me, you alone
are dear. Eros is blind—not only Pluto.
Wolf seeks the lamb; goat, green grass;
dogs, a hare; savage bear, a lamb;
hawk with crooked claws, a sparrow's nestlings;   220

ἐγὼ δέ σοι τὸ φίλτρον αὐξάνω μόνῳ.
Ἀεὶ δὲ νωθρὸς σὺ πρὸς ἡμᾶς καὶ πάλιν·
νικώμενος γὰρ οὐ φρονεῖς τὰ βατράχων·
οὐ γὰρ ἐκεῖνοι τοῖς χανοῦσιν εἰς ὕδωρ
225   ἐπεγκοτοῦσιν ἢ φθονοῦσι· μὴ σύ γε.
Οὐδείς, Χαρίκλεις, εὐλογότροπος φόβος,
τοῦ συζυγέντος, ὡς ὁρᾷς, τεθνηκότος·
τοῖς οὖν ἐμοῖς κέχρησο καὶ τῇ κυρίᾳ·
κάταρχε, σατράπευε, δοξάζου μέγα·
230   ἀντ᾽ αἰχμαλώτου δεσπότης πάντων γίνου
τῶν κειμένων μοι χρημάτων, τῆς οὐσίας·
τὴν σὴν ἀδελφὴν τὴν Δροσίλλαν παρθένον
ἐλευθέραν μοι καὶ συνάρχουσαν βλέπε
οἵῳ θελήσει συζυγεῖσαν σατράπῃ.
235   Τίς μὴ τοσοῦτον ὄλβον ἀνθέλοιτό μοι;
Τοσαῦτα λαβὼν ἀνθυπόσχου τὸν γάμον,
ἄνερ Χαρίκλεις, εὐκλεές μοι νυμφίε.᾽
      Ἔφησε ταῦτα καὶ Δροσίλλαν ἀσμένως
– ἐχρᾶτο καὶ γὰρ ἀγγέλῳ τῇ παρθένῳ –
240   ἐν ἀγκάλαις τίθησι καί ᾽γένοιό μοι·
συνεργός᾽ εἶπε ᾽τοῦ Χαρικλέος γάμου,
πασῶν γυναικῶν ὑπερηγαπημένη·
τὰς δωρεῶν γὰρ αὐτοπίστους ἐγγύας
ἔχεις μαθοῦσα· τί λόγων μοι πλειόνων;᾽
245   Τοιούσδε πικροὺς εἰσδεδεγμένην λόγους
πρηστὴρ κεραυνὸς φεψαλοῖ τὴν παρθένον.
Μερίζεται γοῦν ἀντιπαλαμωμένη
δυοῖν λογισμοῖν ἐμπαθῶς ἀντιρρόποιν·
᾽εἰπεῖν γὰρ αὐτὸν τὸν σκοπὸν τῆς βαρβάρου
250   οὐ βούλομαι νῦν᾽ φησί ᾽πρὸς Χαρικλέα·
ἀνέξεται γὰρ οὐδ᾽ ἐκεῖνος ἂν λέγω·
ὅμως ἀφορμὴ τοῦ τυχεῖν Χαρικλέος·
ἐλεύσομαι πρόθυμος εἰς ὁμιλίαν.᾽
      Προσέρχεται γοῦν ἀμφὶ τὸν Χαρικλέα,
255   τοῦ φωσφόρου κλίναντος ἄρτι πρὸς δύσιν·
ὁ γὰρ Κρατύλος τοῖς ὑπ᾽ αὐτὸν συλλόγοις
τέθαπτο πάντως ὡς ὁ βαρβάρων νόμος.
Ἔφασκεν, ἐξήγγελλε δυσφορουμένη·
ψυχὴν διέσπα τὴν Χαρικλέος μέσην

and I increase my love for you alone.
But you are always indifferent toward me:
though conquered, you are not of the mind of frogs,
for they are not angry with those who look longingly at their water,
or begrudging. Don't you be angry and begrudging! 225
There is no reason to fear my husband,
Charikles, as you see, since he is dead.
Enjoy, then, my goods and me, their mistress;
rule, be satrap, acquire great honor.
Instead of a prisoner, become master of 230
all my goods in store and my property.
See your sister, the maiden Drosilla,
a free woman, sharing in my power
and married to whichever satrap she likes.
Who would not choose such great happiness with me? 235
Take all this and promise marriage in return,
Charikles, my husband, my glorious bridegroom."
        She said these things, took Drosilla
gladly in her arms (for she was using
the maiden as messenger), and added, 240
"Help me marry Charikles,
maiden whom I love beyond all women,
for you have learned that my promises of gifts
are trustworthy by themselves—what need do I have for more words?"
        When the maiden heard these hateful words, 245
a flash of lightning, a thunderbolt burnt her to ashes.
She was torn, then, struggling passionately
with two opposed thoughts.
"I don't want now to tell Charikles," she said,
"the barbarian woman's aim, 250
for he'll not bear it if I tell him.
Nonetheless it's an excuse to meet with Charikles;
I will go eagerly to converse with him."
        She went, then, to Charikles
when the sun had just turned toward the west, 255
for Kratylos had been buried by his own men
gathered together, as was the barbarians' custom.
She spoke, gave the report with great distress,
and tore Charikles' heart in two

260   ξίφει νοητῷ δυσχερῶν ἀκουσμάτων
       λέγοντος· 'οἴμοι τῆς παρούσης ἡμέρας.
       Ὦ γλυκερὸν φῶς, ὦ Δροσίλλα παρθένε,
       ὡς πικρὸν ἦλθες φθόγγον ἀγγέλλουσά μοι.
       Αἴ αἴ, χελιδὼν ἡ γλυκύφθογγος μόνη,
265   ψυχὴν ἐμὴν σοῖς ἐξεπίκρανας λόγοις,
       χρυσοῦν μελιχρὸν ποικιλόγλωττον στόμα.'
       'Αἴ αἴ, Χαρίκλεις, τῆς ἀπανθρώπου τύχης,
       ἥτις με μακραῖς ἐκπιέζει φροντίσιν.
       Ὦ ποῖον ἔσται τῶν καθ' ἡμᾶς κινδύνων
270   καὶ τῶν ἀναγκῶν τῶν πολυτρόπων τέλος;
       Ποῖος θεῶν τις ἀλλὰ καὶ ποίῳ χρόνῳ
       νεμεῖ τελευτὴν τῶν κακοπραγημάτων;
       Ἕως πότε σχῇς, ἀγριαίνουσα Τύχη,
       κινεῖν καθ' ἡμῶν μηχανὰς πολυτρόπους
275   καὶ συνδαμάζειν ἀλλεπαλλήλοις πόνοις;'
           Οὕτως ἐκείνων συστεναζόντων μέγα,
       οὔπω παρῆλθον ἡμέραι δὶς ἐννέα
       μετὰ τελευτὴν Κρατύλου τοῦ βαρβάρου,
       καὶ σατράπης ἄνακτος Ἀράβων Χάγου
280   πρὸς τὴν Χρυσίλλαν γράμμα δουλείας φέρει.
       Ἤκουσεν ἡ Χρυσίλλα καὶ συνεστάλη
       ἰδοῦσα Μόγγον· τοῦτο γὰρ ὁ σατράπης·
       ἐστυφελίχθη τῇ θέᾳ τοῦ σατράπου,
       ἐξεθροήθη, καὶ τὸν υἱὸν Κλεινίαν
285   καλεῖ παρ' αὐτὴν καὶ τὸ γράμμα λαμβάνει
       ταῖς ἔνδον αὐταῖς συλλαβαῖς οὕτως ἔχον·
           ' ὁ τρισμέγιστος Χάγος, Ἀράβων ἄναξ,
       φόρους ἀπαιτῶ καὶ κελεύω λαμβάνειν
       ἀπὸ Χρυσίλλας Παρθάνακτος συζύγου
290   καὶ τῆς ὑπ' αὐτὴν Παρθικῆς φυλαρχίας.
       Ἕλεσθε λοιπὸν θατέραν ὁδῶν δύο,
       ἢ συντετάχθαι τοῖς ἄνακτι τῷ Χάγῳ
       ὑπηρετοῦσιν εἰς ἐτησίους φόρους
       καὶ τὴν ἐμὴν ἂν κερδανεῖν παραυτίκα
295   ταχεῖαν εὐμένειαν, εἰ πείθεσθέ μοι,
       ἢ μὴν ἰδέσθαι τὴν στρατιὰν τοῦ Χάγου
       ὑμῖν ἐπιβρίσασαν οὐ πεπεισμένοις.'
           Τούτων ἀκούσας τῶν λόγων ὁ Κλεινίας

with the spiritual sword of hateful news.   260
"Oh, what a terrible day this is!" he said.
"O sweet light, maiden Drosilla,
what a bitter report you've come and made to me.
Ah, uncommonly sweet-voiced swallow,
with your golden, honey-sweet, subtle-tongued mouth,   265
you've made my soul bitter with your words."
"Ah, Charikles, what a savage misfortune
oppresses me with great cares!
What will be the end of our dangers
and our varied calamities?   270
What god will give an end
to our adventures, and when?
How long shall you be able, angry Fortune,
to move various torments against us
and tame us with continual troubles?"   275
        Thus they lamented greatly together.
Meanwhile eighteen days had not yet gone by
since the death of the barbarian Kratylos,
when the satrap of Chagos, lord of the Arabs,
brought a letter of enslavement to Chrysilla.   280
Chrysilla heard and was downcast
on seeing Mongos (this was the satrap's name).
She was struck and troubled
by his appearance, called her son Kleinias
to her, and took the letter,   285
which read as follows:
        "I, thrice-greatest Chagos, lord of the Arabs,
demand tributes and order that they be taken
from Chrysilla, wife of the lord of the Parthians,
and from the Parthian tribe under her.   290
Choose, then, one of two ways:
either be placed among those
who serve Lord Chagos with annual tributes,
and gain at once my
immediate goodwill, if you obey me,   295
or instead see the army of Chagos
press upon you since you didn't obey."
        When Kleinias heard these words—

- θρασὺς γὰρ ἦν τις καὶ σφριγῶν τὰ πρὸς μάχην –
300   ἐπιστολὴν ἔρρηξε ταύτην εἰς μέσον,
καὶ Μόγγον αὐτὸν τοῦ Χάγου τὸν σατράπην
μεθ᾽ ὕβρεων ἔπεισεν ἀνθυποστρέφειν.
Εἴρηκε ταῦτα πάντα πατρίδα φθάσας
ἄνακτι Χάγῳ Μόγγος αὐτῷ σατράπης·
305   εἴρηκεν, ἐπλήρωσε θυμοῦ τὸν Χάγον·
καὶ τῶν στραταρχῶν συλλεγέντων ἐν τάχει,
πρὸς ἀντιπαράταξιν ἠρεθισμένων
ἐκ τῶν ἄνακτος γραμμάτων ταχυδρόμων,
ἔφιππος ἔστη τοῦ στρατοῦ μέσον Χάγος
310   πεζῇ καταρτίσαντος εὐμήκη κύκλον,
δόξης τε μεστὸς καὶ φρονήματος γέμων,
καὶ δῆλος ἦν τρόπαιον ὑψώσων μέγα,
ἀσπίδα χρυσῆν ἐν μέρει λαιῷ φέρων
στρατηγικῶς ἔχουσαν εἰκονισμένον
315   τὸν Ἡρακλῆν κτείνοντα Λερναίαν ὕδραν,
θυμὸν παροτρύνοντα καὶ νοῦν εἰς μάχην·
ἐχρῆν γὰρ ἐχρῆν τῆς γραφῆς τὸν ἐργάτην
εἰς ἀνδρὸς εὐθώρακος ἀσπίδα γράφειν
μέγιστον ἆθλον εὐσθενοῦς Ἡρακλέος.
320   Τοιοῦτος ἔστη λαμπρὸς ἱππότης Χάγος,
τόξον φαρέτραν καὶ σπάθην ἠρτημένος,
'ἄνδρες στρατηγοὶ καὶ φαλαγγάρχαι' λέγων
'τοῖς Ἄρεως χαίροντες ἄθλων ὀργίοις,
ὁ συστρατηγὸς Μόγγος ἐξ ἐμοῦ κράτους
325   πρὸς Παρθικὴν χθὲς οὐθένειαν ἐστάλη,
ἧς ἐγκρατὴς νῦν ἐστιν υἱὸς Κλεινίας
μετὰ Χρυσίλλας τῆς ἐκεῖνον τεξάσης,
φόρους ἀπαιτῶν καὶ κελεύων αὐτίκα
Ἄραψι Πάρθους ἐκτελεῖν ὑπουργίαν·
330   ἀλλ᾽ οὐκ ἐδέχθη μικρὸν ἐμμεῖναι χρόνον,
οὐ πρὸς Χρυσίλλας, οὐ πρὸς αὐτοῦ Κλεινίου,
μεθ᾽ ὕβρεων δὲ μᾶλλον ἀνταπεστάλη.
Τί φατὲ λοιπόν᾽ Χάγος ἵσταται λέγων,
'ξυναυλία χαίραθλε καὶ ξιφηφόρε;'
335   '"Αναξ μάκαρ᾽ ἔφασαν οἱ στρατηλάται,
'οὗ τὸ κράτος φρίττουσι καὶ τὰ γῆς ἄκρα,
πᾶσα στρατιά, πᾶσα βαρβαραρχία

for he was a bold man and strong in battle—
he ripped this letter in half   300
and with abuse persuaded Mongos,
Chagos's satrap, to leave.
    On arriving at his fatherland, Mongos
told all these things to his lord Chagos,
and his words filled Chagos with anger.   305
The army generals quickly assembled,
having been roused to battle
by speedy letters from their lord,
and Chagos stood on horseback in the middle of the army,
which had formed a large circle of foot soldiers,   310
and he was full of pride and arrogance,
clearly destined to raise up a great trophy.
He carried on his left side a golden shield,
which had embossed on it, appropriately for a general,
a portrait of Herakles killing the Lernaian hydra,   315
which spurred his spirit and mind to battle
(the creator of the picture certainly had
to represent mighty Herakles' greatest contest
on the shield of a well-armored man).
Such was the splendid horseman Chagos,   320
as he stood armed with bow, quiver, and sword
and said, "Generals and phalanx commanders,
who delight in the rites of Ares' contests,
your fellow-general Mongos was sent yesterday
by my authority to the Parthians, mere ciphers,   325
whose master is now the son, Kleinias,
along with Chrysilla, his mother,
to demand tributes and to order
the Parthians at once to submit to the Arabs.
But he was not allowed to remain even a little while,   330
not by Chrysilla or Kleinias himself,
but rather he was sent away with abuse.
What do you say, then," Chagos thus ended his speech,
"my sword-bearing men, who delight in conflict?"
    "Happy lord," said the army leaders,   335
"at whose power even the ends of the earth shudder—
every army, every barbarian kingdom,

καὶ Περσανάκτων ἀρχιπερσοσατράπαι
καὶ πᾶς τις ἐχθρός, πᾶς ἄναξ, πᾶς σατράπης,
340 ὄλεθρος ἡμῖν ἐστι καὶ πλατὺς γέλως
τοῖς μακρὰν ἡμῶν, τοῖς πέριξ καὶ τοῖς πέλας,
καταφρονεῖσθαι Παρθικῇ στραταρχίᾳ,
ἣν οὐδὲ τῆς σῆς χρῄζομεν παρουσίας
κατατροποῦσθαι, τῇ θεῶν συνεργίᾳ.
345 Ἡμᾶς μόνους νῦν ἀντεπιστρατευτέον
ἐπιτραπέντας τῷ μεγίστῳ σου κράτει
ἀντιδρομῆσαι πρὸς τὰ τῶν ἐναντίον,
ὡς μὴ πρὸς αὐτούς, τοὺς ἀνόπλους ἀγρότας,
τοὺς ληστρικῶς ζήσαντας ἐξ ἁρπαγμάτων,
350 τὸ σὸν κινηθῇ παντοτάρβητον κράτος.᾽
Αἰνῶ μὲν ὑμᾶς τῆς τόσης εὐανδρίας᾽
ὁ Χάγος ἀντέφησεν Ἀράβων ἄναξ,
ἐμὸν γένος σύναθλον ἀσπιδηφόρον,
αὐτόχθονες γῆς ὀλβίας ἱπποτρόφου᾽
355 πλὴν οὖν Ἐπαμινώνδας, ἀνὴρ γεννάδας,
ἰδὼν στρατὸν γέμοντα πολλῆς ἀνδρίας,
ἀλλὰ στρατηγὸν ἄνδρα μὴ κεκτημένον,
ἔφη "μέγας θὴρ καὶ κεφαλὴν οὐκ ἔχει."
Λοιπὸν μεθ᾽ ὑμῶν συστρατεῦσαί με πρέπον,
360 ὦ σύμμαχοί μοι καὶ πατρῷοι φίλοι.᾽
Οὕτω μὲν αὐτὸς εἶπεν Ἀράβων ἄναξ
καὶ τὴν ἑαυτοῦ στρατιὰν κατεσκόπει᾽
ὁ πᾶς δὲ λαὸς τοῦ στρατοῦ τῶν Ἀράβων
ἐπευφήμησε τοῦ κρατοῦντος τοῖς λόγοις,
365 ἐκαρτέρει δὲ μὴ διιππεύων ἔτι,
σάλπιγγος ἦχον καὶ βοὴν χαλκοστόμου
τὸν ἵππον ἀσκῶν καὶ καθαίρων τὸ κράνος
καὶ συμβιβάζων εἰς μάχην τοὺς δακτύλους.
Ἔνευσε τοίνυν ὁ κρατῶν προσαλπίσαι᾽
370 ἵππευσεν ἅπας ὁ στρατὸς τῶν Ἀράβων,
καὶ μέχρι Πάρθου τῆς ταλαίνης πατρίδος
εἰς ὄγδοον φθάνουσιν ἡμερῶν δρόμον.
Σκηνοῦσι τοίνυν ἐν μέσῃ πεδιάδι,
Σάρου ποταμοῦ προσρέοντος ἐγγύθεν.
375 Ἡ δυσμενὴς δὲ Παρθικὴ φυλαρχία
Ἄραψιν ἐκτὸς οὐκ ἐθάρρει τὴν μάχην,

the chief satraps of the Persian lords,
every enemy, every lord, and every satrap—
we shall be ruined and objects of total mockery   340
to those far from us, in the area, and nearby
if we are despised by the Parthian army.
With the gods' help, we don't need
your presence to put them to flight.
We alone, under the command of your   345
tremendous power, must now take the field
to attack the enemy.
Not against these men—peasants without shields,
who live, like pirates, from plunder—
should your strength, feared by all, be moved!"   350
      "I praise you for your great courage,"
Chagos, lord of the Arabs, replied,
"my race of shield-bearing comrades in combat,
sprung from a happy, horse-feeding land.
But when Epaminondas, a noble man,*   355
saw an army full of much manly spirit
but lacking a general,
he said, 'A great beast, but it doesn't have a head.'
Then it is fitting that I join in the expedition with you,
my allies and hereditary friends."   360
      The lord of the Arabs spoke thus
and inspected his army.
All the men of the Arab army
assented with a shout to the words of their ruler,
and they waited, not riding yet,   365
accustoming their horses to the noise and sound
of the bronze-mouthed trumpet, cleaning their helmets,
and readying their bodies for battle.
      Then the ruler gave the nod to sound the trumpet,
and all the army of Arabs mounted their horses,   370
and reached the wretched land of Parthia
on the eighth day.
They encamped, then, in the middle of the plain,
near the flowing Saros River.
The opposing Parthian army   375
did not venture a fight outside with the Arabs

πολλῆς παρούσης ἱππικῆς στραταρχίας·
οὐκοῦν περικλείσασα τέχνῃ τὰς πύλας,
τὸ τεῖχος ὠρόφωσε πέτραις χερμάσι
380   καὶ πετροπομποῖς τετρατάρσοις ὀργάνοις·
ἔστησε τοὺς βάλλοντας ἐκ τῶν ὑψόθεν
ἄνδρας ἐνόπλους λιθολεύστας εὐστόχους
καὶ τοξοχαρεῖς σφενδονήτας ὁπλίτας·
ὕψωσε πύργους ἀσφαλεῖς ἀπὸ ξύλων·
385   ἔσφιγξεν αὐτοὺς συμπλοκῇ τῇ τῶν λύγων
πύργους· ἀπῃώρησεν ἐκ τῶν τειχέων
φύλακας αὐτοὺς ἀντιτύπους κεδρίνους·
πᾶσαν κατωχύρωσεν αὐτοῖς τὴν πόλιν
πρὸς Ἀραβικὴν καρτερέμβολον μάχην.
390   Ἀλλ' αἱ κατ' αὐτῆς εἰσδραμοῦσαι μυρίαι
Ἀραβικαὶ φάλαγγες ἀσπιδηφόροι
σφοδρῶς ἐληΐζοντο τοὺς πέριξ τόπους.
Ἃ μὲν κατεστρέφοντο τῶν σφῶν φρουρίων·
ἃ δ' οὐχ ἑλεῖν ἴσχυον εὐθὺς τοῖς ὅπλοις,
395   τὴν ἐν κύκλῳ γῆν, τοὺς κατοίκους ἀγρότας,
ἠνδραπόδιζον, ἠνθράκουν, ἐπυρπόλουν·
οὕτω πολὺν δύσφραστον ἀνθρώπων φόνον
Ἄραβες εἰργάσαντο μακροκοντίαι.
Ἐς αὔριον δὲ μηχανὰς χαλκοστόμους
400   ἔστησαν ἐγγὺς καὶ πρὸς αὐταῖς ταῖς πύλαις·
τεῖχος δὲ συμπλέξαντες ἐκ λύγων μέγα
τοῖς πετροπομποῖς ἀντεπέστησαν σκέπην
τὰς Παρθικὰς εἴργουσαν ἀφέσεις λίθων.
Ἔπεμπον εἰς τὸ τεῖχος Ἄραβες λίθους·
405   ἔβαλλον αὐτοὺς εὐστόχως οἱ τοξόται,
ἐκ τειχέων ἔπιπτον οἱ βεβλημένοι
τόξοις σὺν αὐτοῖς καὶ μετ' αὐτῶν τῶν λίθων.
Ἔρριπτον ἤδη τὰς ἐπάλξεις οἱ λίθοι,
ἔτυπτον, ἐσπάρασσον αὐτὰς εὐστόχως·
410   πλὴν γίνεταί τι σκέμμα νυκτίου δόλου
Πάρθων παρ' αὐτῶν τῶν Ἀράβων ὀργάνοις
– δεινὴ γάρ ἐστι Παρθικὴ φυλαρχία
τρόπους ἐφευρεῖν καὶ καταρτίσαι δόλους
δι' ὧν ἀποστρέψαιτο τοὺς ἐναντίους –
415   οἳ στάντες ὑψοῦ καὶ σκοπήσαντες κάτω,

since there was a large army of horsemen present.
They strategically closed the gates, then,
and covered the wall with rock boulders
and four-sided, rock-throwing machines. 380
They deployed men to shoot from above:
armed stone-throwers with good aim,
and archers, slingers, and hoplites.
They raised secure towers of wood
and bound them fast with entwined flexible branches. 385
They suspended protective coverings from the walls,*
as defenses against blows,
and fortified all the city with them
against the Arabs' powerful war-machine.
But the countless Arab phalanxes of shield-bearing soldiers 390
launched an attack against the city
and violently plundered the places all round.
Some of the forts they conquered,
and those they couldn't seize at once with their weapons—
the surrounding land and the peasant inhabitants— 395
they enslaved, incinerated, and destroyed with fire.
Thus the Arabs with their long lances
accomplished much unspeakable slaughter of men.
The next day they moved their bronze-mouthed war machines
to the gates themselves, 400
wove a great wall from flexible branches,
and set it up as a shelter against rock-throwing machines
since it shut out the Parthian discharges of rocks.
The Arabs sent rocks against the city's wall,
their archers hit the Parthians with accuracy, 405
and those hit fell from the walls,
together with their arrows and rocks.
The rocks were now bringing down the defenses,
striking them, and tearing them apart with accuracy.
But the Parthians unleashed a cunning, night-time plot 410
against the machines of the Arabs,
for the Parthian army is clever
at discovering ways and preparing plots
by which to put their enemies to flight.
They stood on high and looked down so as to aim 415

ὡς εὐστοχῆσαι τὰς βολὰς πρὸς τοὺς λύγους
τοὺς εἰς ᾿Αράβων χρηματίζοντας σκέπην,
σίδηρον ἐκπέμψαντες ἠνθρακωμένον,
τεφροῦσι πάσας μηχανὰς τῶν βαρβάρων·
420 ξηραὶ γὰρ οὖσαι τῶν λύγων αἱ φυλλάδες,
ἑτοιμόφλεκτοι τῇ πυρὸς παρενθέσει
ὤφθησαν· ἐξέκαυσαν ἀλλὰ ῥᾳδίως
ἀμυντικῶν ἅπασαν ὀργάνων θέσιν.
᾿Εντεῦθεν ἦχοι καὶ κρότοι τῶν κυμβάλων
425 ἐκ Παρθικῆς ἤρθησαν ἀγερωχίας.
Πλὴν τοῦ τρίτου φθάσαντος ἡμέρας δρόμου
῎Αραβες ὡπλίσαντο καὶ μεμηνότες
ὅπλοις ἐκυκλώσαντο πᾶσαν τὴν πόλιν
καὶ συρραγείσης καρτερωτάτης μάχης
430 τὸ Παρθικὸν πύργωμα συγκατεσχέθη.
᾿Εκεῖσε πάντως οὐχ ὁ χαλκόδους ῎Αρης
Παρθῶν μεταξὺ καὶ μαχητῶν ᾿Αράβων
ἐμέμψατο στὰς τῆς μάχης κροτουμένης.
Ἡ γοῦν Χρυσίλλα Κλεινίου πεπτωκότος
435 – καὶ γὰρ μεταξὺ τῆς μάχης ἀνῃρέθη –
μάχαιραν ἐξήρπασεν εὖ τεθηγμένην,
καὶ δὴ κατ᾿ αὐτῆς ἐμβαλοῦσα καρδίας
ψυχὴν μετ᾿ αὐτοῦ δυστυχῶς ἐρυγγάνει·
ἡ δὲ Δροσίλλα, καίπερ ἐν μέσῳ φόνων
440 – εἰς γὰρ τὸ κάλλος ἀσθενοῦσι καὶ ξίφη –,
μέσον ξιφῶν ἔμεινεν ἐκτὸς τραυμάτων·
τοὺς πλείονας δὲ τῶν ἔσω φρουρουμένων
τὸ τῆς μαχαίρας ὑπεδέξατο στόμα.
    Καὶ Παρθικῆς μὲν δυσμενοῦς φυλαρχίας
445 πολλὴ κατεκράτησε πανωλεθρία·
ὁ Χαρικλῆς δὲ σὺν Δροσίλλᾳ τῇ κόρῃ,
ναὶ μὴν σὺν αὐτοῖς καὶ Κλέανδρος ὁ ξένος,
δεσμοῖς συνεσχέθησαν, ἀλλὰ δυσλύτοις,
᾿Αραβικὴν μάχαιραν ἐκπεφευγότες,
450 καί, φεῦ, κατακριθέντες οἱ τρεῖς ἐκ τρίτου
τρίτης μετασχεῖν αὖθις αἰχμαλωσίας.

their throws precisely against the flexible branches
that were intended for the Arabs' defense.
They sent forth iron that glowed with heat
and incinerated all the machines of the barbarians,
for the leaves of the withes, being dry, were clearly   420
ready for burning by the application of fire;
and thus they easily burned and destroyed
the whole assembly of defense machines.
Then the Parthians arrogantly celebrated
with great noise and the clashing of cymbals.   425
But when the third day arrived,
the Arabs armed themselves and, in fury,
surrounded all the city,
and when the fiercely violent battle had broken out,
they seized the walled city of the Parthians.   430
Bronze-toothed Ares, standing there
between the Parthians and the warlike Arabs,
did not complain at all of the battle being fought.
Chrysilla, then, since Kleinias was dead
(for he had been killed during the battle)   435
snatched a well-sharpened sword,
thrust it into her heart,
and spit out her soul, unhappily, in company with Kleinias.
Drosilla, however, even in the midst of slaughters,
in the midst of swords, remained free of wounds,   440
for even swords are weak in the face of beauty;
but the majority of those besieged within
received the point of the sword.
      A great and utter ruin overcame
the hostile Parthian army.   445
But Charikles and the girl Drosilla,
and yes, with them also Kleandros, the stranger,
having escaped the Arab sword,
were held together by indissoluble bonds—
alas, all three condemned a third time   450
to share in a third captivity.

ΒΙΒΛΙΟΝ ΕΚΤΟΝ

Ὁ γοῦν κράτιστος Χάγος Ἀράβων ἄναξ
τὰς μὲν γυναῖκας, οἰκτισάμενος τάχα,
καὶ πᾶσαν αὐθύπαρξιν εὖ κινουμένην
ταῖς ἁρμαμάξαις εἶπεν ἐντεθεικέναι,
5   τοὺς δ᾽ αἰχμαλώτους τῶν γυναικῶν χωρίσας
πεζοὺς βαδίζειν ἐγκελεύεται μόνους·
ἤλαυνε λοιπὸν θᾶττον εἰς τὴν πατρίδα.
Καὶ διιόντων εἰς ἐπίκρημνον τόπον
συνηρεφῶς ἔχοντα πολλῆς ἐξ ὕλης
10   κλάδος παρεμφὺς τῇ Δροσίλλας ἀγκάλῃ,
ἐξ ἁρμαμάξης εὐχερῶς ἀφαρπάσας
κατὰ πρανοῦς ἔρριψεν ἐξ ἕδρας μέσης.
Ἦν καὶ θαλάσσης ἀγριαίνων ὁ κλύδων
τὰ πρῶτα τύπτει ταῖς παραλίαις πέτραις
15   – θάλασσα καὶ γὰρ ἀμφὶ τὴν πέζαν ὄρους
οὐ ψάμμον ἀκτῆς εἶχεν ὑπεστρωμένην,
πετρῶν μελαινῶν ἐξοχὰς δὲ καὶ βάθος –,
χαρίζεται δὲ μικρὸν ὕστερον πάλιν
φλοιὸν δρυὸς μήκιστον ἐξηραμμένον,
20   δι᾽ οὗπερ εἰς γῆν ἦλθεν ἠρεμωμένην
ἀκινδύνως πλέουσα μέχρις ἑσπέρας.
Οὔκουν ἐγνώσθη τοῦτο τῷ Χαρικλέει·
οὐ γὰρ κατιδεῖν ἐκ συνηρεφοῦς ὕλης
πεσοῦσαν ἔσχε τὴν Δροσίλλαν ἐξ ἕδρας·
25   ἢ γὰρ ἑαυτὸν εὐθέως συγκρημνίσας
συνῆλθεν αὐτῇ πρὸς θαλάσσης πυθμένα·
ἀλλὰ βραχὺς παῖς ἀπαλόφρων καρδίᾳ
μετὰ Δροσίλλας ἐγκαθήμενος μόνος
εἰς μίαν ἁρμάμαξαν ἀνεκεκράγει
30   ἰδὼν πεσοῦσαν εἰς θαλάττιον βάθος·
ὑφ᾽ οὗ Χαρικλῆς ἐκδραμούσης ἡμέρας
τὴν τῆς κόρης ἔκπτωσιν ἀναμανθάνει·
ὃς καὶ σπαραχθεὶς ἐς μέσην τὴν καρδίαν,
‘ὢ συμφορᾶς’ ἔφασκε ‘δακνοκαρδίου·
35   ὢ δυστυχὴς σύ, δυστυχὴς σύ, Χαρίκλεις.
Ἔμελλες ἄρα καὶ μετὰ πλάνην τόσην,
Τύχη πονηρά, δυσμενής, ποινηλάτις,

BOOK SIX

Most powerful Chagos, lord of the Arabs,
perhaps out of pity, ordered that the women
and all the property that was easy to move
be put in the covered wagons.
But he separated the male prisoners from the women   5
and ordered them to proceed on foot, alone.
He traveled quickly, then, to his fatherland.
And as they were passing through a steep place,
thickly covered by deep forest,
a branch clung to Drosilla's arm,   10
tore her easily from the covered carriage,
and threw her headfirst from her seat.
First a wild wave of the sea
struck her with rocks from the shore
(for even around the foot of the mountain, the sea   15
did not have a stretch of sandy shore,
but only crags and chasms of black rock).
But a little later the wave offered
a piece of oak bark, very large and dry,
on which she sailed without danger until evening,   20
when she came to a deserted land.
Charikles didn't know this
because a thickly covered forest prevented him
from seeing Drosilla's fall from her seat,
for truly he'd at once have thrown himself headlong   25
and gone with her to the bottom of the sea.
But a small, soft-hearted boy,
who sat alone with Drosilla
on the same covered carriage, cried out
when he saw her fall into the depths of the sea.   30
From him Charikles, at the close of day,
learned of the girl's fall,
and, with heart torn in two,
he said, "Oh, misfortune that stings the heart!
Unlucky you, Charikles!   35
O malicious Fortune, hostile, avenging,
were you intending, then, after so great a wandering,

μετὰ φυλακὰς καὶ μετ' αἰχμαλωσίας,
μετὰ θαλάσσης κινδύνους πολυτρόπους,
40   μετὰ τὸν ὄμβρον τῶν τοσούτων δακρύων,
μετὰ φρικώδη λῃστρικὴν ἀστοργίαν,
μετὰ ζυγὸν δούλειον ἀθρόας μάχης
ἀντεισβαλεῖν μοι συμφορὰν βαρυτέραν,
ἣν οὐκ ἐνεγκεῖν ἔστι τῷ Χαρικλέει;
45   Ἔμελλες, αἲ αἴ, καὶ διασπᾶν εἰς τέλος
τὴν ἀδιαχώριστον ἀλληλουχίαν,
τὴν πάντα κατάλληλον εὐαρμοστίαν;
Πῦρ ἐν πυρὶ προσῆξας, ἐν φλογὶ φλόγα,
βάθει προδοῦσα τὴν κόρην θαλαττίῳ
50   καὶ Χαρικλῆν ἐν ζῶσι συντηροῦσά με.
Οὐκ ὄκνος, οὐ μέλλησις, οὐ ῥᾳθυμία
μετὰ Δροσίλλας εὐτυχῶς συντεθνάναι·
τί γοῦν ἀπεστέρησας, ἐγκοτοῦσά μοι,
τοιοῦδε καλοῦ δυστυχῆ Χαρικλέα;
55   Ἢ καὶ Δροσίλλαν ζῶσαν ἤθελον βλέπειν
ἢ μηδ' ἐμαυτόν, τῇσδέ μοι νεκρουμένης.
Ὦ ὦ ποθεινὴ καὶ μόνη μοι τῷ βίῳ,
ὀφθαλμὲ καὶ φῶς καὶ πνοὴ καὶ καρδία,
ἔσβης, ἔδυς, ἔληξας, ἐψύχθης ἄφνω.
60   Ὡς εὐτυχὴς ἦν καὶ πρὸ μικροῦ, παρθένε,
ἔχων σε συμπάσχουσαν εἰς εὐθυμίαν.
Ἐξ ἡλίου φλέγοντος ὡς ὁδοιπόρος
ὑπὸ σκιὰν ἔπιπτον ἐν σαῖς ἀγκάλαις,
χρυσῆ καλὴ πλάτανε, τῆς ἀθυμίας
65   καύσωνα φεύγων καὶ τὸ τῆς λύπης βάρος.
Κεῖσαι τὸ δένδρον καὶ νεαρὸν καὶ μέγα,
πλὴν ξηρὸν ἤδη καὶ νεκρόν, ζῶν οὐκέτι,
οἶκτος μὲν ἄλλοις τοῖς ὁρῶσιν ἐγγύθεν,
εἴ που τὸ κῦμα τῆς θαλάσσης ἐκβράσαν
70   ἔρριψεν ἔξω· καθορῶ δὲ κειμένην·
ἐμοὶ δ' ἀφορμὴ δακρύων ἐπομβρίας.
Ἐπαπορῶ· τὸ πρᾶγμα θαῦμά μοι φέρει·
πῶς ὑδάτων, ὦ δένδρον, ἐψύγης μέσον;
Ἡδύπνοον πῶς ἐξαμαράνθης ῥόδον;
75   Ὡς εἰ πρὸ σοῦ, φεῦ, ἐκ βροτῶν βὰς ᾠχόμην,
τάχ' ἂν θανὼν ἔζησα, κἂν ζῆν οὐκ ἔδει.

after prisons and captivities,
after the varied dangers of the sea,
after the shower of so many tears,   40
after the horrible cruelty of pirates,
after slavery's yoke following a sudden battle,
to throw against me a yet more grievous misfortune,
which Charikles cannot bear?
Did you intend, alas, to tear apart at last   45
our indissoluble union,
the whole perfect harmony between us?
You brought fire to fire, flame to flame
when you delivered the girl to the depths of the sea
and kept me, Charikles, among the living.   50
I should not have hesitated, delayed, or neglected
to die happily with Drosilla.
Why, then, did you, in anger against me,
deprive unlucky Charikles of such a boon?
I should want to see either Drosilla also alive   55
or myself dead if she were dead.
O my only beloved in life,
my eye, light, breath, and heart,
you've burned out, set, ceased, gone suddenly cold.
How lucky I was just a little earlier, maiden,   60
when I had for solace you suffering with me.
Like a traveler out of the blazing sun
into the shade I fell into your arms,
beautiful golden plane tree, as I fled the burning heat
of despair and the heavy weight of grief.   65
You lie untended, a tall, young tree,
but now dry and dead, no longer living,
an object of pity for others seeing you from nearby,
if by chance a wave of the sea threw you out
and cast you ashore; I see you lying there,   70
and this brings an abundance of tears to my eyes.
I have a new doubt; the matter makes me wonder.
How did you stay dry, O tree, in the midst of waters?
How did you fade away, sweet-smelling rose?
If before you, alas, I'd gone, departed from mortals,   75
how quickly after death I'd have returned to life, even if I ought not.

Οὔκουν ἀνεκτὸν οὐδαμῶς οὐδ' ἐν μέρει
νοσφισμὸς ἤδη συμπνεούσης παρθένου.
Αἲ αἴ, προοίχῃ, καὶ συνοίχεσθαι θέλω.
80 Βαβαί, πονηρῶς ἐξ ἐμοῦ διῃρέθης,
ὡς οἷά τις κλὼν συμφυοῦς πτόρθου βίᾳ.
Ὦ προσφιλὴς σύμπνοια καὶ συμφυΐα,
ψυχαῖν δυοῖν ἕνωσις καὶ συμφωνία,
ἓν πνεῦμα, νοῦς εἷς, εἷς λόγος καὶ φρὴν μία,
85 ἓν πανταχοῦ νόημα δυσὶ καρδίαις.
Ποίου σε νηκτοῦ συγκατέκλεισε στόμα;
Ποῖόν σε κῆτος ἐκπέπωκεν ἀθρόον,
ἢ ποῖος ἐξέκαψεν ἑσμὸς ἰχθύων;
Ἆρ' ἐν θαλάσσῃ λῆξιν εὗρες τοῦ βίου,
90 ἢ κρημνὸς ἐζόφωσε σὰς κόρας, κόρη,
κεῖσαι δὲ νεκρὰ θηρίοις προκειμένη
εἰς δυστυχῆ δίαιταν ἠλεημένη;
Ὦ ποῦ ποτ' εἶ νῦν; Οὐ δραμεῖν γὰρ ἰσχύω,
δεσμοῖς κρατηθείς, ψηλαφᾶν σε, παρθένε.'
95   Τούτοις ὁ Χάγος ἀντιπροσχὼν τοῖς λόγοις
– οὔπω γὰρ ὕπνος ἔσχεν αὐτοῦ τὰς κόρας –
καλεῖ πρὸς αὐτὸν ἡκέναι Χαρικλέα,
οἴκτῳ μαλαχθεὶς καὶ παθὼν τὴν καρδίαν.
Ἤκουσεν, ἦλθε πενθικῶς ἐσταλμένος.
100   Ὁ Χάγος εἶπε· 'τίς; Πόθεν; Τί δακρύεις;'
Ἔφη Χαρικλῆς· 'Αἰχμάλωτος Κρατύλῳ,
δοῦλος δὲ σὸς νῦν· ἡ πατρὶς δέ μοι Φθία·
θρηνῶ δ' ἀδελφήν, ἧς ἐγὼ λελειμμένος,
ὡς ἐμπεσούσης, φεῦ, θαλάσσης εἰς ὕδωρ,
105 μισῶ τὸ βιοῦν οὐδὲ φῶς θέλω βλέπειν.'
'Μὴ Πάρθον ὄντα, πατρίδος δ' ἀπὸ Φθίας'
ἔφησε Χάγος 'πῶς κρατεῖ σε Κρατύλος;'
'Οἱ συγγενεῖς με πρὸς τὸ Καρίας πέδον
μετὰ Δροσίλλας' ἦ δ' ὅς 'εἷλκον ἐκ λόγων.
110 Πρὸς οὓς ἀποπλέοντες ὁλκαδοφθόρῳ
ἐμπίπτομεν, φεῦ, λῃστρικῇ ναυαρχίᾳ,
ἐγώ τε καὶ Κλέανδρος, οἱ συνοικέται,
μετὰ Δροσίλλας τῆς ἀδελφῆς, ὡς ἔφην·
οὓς καὶ μόλις φυγόντες, ὡς τῆς ὁλκάδος
115 ἔξω παρ' ἡμῶν ἐντέχνως εἱλκυσμένης,

I cannot bear at all, even in part,
the absence now of the maiden who was my life's breath.
Ah, you have gone first, and I wish I'd gone with you!
Alas, you have been sadly taken from me,   80
like a branch forcibly torn from the sapling that grew with it.
Dearest harmony and natural affinity,
union and concord of two souls,
one spirit, one mind, one reason, and one understanding,
one thought always for two hearts!   85
What swimming creature's mouth engulfed you?
What sea-monster suddenly swallowed you,
or what swarm of fish gulped you down?
Did you find an end of life in the sea,
or did a cliff darken your eyes, girl,   90
and you lie dead, exposed to wild animals
and pitied for your unlucky life?
Ah, wherever are you now? I can't run
to search after you, maiden, since I am held by bonds."
      When Chagos heard these words —   95
for sleep hadn't yet taken hold of his eyes —
he invited Charikles to come to him,
since he was softened by pity and affected in his heart.
Charikles heard and came, dressed in mourning.
      Chagos said, "Who are you? Where are you from? Why are you crying?" 100
      Charikles replied, "I am Kratylos's prisoner
and now your slave. My fatherland is Phthia,
and I am wailing for my sister, who left me behind
when she fell, alas, into the water of the sea —
I hate life; I don't wish to see the light."   105
      "If you are not a Parthian, but your fatherland is Phthia,"
Chagos responded, "how is Kratylos your master?"
"My relatives drew me with their words
to the land of Caria, together with Drosilla," Charikles said.*
While sailing away to them we met, alas,   110
with a pirate fleet, destroyer of ships —
both Kleandros and I, who were prison-mates,
along with my sister Drosilla, as I said.
We escaped them with effort, shrewdly
dragging our merchant ship out of their way,   115

ἄκοντες ἐξήλθομεν εἰς Βάρζον πόλιν·
ἡ Παρθικὴ δὲ δυσμενὴς στραταρχία
συνέσχεν ἡμᾶς αἰχμαλωσίας νόμῳ,
καὶ μέχρι τῆς σῆς εὐτυχοῦς παρουσίας
120   ὑπεντιθέντες τῷ ζυγῷ τοὺς αὐχένας
ἐκαρτεροῦμεν ἀλλεπαλλήλους πόνους·
οὐ γὰρ τοσοῦτον εἶχε τὸ πρᾶγμα θλίβειν
ὁρῶντας ἡμᾶς τῇ βίᾳ νικωμένους,
ὅσον Δροσίλλας ὑπεραλγοῦμεν χάριν
125   γυναικὸς οὔσης καὶ νέας καὶ παρθένου.
Καὶ νῦν δι' αὐτὴν καὶ τὸ φῶς δεδορκότες
στυγοῦμεν οἰμώζοντες ὠδυνημένοι.'
        ' Εἴρηκας εὖ' ὁ Χάγος ἀνταπεκρίθη·
'ποῦ δ' οὗτος ὁ Κλέανδρος; Ἐλθέτω τάχος.'
130   Ἔστη παραχθείς, δακρύων πεπλησμένος·
ὡς ἰδίαν γὰρ συμφορὰν δριμυτάτην
τὴν συμφορὰν ἡγεῖτο τοῦ Χαρικλέος·
ψυχὴ γὰρ ἄλγος ἴδιον κεκτημένη
ἑτοιμοπαθής ἐστι πρὸς τὸ δακρύειν,
135   ἄλλων λεγόντων καὶ στεναζόντων μέγα
τὰς σαφῶν ἑαυτῶν δυσμενεστάτας τύχας.
Οὓς καὶ συναλγήσαντας ᾤκτειρε βλέπων,
τὴν καλλονὴν ἣν εἶχον ἐκπεπληγμένος·
παρεμφερεῖς γὰρ ἦσαν οἱ νεανίαι.
140   Εἴρηκεν οὖν τοιούσδε συμπαθὴς λόγους·
        ' ἐπεὶ προεσχέθητε χειρὶ Κρατύλου
μόλις φυγόντες τὴν θαλαττίαν μάχην,
ἐπεὶ φυλακῆς καὶ πρὸ τοῦ Χάγου τόπος
κατέσχεν ὑμᾶς αἰχμαλώτους ἀθλίους
145   – ἄλλως γάρ ἐστε καὶ φιλάλληλον γένος –
ἐλεύθεροι στέλλεσθε σὺν καλῇ τύχῃ.
Μὴ γὰρ τοσοῦτον ἐκκυλισθείη Χάγος
τῆς συμπαθείας τοῦ καθήκοντος τρόπου,
ὡς αἰχμαλώτους μηδὲν ἠδικηκότας,
150   μὴ τῶν Ἀράβων ἀντιβάντας τῷ κράτει,
ξένους, πρὸ πολλοῦ δυστυχεῖς δεδειγμένους,
δεσμοῖς βιαίοις συγκατασχεῖν εἰσέτι,
τῶν φύσεως ἔξωθεν ἐκπίπτων νόμων.
Μᾶλλον μὲν οὖν δίδωμι καὶ μνᾶς χρυσίου

and we came, unwillingly, to the city of Barzon.
The hostile Parthian army
seized us by the law of captivity,
and until your fortunate arrival
we submitted our necks to the yoke   120
and endured continuous sufferings.
We were not so much distressed
in seeing ourselves conquered by force,
as we were feeling pain for Drosilla's sake
since she was a woman, young, and a virgin.   125
And now, because of her, we hate looking upon the light
and wail aloud in pain."
    "You've spoken well," Chagos answered,
"but where is this Kleandros? Let him come quickly."
    Having been brought in, Kleandros stood there, full of tears,   130
for he considered Charikles' misfortune
as his own most bitter misfortune.
A soul that has its own grief
is easily moved to tears
when others tell and loudly bewail   135
their own cruel misfortunes.*
Seeing them share their suffering, Chagos felt pity,
struck too by the beauty they possessed,
for the young men were somewhat like one another.
He spoke these words, then, in sympathy: 140
    "Since you were held earlier in Kratylos's power
after barely escaping the sea battle
(for even before Chagos, a prison
held you as wretched prisoners),
and since otherwise you are a race of mutual affection,   145
go as free men, with good fortune!
Let Chagos not deviate so far
from the compassion normal to his character
that he violates the laws of nature
by continuing to detain in strong bonds   150
prisoners who have done him no wrong,
who have not opposed the Arabs' power—
strangers who have been unlucky for a long time.
Further, I give you gold minas

155 ὑπὲρ Δροσίλλας τῆς ἐπιθρηνουμένης,
ἢ πρὸς θεῶν ἐν ζῶσι συντηρουμένη
ἕρμαιον ἔσται καὶ Χάγου λαμπρᾶς τύχης.
Καὶ συνδιασώσοιτε τὴν ἐλευθέραν
ὅπου θεοὶ βούλοιντο σῶσαι τῶν κάτω.'
160   Οὐκοῦν Χαρικλῆς καὶ Κλέανδρος οἱ ξένοι
πρὸ τῶν ποδῶν κλίναντες αὐχένας Χάγου
τὴν γῆν ἐποίουν πλημμυρεῖν ἐκ δακρύων.
Μόλις ποτὲ στὰς ὁ Κλέανδρος ἀντέφη,
οὐ γὰρ Χαρικλῆς λῆξιν εἶχε δακρύων·
165   'Ζεὺς αὐτὸς ἄναξ ἀντιχαρίσαιτό σοι,
Χάγε, κραταιὲ τῶν Ἀράβων αὐτάναξ,
ψυχῆς ἅπαν νόημα τῆς σῆς συμφέρον,
δοίη δὲ μακρὸν εὐθαλῆ ζωῆς χρόνον
καὶ δυσμενὲς πᾶν ὑποτάττοι σῷ κράτει.'
170   Τούτοις Χαρικλῆς ἀντέφασκε τοιάδε·
'χαίροις, Ἀράβων ὄλβιε κράτορ, Χάγε,
λύπη δὲ τὴν σὴν μὴ κατάσχῃ καρδίαν,
ἀνθ' ὧν ἀδελφοὺς τληπαθεῖς τρισαθλίους
ἐλευθεροῖς νῦν ἐκ φρενῶν σωτηρίων.'
175   Οὕτως ἀπαλλαγέντες ἐξ Ἀραβίας
ὥδευον ἄμφω τὴν ὀπισθίαν τρίβον,
ποιούμενοι ζήτησιν ἐμμελεστάτην
αὐτῆς ἐκείνης τῆς Δροσίλλας παρθένου,
ὡς ἐντυχεῖν γένοιτο νεκρᾷ κειμένῃ,
180   ἣν τῷ πεσεῖν ᾤοντο μηδὲ ζῆν ἔτι.
Πλὴν ἀλλὰ καὶ πεσοῦσα καὶ σεσωσμένη
καὶ κυκλικοὺς τρεῖς ἡμερῶν περιδρόμους
σὺν ἓξ διανύσασα ταῖς ἐρημίαις
– ὁδοιπορεῖν γὰρ εἶχεν οὐδαμοῦ σθένος
185   τῷ συμπιεσμῷ τῶν μελῶν, τῶν ὀστέων,
ὃν ἐξεκαρτέρησεν ἐκ κρημνισμάτων –,
διατροφὴν ἔχουσα γῆς χλόην μόνην
δένδρων τε καρποὺς τῶν ἀπηγριωμένων·
ἴσχυσεν ἐλθεῖν εἴς τι χωρίον μόλις
190   τῶν πρὸς τὸ βιοῦν ἀφθονωτάτως ἔχον.
Ἐκεῖσε πολλῶν σπερμάτων χορηγία
καὶ παντοδαπῶν θρεμμάτων πανσπερμία,
γυναῖκες, ἄνδρες, παῖδες ὑπὲρ ἀστέρας

for the sake of your lamented Drosilla,   155
who, if the gods preserve her among the living,
will be a boon also of Chagos's splendid fortune.
And may you keep her as a free woman
if the gods should wish to save her from the depths!"
    Charikles and Kleandros, then, the strangers,   160
bent their necks before Chagos's feet
and made the earth overflow with tears.
Then at last Kleandros stood up and replied,
for Charikles couldn't yet stop his tears.
    "May Lord Zeus himself grant you in return,   165
Chagos, mighty lord of the Arabs,
whatever your heart desires;
may he give you a long and prosperous life,
and may he subdue every enemy to your power."
    Charikles added his own words to these: 170
"May you rejoice, blessed ruler of the Arabs, Chagos,
and may grief not afflict your heart
since you're now setting free, with generous heart,
wretched brothers, thrice-unhappy."
    Thus they departed from Arabia,   175
and they traveled the road back together,
diligently searching
for the maiden Drosilla,
in the hope of finding her dead body somewhere,
for they thought that her fall had killed her.   180
But she had emerged from her fall safely
and for nine whole days
had survived in the lonely wilderness
(for she didn't have the strength to walk
because of the bruising of her limbs and bones,   185
which she suffered as a result of her precipitous fall),
with only grass on the ground for food,
and the fruits of wild trees,
until at last she was able to come to a town
that had plenty of what was needed for life.   190
There were plants in abundance, seedlings everywhere,
animals of all types with their young,
women, men, children more plentiful than the stars,

καὶ πανδοχεὺς εὔσπλαγχνος ἀμφὶ τοὺς ξένους.
195   Ἰδοῦσα τοῦτο μακρόθεν τὸ χωρίον
ᾐδεῖτο λοιπὸν εἰσελεύσεσθαι μόνη·
ὅμως πρὸς ἄκρον εἰσδραμοῦσα τοῦ τόπου,
καὶ τοῦτο πολλῇ συστολῇ καὶ δειλίᾳ,
ἔμεινεν ἔνδον ἀστεγοῦς τινος δόμου·
200   ἔφαγεν οὐδὲν ἢ στεναγμοὺς καὶ πόνους,
ἔπιεν οὐδὲν ἢ τὸ δακρύων πόμα·
τὸν γὰρ Χαρικλῆν καὶ τὰ τοῦ Χαρικλέος
ἀμφαγνοοῦσα θρῆνον ἤνυε ξένον,
ἀναιρεθέντα προσδοκῶσα τεθνάναι·
205   'ἇδ' ἐγὼ ἡ τρισάποτμος ἀπὸ σφετέροιο γενέθλου,
ἇδ' ἐγὼ ἡ πολύδακρυς ἀναλθέα πήματα μίμνω.
Κεῖμαι δὲ φθινύθουσα διαμπερὲς ἐγγοόωσα·
ὡς γὰρ μοῖρα μέλαινα δυσώνυμος ἀμφεπέκλωσεν,
οὐδ' ὀλοοῖο χόλοιο πεπαύσεται ἤματα πάντα.
210   Αὐτὰρ ὃν ἡ δύστηνος ἔχον πάρος εἰσορόωσα
ἐκ παθέων ἀνάπαυλαν ἐρωτοτόκου μελεδῶνος,
ὃν ποθέεσκον ἄκριτα, Χαρικλῆς κεῖται ἀνάγκῃ
ὀρφναίοις νεφέεσσιν ἐνειλυμένος θανάτοιο,
κεῖται νεκρὸς ἄελπτος ἀπ' ὄμματος ἡμετέροιο,
215   τόν ῥα φάους ἀπέμερσε κακώνυμος, αἰὲν ἀτειρὴς
Μοῖρα, μέλαινα, φέραλγος, ἀπ' ἔγχεος Ἀραβίοιο.
Χείλεα ἱμερόεντα, τὰ πολλάκις ἐξεφίλησα,
πῦρ μαλερὸν κατέμαρψε καὶ αἰθαλόεντα φαάνθη·
ὄμματα παμφανόωντα ἀείδακρυς ὄρφνα κάλυψε·
220   βόστρυχον ἡλιόωντα μέλαν λύθρον ἐξεμίηνεν.
Ὤμοι ἐγὼ πανάποτμος, ἀεὶ μογέουσα Δροσίλλα.
Ἔτλην φύξιν ἄελπτον ἀπὸ σφετέροιο τοκῆος·
μακρὸν δ' ἐξεπέρησα βαρύβρομον οἶδμα θαλάσσης·
λῃστὰς ὑπεξέφυγον ἀν' οὔρεα μακρὰ βιβῶσα·
225   αἲ αἴ, δακρυόεσσα Χαρικλέος εἵνεκα κούρου,
δούλιον ἦμαρ ὄπωπα· βίῃ δέ τοι ἐστυφελίχθην
κλοιός μ' ἀμφεδάμαζε πυραγροφόροιο μέλημα·
οὔρεϊ ὑψικορύμβῳ ἀμαξόθεν ἔκπεσον αὖθις,
οἴδματι δ' ἀμφεπέλασσα καὶ εἰναλίῃσι πέτρῃσι
230   βένθεος ἀτρυγέτοιο καὶ ἀργαλέῃ στροφάλιγγι·
φλοιός μ' ἐξεσάωσεν ἀπὸ δρυὸς ὅς κεν ἐτύχθη.
Ὤμοι ἐγὼ βαρύδακρυς εἵνεκα σεῖο, Χάρικλεις,

and an innkeeper kindly toward strangers.
She saw this town from far off, 195
but she felt ashamed to enter alone.
Nonetheless she ran to the edge of the place—
and that with great shame and fear—
and stayed in a house without a roof.
She ate nothing but groans and pains 200
and drank nothing but tears;
indeed, not knowing about Charikles and his affairs,
she raised a great lament
since she thought that he was dead, having been killed:
    "Here I am, thrice-unhappy from my birth, 205
weeping many tears, enduring incurable woes.
I lie here, wasting away, groaning continuously,
for a black, hateful fate has spun her web around me,
nor will she ever cease from her deadly anger.
But the man whom before I had only to see, wretched me, 210
to gain relief from the sad sufferings of love,
the man whom I desired ceaselessly, Charikles,
surely lies wrapped in the dark clouds of death,
dead, beyond hope, far from my eyes,
for hateful Fate, always stubborn, black, 215
a bringer of grief, has deprived him of light, through an Arab spear.
Lovely lips, which I often kissed,
were seized by a fierce fire and burnt black,
bright eyes were covered by an ever-tearful darkness,
and hair that shone like the sun was defiled by black gore. 220
Alas for me, unhappy, ever-suffering Drosilla!
I dared unexpected flight from my father,
traversed the immense, loud-roaring sea,
and escaped from pirates by fleeing through tall mountains.
Ah, full of tears for the youth Charikles, 225
I saw the day of slavery; I was abused with violence;
a collar (the work of a blacksmith) tamed me.
On a high mountain I fell, in turn, from a wagon
and tumbled into the swell of the sea, the marine rocks
of the desolate deep, and the terrible whirlpool. 230
A piece of oak bark saved me.
Alas, I am weeping grievously because of you, Charikles,

ὃν πάρος εἰσορόωσα διήνυον ὄλβιον ἦμαρ,
νυνὶ δὲ κρυπτομένοιο πολὺν χρόνον ἄλγεα πάσχω,
235   ἥλιον οὐκ ἐθέλουσα σελασφόρον ἀστέρα λεύσσειν.'
Τοιαῦτα δακρύουσαν ἐκ ψυχῆς μέσης
μαθοῦσά τις γραῦς ἀγαθὴ τὴν καρδίαν
ἤγγισεν, εὗρεν, εἶδεν, ἔστη πλησίον,
ᾤμωξεν, ἠσπάσατο καὶ προσεπλάκη,
240   ἤγαγεν ἔνδον τῆς ἑαυτῆς οἰκίας
καὶ συμμετασχεῖν ἁλάτων κατηξίου.
Ἔφαγε μικρὸν καὶ πρὸς ὕπνον ἐτράπη
– νυκτὸς γὰρ ἤδη τὸ σκότος κατεκράτει –
καὶ συγκλιθεῖσα τῇ χαμαιστρώτῳ κλίνῃ
245   εἶδε γλυκὺν ὄνειρον, ἦλθεν εἰς κόρον
ὕπνου λυσαλγοῦς, παυσολύπου φαρμάκου.
Τὸ φῶς ἐπέστη, καὶ διέστη τὸ σκότος·
ἤγερτο καί 'γραῦ' φησί 'μῆτερ ὀλβία,
ὡς εὐχαριστῶ τῶν φιλοξενημάτων
250   καὶ τῆς χαμαιστρώτου δὲ ταυτησὶ κλίνης,
καθ' ἣν γλυκὺς ὄνειρος ἀντεπῆλθέ μοι,
παρηγορῶν μου τὴν παθοῦσαν καρδίαν.
Ἀλλ' ἀντιφάσκοις εἴ τίς ἐστιν ἐνθάδε
ἀνὴρ ἀγαθὸς πανδοχεὺς Ξενοκράτης.'
255   'Ναί' φησὶν ἡ γραῦς· 'τίς δέ σοι τούτου λόγος;'
'Ἕως ἐκεῖσε, λιπαρῶ, σύνελθέ μοι'
ἔφη Δροσίλλα· 'κατιδεῖν καὶ γὰρ θέλω
εἰ μὴ φανεὶς ὄνειρος ἠπάτησέ με.'
Ὑπεῖξεν ἡ γραῦς καὶ λαβοῦσα κόρην
260   ἐς οἰκίαν ἤγαγε τὴν Ξενοκράτους,
πρὸ τῶν θυρῶν δὲ στᾶσα τῶν τῆς οἰκίας,
ἐκεῖ θελούσης καρτερεῖν τῆς παρθένου,
καλεῖ παρ' αὐτὴν Καλλίδημον ἡκέναι,
τὸν φύντα παῖδα πατρὸς ἐκ Ξενοκράτους,
265   τῆς χειρὸς ἑλκύσασα νεύσει τὸν νέον.
Ὁ δ' ἀνταπελθὼν ἐξερευνᾷ τὴν κόρην·
'τίς καὶ πόθεν σὺ καὶ πατὴρ τίς καὶ πόλις;'
Ὁμοῦ γὰρ αὐτὴν εἶδε καὶ κατεπλάγη,
τὴν καλλονὴν ἣν εἶχεν ἐκπεπληγμένος.
270   Ἡ δὲ Δροσίλλα θᾶττον ἀνταπεκρίθη·
'ἔα με, Καλλίδημε· τοῦτό μοι λέγε,

whom before I had only to see and I'd passed a happy day.
But now, with you gone, I suffer continual grief
and have no wish to see the sun, the light-bringing star."   235
    A good-hearted old woman heard her
as she wept thus from the depths of her soul,
and approached, found the girl, saw her, stood near,
lamented, embraced her, clung to her,
led her into her house,   240
and bid her take some food.
She ate a little and turned to sleep—
for night's darkness was already holding sway—
and lying on a bed made on the ground,
she saw a sweet dream and had her fill   245
of the sleep that relieves grief, the drug that stops pain.
    Light appeared and the darkness retired.
Drosilla arose and said, "Old woman, blessed mother,
how thankful I am for your hospitality
and for this bed made on the ground,   250
in which a sweet dream came to me
and comforted my grief-filled heart.
But tell me whether there is a certain good man here,
Xenokrates, the innkeeper."
    "Yes," the old woman said, "but what business do you have with him?"   255
    "I implore you, come with me to him,"
Drosilla said, "for I wish to know
whether my dream did not deceive me."
    The old woman yielded, took the girl,
led her to the house of Xenokrates,   260
and, standing before the door of the house
(for that's where the maiden wanted to wait),
she called Kallidemos to come to her,
the son born to Xenokrates,
and she drew the young man to her with a gesture of her hand.   265
When he came out, he questioned the girl:
"Who are you, where are you from, who's your father, and what's your city?"
for as soon as he saw her, he was amazed,
struck by her beauty.
    Drosilla quickly answered,   270
"Let me be, Kallidemos. Tell me this,

εἴπερ τις ἔνδον ἐκ ξένης νεανίας,
κλῆσιν Χαρικλῆς, εὐγενὴς τὴν ἰδέαν.'
      Ὁ δ' ἀλλ' ἐρασθεὶς εὐπροσώπου παρθένου,
275   ἔκδηλος ἁλοὺς καλλονῆς ἀσυγκρίτου
      καὶ πρὸς Χαρικλῆν ἐγκοτήσας τῆς κόρης,
      κόπους παρέσχε τῇ Δροσίλλᾳ μυρίους,
      καὶ μηδὲ κλῆσιν ἀντέφασκεν εἰδέναι,
      εἴπερ τίς ἐστι καὶ Χαρικλῆς ἐν βίῳ.
280   'Τί δ' ἀλλά, Καλλίδημε, μὴ ξιφιδίῳ
      πλήττων ἀναιρεῖς; Τί θαλάσσῃ μὴ δίδως;
      Τί μὴ φονεύεις, αὐτόχειρ δεδειγμένος;'
      μετὰ στεναγμῶν ἀντέφη καὶ δακρύων·
      'ὡς νῦν με πικροῖς δεξιούμενος λόγοις
285   τὴν τῆξιν, οἴμοι, προξενεῖς οὐ μετρίαν.'
      Εἰ καὶ Χαρικλῆν παραπώλεσας, κόρη,
      μὴ κάμνε, μὴ στύγναζε, μὴ κατηφία',
      πρὸς τὴν Δροσίλλαν Καλλίδημος ἀντέφη
      'μὴ τοῦ βιῶναι τὸν θάνατον προκρίνῃς.
290   Πολλοὶ παρ' ἡμῶν κρείττονες Χαρικλέος,
      ζῆλον τιθέντες ταῖς ὁρώσαις παρθένοις.'
      Οὕτω μὲν οὖν ἐκεῖνος· ἡ δὲ παρθένος
      Δροσίλλα μικρὰ μειδιάσασα λέγει
      – εἴωθε καὶ γάρ, κἂν κατάσχετος πόνοις
295   ὀφθῇ τις, ἄφνω μειδιᾶν τι πολλάκις,
      ὡς ἂν παρούσης χαρμονῆς, καὶ δακρύειν –·
      'συμπατριωτῶν ἀστικῶν καλῶν νέων
      πῶς ἄρα, Καλλίδημε, παῖ Ξενοκράτους,
      χωριτικοὶ γένοιντο κρείττονες ξένοι;
300   Ἀλγῶ κεφαλήν, Καλλίδημε, καὶ πλέον,
      τὸ νῦν ἔχον, σοὶ προσλαλεῖν οὐκ ἰσχύω.'
      Ὁ γοῦν Χαρικλῆς ἔνδον ἐς Ξενοκράτους
      ὕπνωττε μικρὸν ὕπνον οὐκ ἐγνωσμένος,
      κόπῳ βαρυνθεὶς καὶ πόνῳ καὶ φροντίσιν.
305   Ἡ δὲ Δροσίλλα λεπτὸν ἀσθμαίνουσά τι
      καθῆστο μακρὰν οἰκίας Ξενοκράτους
      'ὦ παῖ Διός' λέγουσα καὶ γοωμένη,
      'ποῦ δή με τὴν τάλαιναν ἄξεις εἰσέτι
      εὑρεῖν Χαρικλῆν; Οὐ γὰρ ἐς Ξενοκράτους·
310   ἢ φάσματος παίζεις με πάντως ἐμφάσει;

whether there is a young man from a foreign land within,
Charikles by name, noble in appearance."
    But he had fallen in love with the maiden's fair face,
had clearly succumbed to her incomparable beauty, 275
and, bearing a grudge against Charikles because of the girl,
caused Drosilla countless troubles,
and replied that he didn't even know the name—
if indeed there even existed a Charikles in the world.
"But why don't you just stab me to death, 280
Kallidemos, with a dagger? Why don't you throw me into the sea?
Why don't you kill me since you've shown you are murderous?"
she answered with groans and tears.
"By greeting me now with cruel words,
you are causing me, alas, to waste utterly away." 285
    "Even if you've lost Charikles, girl,
don't be sick, gloomy, or downcast,"
Kallidemos replied to Drosilla.
"Don't prefer death to living.
Many of our men are superior to Charikles 290
and cause maidens to feel desire when they see them."
    He said these things, but the maiden Drosilla
smiled a little and said
(for even a person clearly overcome by troubles
is liable often suddenly to smile, 295
as if feeling joy, and to weep),
"How could rural strangers,
Kallidemos, Xenokrates' son, be superior
to your compatriots, handsome young city-dwellers?"
But my head hurts, Kallidemos, and I cannot 300
talk with you any more right now."
    Meanwhile Charikles, unrecognized,
was sleeping a little in Xenokrates' house,
oppressed by fatigue, pain, and cares.
But Drosilla, sighing faintly, 305
sat down far from Xenokrates' house
and said with groans, "Child of Zeus,
where will you yet lead this wretched girl
to find Charikles (for it's not to Xenokrates' house)?
Or do you mock me with a phantom's appearance? 310

Ἐχρῆν ἐπαρήγειν σε δυστυχουμένῃ·
ἐχρῆν ἀπαλλάσσειν με δυσπραγημάτων
καὶ τῶν ἐπαχθῶν καὶ μακρῶν στεναγμάτων·
ἐχρῆν ὁδηγεῖν πρὸς τὰ συμφέροντά με,
315   οὐ μὴν ἀνάγκας ταῖς ἀνάγκαις εἰσφέρειν,
ψευδηγοροῦντα τῇ καθ' ὕπνους ἐμφάσει.
Ἀλλ' εἰ θεὸς σὺ καὶ Διὸς γόνος πέλεις,
εἰ ζῇ Χαρικλῆς αὖθις ἐκδίδασκέ με·
καὶ γὰρ παραστὰς τῇ πρὸ ταύτης ἑσπέρᾳ
320   καὶ ζῆν ἐδήλους καὶ πρὸς αὐτοῦ τοῦ Χάγου
ἐλευθερῶσθαι σὺν Κλεάνδρῳ τῷ ξένῳ
καὶ δεξιοῦσθαι πανδοχεῖ Ξενοκράτει·
πρόασμα γοῦν σὸν οὐκ ἀληθὲς εὑρέθη.
Καὶ νῦν ἐπειδὴ μὴ Χαρικλῆς ἐνθάδε
325   οὐδ' ἐστί μοι ζῶν οὐδ' ἐλεύθερος μένει,
ἀλλ' ἢ προεξῴχηκε τοῦ βίου ξίφει,
ἢ δεσμὰ τὸν τράχηλον αὐτοῦ συνθλίβει,
καὶ ζῇ πονηρὸν καὶ πανοίκτιστον βίον.'
Ταύτης ἐπιστὰς Καλλίδημος ἐγγύθεν
330   ἐπηκροᾶτο τῶν κατωδύνων λόγων
καὶ μὴ κατασχεῖν οἷος ὢν οὕτω λέγει·
'τὸ κάλλος ἡμᾶς ἐξελέγχει σου, κόρη,
ἁλόντας οἷς ἔφημεν ἔρρειν ἀθρόον.
Ἀλλ' ὁ τρισανόητος αὐτὸς ᾠόμην
335   σαθροῖς λογισμοῖς ἄσχετος κάλλει μένειν,
ὁμιλιῶν ἄγευστος, ἀτριβὴς πόθου·
διέπτυον δὲ τῶν ἐρώντων τοὺς πόνους,
καὶ τοὺς γάμους σφῶν ὡς ἀπέστεργον τάχα.
Νῦν δ' ἀλλὰ δοῦλος ἄθλιος κατεσχέθην,
340   ὁλοσχερῶς Ἔρωτι θητεύων βίᾳ·
ἄνθος δὲ τὸ πρὶν τὴν παρειὰν φυγγάνει,
τοῦ βλέμματος δὲ σβέννυταί μοι τὸ φλέγον
ἐκ δακρύων ῥύακος ὡς ἐξ ὑδάτων.
Οὕτως ἐγὼ τὸ πάθος οὐκ ἔχω φέρειν·
345   καὶ τὴν Ὁμήρου μέμφομαι Καλλιόπην
εἰποῦσαν εἶναι κοσμικῶν πάντων κόρον,
καὶ φιλοτήτων, ἀκορέστων, ὡς κρίνω·
οὐ πλησμονὴν ἔοικεν εἰσφέρειν ἔρως,
κἂν ἡδονὴ τελοῖτο, κἂν κλύοιτό μοι.

You should have helped an unhappy woman,
freed me from my miseries
and my heavy, long moans,
led me to what would help me,
and not have added to my anguish   315
by deceiving me with an apparition in my sleep.
If you are a god and a son of Zeus,
instruct me whether Charikles still lives,
for yesterday evening you stood by me
and declared that he lived, had been set free   320
along with Kleandros, the stranger, by Chagos himself,
and was being received by the innkeeper Xenokrates.
But your forecast has proved false.
Now, since Charikles is not there,
he is not living, nor yet is he free,   325
but either he was killed with a sword,
or chains press his neck
and he lives a painful and piteous life."
      Kallidemos, standing near her,
heard her sad words   330
and, unable to stop himself, spoke thus:
"Your beauty proves, girl, that I've been conquered
by attractions to which I'd said an abrupt farewell.
I thought, thrice-foolish man,
with faulty reasoning, that I'd stayed immune to beauty—   335
I, who hadn't tasted love-making or experienced desire—
and I spat upon the labors of lovers
and instantly loathed their nuptials.
But now I've been captured, a wretched slave,
forced to be wholly in the service of Love.   340
The former bloom has fled from my cheek,
and the fire of my eye has been quenched
by a stream of tears, as if by a deluge of waters.
Thus I cannot bear my suffering,
and I blame Homer's Kalliope,*   345
who said that there was a satiety of all earthly things,
even of love, which is insatiable, I think.
Eros doesn't seem to bring satiety,
whether the pleasure is being experienced or spoken of.

350   Ῥίψω τὸ λοιπόν, ὡς ὁ γηράσας λόγος,
          ἐν κινδύνοις ἄγκυραν αὖθις ἐσχάτην
          καὶ δεύτερον πλοῦν πλεύσομαι – τί γὰρ πάθω; –
          καί σοι προσείπω τῇ τὸ πᾶν φιλουμένῃ·
          τροφὴν γὰρ οἶδα τὴν σιωπὴν τῆς νόσου.
355   Ὦ πᾶσαν εὐτυχοῦσα καλλονῆς χάριν
          καὶ πᾶν ἀκοντίζουσα καρδίας μέρος,
          χεῖλος μὲν αὐχεῖς ἁπαλώτερον ῥόδου,
          γλυκύτερον δὲ κηρίου σοι τὸ στόμα·
          φίλημα γοῦν σόν, ὡς μελίττης κεντρίον,
360   πικρὸν θανατοῦν φαρμακεῦον ἀλγύνον.
          Ὡς φαρμάκων σοι πλῆρές ἐστι τὸ στόμα,
          κἂν ἐκτὸς ᾖ μέλιτι συγκεχρωσμένον·
          οὗ καὶ φίλημα τῇ δοκήσει κερδάνας,
          αἶ αἶ, περιττὸν ἄχθος ἀντιλαμβάνω.
365   Τὸ στέρνον ἀλγῶ· πάλλομαι τὴν καρδίαν·
          ἀνατραπεὶς ἔοικα σῶμα καὶ φρένας.
          Οὐκ ἐκφύγῃ τις, κἂν δοκῇ πεφευγέναι,
          Ἔρωτα τὸν τύραννον ὁπλοτοξότην,
          ἄχρις ἂν ἐν γῇ φῶς τε καὶ κάλλος μένῃ,
370   καὶ τῶν βροτῶν τὸ ὄμμα πρὸς τοῦτο βλέπῃ·
          Ἔρως γὰρ αὐτός, ὁ θρασύς, ὁ τοξότης,
          καλὸς θεός τις μυθοπλαστεῖται νέος,
          καὶ τόξα πλουτεῖ καὶ φαρέτραν εἰσφέρει.
          Χαίρει τὰ πολλὰ τοιγαροῦν καὶ τοῖς νέοις·
375   ὅπου δὲ κάλλος, ἐκδιώκων προφθάνει
          ἀναπτεροῖ τε καὶ φρένας καὶ καρδίαν·
          οὗ φάρμακόν τις εὗρεν οὐδεὶς ἐν βίῳ,
          εἰ μὴ περιπλοκήν τε καὶ γλυκὺν γάμον.
          Θεὸν βαρύν σε θᾶττον ἐγνώκειν, Ἔρως,
380   εὗρον δρυμῶνος θρέμμα, θηρίου γόνον·
          ὡς ἄγριος σύ, προσχαρὴς δοκῶν μάτην.
          Ἄκουε λοιπὸν καὶ διδάσκου καὶ σύνες,
          ἡ νῦν παρ᾽ ἡμῶν μαργαρόστερνος κόρη,
          φύσει λαχοῦσα χρυσοβόστρυχον κόμην,
385   τὸ κῦμα, τὸν κλύδωνα, τὴν ζάλην ὅσην.
          Λαβεῖν σε πρὸς νοῦν ἱκετεύω τοὺς πάλαι
          ἔρωτι συγκραθέντας εἰς ψυχὴν μίαν·
          συνεννόει μοι τοῖς προλοίποις τῶν πάλαι

I will cast, then, as the old proverb goes,   350
the last-chance anchor in my perils again,
sail a second voyage—for what else am I to do?—
and speak to you, whom I love completely,
for I know that silence nourishes sickness.
You, who possess all of beauty's graces   355
and strike every part of my heart with darts,
boast a lip softer than a rose
and a mouth sweeter than honey.
But your kiss, like a bee's sting,
is cruel, deadly, poisonous, and painful.   360
How full of poison your mouth is,
even if outside it is smeared with honey.
Even if I obtain a kiss from you only in fancy,
alas, I receive in turn a terrible load of grief.
I suffer pain in my chest; I quiver in my heart;   365
I seem agitated in body and mind.
No one will escape—even if one thinks one's escaped—
Eros, the tyrant armed with a bow,
so long as light and beauty exist on earth
and the eyes of mortals look upon them;   370
Eros himself, the insolent archer,
is pictured in myth as a handsome young god,
carrying lots of arrows and a quiver.
He takes great pleasure, then, in young men,
and where there's beauty, he at once pursues it,   375
and he makes both mind and heart take wing.
Against him no one on earth has found a remedy,
except embrace and sweet nuptials.
I at once knew that you were a cruel god, Eros;
I found you to be a creature of the wood, a wild animal's offspring. 380
How fierce you are, who pretend to be kind.
Listen, then, learn, and understand,
O girl now beside me, with your pearly breasts
and naturally golden locks of hair—
comprehend the size of love's waves, rough waters, and storm!   385
I beg you to have in mind the people of long ago
who were united by love into one soul;
consider among the rest

τὸν Ἀρσάκης ἔρωτα πρὸς Θεαγένην,
390   τὸν Ἀχαιμένους πρὸς Χαρίκλειαν πόθον·
κἂν ὡς ἀσέμνους οὐ λαβεῖν πρὸς νοῦν θέλεις,
τοὺς εἰς ἔρωτας σωφρονήσαντας σκόπει,
οὓς ὅρκος αὐτὸς ὁ προβαίνων ὡς δέον
ἀπεῖργειν αἰσχροῦ καὶ προῆγεν ἐνδίκως
395   εἰς ἀσφαλῆ σύζευξιν ἐννόμου γάμου.
Οὐδὲν διοίσειν οἶδε πρὸς μέθην ἔρως·
πλὴν λίθος ἀμέθυσος ἡ Δροσίλλά μοι.
Πρηστήριον πῦρ οἶδεν ἐντίκτειν ἔρως·
ἀλλ᾽ Ἰνδικὴν λίθον σε παντάρβην ἔχω,
400   καὶ φεύξεταί με καὶ τὸ πῦρ φέροντά σε.
Πόνος μὲν ὁ τρύχων με πρὸς τὸ γῆς πλάτος
ὀφθαλμὸν αὐτὸν συγκαθέλκει μοι, κόρη,
ὄψις δὲ τῶν σῶν ἀντανέλκει χαρίτων.
Οὐκ εὐσθενές μοι σωφρονεῖν βλέποντί σε,
405   καὶ συγκινοῦμαι μᾶλλον εἰς τὸ μὴ βλέπειν,
ὡς μήποτε φλὸξ αὐξάνηται τοῦ πόθου
ὅλην ἔχουσα καὶ τροφὴν τὴν σὴν θέαν·
οὕτως ἄφυκτον τὴν σαγήνην τοῦ πόθου
ἐξ ὀμμάτων σῶν ἔσχες εἰς ἐμὴν ἄγραν.
410   Ἀκκίσματός σοι πλῆρες αὐτὸ τὸ στόμα,
ἡ χεὶρ δὲ ναρκᾷ πρὸς τὸ σῶσαι συντόμως
τὸν ἁρπαγέντα τῇ σαγήνῃ τῇ ξένῃ.
Οὕτω τυραννεῖς ὃν κρεμώμενον λάβῃς·
οὔτε πρὸς αὐτὴν γῆν ἐνεχθῆναι θέλεις,
415   οὔτε προσαρπαγέντα σώζεις αὐτίκα.
Ποίαν σοφίαν συγκινήσω καὶ πόθεν
ἐρωτικὰς ἴυγγας εὑρήσω τάλας,

the love of Arsake for Theagenes*
and that of Achaimenes for Charikleia.   390
If you don't wish to consider them since they're unchaste,
look to those who are chaste in love,
whom proper adherence to an oath
kept away from shame and led with justice
to the secure union of a lawful marriage.   395
Love is just like drunkenness,
but Drosilla is an amethyst stone to me.*
Love can cause a burning fire,
but I have you as the Indian stone *pantarbe,*
and so the fire will avoid me if I carry you.   400
The pain that consumes me drags my eyes
down to the ground, girl,
but the sight of your charms draws them back up again.
I can't control myself when I see you,
and I should really rather not see you   405
so that the flame of desire may never increase
through having your sight for its nourishment—
so inescapable is the net of desire
you have trailing from your eyes to catch me.
Your mouth's full of affected indifference,   410
and your hand is loath to save promptly
one who's caught in your strange net.
Thus you tyrannize one you've caught suspended in your net:
you are not willing for him to be brought to the land,
nor do you instantly save the one you've caught.   415
What artifice shall I set in motion, and where,
wretched me, shall I find love charms

ὡς ἄν σε πείσω καὶ παθεῖν ἀναγκάσω
ἑλκτηρίοις ἴυγξι καρδιοστρόφοις;
420   Γυνὴ γὰρ εἶ σύ – γνῶθι τὴν σαυτῆς φύσιν –,
γυνὴ δὲ πασῶν τῶν καθ᾽ ἡμᾶς καλλίων,
τεράστιόν τι πλάσμα φύσεως ξένης,
ὑπερφυές τι χρῆμα θήλεος γένους,
ὡς ἡ σελήνη τῶν προλοίπων ἀστέρων.
425   Δίδου τὸ πᾶν· μὴ βάλλε τοῖς λόγοις μόνοις·
ψυχῆς γὰρ ὡς ἔοικεν ἐγκρύπτειν πάθος,
ἀρνητικοῖς βάλλεις με λοιπὸν ἐν λόγοις.
Ἕλκουσα δῆθεν εὐμένειαν μετρίαν,
ἐμοὶ προεῖπας, ὡς παρηνοχλημένη,
430   ἀλγεῖν κεφαλὴν πολλὰ δυσφορουμένην,
σὲ τὴν κεφαλὴν τὴν ἐμοὶ φιλουμένην.
Καὶ καινὸν οὐδέν, ὦ Δροσίλλα παρθένε·
ἐλθοῦσα καὶ γὰρ εἰς ἄγνωστον χωρίον,
δήμῳ τε πολλῶν ἐμφανισθεῖσα ξένων
435   ἐπεσπάσω βάσκανον ὀφθαλμὸν τάχα·
πλὴν σήμερόν σε τὴν ἐμὴν νόσον θέλω
ἀπαλλαγῆναι τῆς ἐνοχλούσης νόσου·
ἀλλ᾽ ἡ νόσος μοι καὶ πρὸς ὑγείαν δράμοι,
ὡς μὴ καχεκτοίημεν ἄμφω δυσφόρως.
440   Δάφνις ὁ παῖς ἐκεῖνος ἀλλὰ καὶ Χλόη
τρισευτυχῶς συνῆψαν αὐτοὺς εἰς γάμον·
Δάφνις ἐκεῖνος ὁ γλυκύς, ποιμὴν μόνον,
ὁ τῶν ἔρωτος ἀδαὴς τοξευμάτων,
φιλούμενος μέν, ἀντιφιλῶν δὲ πλέον,
445   καὶ μηδὲν εἰδὼς τῶν ἐρώτων τι πλέον·
τῇ παρθένῳ Χλόῃ γὰρ ἐκ τῶν σπαργάνων
ἐρωτικὸν συνῆπτο συμποίμην βρέφος.
Ταύτης ἐρῶν ἦν τῆς καλῆς Χλόης πάλαι,
Χλόης ἐκείνης τῆς ἀπλάστου παρθένου,
450   ἧς πῦρ μὲν ἦν τὸ βλέμμα τῷ νεανίᾳ,
λόγοι δὲ τόξα, καὶ περιπλοκαὶ βέλη.
Χρυσοῦν γένος πρὸς φίλτρον ἦν τὸ προφθάσαν·
ὁ γὰρ φιληθεὶς ἀντεφίλει μείζονως·
οὐχ οἷόν ἐστι τοῦτο χάλκεον γένος·
455   φιλούμενον γὰρ ἀντιφιλεῖν οὐ θέλει.
Ὦ τίς λόγος, τί πρᾶγμα καὶ τίς ἡ φύσις,

that I may persuade you and force you to feel love
though magic spells that draw and whirl the heart round?*
You are a woman—know your own nature!— 420
and a woman more beautiful than all women of our time,
a marvelous creation of exceptional nature,
a creature as far superior to the female race
as the moon to the rest of the stars.
Give me all you've got. Don't strike me with words alone 425
(for it's your way, it seems, to conceal emotion,
and you are striking me further with your words of denial).
Inviting, in truth, a common kindness,
you said to me, as if you were greatly annoyed,
that you felt much pain in your vexed head— 430
you, the precious head that I love.
And this is nothing strange, Drosilla,
for when you came to an unfamiliar town
and were seen by a crowd of many strangers,
you attracted the evil eye perhaps— 435
only, today I wish that you, who are my sickness,
may be released from the sickness that troubles you.
But may my sickness also move quickly toward health
so that we may not both be grievously ill.
Daphnis, that famous boy, and Chloe* 440
united themselves happily in marriage.
Sweet Daphnis, only a herdsman
and ignorant of love's arrows,
was beloved and returned a greater love
and knew nothing more of love, 445
for he'd been united from the cradle
to the maiden Chloe, fellow herder, amorous child.
He loved the beautiful Chloe for a long time,
that unaffected maiden
whose glance was fire to him; 450
whose words, bow and arrows; whose embraces, missiles.
The earlier generation was golden in matters of love,
for the beloved returned the love even more.
This bronze generation is not the same,
for the beloved does not wish to return the love. 455
What is the reason, the need, the natural cause

ἡμᾶς τυραννεῖν τὰς ἐρώσας παρθένους
βληθείσας ἀντέρωτι δακνοκαρδίῳ;
Ἦ γὰρ πρὸς ἡμῶν οὐκ ἐρῶσι παρθένοι;
460   Ἐρῶσι, πλὴν γέμουσι τῶν ἀκκισμάτων·
φιλοῦσι, πλὴν τρύχουσι τοὺς φιλουμένους,
ποιοῦσιν αὐτοῖς ἐκκρεμῆ τὴν καρδίαν,
τήκουσιν, αἲ αἴ, πρὸ χρόνου τὸ σαρκίον,
αὐτὴν διστεύουσι τὴν ψυχὴν μέσην,
465   ὡς ἀγχόνη τὸ πρᾶγμα καὶ πέρας βίου
ἔρωτος εἰς τὸ τραῦμα δυσφορουμένοις.
Βαβαί, πόσος παρῆλθε καιρὸς ἐν μέσῳ,
καὶ τὴν σιδηρᾶν οὐκ ἔπεισα καρδίαν·
πῶς πολλαχοῦ προῆλθον, ἀλλ' ἡ παρθένος
470   ἡ σκληροπετρόστερνος οὐκ ἔνευσέ μοι.
Ἀπόλλυμαι δείλαιος, οἴχομαι τάλας,
εἰ μηδὲ ταῦτα σὴν μαλάξῃ καρδίαν.
Ἡροῦς ἐρῶν Λέανδρος ὁ τλήμων πάλαι,
οἴμοι, θαλασσόπνικτος εὑρέθη νέκυς,
475   φεῦ, τοῦ λύχνου σβεσθέντος ἐκ τῶν ἀνέμων.
Ἄβυδος οἶδε ταῦτα καὶ Σηστὸς πόλις.
Πλὴν ἀλλὰ καὶ θάλασσαν εὑρηκὼς τάφον
σύντυμβον αὐτὴν ἔσχε τὴν ἐρωμένην
ἐκ τείχεος ῥίψασαν αὑτὴν εἰς ὕδωρ·
480   οὓς γὰρ πόθος συνῆψεν εἰς συζυγίαν
τούτους ἐκεῖνος ἦξεν εἰς συντυμβίαν.
Δυστυχὲς ἦν ἐκεῖνο τέρμα τοῦ βίου·
ὡς ὄλβιον κατ' ἄλλον ὡράθη τρόπον·
συντυμβίαν γὰρ ἔσχεν ἰσοψυχία,
485   ἓν φίλτρον, ἓν νόημα σωμάτων δύο.
Ὦ πνεύματος σβέσαντος ἀκτῖνας δύο·
ἔσβεστο λύχνος, καὶ συνεσβέσθη πόθος.
Ὦ πνεύματος ῥίψαντος ἀστέρας δύο,
Ἡρώ τε καὶ Λέανδρον, ἐν βυθῷ μέσῳ.
490   Ὑπέρχεταί μοι σπλάγχνα τῆς μνήμης πόνος·
φλογίζεταί μοι στέρνα πυρὶ τοῦ πάθους.
Οὕτω μὲν οὖν ἐκεῖνος· ἀλλ' ἐγὼ τάλας
οὐ νυκτομαχῶν, οὐ θαλάσσῃ προσπλέων,
ἀποπνιγῆναι κινδυνεύω, φιλτάτη,
495   ἐκ τῆς κατασχούσης με τοῦ πόθου ζάλης,

that we're tyrannized by the maidens who love us
when they're wounded in turn by heart-stinging love?
Or don't maidens return our love?
They love, but are full of affected indifference;   460
they love, but wear out those they love.
They keep the hearts of their lovers hanging,
cause their bodies to waste away, alas, prematurely,
and shoot their souls with arrows—
the situation is like a strangling and death   465
for those who suffer the wound of love.
Alas, how much time has passed
and I haven't persuaded her iron heart.
How often I have gone to her, but the maiden
with the rock-hard heart has not given me her assent.   470
I am lost, poor wretch, I am ruined
if not even these things soften your heart.
The unhappy Leander, who loved Hero long ago,*
was found dead, alas, drowned by the sea
because the lamp had been extinguished, alas, by the winds.   475
Abydos knows this, and the city Sestos.
But although Leander had the sea as a tomb,
still he had his beloved as a tomb-companion
after she threw herself from the wall into the sea,
for whom Love joined into a union   480
he also led into the same tomb.
That death was unfortunate,
but how happy it appeared in another way,
for two like spirits shared the same tomb—
two bodies with one love and one mind.   485
Oh, wind that has blown out two rays of light!
The lamp has been extinguished and the love along with it.
Oh, wind that's caused two stars—
Hero and Leander—to fall into the abyss!
The pain of memory penetrates deep within my body;   490
my breast burns with the fire of passion.
This, then, was Leander's fate. But wretched me,
I am not fighting by night or sailing on the sea,
yet I am in danger of being drowned, dearest,
by the storm of desire that's taken hold of me,   495

εἰ μὴ φθάσῃς σὺ δοῦσα δεξιὰν φίλην.
Σκόπει τὸ ῥεχθέν, ἐννόει μοι τὸν πόθον.
Εὖ οἶδας ὡς γέννημα τοῦ πόθου πόνος.
Ἐμοὶ πύλας ἄνοιγε τῆς σῆς καρδίας,
500   καταστοροῦσα τὸν κλύδωνα τοῦ πόθου,
καὶ τὸν θαλασσόπλαγκτον ἤδη προσδέχου
σαῖς ἀγκάλαις δήπουθεν, ὡς ἐν λιμένι.
Οὐκ ἀγνοεῖς γὰρ ὡς περίφημος πάλαι
ἐρῶν ἐκείνης τῆς Γαλατείας Κύκλωψ
505   προεΐλκεν ἀπειθοῦσαν αὐτὴν τὴν κόρην·
τὸ λάσιον γὰρ ἐβδελύττετο πλέον,
φυγοῦσα τὸν φιλοῦντα· πλὴν ἔστεργέ μοι,
μήλοις μόνοις βάλλουσα μικροῖς τὸν μέγαν.
Ὅμως ἐκεῖνος ἀνθυπισχνεῖτο ξένα·
510   ποθῶν γὰρ αὐτὴν εἰς τὸ πῦρ βαλεῖν ἔφη
καὶ χεῖρας αὐτοῦ καὶ πόδας καὶ κοιλίαν,
ὡς ἐκτεφρῶσαι τὴν λασιώδη τρίχα,
εἰ δυνατὸν δὲ καὶ μέσην τὴν καρδίαν,
εἴ που δοκεῖ καὶ τοῦτο τῇ ποθουμένῃ,
515   κἀκεῖνον ὅνπερ εἶχεν εἰς τὸ φῶς ἕνα
ὀφθαλμὸν εὐρύν, κυκλοσύνθετον, μέγαν.
Οὕτως ἐρῶν προεΐλκεν. Ἐξελιπάρει
εἰς ἄντρον ἐλθεῖν τὴν Γαλάτειαν Κύκλωψ,
ὅπου νέους ἔφασκε νεβροὺς ἐκτρέφειν
520   γαύρους τε μόσχους, ἄρνας, ἄλλας ἀγέλας
κύνας τε πολλάς, ἀγρίας, λυκοκτόνους·
καὶ γλυκερὰς ἔφασκεν ἀμπέλους ἔχειν,
καὶ τυρὸν ἐν χειμῶνι καὶ καιρῷ θέρους
γαυλούς τε τοῦ γάλακτος ἐκκεχυμένους,
525   σμήνη μελιττῶν ὑπὲρ ἑξηκοντάδα
καὶ κισσύβια τεχνικῶς γεγλυμμένα
καὶ δορκάδων ἄμετρα δερμάτων σκύτη.
Τούτοις ἔθελγε τὴν Γαλατείαν Κύκλωψ
ᾄδων μελιχρόν, τῇ θαλάσσῃ προσβλέπων,
530   σύριγγα πρὸς τὸ χεῖλος εὔτεχνον φέρων·
τούτοις ἔθελγε καὶ προσεξελιπάρει
ὡς ἀνθέλοιτο τὴν ἐς ἄντρον ἑστίαν,
χαίρειν ἀφεῖσα τὸν θαλάττιον βίον.
Σὺ δ᾽ οὔτε νεύεις οὔτε μηνύεις λόγον,

unless you first give me your beloved right hand.
Consider what's been done; reflect on my desire.
You know well that suffering is born from desire.
Open the doors of your heart to me
and smooth the wave of desire;   500
receive now in your arms, as in a harbor,
one who's wandered over the sea.
You know well how the famous Cyclops once,*
being in love with Galateia,
tried to entice the girl, who refused him,   505
for she loathed his shagginess more
and fled her lover. But she loved him, I say,
for she was pelting the huge creature with little apples only.
Nevertheless he made extraordinary promises,
for he said that for love of her he'd throw into the fire   510
his hands, feet, and belly
so as to burn to ashes his shaggy hair,
also, if possible, his heart
(if his beloved wanted this too)
as well as that single, wide, round, large eye,   515
which he had for seeing the light.
Thus with his love he was trying to entice her.
He entreated Galateia to come into his cave,
where he said he was rearing new fawns,
skittish calves, lambs, other animals,   520
and many fierce, wolf-slaying dogs;
and he said that he had sweet vines,
cheese in winter and summer,
pails overflowing with milk,
more than sixty beehives,   525
drinking-cups carved with art,
and countless deer hides.
Thus the Cyclops was trying to charm Galateia,
as he sang a honey-sweet song and gazed toward the sea,
lifting a well-made pipe to his lips.   530
Thus he was charming her and entreating her
to choose his home in a cave
and say farewell to her life in the sea.
But as for you, you don't nod or say a word,

535   ἀλλ᾽ οὐδὲ προσπαίζοντι συμπαίζειν θέλεις.
      Οὔκ ἐστιν ἐν σοὶ μῆλον, οὐ γλυκὺς γέλως
      ὁποῖος ἦν τὰ πρῶτα τῆς Νηρηίδος·
      τὸ μειδίαμα προσδοκᾷς δέ μοι μέγα
      χάρισμα πολλῶν ἀντιδιδόναι λόγων.
540   Ὡς εὐχαριστῶ τοῦ χαρίσματος, κόρη·
      πένης κόραξ γάρ, ὡς ὁ δημώδης λόγος,
      οὔσης ἀνάγκης, συμποριζέτω τάλας
      κἂν ἐκ δυσόδμων τὴν τροφὴν ἐντοσθίων.
      Σύννευσον ἔνδον ἀμφὶ τὸν ζητοῦντά σε,
545   ὄψει δὲ πάντως καὶ περιφήμου πλέον
      Κύκλωπος ἁδρὸν Καλλίδημον ἐν βίῳ.
      Ξενοκράτης πρώτιστος ἐν τῷ χωρίῳ·
      ὁ Καλλίδημος οὐκ ἄχαρις τὴν θέαν,
      τῶν εὐγενῶν εἷς ἐστι καὶ τῶν εὐπόρων,
550   ᾧ συζυγεῖσαν οὐ μετάμελος λάβῃ
      τὴν ἐν γυναιξί σε Δροσίλλαν κοσμίαν.
      Βούλει καθιστῶ δῆλα τῷ Ξενοκράτει;
      Καὶ Καλλιδήμου καὶ Δροσίλλας τοὺς γάμους
      λαμπροῖς ἑορτάσειε παστοπηγίοις.
555   Τί μειδιᾷς νεύουσα πρὸς γῆν ἡσύχως,
      ὦ γραῦς ἀγαθή, γραῦς σοφή, γραῦς κοσμία;
      Μέτελθε καὶ σὺ τὴν ἀκαμπῆ παρθένον,
      καὶ Καλλιδήμου μισθὸν ἐκλάβῃ μέγαν.᾽
           Τούτοις ἐνησμένιζεν ὁ Ξενοκράτους·
560   ἡ γραῦς δὲ μικρὰν ἐγκοπὴν ποιουμένη
      τῆς Καλλιδήμου λαλιᾶς πρὸς καὶ τὴν κόρην
      ᾽εἰ καὶ Δροσίλλα μὴ πλανᾶται τῷ βλέπειν᾽
      ἔφασκε, ᾽Καλλίδημε, παῖ Ξενοκράτους,
      οὐκ ἄλλον εἰς γῆν ὄψεταί σου καλλίω.᾽
565   Ἀλλ᾽ οὗτος ἀντέφασκε τῇ κόρῃ πάλιν·
      ᾽ὑπερβαλλόντως ἡδύνεις ὁρωμένη,
      ἀνεκλαλήτως ἀλγύνεις κεκρυμμένη.
      Λειμὼν χαριτόβρυτος ὡράθης μόνη·
      δοκεῖς δὲ θριγκοὺς πολλαχοῦ συνεισφέρειν.
570   Καὶ νῦν ἱμερτὴ σὺ τρυγᾶσθαί μοι, κόρη,
      ὡς ἀκροπρέμνων ἁδροδενδροκαρπία·
      ἄνοιξον οὖν μοι τὰς θύρας τοῦ κηπίου
      καὶ δὸς φαγέσθαι καὶ κορεσθῆναι μόλις.

and you aren't even willing to play with one who's playing. 535
You don't have an apple, nor do you laugh sweetly
as the Nereid used to do;
you think that by smiling you are giving me
a great gift in return for my many words.
How thankful I am for your smile, girl, 540
for, as the popular proverb goes, let a poor raven
when it's necessary take his nourishment—
wretched bird!—even from stinking entrails.
Consent to go to the home of the one who desires you,
and you will certainly see that Kallidemos 545
is more wealthy in property than even the famous Cyclops.
Xenokrates is chief man in the town,
and Kallidemos is not without charm in his appearance:
he is one of the noble, rich people.
If you are united with him, you will not 550
regret it, Drosilla, honorable among women.
Do you wish me to inform Xenokrates?
May he celebrate the nuptials of Kallidemos and Drosilla
with splendid bridal chambers!
Why do you gently smile, with head down, 555
good, wise, honorable old woman?
Approach the unbending maiden, you too,
and you shall receive a great reward from Kallidemos!"
　　Xenokrates' son was pleased with his words,
but the old woman, interrupting briefly 560
Kallidemos's speech to the girl, said,
"If Drosilla's eyes don't deceive her,
she won't see another on earth, Kallidemos,
Xenokrates' son, more handsome than you."
　　But Kallidemos spoke again to the girl: 565
"You give great delight when you are seen,
unspeakable pain when you are hidden from sight.
You alone appeared to me like a meadow full of grace,
but you seem to bring walls with you everywhere.
And now I desire to gather you 570
like ripe fruit at the top of a tree;
open, then, the doors of your garden to me,
and allow me to eat and be sated at last.

Τίς ἦν ἐκεῖνος τῶν χαμαὶ κινουμένων
575   χαλκευτικῆς ἔμπειρος, ὃς λαβὼν φλόγα,
Ἡφαιστικὴν κάμινον ἐκκαύσας νέαν
καὶ τῇ πυράγρᾳ καρδίαν σὴν ἁρπάσας,
ἔδειξε χαλκῆν θεὶς μέσον τῶν ἀνθράκων;
Τίς ἦν ὁ βάψας, ὁ στομώσας εἰς φλόγα
580   τὴν καρδίαν σου τὴν ἀπεσκληρυμμένην;
Ὦ τῶν ἐκείνου δακτύλων δυστεκτόνων·
φεῦ ἐργοχείρων ἀθλίων δυσδαιμόνων,
ὦ δεξιᾶς μοι τεκτονευσάσης βάρη,
χαλκευσάσης σὰ στέρνα καὶ τὴν καρδίαν.
585   Τολμηρὸς ἦν ἐκεῖνος, ὡς Κύκλωψ νέος,
βαρύς, βριαρός, αἱματωπός, παμφάγος,
ὃς εἰς ἐμὴν δείλαιος ἀνθρώπων μόνος
πολλὴν ὀδύνην ἐξεχαλκούργησέ σε.
Τίς τὸν θανόντα ζῶντα δεικνύειν ἔχει;
590   Τίς τὸν πιόντα κόνδυ δηλητηρίου
ᾠδῆς μετασχεῖν φησι κηλητηρίου;
Ὅρα νεκρὸν τὸν ζῶντα. Καὶ τί τὸ πλέον;
Οὕτως ἀπηνήνω με τὸν φιλοῦντά σε.
Τῆς καρδίας σου τῆς λιθοστερεμνίου·
595   Ἔρως, Ἔρως δείλαιε, πῦρ πνέων Ἔρως,
ὡς ἄνθρακές με, φεῦ, τὰ πικρά σου βέλη
καίουσιν. Αἲ αἴ, μὴ τὸ τόξον πῦρ φέρει;
Φέρει μὲν ὄντως· ἀλλὰ τί δράσειν ἔχεις;
Οὐδ' Ἡρακλῆς πρὸς δύο, δημώδης λόγος·
600   πρὸς τρεῖς δὲ σὺ Χάριτας ἁδροδακτύλους
οἷα βραχὺς παῖς, ἀντιπράττειν οὐκ ἔχων,
ἐκεῖθεν ἔνθεν ἐκδραμὼν κατεσχέθης
καὶ δοῦλος οἷα τληπαθεῖς καὶ προσμένεις·
κἂν καὶ πτερύσσῃ πανταχοῦ γῆς ἐκτρέχων,
605   ὅπου τὸ κάλλος, ἐκτελῶν ὑπουργίαν,
αἱ Χάριτες τὸ τόξον ἐντείνουσί σοι·
τὸν σφῶν ἐκεῖναι δοῦλον ὁπλίζουσί σε,
τὸν δραπέτην ἔχουσι πιστὸν οἰκέτην,
τὸν φυγάδα βλέπουσι προσμένοντά σε.
610   Ὡς ἠγρίωσαι, κἂν γλυκὺ γελᾷς, Ἔρως·
ἄφυκτα δεσμὰ συγκροτοῦντά σε βλέπω.
Ὡς ἐξεμάνης, κἂν δοκῇς παίζειν, θέλων.

Who of those walking on earth
was that expert smith who took a flame,   575
kindled a new furnace of Hephaestus,
seized your heart with a pair of fire-tongs,
and revealed it as bronze by placing it amid the coals?
Who dipped in water and tempered for the flame
your hard heart?   580
Oh, what malicious fingers;
alas, what wretched, unlucky labors!
Oh, right hand that created miseries for me,
that forged your breast and heart.
That one was bold, like a young Cyclops,*   585
fierce, strong, bloody, voracious,
who alone, wretched creature,
made you in bronze for my great grief.
Who can make the dead man live?
Who tells the man who's drunk a cup of poison   590
to take part in a charming song?
Behold the corpse that lives. And what is the use?
Thus you rejected me, the one who loves you.
What a stone-hard heart you have!
Wretched, fire-breathing Eros,   595
how your cruel arrows, like coals, alas,
burn me. Ah, surely your bow doesn't carry fire?
Yes, it does, but what can you do with it?
Not even Herakles can fight against two, as the popular proverb goes.
Against three Graces with strong fingers,   600
you, like a little child, can't fight;
running here and there, you were caught
and, like a slave, you endure misery and remain.
Even if you flap your wings and run everywhere on earth,
performing service where there is beauty,   605
the Graces aim their bow at you,
equip you as their slave,
use the fugitive as a trusty servant,
and see you, the runaway, staying.
How savage you are, even if you laugh sweetly, Eros;   610
I see you hammering together inescapable chains.
How furious you are, even if you seem to play gladly.

Ἔχων δὲ χεῖρας εἰς τὸ βάλλειν εὐτόνους
πλήττεις ἀφειδῶς· οὐ γὰρ ἡ τεκοῦσά σε
615   τῆς σῆς διέδρα τοξικῆς τὰ κεντρία.
Τὴν Νιόβην κλαίουσαν ἀγροῖκος βλέπων
"ὢ πῶς ῥέει δάκρυον" εἶπε "καὶ λίθος"·
ἡμᾶς δὲ σὸς νῦν ἔμπνοος λίθος, κόρη,
οὐδὲ βραχὺ στένοντας οἰκτείρειν θέλει.
620   Ὡς ἐν σκοπῷ μοι τόξον ὤφθης ἀθρόον,
ὑπερφερὴς σὺ παρθένων ἐγχωρίων.
Τοῦ σοῦ δὲ κάλλους ἂν συνέστηκε κρίσις,
ἡ Κύπρις οὐκ ἔτυχε πρωτείου πάλιν,
κἂν ὁ κριτὴς ἐκεῖνος ἦν ὧδε κρίνων
625   ἐρωτόληπτος ξανθοβόστρυχος Πάρις.
Σοὶ μαλθακὸν φίλημα, πλέγμα βοστρύχων,
ἡ τῶν μελῶν σου συμπλοκή, τὰ πάντά σοι·
ψυχὴ δ᾽ ἀπειθὴς καὶ νοητὸς ἀδάμας.
Μέσον κακοῦμαι Παφίης καὶ Παλλάδος·
630   τίς Ταντάλειον δίψος ἰσχύει φέρειν;
Καὶ τοῦ Διὸς δὲ νῦν κατήγορος μένω
ὡς ἀνεράστου, μὴ μεταβεβλημένου
πρὸς τὴν καθ᾽ ἡμᾶς εὐπρεπεστέραν κόρην
Λήδας, Δανάης, Γαννυμήδους, Εὐρώπης.
635   Σοῦ καὶ ῥυτὶς μολοῦσα τῷ χρόνῳ μόλις
ἥβης ὁποῦ πρόκριτος, ὡς ἐγὼ κρίνω·
σὸν φθινόπωρον κρεῖττον - ἢ ποῖος λόγος; -
ἔαρος ἄλλης, σὸς δὲ χειμὼν καλλίων
ὀπωροφυοῦς εὐκραοῦς ἄλλου θέρους.
640   Ἀλλ᾽ ἐκδυθείης μέχρις αὐτοῦ σαρκίου
καὶ γυμνὰ γυμνοῖς ἐμπελάσειας μέλη·
ἐμοὶ δοκεῖ γὰρ καὶ τὸ λεπτόν σου φάρος
τεῖχος Σεμιράμιδος. Ὡς γένοιτό μοι.᾽
    Τοσαῦτα λέξας εἰς τὸν οἶκον ἐστράφη,
645   τὴν γραῦν ὀπαδὸν λιπαρῶν ἐκ νευμάτων
ὡς τὴν κόρην πείσειεν ἐνδεδωκέναι·
ἢ καὶ λαβοῦσα τὴν κόρην ὡδοιπόρει·
ἡ νὺξ γὰρ ἠνάγκαζεν ἀνθυποστρέφειν.
    Ὁ γοῦν Χαρικλῆς ἐς Ξενοκράτους μένων
650   πρὸς ὄρθρον ἀντέφασκε ταῖς χελιδόσι·
᾽πᾶσαν μὲν ἤδη νύκτα γρηγορῶν μένω·

With hands strong for hitting,
you strike without mercy: not even your own mother
escaped the stings of your arrows.   615
A peasant seeing Niobe weeping
said, 'Oh, how a stone too lets a tear flow!'
but you, now, girl, a living stone,
aren't willing to pity me even a little as I groan.
You appeared suddenly like a bow, with me as your mark,   620
you who surpass the maidens of the land!
If a contest were held regarding your beauty,
Cypris wouldn't win first prize again*
even if the judge deciding the case were
the love-smitten, yellow-haired Paris.   625
Your kiss, the plaiting of your hair,
the clasp of your limbs, every part of you is soft,
but your heart is unyielding—spiritual steel.
I am trapped between Aphrodite and Pallas.
Who can bear the thirst of Tantalus?*   630
And now I accuse Zeus too
of being unloving, since he's not transformed himself
for the girl among us who's more beautiful
than Leda, Danaë, Ganymede, and Europa.*
Your wrinkles, when at last they appear,   635
are preferable, in my judgment, to youth's sap.
Your autumn is better—what should I say?—
than another's spring, and your winter is more beautiful
than another fruitful, gentle summer.
But may you be stripped to your very flesh,   640
and may you bring your naked limbs near mine,
for even your thin cloak seems to me
like the wall of Semiramis. May this happen to me!"*
    He said these things and returned to his house,
entreating with signs the old woman attending the girl   645
that she persuade her to yield;
and she took hold of the girl and started walking,
for the night was forcing them to turn round.
    Meanwhile Charikles, staying at Xenokrates' house,
towards dawn was responding to the swallows: 650
"For the whole night now I have remained awake,

εἰ δ᾽ ὄρθρος ἥξει μικρὸν ὕπνον ἐγχέων,
χελιδόνες τρύζουσιν, οὐκ ἐῶσί με.
Παύου, κακῶν κάκιστον ὀρνέων γένος.
655   Οὐκ αὐτὸς ἐξέκοψα μίξεως φόβῳ
τὴν Φιλομήλας γλῶτταν, ὡς μή τι φράσοι.
Ἀλλ᾽ εἰς τραχεῖαν καὶ στυγνὴν ἐρημίαν
τὴν Ἴτυος ναὶ συμφορὰν θρηνεῖτέ μοι,
ὡς μικρὸν ὑπνώττοιμι· καὶ κοιμωμένῳ
660   ὄνειρος ἥκοι, χερσὶ τῆς ποθουμένης
ἴσως με τὸν ποθοῦντα συμπλέκειν θέλων.
Τιθωνέ, γηρᾷς· τὴν σὴν Ἠῶ, τὴν φίλην
σὴν εὐνέτιν, ἤλασας ἐκ τοῦ σοῦ λέχους.᾽
Ὧι καὶ πρὸς ὕπνον αὖθις ἐκνενευκότι
665   ὁ καλλίμορφος Διόνυσος ἐγγίσας
δηλοῖ μένειν Δροσίλλαν ἐν τῷ χωρίῳ
εἰς τὸ γραὸς δόμημα τῆς Βαρυλλίδος,
καὶ τῆσδε συζήτησιν αὐτῷ προτρέπει.

ΒΙΒΛΙΟΝ ΕΒΔΟΜΟΝ

Ἤδη μὲν ὄρθρος καὶ κροκόχρως ἡμέρα,
καὶ φῶς ἐναργὲς πανταχοῦ κεχυμένον
ἐκ τοῦ μεγίστου καὶ διαυγοῦς ἀστέρος
ἐξ ὠκεανοῦ προσβαλόντος τῇ κτίσει,
5   ὡς ἡ σοφὴ ποίησις εἰδυῖα γράφει,
σύμμετρα θερμαίνοντος ἐξ ὑψωμάτων
ὀρῶν κορυφὰς καὶ δασυσκίους πόδας
εἰς εὔγονον βλάστημα καὶ τέρψιν βίου·
ἀνίσταται δὲ καὶ Χαρικλῆς ἐξ ὕπνου,
10   καὶ τοῦ δόμου πρόεισι τοῦ Ξενοκράτους,
λαβὼν μετ᾽ αὐτοῦ καὶ Κλέανδρον τὸν φίλον.
Ἡ γραῦς δὲ λοιπὸν δακρύουσαν ὀρθρόθεν
παρηγορεῖσθαι τὴν κόρην πειρωμένη,
ἔφασκε· 'Δεῦρο, τέκνον, ἐξάγγελλέ μοι·
15   πόθεν τίνος σὺ καὶ πατὴρ τίς καὶ πόλις,
τίς ὃν Χαρικλῆν ἐκκαλουμένη στένεις;
Πενθεῖς δ᾽ ἀγεννῶς καὶ στενάζεις ἀφρόνως,
τὸν Καλλιδήμου γάμον οὐ δεδεγμένη,

and if dawn comes and pours a little sleep over me,
the swallows sing and do not let me sleep.
Cease, worst species of wicked birds.
I didn't cut out Philomela's tongue*   655
for fear she'd say something about the intercourse.
Go off in a harsh and gloomy solitude
and lament, yes, the misfortune of Itys,
so that I may sleep a little. And may there come to me,
as I sleep, a dream, which will perhaps enfold me,   660
the lover, in the arms of my beloved!
Tithonos, you grow old: you have driven Dawn,*
your beloved mistress, from your bed."
    When Charikles had fallen again into sleep,
beautiful Dionysus drew near   665
and revealed that Drosilla was staying in the town
at the house of the old woman Maryllis,*
and urged him to search for her.

BOOK SEVEN

    Now it was morning, a saffron-colored day,
and bright light poured forth everywhere
from the immense radiant star
that rose from the ocean and illumined creation
(as learned poetry skillfully describes),   5
and suitably warmed from on high
the tops and shaded feet of mountains
that crops might bear fruit and life be joyous.
Charikles rose from sleep
and went forth from Xenokrates' house,   10
taking with him also his friend Kleandros.
    The old woman, then, trying to comfort
the girl, who had been weeping since dawn,
said, "Come here, child, and tell me
where you're from, who's your father, what's your city,   15
and who is this Charikles you invoke, moaning?
Your lament is unseemly and your moaning foolish
since you've not accepted marriage with Kallidemos,

ὃς ὑπὲρ ἄλλους τοὺς κατοίκους ἐνθάδε
20   ὡραῖός ἐστι καὶ τέθηλε χρυσίῳ.
Οὐκ εὖ γε ποιεῖς, ὦ πένησσα καὶ ξένη,
εἰ Καλλίδημον εὐγενῆ νεανίαν
οὐκ ἄξιόν σοι συμμιγῆναι νῦν κρίνεις.'
Τῆς δὲ Δροσίλλας τοῦ λαλεῖν ἀπηργμένης·
25   'ἐπεὶ μαθεῖν ζητεῖς με, μῆτερ, τὴν ξένην
τὰ κατ' ἐμαυτὴν καὶ τὰ τοῦ Χαρικλέος',
ἤκουσεν ὁ Κλέανδρος, ἔστη τοῦ δρόμου·
ἡ γὰρ Χαρικλοῦς κλῆσις ἔσχε τὸν νέον
ἔμπροσθεν ἐκτρέχοντα τοῦ Χαρικλέος·
30   καί 'δός, Χαρίκλεις, τῆς χαρᾶς τὰς ἐγγύας
ἐμοὶ Κλεάνδρῳ συνταλαιπωροῦντί σοι'
στραφεὶς πρὸς αὐτόν φησι τὸν Χαρικλέα,
ὃν καὶ κατεξέπληξεν αὐτῷ τῷ λόγῳ,
ὃν καὶ κατεθρόησε τῇ φωνῇ μόνῃ.
35   Ἐντεῦθεν ἀντιδόντες ἀλλήλοις χέρας
ἄφνω παρεμβάλλουσιν αὐτῇ τῇ στέγῃ,
ἧς ἔνδον ἡ γραῦς, ἡ φίλοικτος καρδία,
μετὰ Δροσίλλας ἐμπαθῶς προσωμίλει.
Φωνὴ μεταξὺ χαρμονῆς καὶ δακρύων,
40   χειρῶν κρότος, θροῦς καὶ φιλημάτων κτύπος,
ἄμετρος ὄμβρος ἐκραγεὶς τῶν ὀμμάτων,
πρὸς τὸν Σεμέλης φθόγγος εὐχαριστίας,
καλοὶ μὲν εἰς γραῦν ἐκ Χαρικλέος λόγοι
ὑπὲρ Δροσίλλας τῶν φιλοξενημάτων,
45   πολλὴ δὲ πρὸς Κλέανδρον εὐχαριστία
ἀπὸ Δροσίλλας τῆς ἀρίστης παρθένου
τῶν πρὸς Χαρικλῆν συγκακοπραγημάτων.
Τοιοῦτος ἦν θροῦς ἐν μέσῳ τῶν τεσσάρων
σύμμικτος ὄντως χαρμονῆς καὶ δακρύων.
50   Οὐ μὴν ὁ Καλλίδημος ἠγνόησέ τι.
Ἀποσκοπῶν γοῦν καθ' ἑαυτὸν ἀφρόνως
δράσειν φόνιον ἔργον εἰς Χαρικλέα
ἀτραυματίστως, οὐ καθηματωμένως,
ὡς εὐτυχήσοι τῆς Δροσίλλας τὸν γάμον,
55   ἔλαθεν αὐτῷ τὸν βρόχον παραρτύων.
Ὡς εἶδε δ' αὖθις γνόντα τὸν Χαρικλέα
τὴν τῆς κόρης ἄφιξιν ἐν τῷ χωρίῳ

who's handsome beyond all others dwelling here
and exceedingly rich in gold.   20
You're not behaving well, poor stranger,
if you now judge that Kallidemos, a noble youth,
is not worthy of your bed."
    Drosilla began her response,
"Since you seek to learn from me, the stranger, Mother,   25
about my situation and that of Charikles . . . "
At once Kleandros heard her and halted in his tracks,
for the mention of Charikles' name stopped him
as he ran ahead of Charikles;
and, turning back to Charikles,   30
he said, "Give pledges of joy, Charikles,
to me, Kleandros, your companion in misery."
His speech amazed Charikles—
just the sound of his voice disturbed him.
Then they joined hands with one another   35
and went at once to the house
in which the compassionate old woman
was fervently conversing with Drosilla.
There were cries full of joy and tears,
the clapping of hands, murmuring and the sound of kisses,   40
tears flowing from their eyes like torrential rain,
a speech of gratitude to the son of Semele,
fine words from Charikles to the old woman
for her hospitality to Drosilla,
and much gratitude from Drosilla,   45
exceptional maiden, to Kleandros
for being Charikles' companion in misfortunes.
Such was the noise that rose midst the four of them—
a true mixture of joy and tears.
    But Kallidemos was not ignorant of the situation.   50
Contriving with himself, then, foolishly,
to do a bloody deed against Charikles
without getting wounded or bloody himself,
so that he might marry Drosilla,
he was preparing a noose for himself without knowing it.   55
But when he perceived, in turn, that Charikles knew
of the girl's arrival in the town,

πρὸ τοῦ προβῆναι τὸν σκοπούμενον δόλον,
ἀπαυθαδίσας ἐξ ἐρωτομανίας
60   πρὸς ἁρπαγὴν ὥρμησε ληστρικωτέραν·
οὐκ αἰσχύνην γὰρ οἶδε πολλάκις ἔρως.
Σκοπῶν δὲ νυκτὸς ἀμφὶ τὴν ἐρημίαν
ἐπεισπεσεῖν ἄγνωστα τοῖς νεανίαις,
ἔχων σὺν αὐτῷ καὶ συνήλικας νέους,
65   ὡς δῆθεν αὐτὴν τὴν κόρην ἀφαρπάσων
– εἰς γὰρ ἀπόπλουν ηὐτρέπιζεν ὁλκάδα –,
ἀντὶ φλογὸς μὲν ἦν ἀνῆπτον οἱ πόθοι,
πρηστήριον πῦρ ἔσχε τριταίου τρόμου,
ἀνθ' ὁλκάδος δὲ τῆς ἀποπλευσουμένης
70   ἔσχηκεν αὐτὸν ἡ ταλαίπωρος κλίνη,
ἀντὶ δρόμου δὲ τοῦ πρὸς ἄλλο χωρίον,
μακρὰν ποδῶν εὕρηκεν ἀκινησίαν.
      Ὁ γοῦν Χαρικλῆς εἶχεν οὐδένα κόρον
τῶν τῆς Δροσίλλας ἐνδρόσων φιλημάτων·
75   εἰ γὰρ φιλεῖν τις τὴν ποθουμένην λάβοι,
ἄπληστός ἐστιν ἐν μέσῃ τῇ καρδίᾳ
τὴν ἡδονὴν ῥέουσαν εὐκόλως ἔχων·
τὸ χεῖλος οὐκοῦν ἐστιν ἐξηραμμένον,
οὐ γλυκύτητα μετρίαν κεκτημένον,
80   τῆς ἡδονῆς ἐκεῖσε συγκενουμένης.
Ἀπαλλαγέντων τοίνυν ἐκ φιλημάτων,
ἡ γραῦς Βαρυλλὶς ἀντένηψε καὶ λέγει·
'τέκνον Χαρίκλεις, εὖ μὲν ἦλθες ἐνθάδε
εὑρὼν Δροσίλλαν ἐκ θεῶν σεσωσμένην,
85   ἣ μέχρι καὶ νῦν οὐκ ἔληξε δακρύων
καὶ τῶν χάριν σοῦ πενθικῶν ὀδυρμάτων·
ὡς εὖ μὲν ἦλθες – τοῖς θεοῖς πολλὴ χάρις
τοῖς μέχρις ἡμῶν ὑγιᾶ σεσωκόσι
καὶ τῇ ποθούσῃ δεῦρο συμμίξασί σε –
90   ὡς εὖ μὲν ἦλθες, τέκνον, εὖ δὲ καὶ λέγοις
ὅπως μὲν εἰς σύμπνοιαν ἤλθετον μίαν,
ποία δὲ πατρὶς καὶ τὰ τοῦ πόθου πόθεν,
τίς δ' οὗτος ὁ Κλέανδρος αὐτὸς ὁ ξένος,
ποίῳ διεζεύχθητον ἀλλήλων λόγῳ
95   καὶ νῦν ἐπεγνώσθητον ἀλλήλοις πάλιν.
Ἔμελλε πάντως τοῦ λέγειν ἀπηργμένη

before his own stratagem had moved forward,
made reckless by his mad love,
he set out to seize her in the pirate manner,   60
for love often does not know shame.
While he was plotting to attack the young men
secretly in the solitude of night,
with the help of his own young comrades,
in order to steal away the girl   65
(for he was preparing a merchant ship for sailing away),
instead of a flame kindled by desire
the blazing fire of a tertian fever attacked him;
instead of a ship ready to sail
his miserable bed seized him;   70
instead of a course to another place
he found that he couldn't move.
    Charikles, meanwhile, could not get enough
of Drosilla's dewy kisses—
for if a man should kiss his beloved,   75
his heart cannot be sated,
for his pleasure freely flows out of him;
thus his lip becomes dry
and loses its natural sweetness
since his pleasure empties out there.   80
When they had ceased, then, from kisses,
the old woman Maryllis recovered, in turn, and said,
"Charikles, my child, how fortunately you came here
and found Drosilla saved by the gods,
a girl who until now did not cease from tears   85
and mournful laments for your sake.
How fortunately you came—much thanks to the gods
who brought you safe and sound to us
and united you here with your beloved.
How fortunately you came, child, and may you also recount well   90
how you two came to be united together,
where your fatherland is, what the origin of your love is,
who this Kleandros is, the stranger,
and why you two were separated
and now discovered again by one another.   95
The maiden had begun to speak

ἡ παρθένος μοι ταῦτα διεξιέναι,
ναὶ καὶ καθ' εἱρμὸν πάντα τετρανωκέναι
πρὸ τοῦ σὲ τὸ στέγασμα κατειληφέναι.'
100 ''Επωδύνως γοῦν καὶ μετὰ στεναγμάτων
– ἢ πῶς γάρ; –' ὁ Κλέανδρος εἶπεν 'εὖ λέγοις.'
      ' Ἐπεὶ δὲ σύ μου τὴν στέγην, χρυσῆ τύχη,
ἔδυς, θεῶν ἔκ τινος ὡδηγημένος,
ὡς ἂν μικρὸν λήξειε τῶν ὀδυρμάτων
105 ἡ νύκτα δακρύουσα καὶ μεθ' ἡμέραν,
λέγοις ἂν ἡμῖν σὴν ἄφιξιν ἐνθάδε
καὶ τὴν Ἔρωτος μυστικὴν εὐτολμίαν
μεθ' ἡδονῆς πάντως τε καὶ προσχαρμάτων.
Τί γὰρ τὸ λυποῦν τὴν Δροσίλλαν εἰσέτι
110 ἢ τὸ θλίβον τί, σοῦ, Χαρίκλεις, ἱγμένου;
Ὡς γὰρ ἀπόντος ἐστέναζεν, ἐθρόει,
ἔκλαιε πικρῶς, ὠλόλυζε βαρέως,
οὕτω παρόντος, ὡς χαρᾶς συνημμένης
πάντων κρατούσης, ὦ θεῶν σωτηρίων,
115 εὔχρηστον οἶμον ἡ διήγησις λάβοι.
Καθηδυνεῖς δὲ καὶ πλέον τὴν παρθένον,
σοῦ γλυκεροῦ στόματος ἠνεωγμένου,
τὸν ἐξ ἐκείνου φθόγγον ἠνωτισμένην·
θάλψεις δὲ κἀμὲ συμπαθεῖν ἐγνωσμένα
120 οἷς μέχρι δεῦρο δυσχερῶς ἐπλημμέλει.'
      ' Ὡς ἤθελον μὲν πρῶτον αὐτὸς τὴν κόρην,
φίλον Βαρυλλίδιον, ἠρωτηκέναι'
ἔφη Χαρικλῆς 'πῶς σέσωσται καὶ μόνη,
πεσοῦσα πρὸς θάλασσαν ἐξ ὕψους ὄρους.
125 Ὡς νῦν ἐγὼ καὶ θάμβος ἡλίκον φέρω,
εἰ μὴ Δροσίλλαν φασματούμενος βλέπω·
ἐπεὶ δὲ σὸν θέλημα, γραῦ μῆτερ, λέγειν
ἡμῶν τοσαύτας τληπαθεῖς περιόδους
εἰς ἀνταμοιβὴν τῶν φιλοφρονημάτων,
130 ἄκουε· πῶς γὰρ καὶ παραγκωνιστέον
τὴν τῆς τοσαύτης αἰτίαν θυμηδίας
ἐμοὶ Δροσίλλᾳ καὶ Κλεάνδρῳ τοῖς ξένοις;
Εὖ δ' ἴσθι· πατρίς ἐστιν ἡμῶν ἡ Φθία·
μήτηρ ἐμοὶ μὲν Κρυστάλη, πατὴρ Φράτωρ,
135 τῇ δὲ Δροσίλλᾳ Μυρτίων, Ἡδυπνόη.

and was about to tell me these things,
yes, to reveal everything in sequence,
just before you arrived at my house."
    "Painfully, then, and with groans   100
(for how could you otherwise?)," Kleandros said, "may you speak well!"
    "Since you entered my house (oh golden fortune!),"
the old woman continued, "led here by one of the gods
that the girl who was weeping night and day
would cease a little from her laments,   105
tell us of your arrival here
and the mystical courage of Eros
with its pleasure and delights.
Indeed, what still distresses Drosilla,
what afflicts her, now that you've come, Charikles?   110
Just as in your absence she groaned, cried out,
wept bitterly, lamented grievously,
so now since you are present and a shared joy
rules over all (oh savior gods!),
let the narrative take a happy course.   115
You will delight the maiden even more
when you open your sweet mouth
and she hears your voice come out,
and you will rouse me also to sympathize with the troubles
(once known) that she has suffered up to now."   120
    "I should like first to ask the girl
myself, dear little Maryllis,"
said Charikles, "how she, though alone, was saved
when she fell to the sea from the top of a mountain.
How greatly I wonder now, too,   125
whether I'm not seeing a vision when I see Drosilla!
But since it's your wish, old mother, for me to tell
of our many unhappy turns of fortune,
in exchange for your acts of kindness,
listen—for how could I refuse you,   130
the cause of such great rejoicing
for me, Drosilla, and Kleandros, the strangers?
Know this well: our fatherland is Phthia;
my mother is Krystale, my father Phrator,
and Drosilla's father is Myrtion, her mother Hedypnoe.   135

Ταύτην ἑορτῆς εὐαγοῦς τελουμένης
τοῦ τῆς Σεμέλης καὶ Διὸς Διονύσου
ἔξω παρ᾽ αὐταῖς ταῖς πύλαις τῆς πατρίδος
συνεξιοῦσαν ἁπαλαῖς σὺν παρθένοις
140   ἰδὼν ἑάλων· οὐδὲ γὰρ μέμψῃ, γύναι,
ὁρῶντα ταύτης τοῦ προσώπου τὴν θέαν·
εἰς γὰρ τοσοῦτον συρρέον πλῆθος τότε
οὐκ ἦν ἰδέσθαι τῆς Δροσίλλας καλλίω.
Ἁλοὺς προσεῖπον καὶ προσειπὼν ἠξίουν
145   ἐμαυτὸν αὐτῇ τῇ φυγῇ συναρμόσαι.
Ἔνευσεν ἀντέρωτα πάσχουσα ξένον·
καὶ ναῦν ἀποπλέουσαν ἐξευρηκότες,
χαίρειν ἀφέντες συγγενεῖς καὶ πατρίδα
ὁμοῦ συνεισέδυμεν εἰς τὴν ὁλκάδα.
150   Πλὴν ἀλλὰ μικρὸν καὶ πλέοντες εὐδρόμως
ἥλωμεν οὕτως ἀπροόπτως ἀνδράσιν
τοῖς ναυτικῇ χαίρουσι τῇ ληστηρίῳ,
ὧν χεῖρας ἐκφυγόντες ὀψὲ καὶ μόλις,
σεσώσμεθα κρυβέντες ἐς μέσην ὕλην
155   καὶ Βάρζον εἰσέδυμεν ἄστυ σὺν δρόμῳ.
Ὃ καὶ συνεξέδυμεν ἐκτελουμένης
κἀκεῖ μεγίστης τοῦ Διὸς πανδαισίας,
ἐμπίπτομεν δὲ Παρθικῇ στραταρχίᾳ
θήραμα καινόν· καὶ δεθέντες αὐχένας
160   εἰς τὴν ἐκείνων ἀντεπήχθημεν πόλιν.
Ἐκεῖσε πολλῶν ἡμερῶν περιδρόμους
μετὰ στεναγμῶν ἐκμετρήσαντες πόσων
καὶ τὸν καλὸν Κλέανδρον ὃν βλέπεις, γύναι,
προαιχμαλωτισθέντα χειρὶ βαρβάρων
165   συνοικέτην κάλλιστον ἐξευρηκότες
– καὶ γὰρ φυλακῆς εἴδομεν παρ᾽ ἐλπίδα
δούλειον ἦμαρ, ἀλλοφύλους δεσπότας
καὶ δυστυχεῖς ἔρωτας ἀλλὰ καὶ πόσους –
συνηχμαλωτίσθημεν αὖθις ἐκ τρίτου
170   Ἄραψι, Πάρθων κατατετροπωμένων.
Τοίνυν λαχόντες δέσμιοι, παρηγμένοι
ὁδὸν διελθεῖν πανταχοῦ στενουμένην
ἐκ τῆς δασείας καὶ συνηρεφοῦς ὕλης
ἠγωνιῶμεν, ἄλλος ἄλλον ἐκράτει,

During a holy festival of Dionysus,
son of Semele and Zeus, I saw this girl
outside by the gates of the city,
as she was coming out, together with tender maidens,
I saw her and was conquered; you won't blame me, woman,   140
for looking at the vision of this girl's face,
since in the great crowd then flowing together
it was not possible to see a girl more beautiful than Drosilla.
Being conquered, I addressed her
and asked her to join me in flight.   145
She consented since she returned my love with great intensity,
and when we found a ship sailing away,
we said farewell to family and fatherland
and entered the merchant ship.
But after we'd sailed swiftly for a while,   150
we were unexpectedly captured by men
who delighted in piracy,
from whom we fled at last, with difficulty.
We escaped by hiding in the middle of a forest
and then entered the town of Barzon at a run.   155
But when we emerged from Barzon, since there too
a great banquet for Zeus was being held,
we encountered a Parthian army
and became their new booty; bound by our necks,
we were taken to their city.   160
There we filled the course
of many days with great groans,
and we found the noble Kleandros (whom you see here, woman),
who'd been captured earlier by the band of barbarians,
to be an excellent companion in servitude,   165
for we experienced against expectation
prison, slavery, foreign masters,
and unhappy loves (how many!).
Then we were captured again for a third time,
by Arabs, when the Parthians had been defeated.   170
We were led as captives
along a road that was narrowed everywhere
by a leafy and thickly shaded forest,
and we were distressed, holding onto one another,

175 ποιούμενοι δίκαιον εὔλογον φόβον
μή πως ὀλισθήσαντες ἐκ κρημνισμάτων
σχοίημεν αὐτὴν τὴν θάλασσαν εἰς τάφον·
ὃ καὶ πέπονθεν ἡ παροῦσα παρθένος,
ἣν ζῶσαν, ὦ Ζεῦ καὶ θεοὶ πάντες, βλέπω.
180 Ὁ κύριος γοῦν Ἀράβων ἄναξ Χάγος
θρηνοῦντα νύκτωρ ἐκμαθών με τὴν κόρην
μετὰ Κλεάνδρου τοῦ παρόντος εὐθέως
ἐλευθεροῖ, σχὼν οἶκτον ἡμῶν τοῦ πάθους·
οὗ καὶ τὰ συμφέροντα πάντα τῷ βίῳ
185 τὴν τῶν θεῶν πρόνοιαν ἐξῃτηκότες
ἀπηλλάγημεν δουλικῆς ζεύγλης βάρους.
Ἐγγίζομεν δὲ δωδεκαταίῳ φάει
μόλις παρ᾽ αὐτοῦ τῇ στέγῃ Ξενοκράτους·
ἐμέλλομεν δὲ σήμερον τὸ χωρίον
190 παρὰ βραχὺ λιπόντες ἀλλαχοῦ τρέχειν
– τρεῖς γὰρ διηνύκειμεν ἐν Ξενοκράτους
πρὸς παῦλαν ἄχθους ἡμερῶν περιδρόμους –,
εἰ μὴ θεῶν ὄνειρος ἐξαπεστάλη,
ἢ μᾶλλου οὐκ ὄνειρος, ἀλλὰ προφθάσας
195 ὁ καλλίμορφος παῖς Διὸς καὶ Σεμέλης
ἐπέσχεν εἰπών· "μὴ πρόβαινε μηκέτι,
ἕως Δροσίλλαν, ἣν ἰδεῖν ζῶσαν θέλεις,
θρηνοῦσαν εὕρῃς οὖσαν ἐν τῷ χωρίῳ."
Τὰ γοῦν καθ᾽ ἡμᾶς, ὥσπερ ᾔτησας, γύναι,
200 ἔχεις μαθοῦσα· πλὴν τὰ λοιπὰ τοῦ λόγου
αὐτὴν ἐρωτᾶν ἀξιῶ τὴν παρθένον,
πῶς ἔσχεν εἰς θάλασσαν ἐξερριμμένη
ἐνταῦθα πάντως πρός σε κατειληφέναι
αὐτῇ φανεῖσαν δευτέραν Ἡδυπνόην.᾽
205 ᾽ Ἐμοί, Χαρίκλεις, κἂν ὁ βάσκανος μίτος᾽
ἔφη Δροσίλλα ᾽τῆς ἀλάστορος τύχης
ἀεὶ τὰ λυπρὰ συμπερικλώθειν θέλει,
ἀλλ᾽ ἡ θεοῦ πρόνοια τοῦ σωτηρίου,
ἣν καὶ συνεργὸν τῆς καθ᾽ ἡμᾶς ἀγάπης
210 ἐπευτυχοῦμεν – ἀλλὰ μὴ λήγοις, ἄναξ,
τὴν λειπόπατριν συμφυλάττων, ὡς θέλεις –,
ἀεὶ τὰ χρηστὰ βούλεται συνεισφέρειν,
ἥτις πεσοῦσαν – ὦ παλαμναίου κλάδου,

with the just and reasonable fear   175
that we might slip from a precipice
and be buried in the sea,
which happened to the maiden here with us—
whom I see alive, oh Zeus and all the gods!
The ruler of the Arabs, then, Lord Chagos,   180
noticed me wailing at night for the girl,
and quickly freed me, together with Kleandros (who's here with us),
out of compassion for our misfortune.
After asking divine providence
for all that would benefit his life,   185
we were released from the burden of slavery's yoke.
On the twelfth day, after a difficult journey,
we approached Xenokrates' house,
and today we had intended
to leave the village and run elsewhere—   190
for we had spent three days
in Xenokrates' house to rest from our troubles—
if a dream hadn't been sent by the gods,
or rather not a dream but the beautiful
son of Zeus and Semele, who stopped me first,   195
saying, 'Don't go any further
until you find Drosilla (whom you wish to see alive)
weeping in this village.'
     "You have learned, then, what happened to us,
just as you asked, woman. But for the rest of the tale   200
I think you should ask the maiden herself,
how after being cast into the sea
she was able to come here to you,
who appeared to her as a second Hedypnoe."
     "Even if, Charikles," said Drosilla,   205
"the envious thread of avenging Fortune
always wishes to spin painful events,
still, the providence of the savior god,
which also fortunately
favored our love (but don't stop, Lord,   210
protecting, as you will, the one who left her fatherland!),
always wants to bring good things.
This providence, when I fell—oh, murderous branch,

τοῦ χεῖρα συλλαβόντος ἐκ τῆς ἀγκάλης
215   καὶ πρὸς βυθὸν ῥίψαντος ἐξ ἕδρας μέσης –
ἔσωσε πέτραις πολλὰ προσκεκρουμένην
τὰ στέρνα καὶ τὰ σπλάγχνα καὶ τὰς ὠλένας.'
– Καὶ συγκεκυφὼς προσλαλούσῃ τῇ κόρῃ
λευκοὺς ἐρυθροὺς κρυσταλώδεις δακτύλους
220   ταύτης Χαρικλῆς κατεφίλει δακρύων –
'Τίς χερσίν, ἃς σὺ νῦν φιλεῖς καὶ κατέχεις,
τὸν φλοιὸν ἐντέθεικε καὶ δέδωκέ μοι
τοιοῦτον εὐρὺν καὶ παρεκτεταμένον,
ὡς θᾶττον εἰς γῆν ἐμβαλεῖν σεσωσμένην;
225   Ὦ χαῖρε πολλά, Διόνυσε, γῆς ἄναξ,
ὅστις με πολλῶν ἐξέσωσας κινδύνων
καὶ μεῖζον ἄλλο δῶρον ἀντεχαρίσω.
Ὃν ἐν νεκροῖς ἤλπιζον ἐν ζῶσι βλέπω.'
     Καὶ συμπλακέντες τῷ μεταξὺ τῶν λόγων
230   ὡς κισσὸς εἰς δρῦν ἀντεφίλουν ἀσμένως.
Οὕτω δυσαπόσπαστον εἶχον τὴν σχέσιν,
ὡς καὶ δόκησιν ἐμβαλεῖν Βαρυλλίδι
καὶ σῶμα πάντως ἓν γενέσθαι τοὺς δύο,
οἳ τῷ προσλαλεῖν ἦλθον εἰς ψυχὴν μίαν.
235   Τοιοῦτός ἐστι πᾶς ἐρῶν πόθου πνέων·
καὶ γὰρ κατιδὼν ἣν ποθεῖ μετὰ χρόνον
ἄπληστα φιλεῖ πρὸς τὸ λῆξαι τοῦ πόθου.
     Μόλις Χαρικλῆς ἄρτι νήψας ἀντέφη·
'ἀλλ' ὦ τοσοῦτον ὥστε μὴ σθένειν λέγειν,
240   ὦ φῶς ἱμερτόν, ὦ πνοὴ καὶ καρδία,
πῶς τὴν τοσαύτην καὶ διήνυσας τρίβον
καὶ πρὸς τὸ παρὸν ἔσχες ἐλθεῖν χωρίον;'
     ' Ἐκεῖνος αὐτός' εἶπεν αὖθις ἡ κόρη
'ἐλθεῖν καθωδήγησεν εἰς τὸ χωρίον
245   ὁ καὶ θαλάσσης πλημμυρούσης ἁρπάσας
καὶ τὸν Χαρικλῆν ζῶντα νῦν μοι δοὺς βλέπειν.'
     Τούτοις Βαρυλλὶς προσχαρὴς δεδειγμένη
ἔφησεν· 'ὡς καινόν τι δέρκομαι, ξένοι.
Καὶ γραῦς μέν εἰμι καὶ προβᾶσα πρεσβῦτις,
250   χρηστῶν δὲ πολλῶν καὶ κακῶν ἴδρις ἔφυν·
πλὴν ἀλλὰ γὰρ τοσοῦτον οὐκ ἔγνων πόθον
οὐδ' εἶδον οὕτως εὐφυῆ συζυγίαν

which caught my arm by the elbow
and threw me from my seat into the abyss!—   215
saved me, when I'd struck my breast,
belly, and arms many times against the rocks."
(Having bent forward toward the girl as she was talking,
Charikles was kissing her white and rose
fingers like crystals and weeping.)   220
"Who put in my hands—which you now kiss
and hold—the gift of bark
so wide and long that
it could bring me quickly and safely to land?
Hail, Dionysus, lord of earth,   225
who preserved me from many dangers
and favored me with another, greater gift:
whom I expected among the dead, I see among the living."
    Clinging to one another between speeches,
like ivy to oak, they kissed each other gladly.   230
They looked so hard to separate
that they gave Maryllis the impression
that the two of them had become one body,
who in conversation had become one soul.
Such is every lover who breathes desire,   235
for if after a time he sees the girl he loves,
he kisses her insatiably to appease his desire.
    When Charikles at last composed himself, he said,
"You, great beyond words,
dear light, my breath and heart,   240
how did you complete so long a journey
and arrive at this place?"
    "That one himself," replied the girl,
"guided me to this place,
the one who snatched me up from the sea at flood-tide   245
and allowed me now to see Charikles alive."
    Maryllis, showing her pleasure in these things,
said, "What an extraordinary thing I see, strangers!
I am an old woman, advanced in years,
and I have experienced many things, good and bad,   250
but I certainly haven't witnessed so great a love,
nor have I seen such a graceful couple

ἐλθοῦσαν εἰς μέθεξιν οἰκτρῶς ἐκ νέου
οὐ καρτερητῶν ἀλλεπαλλήλων πόνων.
255   Καὶ τὴν μέν, ὦ Ζεῦ, παρθένον τηρουμένην,
καὶ ταῦτα δούλην πολλάκις δεδειγμένην,
τοὺς ἐμμανεῖς ἔρωτας ἐκπεφευγέναι,
τὸν δὲ πρὸς αὐτὰ βαρβάρων γυμνὰ ξίφη
ὡς εἰς θέρους ἄγρωστιν ἐμπεπτωκότα
260   ἐν ζῶσιν εἶναι καὶ συνεῖναι τῇ κόρῃ
ταύτης λαχόντα τὴν διάζευξιν πάλαι,
θεοῦ λέγεις τὸ πρᾶγμα, καὶ καλῶς λέγεις,
σῶφρον Δροσίλλα. Καλλίδημος ἐρρέτω.
Οὓς γὰρ θεὸς συνῆψε τίς διασπάσοι;’
265   Ἔφησε ταῦτα καὶ τράπεζαν εἰς μέσον
τέθεικεν ‘ ὑμῖν συγχαρήσομαι, ξένοι,
τὴν σήμερον’’ λέγουσα ‘συμπάρεστέ μοι
καὶ συγχορεύσω τῷ θεῷ Διονύσῳ
παθόντας οἰκτρὰ προσφυῶς ἡνωκότι.’
270   Οὗτοι μὲν οὖν ἐντεῦθεν ἠσχολημένοι
τροφαῖς κρατῆρσιν ἀμφεγάννυντο πλέον·
ἡ γραῦς δέ – καὶ γὰρ εἶχε καλὴν καρδίαν –
ὅλη φανεῖσα τῆς χαρᾶς καὶ τοῦ πότου
ἤγερτο λοιπὸν τῆς καθέδρας ὀρθία
275   καὶ πρὸς τὸ πρᾶγμα δῆθεν ἐσκευασμένη,
λαβοῦσα χειρόμακτρα χερσὶ ταῖς δύο
ὄρχησιν ὠρχήσατο βακχικωτέραν,
φθόγγον κορύζης οὐ μακρὰν ποιουμένη
χαρᾶς τελεστὴν καὶ γέλωτος ἐργάτην.
280   Ἔσφαλλε μέντοι θαμὰ συγκινουμένην
τὸ συνεχὲς λύγισμα τὴν Βαρυλλίδα,
πίπτει δὲ πάντως ἡ ταλαίπωρος κάτω
τῷ συμποδισμῷ τῶν σκελῶν τετραμμένη·
ὑψοῖ δὲ θᾶττον εἰς καφαλὴν τοὺς πόδας,
285   καὶ τὴν καφαλὴν ἀντερείδει τῇ κόνει·
τοῖς συμπόταις ἐπῆρτο μακρός τις γέλως.
Οὕτως ἐκείνη συμπεσοῦσα κειμένη
ἡ γραῦς Βαρυλλὶς ἐξεπόρδησε τρίτον
τῷ συμπιλησμὸν τῆς κεφαλῆς μὴ φέρειν.
290   Οὔκουν ἐπεξήγερτο· μὴ γὰρ ἰσχύειν
ἔφασκεν ἡ δύστηνος, καὶ προκειμένη

come to share pitiably from a young age
such unbearable, unremitting sufferings.
That the girl, O Zeus, who kept herself a maiden, 255
and this when often made a slave,
has escaped mad loves,
and the boy, who fell among drawn swords
of barbarians as if into summer grass,
is among the living and united with the girl 260
after having been long separated from her,
you say this is a god's work and you are right,
wise Drosilla. Let Kallidemos be damned!
Who could separate those whom a god has joined?"*
    She said this and set a table 265
in the middle, saying, "Today I will celebrate with you,
strangers. Be my guests,
and I will dance with the god Dionysus,
who has inseparably united those who've suffered pitiably."
    They were then occupied with their food 270
and rejoiced even more in their cups,
but the old woman (for she had a good heart),
when she was clearly full of joy and wine,
rose up from her seat,
and having prepared herself 275
by taking napkins in her hands,
engaged in a frenzied, Bacchic dance,
while making a wheezing sound from her nose
that produced joy and caused laughter.
But her continuous twistings and turnings tripped Maryllis up 280
as she moved ceaselessly along,
and the poor woman fell down,
overturned by an entanglement of her legs;
then she lifted her feet at once to her head
and pressed her head into the dust. 285
Her drinking companions were convulsed in laughter.
As that old woman, Maryllis, lay there after her fall,
she broke wind three times,
not able to bear the compression of her head.
She didn't rise up, then, for the wretched woman said 290
that she didn't have the strength, and so lying in front of them,

τὰς χεῖρας αὐτῆς ἀντεφήπλου τοῖς νέοις.
Ἀλλ' ὁ Κλέανδρος συγκατασχεῖν οὐκ ἔχων,
ἐξυπτιάσας τῷ γέλωτι καὶ μόνος
295   ὡς ἡμιθνὴς ἔκειτο πυκνὸν ἐμπνέων.
Τί γοῦν Χαρικλῆς; Τῶν γελώτων ἐν μέσῳ
καλῆς ἀφορμῆς τῷ δοκεῖν δεδραγμένος,
ἐπεισκεκυφὼς τῷ Δροσίλλας αὐχένι
ἐπεγγελάσων τῇ καλῇ Βαρυλλίδι,
300   οὐκ εἶχε πάντως τῶν φιλημάτων κόρον,
τῶν χειλέων ἐκεῖσε προσκολλωμένων.
Πλὴν ἀλλ' ἀναστὰς ὁ Κλέανδρος καὶ μόλις
ἔδειξε τὴν γραῦν συμπεσοῦσαν ὀρθίαν,
οἶμαι, πτοηθεὶς ἐκ προσυμβεβηκότων
305   ὡς μή τι γ' αὖθις ἐκφορήσοι καὶ κόπρους
ἢ τὴν κεφαλὴν ἀλοηθῇ κειμένη,
μισθὸν λαβοῦσα τῶν φιλοξενημάτων
τὴν θρύψιν αὐτὴν ἐν πόνοις τοῦ κρανίου.
Ἥ καὶ συνιζήσασα τοῖς νέοις ἔφη·
310   'μὰ τοὺς θεούς, ὦ τέκνα, καὶ σκοπεῖτέ μοι·
ἐξ οὗ καλὸς παῖς τῆς Βαρυλλίδος Χράμος
τέθαπτο – καὶ γάρ ἐστιν ὄγδοος χρόνος –,
οὐκ ἦλθον εἰς γέλωτας, οὐκ ὠρχησάμην·
ὑμῖν δὲ ταῦτα λοιπὸν ἐξ ἐμοῦ χάρις·
315   παισὶ πλανηθείς φασι καὶ γέρων τρέχει.'
        'Μὰ τὸν σὸν υἱόν' ἀντέφησαν οἱ νέοι
' ἤδυνας ἡμᾶς, ὦ Βαρυλλὶς κοσμία,
ἄλλοις τε πολλοῖς καὶ τροφῇ σῇ καὶ πόσει·
ὄρχημα δ' οὖν σὸν καὶ τέχνη λυγισμάτων
320   καὶ σῶν ποδῶν κίνησις ἀφθονωτέρα
καὶ πυκνὸν ἀντίλοξον εὔστροφον τάχος
ὑπὲρ τροφὴν ἥδυνεν, ὑπὲρ τὴν πόσιν,
ὑπὲρ τράπεζαν τὴν πολυτελεστάτην,
ὑπὲρ φιάλην τὴν ὑπερχειλεστάτην.
325   Καὶ καινὸν οὐδέν, μῆτερ, ὧν κατειργάσω·
ἡμεῖς δὲ κἂν γέροντες ἦμεν τρισσάκις,
συμμετριάζειν οὐκ ἂν εἴχομεν φόβον,
πάντως τὰ λῷστα τῶν θεῶν δωρουμένων.'
        Τοιαῦτα πρὸς γραῦν εἶπον οἱ νεανίαι,
330   καὶ τῆς τραπέζης ἐκ ποδῶν τεθειμένης

she stretched out her hands to the young men.
Kleandros couldn't control himself,
fell back with laughter, and lay by himself
as if half-dead, gasping for breath.   295
What about Charikles, then? In the midst of all the laughter
he seized what seemed to him a good opportunity,
and, bending forward toward Drosilla's neck
to laugh at the good Maryllis,
he was kissing Drosilla insatiably,   300
with their lips stuck fast together.
But Kleandros stood up and with effort
raised to her feet the old woman who'd fallen,
since he feared from what had just happened, I think,
that she'd also soil herself   305
or have her head smashed as she lay there,
taking as reward for her hospitality
the painful crushing of her skull.
She sat together with the young men and said,
"By the gods, children, hear my words: 310
ever since Maryllis's beautiful child Chramos
was buried—it has been eight years—
I have not laughed or danced.
I thank you, then, for these things;
they say that even an old man runs when playing with children."   315
      "By your son," answered the young men,
"you have given us pleasure, honest Maryllis,
with many things, and especially your food and drink,
but then your dancing—the skill of your twisting movements,
the continuous action of your feet,   320
and your constant, slantwise, nimble quickness—
has given us pleasure beyond food, beyond drink,
beyond the extravagant table,
beyond the overflowing wine bowl.
And there is nothing strange, mother, in those things you've done.   325
Even if we were three times as old,
we would not be afraid to jest together
when the gods give wonderful gifts."
      The young men said these things to the old woman,
and when the table was removed,   330

ὁ μὲν Κλέανδρος εἰς τὸν ὕπνον ἐκλίθη,
ἡ γραῦς δὲ λοιπὸν ἔνθεν ἀντανεκλίθη.

ΒΙΒΛΙΟΝ ΟΓΔΟΟΝ

Ὁ γοῦν Χαρικλῆς χεῖρα δοὺς τῇ παρθένῳ
εὐθὺς μετ' αὐτῆς ἦλθεν εἰς τὸ κηπίον
ἐγγύθεν ὄν· προβὰς δὲ μικρὸν ἱστόρει
τὰ δένδρα, τὴν ὀπώραν, ἄνθη ποικίλα,
5   καλόν τι χρῆμα τοὺς ὁρῶντας ἡδύνον.
Καὶ δὴ συνιζήσαντες ὑπὸ μυρρίνην
συνῆλθον ἄμφω πρὸς λόγου κοινωνίαν.
Καί 'τίς, φίλον μέλημα' Χαρικλῆς ἔφη,
'ὃν εἶπε Καλλίδημον ἡ γραῦς ἐν πότῳ;
10   Μή σου κατηξίωτο βασκάνῳ τύχῃ
κατατρυφῆσαι καλλονῆς καὶ τοῦ γάμου
δεινὸς βιαστὴς καὶ τύραννος ὠμόνους;
Μή τις τὸ πῦρ ἔφθασεν ἐγκατασβέσαι,
ὃ πρὸς Χαρικλῆν ἔσχες ἐν ψυχῆς βάθει;
15   Ὦ ὦ ποθεινὸν ὄμμα, μὴ σύγκρυπτέ τι·
πρὸς γὰρ Χαρικλῆν ἐξερεῖς, οὐ πρὸς ξένον.'
'Πῶς εἶπας; Εὐφήμησον' ἀνταπεκρίθη
πρὸς τὸν Χαρικλῆν ἡ Δροσίλλα παρθένος,
'ἄνερ Χαρίκλεις· ναὶ γὰρ εἶ σὺ καὶ μόνος
20   ἀνὴρ ἐμοί· καὶ τοῦτο μὴ ψευδὴς λόγος.
Παρεσφάλη σοι τὸ φρονοῦν καὶ τὸ κρίνον
ἐκ τῆς περισχούσης σε μακρᾶς ἀνίας·
καὶ γὰρ παρακόπτουσι λῦπαι καὶ φρένας.
Ἦ γάρ, πάτερ Ζεῦ καὶ θεῶν γερουσία,
25   εἰ μὴ Δροσίλλα μέχρι καὶ νῦν παρθένος
τὸ πρᾶγμα πάντως ἐξελέγξει καὶ μόνον.
Οἷος λόγος, κάλλιστε Χαρίκλεις ἄνερ,
τὸ τῶν ὀδόντων ἕρκος ἐξέφυγέ σου.
Ἐρῶ δέ σοι· καὶ μάρτυς ἔστω τοῦ λόγου
30   ὁ τοῦ Διὸς παῖς, ὃς πρὸ τῆς χθὲς καθ' ὕπνον
δηλοῖ παραστὰς κειμένῃ κοιμωμένῃ
τὴν σὴν κατασκήνωσιν εἰς Ξενοκράτους,
οὗ προσταγῇ πεισθεῖσα - πῶς γὰρ οὐκ ἔδει; -

Kleandros lay down to sleep,
and the old woman, then, reclined in turn.

BOOK EIGHT

Charikles, then, gave his hand to the maiden
and at once went with her into the garden
nearby, and stepping forward a little, he gazed
at the trees, the fruit, and the varied flowers,
a beautiful spectacle that delighted those who saw it.   5
And so, sitting down together beneath a myrtle,
they joined in conversation.
Charikles said, "Who, dearest darling,
is that Kallidemos the old woman mentioned while we were drinking?
Can it be that envious Fortune deemed   10
a terrible, violent man, a cruel-minded tyrant,
worthy to revel in your beauty and marriage?
Surely someone didn't manage to quench the fire
that you had for Charikles in the depth of your soul?
Oh beloved eye, don't conceal anything,   15
for you will be speaking to Charikles, not a stranger."
    "What did you say? Be still, Charikles, my spouse,"
replied the maiden Drosilla to Charikles,
"for you alone are my husband,
and I am not speaking falsely.   20
Your thinking and judgment are in error
from the long grief that has enveloped you,
for sorrows unsettle the mind also.
Truly, Father Zeus and council of the gods,
if Drosilla has not remained a virgin up to now,   25
the deed itself will certainly prove it.
What a word, beautiful Charikles, my spouse,
has escaped the barrier of your teeth!
But I will tell you, and let Zeus's child
be a witness of my word, who day before yesterday   30
stood by me as I lay in bed sleeping
and revealed that you were staying in Xenokrates' house.
Obeying his command—for how could I not?—

πολλῆς χαρᾶς πλησθεῖσα τὴν γραῦν ἠρόμην,
35   εἴ τις παροικεῖ πανδοχεὺς τῷ χωρίῳ.
Δηλωσάσῃ πάντως δὲ τὸν Ξενοκράτην
ταύτῃ πρὸς αὐτοῦ τοὺς δόμους συνειπόμην.
Εἰδυῖα δ' αὕτη καὶ πρὸ τῆς σῆς παρθένου
τὸν Καλλίδημον παῖδα τοῦ Ξενοκράτους,
40   ἐλθεῖν πρὸς ἡμᾶς ἱκέτευε τὸν νέον,
ὡς ἐκπυθέσθαι σὴν ἔλευσιν ἐνθάδε·
οὐ γὰρ συνεισέδυμεν ἄμφω τὴν στέγην·
καὶ τοῦτο δεῖγμα τῆς ἐμῆς εὐκοσμίας.
Ὡς εἴθε πάντως εἰσέδυν τὴν οἰκίαν.
45   Καὶ χαρμονὴν εὕρηκα συντομωτέραν,
καὶ τηλικαύτην ἔσχον εὐετηρίαν,
θησαυρὸν ἁβρὸν γνοῦσα τὸν Χαρικλέα.
Ὁ γὰρ προλεχθεὶς Καλλίδημος εὐθέως
ἡμᾶς ἰδὼν ἔξεισι τοῦ δωματίου
50   καί μοι φθονήσας ἐξ ἀποφράδος τύχης
τῆς δεῦρό μοι σῆς εὐτυχοῦς παρουσίας
καὶ τήν, Χαρίκλεις, κλῆσιν ἐξηρνεῖτό μοι·
ἐγγὺς γὰρ ἑστώς, ἐκ κεφαλῆς εἰς πόδας
γεωμετρῶν με καὶ πυκνὸν μεταβλέπων
55   καὶ τὴν πνοὴν ἔοικεν ἐκλελοιπέναι.
Εἰ γὰρ τὸ κάλλος δεινόν ἐστιν ἑλκύσαι
καὶ τοὺς παρακμάσαντας ἄνδρας πολλάκις,
πόσῳ τὸν ἀκμάζοντα καὶ νεανίαν;
Οἵους μὲν οὖν προεῖπεν εἰς μάτην λόγους,
60   ὅσας δὲ κατέλεξε τὰς ὑποσχέσεις,
οὐκ ἔστιν εἰπεῖν, ὦ Χαρίκλεις, κἂν θέλω·
καὶ πῶς γάρ, οἷς προσέσχον οὐδὲ μετρίως;
Ἓν οἶδα τοῦτο – μάρτυς ἡ γραῦς τοῦ πάθους –
ὡς σῆς ἐνωτισθεῖσα δακνοκαρδίου
65   ἐλεύσεως ἄρνησιν – αἶ αἴ σοι φθόνε –
αὐτὴν ἑῴκειν ἐκκοπῆναι καρδίαν,
ψυχὴν ἐρυγεῖν θᾶττον ἠναγκαζόμην,
ἄψυχος ἦν, ἄναυδος, ἀνδριὰς ὅλη,
καὶ τοὺς θεούς, φεῦ, παγγενῶς ἐμεμφόμην,
70   ῥαίνουσα θερμὰ ῥεῖθρα πολλῶν δακρύων,
θρηνοῦσα πικρῶς ὑπὲρ ἀνδρὸς γνησίου.
Τοῦ τίνος; Αἶ αἴ, τοῦ καλοῦ Χαρικλέος.'

and filled with much joy, I asked the old woman
whether an innkeeper lived in the village,   35
and when she named Xenokrates,
I followed along with her to his house.
And this woman, knowing Kallidemos,
Xenokrates' son, even before she knew your maiden,
asked the young man to come to us   40
that we might inquire about your arrival here,
for neither of us entered the house,
and this is proof of my modesty.
If only I had entered the house anyway!
I should have found joy more quickly,   45
and what great happiness I should have had
when I recognized Charikles, my splendid treasure.
Kallidemos (whom I mentioned earlier), on seeing us,
exited at once from the house
and, refusing to admit to me (by an unlucky fate)   50
your fortunate presence here with me,
denied that he knew even your name, Charikles.
As he stood near, measuring me
from head to foot and examining me closely,
he seemed to have even lost his breath,   55
for if beauty often can attract
even men past their peak,
how much more the young man in his prime?
What words, then, he spoke in vain,
and how many promises he made,   60
I couldn't say, Charikles, even if I wanted to,
for how could I when I gave them not the slightest attention?
I know this one thing—and the old woman is witness to my suffering—
that having heard his denial
of your arrival (ah, cruel envy!),   65
I thought I'd had my very heart cut out,
I was being forced at once to disgorge my soul,
I was lifeless, voiceless, altogether a statue,
and I blamed all the gods, alas,
as I wept warm streams of many tears,   70
lamenting bitterly for my rightful spouse.
For whom? Ah, for the beautiful Charikles."

Τούτοις Χαρικλῆς ἀντεπεῖπε· 'σοὶ χάρις,
ὦ τοῦ μεγίστου τῶν θεῶν Διὸς γόνε,
75   τῷ Καλλιδήμου τὴν ἐπίφθονον σχέσιν
ἣν πρὸς Δροσίλλαν ἔσχεν ἠφανικότι
καὶ καθοδηγήσαντι τὸν Χαρικλέα
πρὸς τὸ γραὸς δόμημα τῆς Βαρυλλίδος.
Εἰ μὴ γὰρ ἐφθόνησεν ἡμῖν τοῦ πόθου,
80   οὐκ ἐκ θεῶν ἂν ἀντεπέσχε τὴν νόσον.'
Καὶ συγκεκυφὼς εἰς τὸν αὐτῆς αὐχένα
καὶ τρὶς φιλήσας, θεὶς ὑπ' αὐτὴν ἀγκάλην
τὰ τῶν γυναικῶν ἀντιπάσχειν ἠξίου
'ὁρᾷς' λέγων 'τὰ δένδρα' – δείξας δακτύλῳ –
85   'ὅσας νεοττῶν καλιὰς ὑπερφέρει·
ἐκεῖ τελεῖται στρουθίων πάντως γάμος·
παστὰς τὸ δένδρον ἐστί, νυμφὼν ὁ κλάδος,
κλίνην ἔχει δὲ τὰς ἑαυτοῦ φυλλάδας·
ναὶ καὶ τὸν ὑμέναιον ἐξᾴδει μέγα
90   τὰ πτηνὰ συρρέοντα τοῦ κήπου πέριξ.
Δός μοι, Δροσίλλα, καὶ σὺ τὸν σαυτῆς γάμον,
δι' ὃν διυπήνεγκα μυρίους πόνους,
δι' ὃν φυγήν, δούλωσιν, αἰχμαλωσίαν,
δι' ὃν στεναγμοὺς καὶ θαλάσσας δακρύων.
95   Ὦ φίλα δεσμὰ καὶ πλοκαὶ τῆς ἀγκάλης
καὶ δακτύλων ἕλιγμα καὶ ποδῶν στρέβλα.
Ἔγνων, ἐπέγνων, Ἄρες, ἐκ τῶν πραγμάτων,
ὡς οὐδ' ἂν αὐτὸς ἀπρεπῶς ἐδυσφόρεις,
ἁλοὺς σιδηρώμασιν, Ἡφαίστου πόνοις,
100   τῇ ποντογενεῖ συγκαθεύδων ἀσμένως.
Ἀλλ', ὦ φίλον πρόσφθεγμα, μὴ κώλυέ με.
Ἔρως, συνέργει συμπνέων τῇ παρθένῳ·
τὸν πτηνὸν οὐδεὶς φεύξεται πεζὸς τρέχων.
Ὦ φῶς ἐμὸν σύνθαλπε καὶ τὴν καρδίαν·
105   ἄχαρι τέρπει κάλλος, ἀλλ' οὐ κατέχει,
δελήτιον καθώσπερ ἀγκίστρου δίχα.
Ἥρα δέ σε βλέπουσα καὶ Παλλὰς κόρη
"γυμνούμεθα" προσεῖπον "ὡς πρὶν οὐκέτι·
ἀρκεῖ γὰρ ἡμῖν ποιμένος κρίσις μία."
110   Εἴθε ζέφυρος νῦν γενοίμην, παρθένε,
σὺ δ' εὐκραὲς βλέπουσα προσπνέοντά με,

Charikles replied to these things, "I give thanks to you,
son of Zeus, the greatest of the gods,
for destroying Kallidemos's   75
jealous attachment to Drosilla
and guiding Charikles
to the house of the old woman Maryllis,
for if Kallidemos had not grudged us our love,
the gods would not have made him sick in return."   80
        He bent forward toward her neck,
kissed her three times, and placing his arm beneath her,
asked to receive in turn the favors wives give.
"You see the trees," he said and pointed with his finger,
"how many nests of young birds they bear.   85
There the marriage of sparrows is consummated:
the tree is the wedding hall; the branch, the bridal chamber;
and the leaves, the marriage bed—
yes, and the birds flying around the garden
loudly sing out the wedding song.   90
You too, Drosilla, grant me your nuptials,
for which I endured countless sufferings,
flight, slavery, imprisonment,
groans, and seas of tears.
Oh beloved bonds, intertwined arms,   95
interlaced fingers, and interlocked feet!
I know, Ares, from your deeds,*
that not even you would be very distressed
if caught by iron chains, the works of Hephaestus,
when sleeping gladly with the seaborn goddess.   100
But, name that I love, don't thwart me!
Eros, assist me by breathing love into the maiden;
no one running on foot will escape the winged god.
Oh my light, warm also my heart;
ungracious beauty gives delight but doesn't hold,   105
like bait without a hook.
Hera and the maiden Pallas, on seeing you,*
said, 'We do not disrobe ourselves any more, as before,
for one judgment of a shepherd is enough for us.'
If only I were now the west wind, maiden,   110
and you, seeing me blowing gently upon you,

τὰ στέρνα γυμνώσασα προσλάβοις ἔσω.
Σὺ γοῦν, Σελήνη γλαυκοφεγγὴς ὀλβία,
ἄθρει ποδήγει φωταγώγει τὸν ξένον·
115   Ἐνδυμίων ἔφλεξε καὶ σὴν καρδίαν.
Ἔρροιεν ἄργυρός τε καὶ λαμπρὸς λίθος,
καὶ χρυσὸς αὐτὸς κατασκώπτων καρδίας·
φθείροιντο ταῦτα, πλοῦτος, ὄλβος μυρίος,
ὁ πρὸς Χρυσίλλας ἐγγυώμενος πάλαι·
120   σύ μοι τὰ πάντα ταῦτα, σῶφρον παρθένε.
Τὸ ξανθὸν αὐχεῖς· ἔρρε, χρυσίου βάρος·
ἔχεις τὸ λευκόν· χαῖρε, μαργάρων χάρις·
περιπλοκὴ σὴ κόσμος ἐστὶν αὐχένος,
ἐπὶ πτυχὶ σῶν χειλέων ἄνθραξ λίθος.
125   Ὁ σὸς δὲ πάντως οὐκ ἀκόσμητος γάμος·
ἀηδόνες γὰρ ἐγχορεύουσαι κύκλῳ
ᾄδουσιν, ἀντᾴδουσιν αἱ χελιδόνες.
Σὸς Ὑμέναιος ταῦτα· δός μοι τὸν γάμον.
Ὁ στρουθὸς οἶδε μῖξιν, οἶδε τὸν γάμον·
130   ἡμεῖς δὲ καὶ ποθοῦντες οὐ μιγνύμεθα;'
     Τοιαῦτα πολλὰ τῇ κόρῃ προσωμίλει·
ὁ γὰρ φιλῶν πᾶς τὴν ποθουμένην βλέπων
καὶ νοῦν πρὸς αὐτὴν ἐξανατείνων ὅλον
οὐδὲν τὰ λοιπὰ πάντα τοῦ βίου κρίνει.
135   Ἀλλ' ἡ Δροσίλλα τὸν καλὸν Χαρικλέα
καίτοι κρατοῦσα καὶ φιλοῦσα τὸν νέον
ἐδεξιοῦτο τῇ περιπλοκῇ μόνῃ
καὶ τῇ μελιχρότητι τῶν φιλημάτων.
Ἔφασκε καὶ γάρ· 'ὦ Χαρίκλεις, καρδία,
140   τοῦ συνδυασμοῦ τῆς Δροσίλλας οὐ τύχῃς.
Μὴ κάμνε, μὴ βίαζε, μὴ μάτην πόνει·
ἀσχημονεῖν γὰρ σωφρονοῦσαν οὐ θέμις.
Φιλῶ μὲν οὖν σε· πῶς γὰρ οὔ; Ποῖος λόγος;
Φιλῶ Χαρικλῆν καὶ ποθῶ πάντων πλέον·
145   πλὴν ὡς ἑταιρὶς οὐ προδῶ τὸ παρθένον
γνώμης τε χωρὶς μητροπατρῴου γένους.
Τῇ δὲ προνοίᾳ τῶν θεῶν θαρρῶν ἔσο·
μαρτύρομαι γὰρ οὐρανόν, γῆν, ἀστέρας,
ὡς οὐκ ἂν ἄλλοις ἐκδοθείην εἰς γάμον,
150   εἰ μὴ Χαρικλεῖ· πῶς γὰρ εἰκὸς ἐννόει.

would strip your breast naked and receive me within.
You, then, blessed Moon with your gleaming light,
look at the stranger, lead him, guide him with your light;
Endymion inflamed your heart too with passion.* 115
Away with silver and brilliant stones,
and gold itself, which mocks hearts;
let these things perish—the riches, the infinite wealth
that Chrysilla promised me long ago;
you are all these things to me, chaste maiden. 120
You boast of yellow hair—away, weight of gold.
You have white skin—farewell, grace of pearls.
The twining of your arms is an ornament for my neck,
and in the fold of your lips is a red ruby stone.
Your wedding is certainly not unadorned: 125
a choir of nightingales in a circle are singing,
and the swallows sing in response.
These things are your wedding song; grant me your nuptials!
The sparrow knows love-making and marriage;
but we, who love one another, do not make love?" 130
    He said many such things to the girl,
for every lover when he sees his beloved
and directs his whole mind toward her
judges that all the rest of his life is nothing.
But Drosilla, although holding the beautiful Charikles 135
and kissing the young man,
welcomed him with her embrace alone
and the sweetness of her kisses.
"Charikles, my heart," she said,
"you shall not obtain coition from Drosilla. 140
Don't complain, use force, or labor in vain,
for it's not right for a chaste woman to behave shamefully.
I love you! How could I not? For what reason?
I love and desire Charikles more than anything,
but I will not give up my virginity, as a prostitute does, 145
without thought for my family, my parents.
Have confidence in the foresight of the gods,
for I call the sky, earth, and stars to witness
that I should not be given in marriage to any others
except Charikles. How could I be? Think about it. 150

Πλὴν ἴσθι λοιπὸν ὡς ἀπ᾿ αὐτῆς ἑσπέρας,
καθ᾿ ἣν μένειν ἐνταῦθα μηνύων, ἄνερ,
ὄνειρος ἦλθέ σε, τριφίλητον κέαρ,
εὔελπίς εἰμι τῇ θεοῦ ξυνεργίᾳ,
155   ὡς πάτραν αὐτὴν ὄψομαι μετὰ χρόνον
καὶ Μυρτίωνα καὶ φίλην Ἡδυπνόην
καὶ συγχορεύσω ταῖς φίλαις συμπαρθένοις
εἰς βωμὸν αὐτὸν τοῦ θεοῦ Διονύσου,
πίω δὲ νᾶμα τοῦ καλοῦ Μελιρρόου
160   καί σοι, Χαρίκλεις, συμμετάσχω τοῦ γάμου.
Ἀμήχανον γάρ, οὐκ ἀνάσχωμαι κλύειν
μὴ σωφρονεῖν με μᾶλλον ἐν ξένοις τόποις.᾿
‘ Ὦ σώφρονος νοῦ καὶ καλῶν βουλευμάτων
τῶν σῶν᾿ Χαρικλῆς πρὸς Δροσίλλαν ἀντέφη·
165   ‘ὡς εὖ τὸ χρυσοῦν νῦν ἀπαγγέλλει στόμα·
ὡς εὖ κελαδεῖ γλῶσσά σοι τρισολβία.
Πλὴν ταῦτα χρηστά, ταῦτα σεμνά, παρθένε,
εἰ μὴ πρὸς αὐτὴν συγκινούμενοι Φθίαν
παρεμποδισθείημεν αὖθις ἐκ Τύχης.
170   Καταδρομὰς δὲ ληστρικὰς τὰς ἐν μέσῳ
καὶ βαρβάρων μάχαιραν ὠμοκαρδίων
καὶ τῆς θαλάσσης ἀγριώτατον στόμα
οὐκ ἀγνοεῖν ἔοικας· οὐ γὰρ λανθάνει
ἡμῖν τὰ συμπίπτοντα δεινὰ τῆς Τύχης·
175   τί γοῦν, ἄν – ἀλλ᾿ ἵλαθι, δυσμενὴς Τύχη,
καὶ στῆσον ὀψὲ τὴν καθ᾿ ἡμῶν μανίαν –
παρεμπεσεῖν μέλλωμεν αὖθις εἰς νέαν
πολύτροπον κάκωσιν αἰχμαλωσίας
ἢ καὶ διαζευχθῶμεν ἀλλήλων; Λέγε.᾿
180   ‘ Ἀλλ᾿, ὦ Χαρίκλεις᾿ ἀντέλεξεν ἡ κόρη,
‘οὐ τὴν Δροσίλλαν, ἀλλ᾿ Ἔρωτος ἀγρίου
ἔοικας ἔργον τερπνὸν ἐνστερνικέναι.᾿
Οὕτως ἐκείνων συλλαλούντων τῶν δύο
Κλέανδρος ἦλθε τρίτος ἠρέμα στένων
185   ‘ὤμοι᾿ λέγων, ‘τέθνηκεν ἡ Καλλιγόνη.᾿
Καί ‘τίς, φίλε Κλέανδρε, τοῦτο μηνύει
ἄγγελμα πικρόν;᾿ ἀντέφησαν οἱ νέοι.
‘Γνάθων τις ἐλθὼν ἐμπορικὸς Βαρζόθεν᾿
ἀντεῖπεν ὁ Κλέανδρος· ἀλλ᾿ ‘ὦ τοῦ πάθους᾿

Know, then, that since that very evening
when a dream came revealing that you,
my husband, my thrice-loved heart, were staying here,
I have trusted in god's help
that I shall see my fatherland and Myrtion   155
and dear Hedypnoe after a time,
join in the dance with my dear fellow-maidens
at the altar of the god Dionysus,
drink the stream of the beautiful Melirroas,
and with you, Charikles, be united in marriage.   160
It is impossible—I will not endure it to be said that
I wasn't chaste, especially in foreign lands!"
        "Oh, what a prudent mind and what noble counsels,"
Charikles replied to Drosilla.
"How well your golden mouth now speaks;   165
how well your thrice-blessed tongue resounds.
But these resolutions would be good, would be fine, maiden,
unless, while we are moving together toward Phthia,
Fortune should impede us again.
You're not ignorant, I think, of pirate raids   170
that intervene, the sword
of cruel barbarians, the savage
mouth of the sea, for the terrible accidents
of fortune are not unknown to us.
What, then, if—but be gracious, cruel Fortune,   175
and stop at last your fury against us!—
we fall again into a new,
diverse misfortune of captivity
or even become separated from one another? Tell me."
        "But, Charikles," replied the girl,   180
"you seem to cherish in your heart
not Drosilla, but the delightful work of wild Eros."
        While the two of them were thus conversing,
Kleandros came, making a third, and groaning softly
said, "Alas, Kalligone is dead."   185
        And the young persons replied, "Who,
dear Kleandros, told you this bitter news?"
        "Gnathon, a merchant here from Barzon,"
answered Kleandros. "Oh, what a calamity!"

190	ἔφησαν αὖθις, δάκρυον πεπομφότες.
	Καὶ γοῦν μονῳδεῖν ὁ Κλέανδρος ἠργμένος
	συνδακρύοντας αὖθις εἶχε τοὺς δύο.
	Ἔφασκε τοίνυν ἐν στεναγμῷ μυρίῳ
	τοιαῦτα καὶ πάνοικτρα καὶ τυχὸν τόσα,
195	ὡς οὐκ ἐώσης τῆς βαθείας ἑσπέρας
	μακρὰν πρὸς αὐτὴν ἐξερεῖν τραγῳδίαν·
	‘ ἰαταταιὰξ τῆς παρούσης ἡμέρας,
	καθ᾿ ἣν ἐγώ, δείλαιος ἀνθρώπων μόνος,
	τὴν σὴν τελευτὴν μανθάνω, Καλλιγόνη.
200	Νοσφίζομαί σου τῆς συνοικίας πάλαι,
	Πάρθων φανείς, φεῦ, δοῦλος ἀγκυλοφρόνων·
	εἶχον δὲ μικρὰν ἐλπίδα ζωοτρόφον,
	ὡς χεῖρας ἀνδρῶν ἐκφυγοῦσαν βαρβάρων
	σχοίην ποτ᾿ αὖθις κατιδεῖν σε, παρθένε.
205	Καὶ νῦν δὲ μᾶλλον σωφρόνως ἠγαλλόμην,
	ἐλεύθερον φῶς, ὦ θεοί, λαχὼν βλέπειν·
	εὑρεῖν γὰρ εἰς νοῦν εἶχον ἀνθυποστρέφων.
	Καὶ νῦν ἐμὸν φῶς ἐσκοτίσθης ἀθρόον.
	Καὶ πῶς ὁδεύσω; Ποῦ καταντήσω μόνος;
210	Οὐκ ὤφελον, γῆ, πῦρ, ὕδωρ, ἀήρ, νέφος
	καὶ πανδεχὲς σφαίρωμα καὶ φῶς ἡλίου,
	ἐκ γαστρὸς ἐλθεῖν καὶ προελθεῖν εἰς βίον.
	Εἰ δ᾿ ἦν ἀνάγκη πᾶσα φῦναι μητρόθεν,
	ἐχρῆν δι᾿ αὐτὰς τὰς ἀποφράδας τύχας
215	διαφθαρῆναι καὶ λυθῆναι πρὸς τέφραν,
	πρὶν ἂν λαβεῖν αἴσθησιν ἐντελεστέραν
	καὶ πρὶν ἰδεῖν με τὴν παροῦσαν ἡμέραν.
	Αἲ αἴ, στένω θνήσκουσαν ὡς τρυγουμένην,
	ὄμφακα βότρυν ἢ παρήμερον στάχυν
220	ἐν ἀγρῷ τοῦ Χάρωνος ἐχθρῷ δακτύλῳ.
	Πῶς ὑπενέγκω τὴν ἀπευκταίαν τύχην,
	ἄλλης ἐπ᾿ ἄλλης συμφορᾶς νεωτέρας
	καταστρεφούσης τὴν κεφαλήν μου κύκλῳ;
	Χεῖρας μὲν ἐξέφυγες ἀνδρῶν βαρβάρων,
225	οὐ μὴν δὲ καὶ Χάρωνος ἀνθρωποκτόνου.
	Ὄλωλεν ἐλπὶς μέχρι νῦν τρέφουσά με,
	ὄλωλε καὶ Κλέανδρος ὡς Καλλιγόνη.
	Ὦ δυστυχὲς σὺ Βάρζον, ἀθλία πόλις,

they replied with tears. 190
Then Kleandros started to raise a lament
and had the two of them weeping with him in turn.
He spoke, with much groaning,
such pitiable words as follows (and perhaps only these,
since the late evening did not permit 195
him to give a long tragic speech):
"Alas for this day
on which I, most wretched of men, alone,
have learned of your death, Kalligone.
I have long been separated from your company, 200
having become a slave, alas, of the treacherous Parthians,
but I had a great hope sustaining my life,
that I should escape the hands of the barbarians
and be able to see you again one day, maiden.
And just now I was rejoicing with more reason, 205
having obtained freedom's light (oh gods!) to look upon,
for I had in mind to find you when I returned.
Now, my light, you have become darkened all at once.
How shall I travel? Where shall I go, alone?
Oh earth, fire, water, air, cloud, 210
all-receiving sphere, and light of the sun,
if only I'd not left the womb and come to life!
But if it was necessary that I be born from a mother,
I should have been destroyed through unspeakable misfortunes
and dissolved to ashes 215
before I gained full perception
and before I saw this day.
Ah, I bewail the maiden dying like an unripe
bunch of grapes or an immature ear of corn,
gathered in a field by Charon's hateful hand. 220
How shall I endure this terrible fate,
when one new misfortune after another
encircles my head?*
You escaped the hands of barbarians
but not those of Charon, killer of men. 225
The hope that sustained me until now has perished;
Kleandros too has perished, like Kalligone.
Oh, unlucky Barzon, wretched city

καθ᾽ ἣν διεζεύχθημεν ἀλλήλων βίᾳ.
230   Ὡς κρεῖττον ἦν μοι συνθανεῖν τῇ παρθένῳ,
ἢ ζῆν ἀμυδρῶς καὶ στενάζειν ἐκ βάθους,
οἰκεῖν δὲ τὴν γῆν ὡς σκιὰ κινουμένη.
Τὰ πάντα φροῦδα τῶν παλαιῶν ἐλπίδων.
Οὐδὲ προσεῖπον ἐν πνοαῖς ταῖς ἐσχάταις,
235   Καλλιγόνη, θάμβημα, σεμνὴ παρθένος.
Ὦ θαῦμα μακρὸν τὰς ἐμὰς ἔχει φρένας,
πῶς αἱ τοσαῦται συμφορῶν καταιγίδες
εἰς οἶκτον οὐκ ἔκαμψαν οὐδ᾽ εὐσπλαγχνίαν
τήν, φεῦ, καθ᾽ ἡμῶν δυσμεναίνουσαν Τύχην.᾽
240   Οὕτως ἐποιμώζοντα τὸν νεανίαν
συνδακρύοντες οἱ νέοι παρηγόρουν
ἐξ ἱλαρῶν ἴυγγος ἡδέων λόγων.
Ὡς δ᾽ ἦλθεν ἡ νὺξ συγκρυβείσης ἡμέρας,
ὁμοῦ συνῆλθον εἰς τὸ τῆς Βαρυλλίδος
245   οἴκημα καὶ τράπεζαν ἡτοιμασμένην
εὑρόντες ἐκλίθησαν· ἡ δὲ γραῦς πάλιν
τροφὰς ἐτίθει καὶ τὸν οἶνον εἰς μέσον.
Ἦν οὖν παρ᾽ αὐτοῖς ὁ ξένος συνιζάνων·
διπλῶν γὰρ ἦλθεν ἄγγελος μηνυμάτων,
250   πικροῦ Κλεάνδρῳ καὶ Χαρικλεῖ γλυκέος.
Καὶ χεῖρας εἰς τὸ δεῖπνον ἐμβεβληκότες
τὴν γραῦν κατηνάγκαζον ἐγκλῖναι γόνυ·
αὐτὴ δὲ πρὸς τὸν λύχνον ἀσχολουμένη,
μέριμναν εἰς ὕφαψιν εὖ ποιουμένη
255   ἔφησε· ᾽τέκνα, σὺ Κλέανδρε καὶ Γνάθων
καὶ σὺ Χαρίκλεις καὶ Δροσίλλα παρθένε,
οἱ τέσσαρες χαίροντες ἑστιᾶσθέ μοι -
φιλῶ γὰρ ὑμᾶς, ὡς ἐκεῖνον τὸν Χράμον,
ὃν υἱὸν εἶχον, ὃς προήχθη μου μόνος,
260   οὗ μικρὸν ἀπήλαυσα τῶν χαρισμάτων,
καὶ μακρόν εἰμι δυσφορουμένη χρόνον -᾽
οἱ τέσσαρες χαίροντες ἑστιᾶσθέ μοι,
οἱ τέσσαρες τὸν οἶνον ἐκροφεῖτέ μοι·
τροφὴν ἐγὼ γὰρ τὴν ὑμῶν ἔχω θέαν.᾽
265   Ὡς δὲ Δροσίλλαν καὶ Χαρικλῆν ὁ Γνάθων
τεραστικῶς ἤκουσεν ἐκ Βαρυλλίδος,
ὥρμησεν εἰπεῖν καὶ συνεστάλη πάλιν·

in which we were forcibly separated from one another.
How much better it would have been for me
to have died with the maiden   230
than to live in darkness, groaning from deep within,
and inhabit the earth like a moving shadow.
All of my old hopes are gone.
I didn't even salute you at the time of your last breath,
Kalligone, wonder of my life, noble maiden.   235
Oh, a great astonishment grips my mind
that so many storms of adversities
did not move Fortune to pity or even compassion,
Fortune, who, alas, was hostile against us!"
       The young people wept with Kleandros   240
as he lamented thus, and consoled him
with the charm of kind, sweet words.
When night came and day had set,
they went together to Maryllis's house
and, finding a table prepared,   245
they reclined, and the old woman again
placed food and wine out for them.
There was, then, a stranger sitting beside them,
for a messenger had come with two pieces of news,
bitter for Kleandros, sweet for Charikles.   250
They reached out their hands to dinner
and tried to coerce the old woman to recline with them,
but she, occupied with the lamp
and thinking about lighting it,
said, "Children—you, Kleandros and Gnathon,   255
and you, Charikles and the maiden Drosilla—
you four rejoice and feast for me,
for I love you as I loved that Chramos,
who was my only son and was taken from me,
whose gifts I enjoyed but a brief moment,   260
while for a long time I've been miserable.
You four rejoice and feast for me;
you four drink down wine for me;
the sight of you is food enough for me."
       When Gnathon heard the names   265
Drosilla and Charikles from Maryllis, he marveled,
started to speak, and broke off again.

ἀλλὰ πρὸς αὐτοὺς ἐντρανέστερον βλέπων
καὶ γνοὺς ἐναργῶς ἐν φιλαλλήλῳ σχέσει
270   αὐτοὺς ἐκείνους τυγχάνειν τοὺς φυγάδας
ἐνθουσιωδῶς εἶπεν ἐν θυμηδίᾳ·
'ὡς ἀγαθή, Ζεῦ καὶ θεοί, νῦν ἡμέρα.
Εἰληφέναι γοῦν ἐκ δυοῖν ἀνδρῶν ἔχω
πάντως μεγίστας τῆς χαρᾶς τὰς ἐγγύας.
275   Ὦ χαῖρε, Φράτωρ, ἀλλὰ καὶ σὺ Μυρτίων·
τοὺς παῖδας ὑμῶν ζῶντας ἀντιμηνύσω.'
'Μεμιγμένον μέλιτι σόν, Γνάθων, στόμα,'
εἰπόντες ἠρώτησαν οὗτοι τὸν ξένον
'ποῦ δὲ Φράτωρ πάρεστι καὶ ποῦ Μυρτίων
280   καὶ πῶς ἐκείνων παῖδας ἡμᾶς τοὺς δύο
εἶναι διέγνως ἀντιφάσκοις ἡδέως.'
' Ἐγὼ διδάξω τοὺς διηπορηκότας'
ἔφησεν αὐτοῖς ὁ Γνάθων συνεσθίων·
'αὐτοὶ γὰρ ἄνδρες, οὓς δεδήλωκα, ξένοι,
285   οὓς εἶδον, οἷς συνῆλθον εἰς ὁμιλίαν,
πάλαι μετηνέχθησαν εἰς Βάρζον πόλιν,
πεμφθέντες, ὡς ἔφασκον, ἐξ ὀνειράτων,
βαρὺν μὲν ὄγκον εἰσφέροντες χρυσίου
ποιούμενοι δὲ τῆς πολίχνης ἐν μέσῳ
290   πολὺν Δροσίλλας καὶ Χαρικλέος λόγον·
σφοδρῶς δ' ἐδυσχέραινον οἱ γηραλέοι,
λέγοντες αὐτοὺς τὸν Διὸς θεοῦ γόνον
ἀπὸ Φθίας εἰς Βάρζον ἀπεσταλκέναι,
καὶ τοὺς ἑαυτῶν παῖδας ἐξευρηκέναι.
295   Ὡς γοῦν ἐφευρεῖν εἶχον ὑμᾶς οὐδέπω,
"ἡμεῖς μέν" εἶπον "- ποῦ γὰρ ἄν τις ἐκδράμοι;
Καὶ ποῦ πλανηθῇ; Ποῦ δ' ἐκείνους συλλάβῃ; -
μενοῦμεν ὧδε τῷ θεῷ πεπεισμένοι·
ἴσως καταλάβοιεν ὀψὲ τὴν πόλιν.
300   Ὁ καθοδηγήσας γὰρ ἡμᾶς ἐνθάδε,
ἐκεῖνος αὐτοὺς ἐκδραμεῖν ἀναγκάσει,
καὶ λῆξιν ὀψὲ τῆς πλάνης εὑρηκέναι.
Σὺ δ', ὦ φίλων ἄριστε, Βαρζίτα Γνάθων"
- εἶδον γὰρ ὡς ἔσαττον αὐτὰς τὰς ὄνους,
305   τὸ χωρίον φθάσαι δὲ κατηπειγόμην -
"ἔννοιαν αὐτῶν τῶν πλανωμένων ἔχε,

But looking at them more keenly
and recognizing clearly by their display of mutual love
that they were themselves those fugitives, 270
he spoke with happy excitement:
"What a good day this is, Zeus and the gods!
I am able to obtain, then, from two men
the richest rewards for their joy.
Rejoice, Phrator, and you too, Myrtion; 275
I shall announce to you that your children are alive."
        "Your mouth, Gnathon, is coated with honey,"
they said, and then questioned the stranger,
"Where is Phrator? Where is Myrtion?
And how did you know that we are 280
their children? Please answer!"
        "I will teach you what you don't know,"
Gnathon said to them as he ate,
"for those men whom I indicated,
strangers whom I saw, with whom I conversed, 285
had been transported long ago to the city of Barzon,
sent, they said, by dreams.
They carried with them a heavy weight of gold
and spoke much, in the midst of town,
about Drosilla and Charikles. 290
The old men were very upset,
saying that the son of the god Zeus
had sent them from Phthia to Barzon
to seek their children there.
When they could find you nowhere, 295
they said, 'We shall remain here,
in obedience to the god—for where should we run from here?
Where should we roam? Where should we overtake them?
Perhaps at length they will arrive at this city,
for the one who guided us here 300
will compel them to come quickly
and make an end at last of their wandering.
But you, best of friends, Gnathon of Barzon'—
for they saw that I was loading my asses
and hastening to reach the village— 305
'take thought for our wandering children,

εἴ πως ἐφευρεῖν σὺν θεοῖς κατισχύσῃς·
καὶ μηνύσας μνᾶς χρυσίου λάβῃς δέκα".
Καὶ νῦν ὁμαρτήσασα χρηστή τις τύχη
310   ὑμῖν ἐπεγνώρισεν, ὡς ὁρᾶτέ, μοι.'
      'Καλλιγόνη δὲ καλλίμορφος παρθένος
τέθνηκεν· αἲ αἲ τῆς ἀπανθρώπου Τύχης·
Κλέανδρος εἰπὼν τὸν πανύστατον λόγον
καὶ τὴν πνοὴν ἀφῆκεν ἅμα τῷ λόγῳ.
315   Σφάττειν γὰρ οἶδεν ὑπὲρ εὔθηκτον ξίφος
ὀξεῖα συμπεσοῦσα λύπη πολλάκις.
Οὕτω, Δροσίλλας καὶ Χαρικλέος μέσον
οὐκ ἠμέλησε δυσμένεια τῆς Τύχης
πολὺν φορυτὸν συμφορῶν συνεισφέρειν
320   καὶ λυπρὰ χρηστοῖς ἐμπαθῶς συμμιγνύειν.

BIΒΛΙΟΝ ΕΝΑΤΟΝ

      Ἤδη μὲν ὄρθρος καὶ τὸ φῶς τῆς ἡμέρας
ηὔγαζε λαμπρῶς πανταχοῦ γῆς ἐξ ἕω·
σφοδρῶς δὲ δακρύσαντες, ὡς φίλοις ἔθος,
τὸ σῶμα συγκαίουσιν Ἑλλήνων νόμῳ,
5   χοὰς ἐπισπείσαντες ἐξ ὠπτημένων
κρεῶν συνάμφω καὶ ῥοὸς μελικράτου.
Ἐκεῖ συνῆλθε πᾶς νομεύς, πᾶς ἀγρότης,
πᾶς συμπαθὴς ἄνθρωπος εἰς ξένου τάφον,
καὶ τῶν γυναικῶν πᾶσα τληπαθεστέρα,
10   μεθ᾽ ὧν Βαρυλλὶς καὶ προῆρχε τοῦ γόου.
Ἐκεῖνον ἐθρήνησε καὶ δρῦς καὶ πέτρα
καὶ κοιλάδων ῥοῦς καὶ βαθύσκιοι νάπαι·
καὶ γὰρ ἱκανὸς ἦν Κλέανδρος τῷ τότε
κάμψαι πρὸς οἶκτον καὶ πετρῶν σκληρὸν γένος.
15   Ἡ δὲ Δροσίλλα, καίπερ οὖσα παρθένος,
πασῶν γυναικῶν μεῖζον ἐθρήνει τότε.
Ὡς γὰρ θαλάσσης κυματωθείσης νότῳ
ἡ κυμάτων σύρροια κυλινδουμένη
ναῦν συσχεθεῖσαν τῇ φορᾷ περιτρέπει,
20   κἂν εὔτροπίς τίς ἐστιν εὖ δ᾽ ἔχει τέχνης,
ἄλλου μετ᾽ ἄλλο συμφυῶς γεννωμένου,

if somehow, with the gods' help, you may find them,
and when you inform us, you shall receive ten minas of gold.'
And now a good fortune has accompanied you
and made you known to me, as you see."   310
    "But Kalligone, the beautiful maiden,
is dead. Ah, what a savage Fortune!"
These were Kleandros's last words,
and with these words he emitted his last breath,
for a sharp grief that has fallen upon one
often has a power to kill beyond that of a sharpened sword.   315
Thus, in the midst of Drosilla and Charikles' reunion
hostile Fortune did not neglect
to bring a great heap of misfortunes
and avidly mix painful things with the good.   320

BOOK NINE

    It was now dawn and the light of day
was illuminating brightly from the east all parts of the earth.
Weeping copiously, as friends are inclined to do,
they burnt up the body in the Greek manner,
both of them pouring libations   5
from roasted meat and honey drink.
There for the stranger's funeral, came every herdsman,*
every peasant, every man of compassion,
and every woman prone to commiserate,
among whom Maryllis began the lamentation first.   10
For Kleandros the oak lamented, and the rock,
and streams in deep valleys, and shady glens,
for truly Kleandros could make
even the hard race of rocks feel pity.
Drosilla, although she was a maiden,   15
was lamenting then more loudly than all the women,
for just as, when the south wind disturbs the sea,
the rolling confluence of waves
capsizes a ship overcome by the motion,
even if the ship has a good keel and skilled sailors,   20
for waves come up one after another,

οἷς οὐδαμῶς ἔλλειμμα καὶ πλήθους μέτρον,
εἰ μή τίς ἐστιν ἐκ Κοροίβου μαινόλου
ὅμοιος υἱὸς καὶ πατρῴζει τὰς φρένας,
25   πειρώμενος μάταιος εἰς οὐδὲν δέον
φορὰς ἀμέτρους ἐκμετρῆσαι κυμάτων
ὅτε πρὸς ὥραν τῆς ὀπωροφθισίας
ὁ μὲν Ποσειδῶν ἐξεγείρει τὸν νότον,
νότος δὲ τὴν θάλασσαν ἀντικορθύει,
30   θάλασσα δ᾽ αὐτὴ συνταράσσει τὰ σκάφη,
σκάφη δὲ πάντως τὰς πλεόντων καρδίας,
οὕτως ἀμέτρως ἐκχυθεῖσαι μυρίαι
ζάλαι ζεουσῶν συμφορῶν ἀνενδότων
τὰς τῆς Δροσίλλας ἀντεπέκλυζον φρένας,
35   ὡς ναῦν ἀνερμάτιστον ἰσχυρὸς κλύδων.
Ἔφασκεν οὖν κλαίουσα τὸν νεανίαν·
    ῾ὤμοι, Κλέανδρε, τίς βριαρόχειρ δαίμων,
δαίμων ἀλάστωρ εἰς λυπρὰς ὥρας φέρων,
βαρὺς καθ᾽ ἡμῶν ἐμπεσὼν καὶ μηνίσας;
40   Ἐκ συμφορῶν γὰρ συμφορὰς ἄλλας ἄγει,
ἀεὶ δὲ τὴν γραῦν ἡ νέα νικᾶν θέλει.
Τί ταῦτα, Τύχη; Ποῖ ποτε σταῖεν τάδε;
Τίς τῶν καθ᾽ ἡμᾶς λῆξίς ἐστι δακρύων;
Ὦ γλυκίων Κλέανδρε συμφυλακίτα,
45   σύνδουλε, συνέριθε, συννεανία,
συναιχμάλωτε, συνελεύθερε, ξένε,
οἴχῃ πρὸ ὥρας χλωρὸς ὡραῖος στάχυς,
οὐδὲ προσειπὼν τὸν σεαυτοῦ πατέρα
ἐν τῷ παραπνεῖν τὰς πνοὰς τὰς ἐσχάτας.
50   Ὦ κλὼν φανεὶς ὄρπηκος ἁδροῦ Λεσβίου,
ἔφυς μὲν ἁδρὸς καὶ καλὸς καὶ γλυκίων,
μικρὸν δὲ μικρὸν ὡς ἀπὸ φλογὸς ξένης
ἐπὶ φθορὰν νένευκας ἐξηραμμένος.
Χθὲς ἦς παρ᾽ ἡμῖν, ἀλλὰ νῦν ἐν νερτέροις·
55   χθὲς ἦς λαλῶν μοι, σήμερον δὲ μὴ κλύων·
συνωμίλεις χθὲς εἰς ἐμὴν εὐθυμίαν,
ἄφωνος εἶ νῦν εἰς ἐμὴν ἀθυμίαν·
οὐκ ἔστι δεινῶν τῶν καθ᾽ ἡμᾶς τις κόρος.
Καὶ ποῦ προβῶμεν τῶν κακῶν περαιτέρω;
60   Ὦ δυστυχὲς σύ, δυστυχὲς Καλλιστία.

with no intermission or limit to their number—
unless there is some raving fool's son,
similar to his father in wits,
who tries in vain, for no needful purpose,   25
to measure the countless onslaughts of waves
when towards the end of the autumn season
Poseidon brings on the south wind,*
and the south wind lifts up the sea,
and the sea troubles the boats,   30
and the boats the hearts of those sailing—
thus without measure, countless storms
of seething, relentless misfortunes poured forth
and deluged Drosilla's heart,
just as a strong wave swamps a ship without ballast.   35
    Then, weeping for the young man, she said,
"Oh, Kleandros, who is that strong-handed demon,
that spiteful spirit bringing painful times,
attacking us with violence and anger?
He brings misfortune after misfortune,   40
and the new always exceeds the old.
Why are these things happening, Fortune? Where will they stop?
What end is there for our tears?
O sweet Kleandros, comrade in captivity
and in slavery, fellow-worker, agemate,   45
companion in prison and in freedom, stranger,
you are gone before your time, a beautiful unripe ear of corn,
without even having saluted your own father
as you yielded your last breath.
O branch of a sturdy sapling of Lesbos,   50
you are strong, beautiful, and sweet,
but too soon, as if scorched by a strange flame,
you've succumbed to death.
Yesterday you were with us; now you are among the dead.
Yesterday you were talking with me; today you do not hear.   55
Yesterday your conversation cheered me;
now your silence makes me lose heart.
There's no end of terrible things for us—
where are we to escape from evils?
O unlucky Kallistias,   60

Καὶ γὰρ τὸ τέκνον, ὁ Κλέανδρος, ὁ ξένος,
ὡς πτηνὸν ἐκπτὰς πατρικῆς ἐξ ἀγκάλης
κεῖται πεσὼν οἴκτιστος ἐν ξένοις τόποις.
Ὦ ποῦ τρέφεις, δείλαιε, χρηστὰς ἐλπίδας
65   εὑρεῖν τὸν υἱὸν καὶ λαβεῖν ἀπὸ πλάνης
καὶ πῦρ ἀνάψαι καὶ δᾷδας γαμηλίους
στῆσαί τε λαμπρὰ καὶ χοροὺς καὶ παστάδα
καὶ συγχαρῆναι τῇ Κυδίππῃ τὰς φίλας
τῷ τὸν καλὸν Κλέανδρον ἀπειληφέναι;
70   Πλὴν ὀψὲ μαθὼν τὴν κατὰ φρένας πλάνην
καὶ τοῦ λογισμοῦ τὴν ἀσύστατον ῥύμην
καὶ γνοὺς τὸν υἱὸν συμπεσεῖν ἐπὶ ξένης
– διδάσκαλος γὰρ ὁ χρόνος τῶν πραγμάτων –
καὶ πολλὰ κλαύσεις καὶ στενάξεις ἐκ βάθους,
75   ῥαίνειν πολύρρουν ὄμβρον ἐκ τῶν ὀμμάτων
ὑπὲρ τὸ πρὶν δάκρυον ἠναγκασμένος·
πρῴην γὰρ ἴσως ἐλπὶς εἶρξε μετρία
τὴν τῶν ῥεόντων δακρύων ἀμετρίαν·
μικρὸν δὲ μικρὸν καὶ τακήσῃ τῷ χρόνῳ
80   ἄνθραξι λύπης, ὡς χιὼν δι᾽ ἡλίου.
Αἲ αἴ, συναιχμάλωτε, συνοδοιπόρε,
εἰ γοῦν Χαρικλῆς ἐξ ἀποφράδος τύχης
ἐμὲ Δροσίλλαν τληπαθῆ τρισαθλίαν
ἀφαρπαγῆναι κινδυνεύσοι καὶ πάλιν,
85   τίς, τίς νεμεῖ κούφισμα τῆς λύπης βάρους;
Ποῖος κατασταίη τις εἰς παῦλαν πόνων
λόγῳ μελιχρῷ καὶ τρόπῳ σωτηρίῳ;
Ἡ ψυχαγωγία γάρ, ἡ σωτηρία,
ἡ πᾶσα παράκλησις ἐξόλωλέ μοι.
90   Τίς αὔρα λεπτὴ καὶ δρόσος φλογοφθόρος
ἀκάματον πῦρ καὶ διηρμένην φλόγα
ἐμῶν παθῶν σβέσαιεν οὐ κοιμωμένων;
Στάσις δὲ τίς γένοιτο καὶ λῆξις πόνων·
καὶ νήνεμος νοῦς ἐκ παθῶν τρικυμίας;
95   Ὦ τίς, Χαρίκλεις, παραμυθήσαιτό σε,
εἴ τι Δροσίλλα τῶν ἀπευκταίων πάθοι;
Βαθεῖα γὰρ νὺξ καὶ βαθέσπερος γνόφος
καὶ χοῦς ἀμυδρός – ὦ κακῶν συγκυρμάτων –
ἔχουσι, φεῦ φεῦ, τὴν Κλεάνδρου καρδίαν.

your son Kleandros, the wanderer,
having flown, like a bird, from his father's arms,
lies dead, most pitiably, in a foreign land.
How do you maintain happy hopes, wretched man,
that you may find your son, welcome him from his wandering,   65
light the fire and the wedding torches,
and organize a splendid ceremony, with choruses and bridal chamber;
and that Kydippe's friends may rejoice with her
for having recovered the beautiful Kleandros?
But in the end, you'll learn of the wandering of his mind   70
and the chaotic impulse of his thought,
you'll learn that your son has died in a foreign land,
for time is a teacher of all things,
and you'll lament greatly and groan from deep within,
compelled to shed streams of tears   75
from your eyes (far beyond what flowed before)—
for earlier, perhaps, a modest hope blocked
the infinite streams of tears,
but soon you'll be dissolved
by coals of grief, like snow by the sun.   80
Ah, companion in prison, fellow traveler,
if Charikles, then, by unlucky fortune,
may possibly be snatched away yet again
from me, miserable Drosilla, thrice-wretched,
who will relieve the weight of my pain?   85
Who will come to end my sufferings
with honey-sweet word and healing manner?
Comfort, salvation,
all consolation has perished for me.
What light breeze and flame-destroying dew   90
could quench the tireless fire and blazing flame
of my sufferings, which don't sleep?
What rest, what end of sufferings, what calm mind
could there be after this third wave of troubles?
Oh, Charikles, who would console you   95
if Drosilla should suffer some terrible misfortune?
Profound night, deep evening's gloom,
and dark earth—oh, evil fortune!—
hold fast Kleandros's heart, alas.

100 Ὦ πῶς κλείσεις τὴν Κυδίππην μητέρα
ἐν ἀλλοδαπῇ δυστυχῶς τεθαμμένος
καὶ τοῖς στεφάνοις εὐφρανεῖς καὶ δοξάσεις
τὴν ὀσφὺν ἐξ ἧς εἰς τὸ φῶς ἦλθες τόδε,
σχοίη δέ σε σκίπωνα καὶ βακτηρίαν
105 εἰς γῆρας ἐλθὼν ὁ σπορεὺς ἀπὸ χρόνων;
Ὦ φῶς θρυαλλὶς χαρμονῆς, σέλας γένους,
ἔσβης, ἐθραύσθης, ἐφθάρης, ἀπεκρύβης.᾿
    Οὕτω Δροσίλλας κωκυούσης τὸν ξένον
'τῆς μὲν περιττῆς τῷ νεκρῷ τύρβης ἅλις
110 καὶ τῶν ἀμέτρων δακρύων καὶ τοῦ γόου᾿
ἔφη μέσον στὰς ἔμπορος Γνάθων ξένος˙
'εἰ γὰρ μεταξὺ χαρμονῆς παρεμπέσοι
λυπρὸν τυχηρὸν δάκνον ἀλγῦνον φρένας,
τὸν εὖ φρονοῦντα τῇ χαρᾷ χρὴ διδόναι˙
115 ὅταν μὲν οὖν ἄκρατόν ἐστι τὸ θλίβον,
οὐ μεμπτὸν εἴ τις καὶ κατ᾿ ἄκρας δακρύει˙
εἰ συμμιγῇ δὲ χρηστὰ ταῖς ἀλγηδόσι,
τὸ κρεῖττον, οἶμαι, τῆς τύχης εἰσελκτέον˙
ὑπερφερῇ γὰρ δυστυχῆ τῶν κρειττόνων,
120 πλείω τὰ λυπρὰ τῶν καλῶν τῶν ἐν βίῳ.
Τῶν θλίψεων γοῦν εὖ καταφρονητέον,
εἴ πού τι χρηστὸν ἐν μέσῳ παρεμπέσοι
ἀπροσδοκήτως ἐκ τύχης παρηγμένον˙
οὐ γὰρ τοσοῦτον αἱ κατ᾿ ἐλπίδας τύχαι
125 τοῖς εὖ παθεῖν μέλλουσιν ἀνθρώποις ἄρα
τὸ τερπνὸν εἰσφέρουσιν ἄν, ὡς εἰδόσιν,
αὐτοῖς ἐκείνοις προσδοκῶνται πρὸ χρόνων,
ὅσον τὸ συμβὰν ἀγαθὸν παρ᾿ ἐλπίδα
ψυχὴν διογκοῖ καὶ πλατύνει καρδίαν,
130 καὶ πάντα λυπρὰ τὰ προσυμβεβηκότα
ἐκ τῶν νοητῶν ἐξελαύνει πυθμένων
καὶ τῶν ἀδήλων τοῦ λογισμοῦ χωρίων
καὶ τοὺς παθόντας εἰς ἀνάπλασιν φέρει,
τῶν ἀλγυνόντων ἐξαλεῖφον τοὺς τύπους
135 εἰς εἶδος ἄλλο καὶ κατάστασιν νέαν,
καὶ χρωματουργεῖ τοῦ προσώπου τὴν θέαν
εἰς ἐντελῆ μόρφωσιν ὡραϊσμένην.
Πλὴν λῆξον ὀψὲ τῶν μακρῶν ὀδυρμάτων

How will you glorify your mother, Kydippe,   100
now that you've been buried, unfortunately, in a foreign land,
how will you cheer her with wreaths and extol
the loins from which you came into this light,
and how will your father have you as a staff and cane
when he's come to old age years from now?   105
O torch, candle of joy, bright light of the family,
you've been quenched, broken, destroyed, and hidden away."
        While Drosilla thus wailed over the stranger,
the merchant Gnathon stood in the middle and said,
"Enough of excessive lamentation for the dead   110
and endless tears and groaning!
If in the midst of joy something painful happens
that stings and grieves the mind,
still the wise man should give himself to joy.
But when distress is unmixed,   115
a man cannot be faulted if he weeps without restraint.
Yet if good things are mixed with sufferings,
one must seize the better part of fortune, I believe,
for misfortunes surpass happier moments,
and adversities outnumber good things in life.   120
One must think lightly of afflictions, then,
if something good should slip in the midst—
an unexpected gift of fortune.
Desired fortunes do not bring
so great a joy to men   125
destined to prosper, if they know
and expect them beforehand,
as the good that happens unexpectedly,
for it swells the spirit, expands the heart,
drives out from the depths of thought   130
and the dark recesses of the mind
all the painful things that happened before,
restores those who have suffered
by wiping out the traces of afflictions
to give another appearance and a new condition,   135
and colors the complexion of the face
to a perfect semblance of beauty.
But cease at last from your great wailings

ἄγουσα σαυτὴν εἰς ἀνάκτησιν, κόρη.
140   Ἄφες, Χαρίκλεις, καὶ σὺ τὴν θρηνῳδίαν·
γενοῦ σεαυτοῦ, μή τι φαῦλον ἐμπέσοι·
χρὴ γὰρ τὰ συμπίπτοντα γενναίως φέρειν.᾿
Οὕτως ἐκεῖνοι τοῖς πόνοις ἐκαρτέρουν.
Οὔπω δὲ διτταὶ συμπαρῆλθον ἡμέραι,
145   καὶ πάντας οὓς ἤνεγκε φόρτους ὁ Γνάθων
ἀπεμπολήσας τοῖς ἐποίκοις ἀγρόταις,
λαβὼν μετ᾿ αὐτοῦ τὴν φίλην συζυγίαν
ὤδευε πρὸς τὸ Βάρζον ἀπτέρῳ τάχει·
οὗ καὶ φθάσαντες τὴν πύλην τῆς εἰσόδου
150   ὁρῶσι τοὺς σφῶν ἀθλίους φυτοσπόρους
αὐτὸς Χαρικλῆς καὶ Δροσίλλα παρθένος
εἰς πέτραν, ἕδραν εὔξοον, καθημένους,
καὶ θάμβος ἔσχον καὶ καλῆς αἰδοῦς τύπον.
Ἀλλὰ προλαβὼν ὁ Γνάθων καὶ προφθάσας
155   ἄμφω κατησπάσατο τοὺς γηραλέους
καὶ τὴν τέκνων ἄφιξιν αὐτοῖς μηνύσας
χρυσοῦ δέκα μνᾶς δῶρον ἀντιλαμβάνει.
Οἳ δ᾿ ἀλλ᾿ ἐπεὶ προσέσχον αὐτοῖς τοῖς τέκνοις,
ὁποῖον ἔσχον γῆθος οὐκ ἔχω λέγειν,
160   ὡς εἶδον αὐτὴν τὴν καλὴν ξυνωρίδα
τὴν Βαρζικὴν γῆν συμπατοῦσαν ἀθρόον·
οἳ πρῶτα δακρύσαντες, ὡς γήρᾳ νόμος,
τὰς σφῶν κεφαλὰς κατεφίλουν ἀσμένως,
ἔχαιρον, ἤλγουν, εὐθύμουν, ἐδυσφόρουν,
165   ἠγαλλίων, ἔκλαιον, ἐκρότουν μέγα·
τὸ τῆς χαρᾶς δάκρυον ἔρρει πλησμίως,
τῆς χαρμονῆς ὁ θρῆνος ὑψοῦτο πλέον.
Πληθὺς δὲ πᾶσα Βαρζιτῶν κοινῷ δρόμῳ,
ἐπεὶ τὸ συμβὰν ἐκ βοηδρόμων μάθοι,
170   ἐξήλθοσαν χαίροντες οἰκείους δόμους,
οἱ παῖδες, ἡ γραῦς, ὁ σφριγῶν, ἡ παρθένος,
μεῖραξ, γυνή, παῖς ἁπαλὴ καὶ πρεσβῦτις,
πάντες προσεπτύσσοντο πυκνὰ τοῖς νέοις.
Ὁ θρῆνος ἠκόντιζε τὸν πολὺν κρότον,
175   ἡ χαρμονὴ δ᾿ ἔκλινε τὴν θρηνῳδίαν·
οὕτω συνήλγουν καὶ συνεσκίρτων πάλιν
τοῖς πατράσι σφῶν πᾶσα κοινῶς ἡ πόλις.

and compose yourself, girl.
You too, Charikles, cease your lamentation.   140
Control yourself, that something bad not happen,
for one should bear nobly the accidents of fate."
    Thus they tried to hold up against their troubles.
And two days had not yet passed
when Gnathon sold to the peasants of the region   145
all the cargo that he'd brought
and, taking the dear couple with him,
traveled to Barzon with winged speed.
Charikles and the maiden Drosilla
arrived at the entrance gate   150
and saw their wretched fathers
sitting on a rock, a well-polished seat;
and they were amazed, their faces tinged with noble shame.
But Gnathon, having gone ahead,
embraced the two old men first,   155
and, informing them of the arrival of their children,
received a gift of ten minas of gold in return.
But what joy the old men felt when they turned
to the children themselves, when they saw
the lovely pair suddenly treading   160
the earth of Barzon, I cannot say!
First they wept, as old people do;
then they kissed their children's heads gladly,
rejoiced, grieved, were cheerful, distressed,
exulted, lamented, and loudly clapped their hands.   165
Tears of joy flowed in abundance,
and lament seemed to surpass the joy.
All the people of Barzon, when they learned from messengers
what had happened, came running out
together, rejoicing, from their homes: 170
children, old women, fresh lads, maidens,
youths, wives, tender girls, elderly ladies,
all were embracing the young persons continuously.
Their laments released a great sound,
and their joy replaced their lamentation;   175
thus the whole community was grieving
and leaping for joy together with the fathers.

Αὐτὸς δὲ Φράτωρ τῇ Δροσίλλᾳ παρθένῳ
ἀντεμπλακεὶς ὡς ⟨τῷ⟩ τέκνῳ προσωμίλει·
180   'γάννυσθε, παῖδες, πρὸς γονεῖς σεσωσμένοι·
διπλοῦς γὰρ ὑμεῖς εὐτυχεῖτε πατέρας,
οὓς αὖθις ἡμεῖς εὐτυχοῦμεν τεκνία.
Ὡς δεξιὸν τὸ τέρμα τῆς ὑμῶν πλάνης,
ὡς εὐτυχὴς ἡ λῆξις ἡ τῶν δακρύων.
185   Σώζεσθε καὶ τηρεῖσθε πρὸς συζυγίαν,
οὓς οἱ θεοὶ συνῆψαν ὡς νυμφοστόλοι.'
Ἐπεὶ δὲ μακροῖς τοῖς μετ' ἀλλήλων λόγοις
καὶ μέχρι νυκτὸς ἦσαν ἠσχολημένοι,
μνήσαντο δόρπου· καὶ καθίσας ὁ Γνάθων
190   αἰτεῖ παρ' αὐτὸν ὡς καθίσοι καὶ Φράτωρ.
Φράτωρ δὲ τοῖς Γνάθωνος ὑπείξας λόγοις
καὶ Μυρτίωνα συνθακεύειν ἠξίου·
ὁ Μυρτίων δὲ νυμφίον Χαρικλέα
καὶ γοῦν Χαρικλῆς τὴν Δροσίλλαν παρθένον.
195   Οἱ τρεῖς μὲν ἐκλίθησαν ἐξ εὐωνύμων,
ἐν δεξιοῖς δὲ προσφιλὴς συζυγία,
αὐτὸς Χαρικλῆς δηλαδὴ καὶ παρθένος·
ὃς οὐ μετρίας μέμψεως κατηξίου,
ἀλλ' ὕβρεων μᾶλλον δὲ καὶ τωθασμάτων,
200   τὸν αἴτιον Γνάθωνα τῶν ξενισμάτων,
ὡς μὴ Δροσίλλαν ἀπέναντι καθίσοι
τῶν ἐκτακέντων ἐξ ἔρωτος ὀμμάτων
καὶ Μυρτίωνα τὸν φύσαντα τὴν κόρην
ἐγγὺς παρ' αὐτοῦ τῆς καθέδρας τῷ τόπῳ,
205   ὅπως τοσαύτης χαρμονῆς τελουμένης
ἀντιπροσωπῶν ἐμβλέποι τῇ παρθένῳ.
Οὐ μὴν ἐπεφθόνει δέ – πῶς τις ἐκφράσοι; –
καὶ τῷ κυπέλλῳ τηλικούτων χειλέων
ἄριστα θιγγάνοντι τῶν τῆς παρθένου·
210   ἐζηλοτύπει καὶ πρὸς οἴνου τὴν πόσιν,
ὡς εἰς Δροσίλλας πλησιάζοντος στόμα.
Οὕτω μὲν εἶχε καὶ τὰ τῆς πανδαισίας·
καὶ νὺξ μελάμπους ἐγχυθεῖσα τοῖς ξένοις,
κατεσπακυῖα τὴν τάσιν τῶν ὀφρύων
215   τὸν νήδυμον σφῶν ἦγεν ὀφθαλμοῖς ὕπνον.
Ἀλλὰ πρὸς ὄρθρον ἡ καλὴ καὶ παγκάλη,

Phrator embraced the maiden Drosilla
and spoke with her as if she were his own child,
"Be happy, children, having returned safe to your fathers: 180
you are fortunate in having two fathers,
and we are fortunate in having you as children.
How happy is the end of your wandering;
how fortunate the cessation of our tears!
You've been preserved and protected for your nuptials,   185
you whom the gods have united, acting as your bridal escorts."
      After they had conversed with one another
at length, until nightfall,
they thought of dinner. Gnathon sat down
and asked that Phrator sit down beside him;   190
Phrator complied with Gnathon's request
and asked Myrtion to sit with him;
Myrtion asked the bridegroom Charikles,
and then Charikles asked the maiden Drosilla.
The three men reclined on the left,   195
and on the right the beloved couple,
that is, Charikles and the maiden.
Charikles felt that Gnathon, the evening's host,
deserved no small blame
but rather insults and jeers   200
since he did not seat Drosilla opposite
Charikles' eyes, which were melted with love,
but instead placed Myrtion, the girl's father,
near his seat
so that, during the celebration of such great joy,   205
Myrtion might gaze at the maiden's face.
Moreover, Charikles envied—how should one describe it?—
even the cup that touched (most excellently)
the lovely lips of the maiden;
he felt jealousy even toward the wine being drunk,   210
since it was entering Drosilla's mouth.
Thus the lavish banquet progressed,
and black-footed night flowed over the guests,
releasing the tension of their brows
and bringing sweet sleep to their eyes.   215
But towards dawn the very beautiful

ἡ τοῦ γέροντος Μυρτίωνος θυγάτηρ,
καταλαβοῦσα τὴν σορὸν Καλλιγόνης
ἔλουεν αὐτὴν ἄλλο λουτρὸν δακρύων.
220   Τὸ γὰρ γυναικῶν συμπαθέστατον φύλον
ἑτοιμοπενθές ἐστι καὶ ξένοις πόνοις
καὶ φιλόδακρυ γίνεται παραυτίκα·
οὐκ ἐν μόνῃ γὰρ συμφορῶν περιστάσει
φιλεῖ τὸ πενθεῖν καὶ τὸ μακρὸν δακρύειν,
225   καὶ μᾶλλον εἴ τις ἐκπεράσοι τὸν βίον·
διηνεκῶς δὲ καὶ χρόνων περιδρόμοις
σῶζον κακῶν ἔννοιαν ἀμφιδακρύει.
Οὕτως ἐκείνη συμπαθῶς ἡ παρθένος
λαθοῦσα τοὺς τέσσαρας, ὡς κοιμωμένους,
230   Γνάθωνα, Μυρτίωνα τὸν φυτοσπόρον,
ναὶ μὴν Χαριλῆν καὶ τὸν αὐτοῦ πατέρα,
ἔκραζε κυπτάζουσα πρὸς Καλλιγόνην,
ἔτυπτεν εἰς τὸ στέρνον, ἀνεκεκράγει
μετὰ στεναγμῶν καὶ μετ' ὄμβρου δακρύων·
235   'ὦ πολλὰ βασκαίνουσα, δυσμενὴς Τύχη,
οὐκ ἤρκεσάν σοι τὰ προσυμβεβηκότα
ἀλγεινὰ πικρὰ τῇ Δροσίλλας καρδίᾳ·
ἀλλὰ πρὸς αὐτοῖς καὶ τὸ λοιπὸν εἰσφέρεις.
Σὺ μὲν θανατοῖς παρθένον Καλλιγόνην,
240   Καλλιγόνη δὲ τὸν Κλέανδρον κτιννύει·
ὁ δὲ Κλέανδρος τοὺς ἐκείνου γνησίους
οὐ συνθανατοῖ, τῇ δὲ τούτων καρδίᾳ
λύπης τοσαύτης ἀντιπέμπει πικρίας.
Θρηνῶ σε λοιπόν, ὦ κόρη Καλλιγόνη,
245   συμπαρθένε, κλαίω σε γῇ κεχωσμένην
ἀντὶ Κλεάνδρου τοῦ προεξῳχηκότος,
τοῦ συγξενιτεύσαντος ἡμῖν ἐν ξένοις·
θρηνῶ σε μητρὸς καὶ πατρὸς στερουμένην,
καὶ φεῦ θανοῦσαν ἀλλὰ μακρὰν πατρίδος,
250   ἣν οὐ κατεῖδον, οὐ συνῆλθον εἰς λόγους,
οὐκ εἰς χαρὰν ἔστερξα καὶ προσεπλάκην,
ἐν συμφοραῖς οὐκ ἔσχον εἰς λύπης ἄκος.
Ὡς εἴθε καὶ Κλέανδρον οὐκ εἶδον πάλαι
καὶ συμμετέσχον καὶ τροφῶν καὶ δακρύων.
255   Σὺ δ' ἀλλὰ δέξαι τὴν ἐμὴν θρηνῳδίαν,

daughter of old Myrtion
arrived at Kalligone's tomb
and gave it another bath of tears.
The race of women, full of compassion,   220
is ready to mourn for even the sufferings of strangers
and prone to sudden tears—
for not only in circumstances of misfortunes
are women inclined to lament and weep at length
(particularly if someone should die),   225
but continuously in the course of time,
preserving the memory of evils, they weep profusely.
Thus that maiden, in sympathy,
unseen by the four of them as they slept
(Gnathon, her father Myrtion,   230
and also Charikles and his father),
moaned loudly as she bowed in sorrow toward Kalligone's tomb,
beat on her breast, and cried out
with groans and a shower of tears:
"Oh, envious, cruel Fortune,   235
the painful, bitter things that fell upon
Drosilla's heart before weren't enough for you,
but to them you add the rest:
you murder the maiden Kalligone,
and Kalligone's death kills Kleandros,   240
but Kleandros's death does not kill his friends in turn—
instead he sends to their hearts
the bitterness of great grief.
I lament for you, then, maiden Kalligone,
fellow-virgin. I weep for you covered with earth,   245
since Kleandros cannot, who left home
and lived in foreign lands with us, among strangers.
I wail for you deprived of mother and father,
and, alas, dead far from your fatherland—
whom I didn't see, with whom I didn't speak,   250
whom I didn't joyously kiss and embrace,
whom I didn't have in misfortunes as grief's remedy.
Oh, if only I hadn't ever seen Kleandros
and shared with him food and tears!
But you, receive my lamentation,   255

ἦν ὡς χοὰς νῦν πενθικὰς ἔσπεισά σοι.'
Εἴρηκε ταῦτα, καὶ μετ' αἰδοῦς κοσμίας
Γνάθωνος αὖθις ἀντεισῆλθε τὴν στέγην,
ὅθεν ξενίσας τοὺς γέροντας ὁ Γνάθων
260   σὺν τοῖς τέκνοις σφῶν ἀμφὶ πρώτην ἡμέραν,
ἐκεῖ θέλοντας καρτερῆσαι μὴ πλέον
τέλος προσελθὼν καὶ προσειπὼν ἀσμένως
καὶ γνήσιον φίλημα δοὺς τοῖς ἀνδράσιν
εἰς δευτέραν ἔπεμψε πρὸς τὴν πατρίδα.
265   Τῆς οὖν θαλάσσης εὖ κατεστορεσμένης,
οὐ πνεύματος πνέοντος ὠλεσισκάφου,
οὐ τῶν κυμάτων ἀμφικυλινδουμένων,
οὗτοι προσηνοῦς ἡμερωτάτου πλόου
τυχόντες ἐστέλλοντο πρὸς γῆν φιλτάτην.
270   Ἐπεὶ δὲ προσπλεύσαντες ἡμέρας δέκα
φθάσαιεν ὀψὲ καὶ πρὸς αὐτὴν πατρίδα
καὶ τοῖς ἐπευκτοῖς ἐμπατήσαιεν τόποις,
ὁ μὲν Χαρικλῆν ἀπογεννήσας Φράτωρ
μεθεῖλκε Μυρτίωνα πρὸς τὴν οἰκίαν,
275   ὁ δὲ Δροσίλλαν ἐκτοκεύσας Μυρτίων
ἀντιμεθεῖλκε τοῦτον ἀμφὶ τὸν δόμον,
αἱ μητέρες δὲ τοῦ νέου καὶ τῆς κόρης,
Ἡδυπνόη τε καὶ σὺν αὐτῇ Κρυστάλη,
ἐπεὶ τὸ συμβὰν ἐκμάθοιεν, εὐθέως
280   ἐκεῖ δραμοῦσαι, προσπλακεῖσαι τοῖς νέοις
τοῖς τῆς χαρᾶς ἔλουον αὐτοὺς δακρύοις.
Τὸ προσφιλὲς δὲ μητροπάτρῳον γένος,
ὁ πατριώτης ὄχλος, ὁ ξυμφυλέτης,
συνεκρότουν, ἔχαιρον, ἐσκίρτων μέγα,
285   ἠγαλλίων ὁποῖον ἀλλὰ καὶ πόσον.
Οὗτοι μὲν οὕτως εἶχον· εἷς δέ τις φθάσας
ὁ πρῶτος αὐτῶν, ἱερεὺς Διονύσου,
ἐπιτρέπει τάχιστα κατειληφέναι
εἰς τὸν νεὼν ἅπαντας αὐτοὺς τοὺς ὄχλους,
290   ὡς μὲν ἂν συναρμόσαιτο τῷ Χαρικλέι
νύμφην Δροσίλλαν εἰς ὁμιλίαν γάμου.
Εἴρηκε ταῦτα καὶ διπλοῦς παραυτίκα
κλάδους παρασχὼν ἀμπέλου τοῖς νυμφίοις
εἰς τὸν νεὼν εἰσῆξεν ἅμα τοῖς ὄχλοις.

which I've poured forth for you now like mourning libations."
    She said these things, and with proper modesty
entered Gnathon's house again.
There Gnathon had entertained the old men
with their children the first day,   260
and when they were willing to stay no longer,
he approached at last, addressed them warmly,
gave the men a friendly kiss,
and sent them the next day to their fatherland.
The sea, then, was calm—   265
winds that destroy ships were not blowing,
and menacing waves were not rolling around;
these travelers met with gentle, quiet sailing
when they set forth toward their beloved land.
    After sailing for ten days,   270
they arrived at last in their fatherland
and walked in the places they'd missed;
Charikles' father, Phrator,
took Myrtion to his home;
and Drosilla's father, Myrtion,   275
took Phrator in turn to his house.
The mothers of the young couple—
Hedypnoe and Krystale—
when they learned what had happened,
quickly ran up, embraced the young persons   280
and bathed them with tears of joy.
And the dear families of the fathers and mothers,
and the citizens and fellow-clansmen
applauded, exulted, and leaped for joy—
with such great enthusiasm they rejoiced!   285
    While all this was happening,
the chief man among them, Dionysus's priest, arrived,
bid all the people
go to the temple as quickly as possible
so that he might join Drosilla   290
with Charikles, to be his wife in the union of marriage.
    He said these things and at once
gave the bridal couple two vine-branches
and led them into the temple together with the people.

295   Τί γοῦν τὸ λοιπόν; Συζυγεῖσα πρὸς γάμον
νύμφη Δροσίλλα τῷ Χαρικλεῖ νυμφίῳ
καὶ πρὸς δόμους ἀχθεῖσα τῶν γεννητόρων,
μετὰ στεφάνων καὶ κρότων καὶ κυμβάλων,
ἐν ἑσπέρᾳ μένουσα παρθένος κόρη
300   γυνὴ πρὸς ὄρθρον ἐξανέστη τῆς κλίνης.

What then is left? Drosilla was joined   295
to Charikles in marriage, a bride to a groom,
and led to the family house,
with wreaths, applause, and cymbal crashes.
      And the girl who was still a virgin in the evening
was a woman when she rose at dawn from her bed.   300

EXPLANATORY NOTES

1.22. "Mysian plunder" was a proverbial expression meaning "easy prey" due to cowardice or weakness. Cf. Aristotle *Rhetoric* 1372b20. Mysia, a region in northwest Asia Minor, had Telephus as one of its legendary kings (see note 3.251). On "proverbial contempt for the Mysian character," see Edward M. Cope, *The Rhetoric of Aristotle with a Commentary*, rev. John E. Sandys (1877; reprint, 3 vols. in 1, New York: Arno Press, 1973), 235–36 (quotation from p. 236). For Eugenianos's model here, cf. Prodromos *Rhodanthe and Dosikles* 1.26 (for discussion see Panagiotis A. Agapitos, "Narrative, Rhetoric, and 'Drama' Rediscovered: Scholars and Poets in Byzantium Interpret Heliodorus," in *Studies in Heliodorus*, ed. Richard Hunter [Cambridge: The Cambridge Philological Society, 1998], 151).

1.102–3. Pheidias and Praxiteles were famous Athenian sculptors who worked in the fifth and fourth centuries B.C. respectively. Zeuxis of Herakleia, a famous Greek painter of the late fifth and early fourth centuries B.C., is also said to have made statues in clay (Pliny *Natural History* 35.66). Zeuxis is often included in trios representing great artists of the past, e.g., Michael Psellus *Chronographia* 3.14: "the workers on these stones were reckoned with the like of Pheidias and Polygnotus and Zeuxis" (E. R. A. Sewter, trans., *Fourteen Byzantine Rulers: The* Chronographia *of Michael Psellus*, rev. ed. [London: Penguin Books, 1966], 72).

2.203. The Sirens were mythological females whose song lured sailors to their death.

2.308. Pandora, the original human female, was created and given gifts by the gods that she might be a punishment for mankind. For the story of her making, see Hesiod *Works and Days* 57–105, esp. 60–82: Zeus had Hephaestus make her with a goddess's face and maidenly form; Aphrodite was to shed grace and cruel desire upon her; the Graces and Persuasion put gold necklaces on her; the Hours crowned her with spring flowers; and so forth.

2.327–28. For Niobe, see "List of Gods and Legendary Figures" (gods and figures that appear more than once in the novel are identified there).

2.329.   For Pandion's daughter, see "List of Gods and Legendary Figures," under Pandion.

3.86.   While crossing Lydia on his way to attack Greece (480 B.C.), Xerxes, the king of Persia, came across a beautiful plane tree, which he decorated with gold and furnished with a guardian (thus Herodotus 7.31). This story becomes proverbial. On Asian and Mediterranean reverence for big, shady trees, see Frank H. Stubbings, "Xerxes and the Plane-Tree," *Greece and Rome* 15 (1946), 63–67. (Like Xerxes' plane tree, Eugenianos's too has a guardian assigned.) Plato's *Phaedrus* features another famous plane tree: after leaving the city, Socrates and Phaedrus come across a tall, shady plane tree by the banks of a river, sit beneath it, and talk of love. Similarly in Eugenianos's novel, after leaving the city, the hero and his friends sit beneath a large plane tree by the banks of a river and talk of love. The setting of Plato's *Phaedrus* was famous and much-evoked. On its use during the Second Sophistic, see M. B. Trapp, "Plato's *Phaedrus* in Second-Century Greek Literature," in *Antonine Literature*, ed. D. A. Russell (Oxford: Clarendon Press, 1990), 141–73; for its use later, e.g., in the tenth century A.D., John Geometres *Progymnasmata*, "A letter describing Geometres' garden" (text and discussion: A. R. Littlewood, *The Progymnasmata of Ioannes Geometres* [Amsterdam: Adolf M. Hakkert, 1972], 8.23–29, with pp. 48–49 n. 8.23–29).

3.115.   Kronos was chief among the "old gods," the Titans, who were overthrown by Zeus's generation of Olympian gods. At 2.365, the adjective "Kronikos" is translated as "old-fashioned." For Eros as a primordial being, see also Hesiod *Theogony* 116–22, Longus 2.5.

3.155.   Lais, the Corinthian, was one of (at least) two celebrated courtesans named Lais linked with prominent men of the fifth and fourth centuries B.C. (see, e.g., Athenaeus 13, 570b–e, 588c–589b; Pausanias 2.2.4). On the theme of an aging Lais, cf. *Anthologia Palatina* 6.1 (Plato), 6.18 and 20 (Julianus, prefect of Egypt).

3.212.   Priapos was a minor, phallic god associated with sexuality and lewd behavior. For Herakles (3.211), see "List of Gods and Legendary Figures."

3.251.   According to legend, Telephus, king of Mysia, was wounded by the Greek hero Achilles when the Greeks mistook Mysia for Troy. Having learned that his wound could be cured only by the wounder, Telephus went to Achilles, who cured him with rust from the spear that wounded him (Apollodorus *Epitome* 3.17–20). For the analogy with love, cf. *Anthologia Palatina* 5.225.5–6 (Macedonius the Consul), 291.5–6 (Paulus Silentiarius).

3.264–85.   The story of Rhodope is also told at Achilles Tatius 8.12. Barbition sings two mythological songs (3.263–88, 297–322), both in hexameter verse with Theocritean refrains. These are remarkable, both in the context of the novel (the rest of which is in twelve-syllable verse) and also in the context of the history of the pastoral in Byzantium. On these songs, see Antonino M. Milazzo, "Motivi bucolici e tecnica alessandrina in due 'idilli' di Niceta Eugeniano," *Studi di filologia bizantina* 3 (1985), 97–114; see also my article in *A Companion to Greek and Latin Pastoral*, ed. Marco Fantuzzi and Theodoros Papangelis (Leiden: Brill, forthcoming).

3.298. For the story of Syrinx and Pan, see also Achilles Tatius 8.6.7–10, Longus 2.34. Pan, with his goat legs and horns, was a Greek god of shepherds.

3.316. Phoebus, "radiant one," is a synonym of the Olympian god Apollo. Apollo's amorous pursuit of Daphne, daughter of a river god, ended with her transformation into a laurel tree to escape him (Parthenius 15, Ovid *Metamorphoses* 1.452–567).

3.367–86. The hero's initial impulse here to abduct the maiden even without her prior consent is unprecedented in the ancient Greek novel (in which only villains or rogue suitors are involved in such activities). Eugenianos is following Theodore Prodromos, his Byzantine mentor, who has his hero actually carry out a violent, non-consensual abduction of the heroine. On the significance of this striking innovation in relation both to the ancient novel and also to Byzantine custom and laws, see Joan B. Burton, "Abduction and Elopement in the Byzantine Novel," *Greek, Roman, and Byzantine Studies* 41 (2000): 377–409; cf. Corinne Jouanno, "Les jeunes filles dans le roman byzantin du XIIe siècle," in *Les personnages du roman grec*, Actes du colloque de Tours, 18–20 novembre 1999, ed. Bernard Pouderon, with Christine Hunzinger and Dimitri Kasprzyk (Lyon: Maison de l'Orient Méditerranéen, 2001), esp. 336–37.

4.62. In book one, the festival that the Barzians are celebrating when the Parthians attack is explicitly identified (by the narrator) as the festival of Dionysus (1.113; see also 107, 151). But in telling his story later Charikles calls it a festival of Zeus (4.62 and 7.157). On the conflation of Zeus and Dionysus, father and son, and Christian resonances in Eugenianos's novel, see Joan B. Burton, "Reviving the Pagan Greek Novel in a Christian World," *Greek, Roman, and Byzantine Studies* 39 (1998): 205–8 (with attention to linkages between Dionysus and Jesus).

4.145–8. The Peloponnesian river-god Alpheios fell in love with the nymph Arethusa; she fled to Ortygia, an island near Syracuse, and was transformed into a spring, but the river Alpheios pursued her across the sea and mingled his waters with hers. For this story, see Achilles Tatius 1.18.1–2, Pausanias 5.7.1–3. (Kleinias's description here of Eros's power [Eugenianos 4.135–48] is modeled on Achilles Tatius 1.17.1–18.2.)

4.248–49. The youth Narcissus, a scorner of love, fell in love with his own reflection in the water and died as a result; his body disappears and a flower is found in its place. Another version of the story has Narcissus wasting away beside the water rather than throwing himself within (see Ovid *Metamorphoses* 3.339–510, Pausanias 9.31.6, Nonnus *Dionysiaca* 48.581–86).

4.250–53. This is a reference to the story of Apollo's tragic slaying of his beloved youth Hyacinth. In this version, the West wind Zephyros, Hyacinth's unrequited lover, in jealousy blows Apollo's javelin into Hyacinth while Apollo and Hyacinth are exercising together (see Lucian *Dialogues of the Gods* 14: "Hermes and Apollo"). From Hyacinth's blood arose the flower named for him. (In other, earlier versions, Apollo's javelin kills Hyacinth by accident.)

4.258. This is a reference to the story of Aphrodite's love for Adonis, who dies young. This version of Adonis's death, with the god Ares killing him from jealousy and Aphrodite's blood turning the rose red, is also given in Aphthonius *Progymnasmata* 2, late-fourth / early-fifth century A.D. (Hugo Rabe, ed., *Aphthonii Progymnasmata* [Leipzig: B. G. Teubner, 1926], p. 3.5–19). For this aetiology of the red rose cf. Philostratus *Letters* 1 and 4; John Geometres *Progymnasmata*, "A Second Encomium of the Apple" (Littlewood, *Progymnasmata of Ioannes Geometres*, 21.9–13, with p. 81 n. 21.9–13); *Kallimachos and Chrysorrhoe* 834–35 (Michel Pichard, ed., *Le roman de Callimaque et de Chrysorrhoé* [Paris: Société d'édition "Les Belles-Lettres," 1956], with French trans.). A common earlier version of Adonis's story had him die in a hunting accident (Bion *Lament for Adonis* 7–66; Apollodorus *Bibliotheca* 3.14.4; Ovid *Metamorphoses* 10.709–39). The flower transformations also differed: Ovid has an anemone arising from Adonis's blood; Bion, an anemone from Aphrodite's tears and a rose from Adonis's blood (for the suggestion that Bion "perhaps invented the story of the rose," see J. D. Reed, ed., *Bion of Smyrna: The Fragments and the* Adonis [Cambridge: Cambridge University Press, 1997], 233 n. 66).

4.277–88. On parallels with erotic imagery of the Song of Songs, see Burton, "Reviving the Pagan Greek Novel," 201–3 (with notice also of Eugenianos 6.570–73).

4.381–86. Polyphemos is the same monstrous Cyclops (one-eyed giant) who encounters Odysseus in Homer's *Odyssey*, book 9. The reference here, however, is to the adolescent Polyphemos in love with the Nereid Galateia (a sea-nymph). Charikles is recalling Theocritus's Eleventh Idyll (early third century B.C.). On how Charikles' retelling of Polyphemos's story reveals Charikles as a sophisticated reader of past texts, see Joan B. Burton, "A Reemergence of Theocritean Poetry in the Byzantine Novel," *Classical Philology* 98 (2003): 253–56. Cf. the later, more extensive reworking of Theocritus's poem at Eugenianos 6.503–46.

5.355.   Epaminondas was a famous Theban general of the fourth century B.C.

5.386.   (5.387 in Greek text). The Greek text is uncertain. Conca prints the reading of MUL, κεδρίνους, "cedar-wood," but as a *locus corruptus*. P has κωδώνους, "trumpets" (but, Boissonade notes, with the scholium κωδώνιον, δέρμα, "hide"; for discussion, see Boissonade[1] 2:276–77); thus too Boissonade[1], with κώδωνας in Boissonade[2] and Hercher. Dawe suggests κνώδοντας for "the ancient equivalent of barbed wire" (R. D. Dawe, "Notes on Theodorus Prodromus *Rhodanthe and Dosicles* and Nicetas Eugenianus *Drosilla and Charicles*," *Byzantinische Zeitschrift* 94 [2001]: 17–18). I have translated somewhat ambiguously as "protective coverings" since in any case the next line describes their purpose as "defenses against blows." For descriptions of manuscripts MPUL, see Fabrizio Conca, ed., *Nicetas Eugenianus, De Drosillae et Chariclis amoribus* (Amsterdam: J. C. Gieben, 1990), 7–11.

6.109.   Caria was a mountainous region located in the southwest corner of Asia Minor.

6.136.   (Greek text). For σαφῶν read σφῶν here (as in Conca, *Nicetas Eugenianus*, 149).

6.345.   Kalliope was the muse of epic poetry; Homer the epic poet credited with the two great ancient Greek epics the *Iliad* and the *Odyssey*. Eugenianos is echoing Heliodorus 4.4.3 here; the Homeric reference is *Iliad* 13.636–39.

6.389–90. This is the first of Kallidemos's awkward series of amatory examples. The figures named here are all characters in Heliodorus's earlier Greek novel, *The Ethiopian Story* (third or fourth century A.D.). In the tradition of the Greek novel (ancient and Byzantine), this is the first direct reference to an earlier novel. The examples given are of unrequited not requited love, however: Arsake is a satrap's wife, in love with the hero, Theagenes; Achaimenes is Arsake's maid's son, in love with the heroine, Charikleia. On the stunning inappropriateness of Kallidemos's examples here and his obsession with fictive love narratives, see Burton, "Theocritean Poetry in the Byzantine Novel"; cf. Corinne Jouanno, "Nicétas Eugénianos: Un héritier du roman grec," *Revue des études grecques* 102 (1989): 350–51.

6.397.   The Greek verb μεθύω means "I am drunken with wine"; hence the adjective ἀμέθυστος means "not drunken." On the power of the stone amethyst against drunkenness, see Heliodorus 5.13.4; *Anthologia Palatina* 9.748 (Plato the Younger); cf. Plutarch *Table-Talk* 647b–c.

6.399.   On the power of the precious stone *pantarbe* against fire, see Heliodorus 8.11–12.

6.419   (Greek text). I read ἑλκτηρίοις with Hercher, rather than Conca's ἑλκτηρίος (M has ἑκτηρίοις; P omits this section).

6.440–51.   Kallidemos's second amatory example is from Longus's pastoral novel, *Daphnis and Chloe* (usually dated to the late second or early third century A.D.); this is also the second direct reference in Eugenianos's novel to an earlier novel. Daphnis and Chloe's example of requited love suits Kallidemos's rhetorical aim more closely, and it is expanded further than the examples cited from Heliodorus's novel.

6.473–92   Kallidemos's third amatory example is from Musaeus's short hexameter poem *Hero and Leander* (late fifth or early sixth century A.D.). The mythological lovers Hero and Leander lived across the Hellespont from one another, Hero in Sestos and Leander in Abydos (on the Asian side of the Hellespont). Leander swam across the Hellespont at night to visit Hero, and when he drowned during a storm and his body swept ashore to her tower, Hero fell from her tower to her death. For earlier versions of their story, see Ovid *Heroides* 18–19, Virgil *Georgics* 3.258–63; cf. Marlowe's *Hero and Leander*.

6.503–46.   The primary model for Kallidemos's fourth and final amatory example, the adolescent Cyclops's courtship of the beautiful nymph Galateia, is Theocritus's *Idyll* 11. On the identity of this Cyclops, see the note at 4.381–86. On how Kallidemos's lengthy reworking of the Cyclops's courtship reveals his own lack of literary and social sophistication (with attention to issues of intertextuality), see Burton, "Theocritean Poetry in the Byzantine Novel."

6.585–86.   Kallidemos introduces a new, monstrous mode of Cyclops here; he does not look to Theocritus again. For discussion of how "Kallidemos can be seen as a fictive character trying out roles," see Burton, "Theocritean Poetry in the Byzantine Novel."

6.623–25.   This is a reference to the famous beauty contest between the three goddesses Hera, Athena, and Aphrodite. The judge, the Trojan king Priam's son Paris, awarded the prize to Aphrodite because she offered him as bribe the beautiful Helen (which led to the Trojan War). See 8.107–9 for another reference to the judgment of Paris.

6.630.   For a crime against the gods, Tantalus is punished in Hades with eternal thirst and hunger: he stands in a pool of water that drains whenever he tries to drink; fruit hangs before him but moves away whenever he tries to seize it (see, e.g., Homer *Odyssey* 11.582–92; hence the word "tantalize"). For a similar comparison of love to Tantalus's thirst, see *Anthologia Palatina* 5.246.5–6 (Paulus Silentiarius).

6.634.   The god Zeus, a notorious philanderer, transformed himself into a swan to seduce Leda, a shower of gold to seduce Danae, and a bull to seduce Europa. In one version of Ganymede's abduction, Zeus in the form of an eagle carries him off. For a similar comparison, see *Anthologia Palatina* 5.257 (Palladas).

6.643.   On the magnitude of the walls around Babylon, see Herodotus 1.178–81, Diodorus Siculus esp. 2.7.2–5 (whose account reflects the tradition that Queen Semiramis built these walls). For a similar comparison, see *Anthologia Palatina* 5.252.1–4 (Paulus Silentiarius).

6.655.   For the story of Philomela, Itys, and the swallow, see "List of Gods and Legendary Figures," under Pandion (Philomela's father).

6.662–63. Dawn, having fallen in love with Tithonos, a mortal youth, asked Zeus to make him immortal but forgot to ask that he not age. For their story, see *Homeric Hymn to Aphrodite* 218–38.

6.667.   (Greek text). Conca has Baryllis as the old woman's name; I use the name Maryllis instead (as in manuscripts PUL and editions prior to Conca). Conca, with hesitation, follows manuscript M in using the name Baryllis; he suggests the name may underscore the old woman's crude character (Conca, *Nicetas Eugenianus*, 26; see also Andrea Giusti, "Nota a Niceta Eugeniano [Dros. et Char. VII 247–332]," *Studi italiani di filologia classica* 3 [1993]: 220 n.16). The name Maryllis, however, has its own resonance, as Beaton notes: "a comical transformation of Theokritos' Amaryllis" (Roderick Beaton, *The Medieval Greek Romance*[2] [London: Routledge, 1996], 77). For the name Amaryllis used of lovely young girls in a bucolic context, see Theocritus Idylls 3, 4.36–40; Longus 2.7.4–7 (with 2.7.7 echoed at Eugenianos 6.377–78); cf. Virgil Eclogues 1.5. In light of Eugenianos's repeated echoes of Theocritus's poetry and Longus's pastoral novel, an ironic evocation of the memorable bucolic name Amaryllis, featured in both their works, does not seem out of place (Maryllis, an Amaryllis grown old).

7.264.   On how "Eugenianos is having Maryllis respond to the lovers' embrace and reunion in Christian terms, with Christian imagery," see Burton, "Reviving the Pagan Greek Novel," 203–4 (quotation from p. 204); on the old woman's echo at 7.264 of the famous biblical line "Therefore what God has joined, let no one separate"

(Matthew 19.6, Mark 10.9), see also Alexander P. Kazhdan, "Bemerkungen zu Niketas Eugenianos," *Jahrbuch der österreichischen byzantinischen Gesellschaft* 16 (1967): 116.

8.97–100. For the story of how the god Hephaestus trapped with bonds his wife, Aphrodite, and her lover Ares as they slept together in Hephaestus's bed, see Homer *Odyssey* 8.267–366.

8.107–9. A second reference to the famous beauty contest between the three goddesses Hera (Zeus's wife), Pallas Athena, and Aphrodite (cf. 6.622–25). While shepherding flocks on Mount Ida, Paris was chosen to be judge.

8.115. The reference is to the moon-goddess's love for the handsome mortal Endymion.

8.223. (Greek text). The Greek should read καταστεφούσης here (as in Conca, *Nicetas Eugenianus*).

9.7–14. On the significance of Kleandros's pastoral funeral and Drosilla's excessive lamentations (9.15–107, 216–56) for the ending of the novel, see Burton, "Theocritean Poetry in the Byzantine Novel."

9.28. Poseidon, Zeus's brother, god of the sea, both stirs up storms at sea and also stills waters.

SELECT BIBLIOGRAPHY

Agapitos, Panagiotis A. "Narrative, Rhetoric, and 'Drama' Rediscovered: Scholars and Poets in Byzantium Interpret Heliodorus." In *Studies in Heliodorus*, edited by Richard Hunter, 125–56. Cambridge: The Cambridge Philological Society, 1998.

Agapitos, Panagiotis A., and Diether R. Reinsch, eds. *Der Roman im Byzanz der Komnenenzeit*, Referate des Internationalen Symposiums an der Freien Universität Berlin, 3. bis 6. April 1998. Meletemata 8. Frankfurt am Main: beerenverlag, 2000.

Alexiou, Margaret. "A Critical Reappraisal of Eustathios Makrembolites' *Hysmine and Hysminias*." *Byzantine and Modern Greek Studies* 3 (1977): 23–43.

———. "Literary Subversion and the Aristocracy in Twelfth-Century Byzantium: A Stylistic Analysis of the *Timarion* (ch. 6–10)." *Byzantine and Modern Greek Studies* 8 (1982–83): 29–45.

Angold, Michael. *The Byzantine Empire, 1025–1204: A Political History*. 2nd ed. London: Longman, 1997.

———. "The Interaction of Latins and Byzantines during the Period of the Latin Empire (1204–1261): The Case of the Ordeal." *Actes du XVᵉ Congrès international d'études byzantines, Athènes septembre 1976* 4 (1980): 1–10.

———. *Church and Society in Byzantium under the Comneni, 1081–1261*. Cambridge: Cambridge University Press, 1995.

Baldwin, Barry, trans. *Timarion*. Detroit: Wayne State University Press, 1984.

Bartlett, Robert. *Trial by Fire and Water: The Medieval Judicial Ordeal*. Oxford: Clarendon Press, 1986.

Beaton, Roderick. *The Medieval Greek Romance*. 2nd ed. London: Routledge, 1996.

———. "The World of Fiction and the World 'Out There': The Case of the Byzantine Novel." In *Strangers to Themselves: The Byzantine Outsider*, Papers from the Thirty-second Spring Symposium of Byzantine Studies, University of Sussex, Brighton, March 1998, Society for the Promotion of Byzantine Studies 8, edited by Dion C. Smythe, 179–88. Aldershot: Ashgate, 2000.

Beck, Hans-Georg. "Marginalia on the Byzantine Novel." In *Erotica Antiqua*, Acta of the International Conference on the Ancient Novel held under the auspices of the Society for the Promotion of Hellenic Studies at the University College of North Wales, Bangor, Wales, U.K., 12th–17th July 1976 to mark the centenary of the publication of E. Rohde, *Der griechische Roman*, edited by B. P. Reardon, 59–65. Bangor, 1977.

———. *Byzantinisches Erotikon: Orthodoxie-Literatur-Gesellschaft*. Munich: Bayerische Akademie der Wissenschaften, 1984.

Betts, Gavin. *Three Medieval Greek Romances:* Velthandros and Chrysandza, Kallimachos and Chrysorroi, Livistros and Rodamni. New York: Garland, 1995.

Boissonade, Jean F. *Nicetae Eugeniani narrationem amatoriam et Constantini Manassis fragmenta*. 2 vols. Leiden: Apud S. et J. Luchtmans, 1819.

———. "Nicetas Eugenianus." In *Erotici scriptores*, edited by Wilhelm A. Hirschig. Paris: Ambrosio Firmin Didot, 1856.

Burton, Joan B. "Reviving the Pagan Greek Novel in a Christian World." *Greek, Roman and Byzantine Studies* 39 (1998): 179–216.

———. "Abduction and Elopement in the Byzantine Novel." *Greek, Roman and Byzantine Studies* 41 (2000): 377–409.

———. "A Reemergence of Theocritean Poetry in the Byzantine Novel." *Classical Philology* 98 (2003): 251–73.

———. "Byzantine Readers of the Novel." In *The Cambridge Companion to the Greek and Roman Novel*, edited by Tim Whitmarsh. Cambridge: Cambridge University Press, forthcoming.

Clucas, Lowell. *The Trial of John Italos and the Crisis of Intellectual Values in Byzantium in the Eleventh Century*. Munich: Institut für Byzantinistik, Neugriechische Philologie und Byzantinische Kunstgeschichte der Universität, 1981.

Conca, Fabrizio. "Il romanzo di Niceta Eugeniano: Modelli narrativi e stilistici." *Siculorum gymnasium* 39 (1986): 115–26.

———, ed. *Nicetas Eugenianus, De Drosillae et Chariclis amoribus*. Amsterdam: J. C. Gieben, 1990.

———, ed. and trans. *Il romanzo bizantino del XII secolo*. Turin: Unione Tipografico-Editrice Torinese, 1994.

Cupane, Carolina. "Un caso di giudizio di Dio nel romanzo di Teodoro Prodromo (I 372–404)." *Rivista di studi bizantini e neoellenici* 10–11 (1974): 147–68.

Dawe, R. D. "Notes on Theodorus Prodromus *Rhodanthe and Dosicles* and Nicetas Eugenianus *Drosilla and Charicles*." *Byzantinische Zeitschrift* 94 (2001): 11–19.

Deligiorgis, Stavros. "A Byzantine Romance in International Perspective: The *Drosilla and Charikles* of Niketas Eugenianos." *Neo-Hellenika* 2 (1975): 21–32.

Dyck, Andrew R., ed. *Michael Psellus: The Essays on Euripides and George of Pisidia and on Heliodorus and Achilles Tatius.* Vienna: Der österreichischen Akademie der Wissenschaften, 1986.

Garland, Lynda. "'Be Amorous, But Be Chaste . . . ': Sexual Morality in Byzantine Learned and Vernacular Romance." *Byzantine and Modern Greek Studies* 14 (1990): 62–120.

Giusti, Andrea. "Nota a Niceta Eugeniano (*Dros. et Char.* VII 247–332)." *Studi italiani di filologia classica* 3 (1993): 216–23.

Hägg, Tomas. *The Novel in Antiquity.* Berkeley: University of California Press, 1983. Originally published as *Den antika romanen* (Uppsala: Bokförlaget Carmina, 1980; revised by author for English edition).

Hercher, Rudolph. *Erotici scriptores Graeci.* Vol. 2. Leipzig: B. G. Teubner, 1859.

Hunger, Herbert. "Die byzantinische Literatur der Komnenenzeit: Versuch einer Neubewertung." In *Byzantinistische Grundlagenforschung: Gesammelte Aufsaetze,* 59–76. London: Variorum Reprints, 1973.

———. "Byzantinische 'Froschmänner'?" In *Antidosis: Festschrift für Walther Kraus zum 70. Geburtstag,* edited by Rudolf Hanslik, Albin Lesky, and Hans Schwabl, 183–87. Vienna: Hermann Böhlaus Nachf., 1972.

———. *Die hochsprachliche profane Literatur der Byzantiner.* Vol. 2. Munich: C. H. Beck, 1978.

———. *Antiker und byzantinischer Roman.* Heidelberg: Carl Winter Universitätsverlag, 1980.

Jeffreys, Elizabeth M. "The Attitudes of Byzantine Chroniclers towards Ancient History." *Byzantion* 49 (1979): 199–238.

———. "The Comnenian Background to the *Romans d'Antiquité.*" *Byzantion* 50 (1980): 455–86.

———. "Western Infiltration of the Byzantine Aristocracy: Some Suggestions." In *The Byzantine Aristocracy, IX to XIII Centuries,* British Archaeological Reports International Series 221, edited by Michael Angold, 202–10. Oxford: British Archaeological Reports, 1984.

———. "The Novels of Mid-Twelfth Century Constantinople: The Literary and Social Context." In *ΑΕΤΟΣ: Studies in Honour of Cyril Mango, presented to him on April 14, 1998,* edited by Ihor Ševčenko and Irmgard Hutter, 191–99. Stuttgart: Teubner, 1998.

Jeffreys, Michael J. "The Nature and Origins of the Political Verse." *Dumbarton Oaks Papers* 28 (1974): 141–95.

Jouanno, Corinne. "Nicétas Eugénianos: Un héritier du roman grec." *Revue des études grecques* 102 (1989): 346–60.

———. "Les barbares dans le roman byzantin du XIIe siècle: Fonction d'un topos." *Byzantion* 62 (1992): 264–300.

———. "Les jeunes filles dans le roman byzantin du XIIe siècle." In *Les personnages du roman grec*, Actes du colloque de Tours, 18–20 novembre 1999, edited by Bernard Pouderon, with Christine Hunzinger and Dimitri Kasprzyk, 329–46. Lyon: Maison de l'Orient Méditerranéen, 2001.

Kazhdan, Alexander P. "Bemerkungen zu Niketas Eugenianos." *Jahrbuch der österreichischen byzantinischen Gesellschaft* 16 (1967): 101–17.

———. "Theodore Prodromus: A Reappraisal." In *Studies on Byzantine Literature of the Eleventh and Twelfth Centuries*, in collaboration with Simon Franklin, 87–114. Cambridge: Cambridge University Press, 1984.

Kraemer, Ross S., ed. *Maenads, Martyrs, Matrons, Monastics: A Sourcebook on Women's Religions in the Greco-Roman World*. Philadelphia: Fortress Press, 1988.

Kyriakis, Michael J. "Of Professors and Disciples in Twelfth Century Byzantium." *Byzantion* 43 (1973): 108–19.

Labarthe-Postel, Judith. "Hommes et dieux dans les *ekphraseis* des romans byzantins du temps des Comnène." In *Les personnages du roman grec*, Actes du colloque de Tours, 18–20 novembre 1999, edited by Bernard Pouderon, ᴖh Christine Hunzinger and Dimitri Kasprzyk, 347–71. Lyon: Mai᷄ de l'Orient Méditerranéen, 2001.

MacAlister, ᴢanne. "Byzantine Twelfth-Century Romances: A Relative Chronᴄ ᷄y." *Byzantine and Modern Greek Studies* 15 (1991): 175–210.

———. Dr ᷄s and Suicides: *The Greek Novel from Antiquity to the Byzantine Emp᷄* London: Routledge, 1996.

Macriᵈ Ruth, and Paul Magdalino. "The Fourth Kingdom and the Rhetoric oᶠ ellenism." In *The Perception of the Past in Twelfth-Century Europe*, edited ᵇy Paul Magdalino, 117–56. London: The Hambledon Press, 1992.

Mᵃ ᴬalino, Paul. "Eros the King and the King of *Amours*: Some Observations ᴖn *Hysmine and Hysminias*." *Dumbarton Oaks Papers* 46 (1992): 197–204.

———. *The Empire of Manuel I Komnenos, 1143–1180*. Cambridge: Cambridge University Press, 1993.

Marcovich, Miroslav, ed. *Theodori Prodromi de Rhodanthes et Dosiclis amoribus libri IX*. Stuttgart: Teubner, 1992.

———, ed. *Eustathius Macrembolites: De Hysmines et Hysminiae amoribus libri XI*. Munich: Teubner, 2001.

Mazal, Otto. *Der Roman des Konstantinos Manasses*. Vienna: Hermann Böhlaus Nachf., 1967.

Milazzo, Antonino M. "Motivi bucolici e tecnica alessandrina in due 'idilli' di Niceta Eugeniano." *Studi di filologia bizantina* 3 (1985): 97–114.

Mullett, Margaret. "Aristocracy and Patronage in the Literary Circles of Comnenian Constantinople." In *The Byzantine Aristocracy IX to XIII Centuries*, British Archaeological Reports International Series 221, edited by Michael Angold, 173–201. Oxford, 1984.

Nilsson, Ingela. *Erotic Pathos, Rhetorical Pleasure: Narrative Technique and Mimesis in Eumathios Makrembolites' Hysmine and Hysminias*. Uppsala: Acta Universitatis Upsaliensis, 2001.

Petit, L. "Monodie de Nicétas Eugénianos sur Théodore Prodrome." *Vizantiiskii vremennik* 9 (1902): 446–63.

Petrovskii, Fedor A., trans. *Nikita Evgenian: Povest' o Drosille i Kharikle*. Moscow, 1969.

Plepelits, Karl, trans. *Eustathios Makrembolites, Hysmine und Hysminias*. Stuttgart: Anton Hiersemann, 1989.

Podestà, Giuditta. "Le satire lucianesche di Teodoro Prodromo." Parts 1 and 2. *Aevum* 19 (1945): 239–52; 21 (1947): 3–25.

Reardon, Bryan P., ed. *Collected Ancient Greek Novels*. Berkeley: University of California Press, 1989.

Stephens, Susan A., and John J. Winkler, eds. *Ancient Greek Novels: The Fragments*. Princeton: Princeton University Press, 1995.

Svoboda, Karel. "La composition et le style du roman de Nicétas Eugénianos." In *Actes du IVe congrès international des études byzantines, Sofia, septembre 1934*. 2 vols. Edited by Bogdan D. Filov, 1:191–201. Sofia: Imprimerie de la Cour, 1935–36.

Wilson, Nigel G. *Scholars of Byzantium*. Baltimore: The Johns Hopkins University Press, 1983.

———. *Photius, The Bibliotheca: A Selection*. London: Duckworth, 1994.

BOLCHAZY-CARDUCCI PUBLISHERS, INC.

THE MEANING OF HELEN
In Search of an Ancient Icon
Robert Emmet Meagher

"The Story of Helen is the Story of Woman"

Helen's face launched a thousand ships, to say nothing of countless books, dramas, poems, paintings, and operas. She is arguably the most notorious woman in western culture. What makes her so engaging, so consequential? Helen, for better or for worse, in all her metamorphoses, represents the complex, intact fossil record of woman in western culture.

CHAPTERS ON

- Helen and History
- The Many Helens
- The Duality of Helen
- The First Helen
- The Truth of Helen

The Meaning of Helen: x + 191 pp. (2001) 6" x 9" Paperback, ISBN 0-86516-510-6

THE ESSENTIAL EURIPIDES
Dancing in Dark Times
Robert Emmet Meagher

*Plays and Interpretation
in One Affordable Volume*

THIS UNIQUE VOLUME INCLUDES

- A monograph on Euripides entitled "Mortal Vision: the Wisdom of Euripides"

- Five plays in translation: *Hekabe, Helen, Iphigenia at Aulis, Iphigenia in Tauris,* and *Bakkhai*

- A concluding essay entitled "Revel and Revelation: the Poetics of Euripides"

The Essential Euripides: xii + 556 pp., 4 B&W illustrations (2001) Paperback, ISBN 0-86516-513-0

WWW.BOLCHAZY.COM

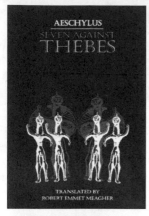
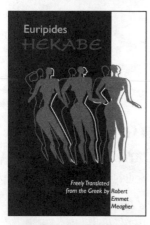

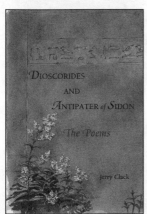

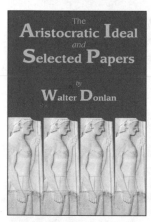